SURVIVOR

The last time Jack Hardy had seen the *Candle-fish,* he had been a young Navy lieutenant, fighting for his life in the waters of the Pacific while his submarine was torn apart by violent tremors and gigantic charges of electrical energy.

Now Jack Hardy was back aboard the *Candlefish,* a middle-aged man haunted by nightmares of a war concluded long ago, and by the memory of a voyage that had almost destroyed him as a man.

Only Jack Hardy knew what had happened aboard the *Candlefish* thirty years before. Only he at first recognized what was happening now.

And somehow he had to find a way to do now what he had not been able to do then. Somehow he had to change the course of the satanic drama that was inexorably unfolding— or he would not survive a second time . . .

GHOSTBOAT

"This story, like the ghostly sub itself, exerts a magnetic pull over the reader by means of sheer fascination coupled with horror. Just as it held every member of the crew, so GHOSTBOAT will not let you go until the last moment of its fateful journey."

—Adi-Kent Thomas Jeffrey,
THE BERMUDA TRIANGLE

Ghostboat

**George E. Simpson
and
Neal R. Burger**

A DELL BOOK

Published by
Dell Publishing Co., Inc.
1 Dag Hammarskjold Plaza
New York, New York 10017

Dell ® TM 681510, Dell Publishing Co., Inc.
Printed in the United States of America
First printing—February 1976

For Jean and Maureen

ACKNOWLEDGMENTS

To the men of the United States Submarine Force, whose exploits provide the background of this book.

For valuable and unselfish assistance: Lt. (j.g.) Cynthia Ellis, USNR, Navy Office of Information, Los Angeles Branch, California; Donald E. Baruch, Chief, Audio-Visual Production Branch, Department of Defense; Jeanne F. Bernkopf, manuscript editor; Mel Bloom, authors' agent; Jack Brodsky, motion-picture producer; Kenneth Dorward, friend and consultant; William R. Grose, Executive Editor, Dell Publishing Co.; John Guillermin, motion-picture director; Gary Hamner, typist; Daryl Henry, friend and consultant; Stuart Miller, authors' agent; Karen A. Pritchard, Curator, Pacific Submarine Museum, Pearl Harbor, Hawaii.

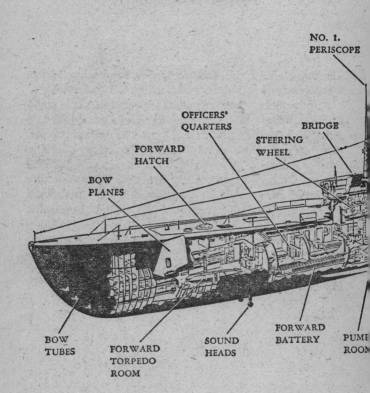

NO. 1.
PERISCOPE

OFFICERS'
QUARTERS

BRIDGE

STEERING
WHEEL

FORWARD
HATCH

BOW
PLANES

BOW
TUBES

FORWARD
TORPEDO
ROOM

SOUND
HEADS

FORWARD
BATTERY

PUMP
ROOM

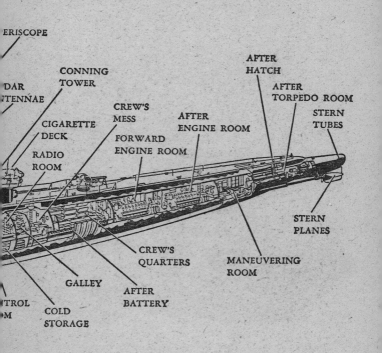

ERISCOPE

DAR
NTENNAE

CONNING
TOWER

CIGARETTE
DECK

RADIO
ROOM

CREW'S
MESS

FORWARD
ENGINE ROOM

AFTER
ENGINE ROOM

AFTER
HATCH

AFTER
TORPEDO ROOM

STERN
TUBES

STERN
PLANES

CREW'S
QUARTERS

MANEUVERING
ROOM

NTROL
M

GALLEY

COLD
STORAGE

AFTER
BATTERY

U. S. S. CANDLEFISH, #284

PART I

CHAPTER 1

December 11, 1944

Five hundred miles southeast of Tokyo Bay, night lay raven-black over a lackluster sea, its languorous movement unusual for that time of year. A long, inky shape slipped invisibly across the Pacific, stroking the surface of the watery desert. The boat cut a path through a hush so vast that even the men keeping watch on deck were moved to a reverent peace.

Below decks, Captain Basquine checked his watch and listened to the gentle whine of the diesels as he waited for Dusty Rhodes to finish his hammering. "How about it?" he asked. Rhodes gave the plug one more whack with the hammer, took a deep breath, and came out of his crouch slowly, muscle-weary, fatigue etched on his face.

"That's the last one, sir," he mumbled, and wiped his sweating chin and chest. He watched the Captain straighten, clear his throat, and stroll forward through the crowded torpedo room.

Billy G. Basquine, Lieutenant Commander, U.S. Navy, went as far forward as he could, turned at the torpedo-tube doors, and glanced down into the below-decks storage bays. His eyes traveled up, lingered on the torpedoes nesting on their skids; he felt the adrenalin start to pour through his body. The men settled into position and waited as he took three steps to the center of the room, then faced them again. His arms shot out sideways, and he braced himself between two torpedoes.

An auxiliaryman opened the intercom line so the Captain's voice would carry to all compartments. And Basquine launched into his speech: "All right, here's the poop. The Exec and I have been through the entire boat, and everything is up to snuff again. The Japanese had a go at us this afternoon with the MADs, and I have to admit they're getting better. Maybe if the war lasts another three years . . ."

There were some titters and some groans. Basquine let them die out and then roared: "They might learn to hit their own asses with a bull fiddle!"

The men laughed. Basquine knew they liked to hear him use their own language. And they liked it loud.

"NOW THEN! Four points! In order. One: The clowns in those planes, those cockeyed little Nips, are already taking bows for sinking a big fat American submarine! That's us—*Candlefish*. They're probably collecting medals right now. Two: Tomorrow, Tokyo Rose is going to tell the world we've been sunk . . . *again*. That's *twice* on the same patrol."

Quinn, a throttleman from New Jersey, shouted out, "Dat's a new record for stupidity!"

"Matched only by yours, bub." Basquine grinned, and the laughter came at Quinn's expense. "Point number three! They're hitting oh-for-two and we're on a streak, five-for-five, and we still have our turn at bat!"

That was sure-fire. Baseball always got to them. Three men beat on the bulkheads with tin cups and added to the din.

Basquine watched, satisfied. Those Jap peckerheads with their Magnetic Airborne Detectors had almost done them in, but they were still functioning, and that was all Basquine wanted. He took on a grim look and started aft. The men, all smiles now, scrunched back to let him pass.

"Skipper? What about point number four?"

Basquine stopped, looked around, finally located the voice. "What about it, Ramos?"

"Well, what is it, sir?"

Billy G. Basquine gazed hard at the grinning faces, and they slowly withered.

"Number four," said Basquine softly. "Tomorrow we are changing course, and we're changing orders. We will not proceed to the Kuriles. Instead, we will take up a station right inside Tokyo Bay." His voice thickened. "Then I am going to shoot the living hell out of anything flying the meatball, as long as it floats."

Smiles crumbled and men sagged as the meaning of his statement sank home. Then there was an explosion of cheers, started by four war-rabid torpedomen. But Basquine was already moving through the hatch to officers' country.

A stream of men moved aft, clearing the corridor for the Captain. He entered his cabin and slowly sank into the chair by his desk. He sat and reflected over the patrol up to date. He knew they were on a streak. More ships? More tonnage? Why not? The *Candlefish* could move right up alongside all the other big ones. Mush Morton's *Wahoo,* Dick O'Kane's *Tang*—Billy G. Basquine's *Candlefish.* Just the thought of it brought a proud smile to his lips. He pulled down his drop-leaf desk top and drew the day-to-day log out of one of his stuffed cubbyholes. He flipped through the pages with their heavy ink scrawl, stopping at December 11th. He started to write his version of their afternoon encounter with the MADs.

* * *

Lieutenant Jack Hardy had telescoped his too-long frame into the too-short bunk that was his living space aboard the *Candlefish*. The navigation officer was in a nether state, between sleep and wakefulness, aware of the sounds of the sub but not taking particular note of any one thing . . . except the pumps . . .

Then the sweat began. First the hands, then under his arms. The hum of machinery blended into nothingness. He felt himself sliding over . . . again.

"God in heaven," he murmured, "no more, please . . ."

Once more: the sharp hiss of compressed air, followed by the rending of metal, the tube door ripping open, slamming Kenyon back against the bays, crushing the life out of him. The gush of sea water that slammed through the after torpedo room, sweeping Hardy off his feet along with the torpedomen. The sudden knowledge of responsibility—

The hand shaking his shoulder pulled him back to reality. Jack's eyes snapped open. He looked around for the hand and heard only a voice: "Twenty-one hundred hours, Mr. Hardy."

Hardy pulled the curtain aside and gazed up into the somber, unsmiling face of the executive officer, William Bates.

"Disturb your nap, mister?"

"No . . . I was awake." Hardy threw his legs over the side and hit the deck.

Bates permitted himself the smallest of smiles, his own precious sneer. "Captain wants a position report. For some reason, he still thinks you're qualified."

"Well, sir, I suppose he knows best."

Bates blinked but let it slide by. This cat-and-mouse game was so familiar to both of them that each knew how far the other would go. Hardy had just reached his limit. Now it was the Exec's turn.

"I'm feeling charitable tonight, Hardy. So just get your ass up on the bridge."

Hardy glared at him. "Walinsky's checking out Cyclops—"

"Get your ass aft, get your one-eyed wonder, and get up to the bridge—on the double!" Bates spun on his heel, stepped out into the passageway, and was gone.

Jack Hardy ripped open his locker, shrugged into his black watch sweater, and tore his foul-weather jacket off its hook. He slammed the locker door shut, promising to do the same to Bates's face some day when the war was over. Then he stalked out of his quarters, heading aft.

He was in no mood to appreciate the complexity of this mechanism he was a part of, this fleet boat. Basquine's Boomers. "Three hundred twelve feet of lean and mean," as the Captain put it.

What bullshit! Too often Hardy found Basquine an insufferable bore.

He ducked through the hatch into the control room. A petty officer was leaning over the plotting desk, studying a chart. He looked up and smiled at Hardy, but from here on the smiles would be fewer and further apart.

Past the radio room and into the galley. Slugger was busy fortifying his peanut-butter habit, loading up crackers with the brown goop. He glanced up at Hardy, turned suddenly cold, then marched around to the crew's mess, careful to back out with his plate so he wouldn't have to offer Hardy any.

Hardy followed and slipped quickly through the crew's quarters, the one compartment aboard ship he wished were located somewhere below, so he wouldn't have to traverse it so frequently. But what difference did it make? He was trapped aboard this floating cocoon with eighty-three other men, and three-fourths of them considered him the scapegoat for all their ills. Especially since Kenyon's death.

In the crew's quarters, most of the men simply ignored him. Corky Jones, poring over his Ann Sheridan scrapbook, started to say something but caught himself in time. Hardy continued through to the forward engine room, looking for his one friend among the lower ranks: Anton Walinsky, King of the Diesels. The Chief had served aboard the old S-boats before the rest of the crew had their first teeth.

The Fairbanks-Morse engines were immense, each one covering deck space nearly the entire length of the compartment, some twenty feet. As usual, the *Candlefish* was charging her batteries on the forward diesels, main engines one and two, while running surfaced at night. The sheer power of those giant pistons, coupled with the heat they threw off, was overwhelming.

Walinsky was aft, near the engine stand, a diminutive figure bathed in sweat, securing a wooden cabinet to the bulkhead over one of the engines. It was a handmade, felt-lined, carved mahogany pipe rack. And the pipes it contained were Walinsky's pride and joy: Danish Larsens, British Charatans, Dunhills, and a couple that Walinsky had carved himself.

The Chief straightened and surveyed the cabinet, admiring his collection. He felt Hardy's presence and turned to him.

"Mighty handsome, Chief."

"Me or the pipes?"

Hardy smiled and inquired about Cyclops.

"All fixed," Walinsky said, and called to one of the oilers tending main engine number two, "Hey, Rieser, bring me Mr. Hardy's sextant!"

Rieser looked up dully from the gauges he was reading, regarded Hardy coldly, then turned away and winked at his cronies. His eyes scanned the small work-bench, passing right over the sextant. Stooping, he opened one of the drawers in the bench and made a show of rummaging through the tools. Hardy took it all in stoically. Walinsky built up steam. He approached Rieser from behind as the greasy oiler went on fumbling around the workbench.

"Can't seem to find it, Chief . . . I . . ." He saw Walinsky coming and, at the last second, scooped up the sextant like a prospector discovering a gold nugget. "Here it is! Right in front of me all the time."

Walinsky snatched it out of Rieser's hand. He ran a practiced eye over the tangent screw, tested the clamp screw, then turned and marched back to Hardy.

"Okay, sir. She's as good as new. Like the day we put her together. You won't drop her again, will you?"

Jack smiled and took the strange device from Walin-sky, palming it in his left hand. Cyclops looked like any other sextant, but with one variation: Instead of the standard eyepiece, one half of a pair of 7x35 binoculars had been secured to the clamp.

"Thanks, Chief. Maybe coffee later, hm?"

Walinsky nodded and watched Hardy walk forward, past the gazes of the men, his eyes straight ahead. Walinsky swept a gaze over his domain. The men were working. Rieser was taking readings from the gauges as if his life depended on it.

Walinsky sidled over to him and spoke just at the level of the diesels, a mere shout, but low enough so Rieser had to strain to hear.

"You pull a stunt like that again and I'll kick your butt from one end of this boat to the other, inside and then outside. Hear me?"

Rieser tried ignorance: "Honest, Chief, I just couldn't find the lieutenant's goddamned sextant."

"That's because you're stupid, Rieser. You're the stupidest creep on this boat. Well, I got something you *can* find. The stop valve on the number two sanitary tank. Check it. It's sticking."

Rieser relaxed. That wasn't too bad.

"From the *inside*." Walinsky purred like a cat lapping cream from a saucer. He watched with great satisfaction the look of horror and dismay that spread over Rieser's face. "If I don't smell something mighty strange inside of ten minutes, we're gonna talk some more! *Capisce?*"

Hardy, Cyclops clutched in his left hand, pulled himself up the control-room ladder to the conning tower. Because the bridge hatch was open, the con was bathed in a red glow from the combat lights. As his eyes adjusted, Hardy became aware of the other people sharing this, the topmost part of the sub's interior.

Jenavin, the quartermaster of the watch, was positioned right behind the helmsman, an Officer Candidate School prep manual poking out of his back pocket.

Bates, Basquine, and Ensign Jordan, the gunnery officer, were hanging over the chart table playing war games.

The young ensign cleared his throat, looked from the Captain to the Exec, then jumped in feet first: "Supposing we did get through the mine fields, sir. Suno Saki here has suspected shore batteries, and the Japs have airfields ringing Tokyo. After all, it *is* their capital."

Basquine had been following Jordan's pointing finger on the chart. Now he froze and raked the top of the con with a withering look. "Who told you I needed a geography lesson?" His fingers started drumming on the charts. He wanted tonnage. "Don't you guys understand? It's *because* of the mine fields!"

Hardy smiled. He had to admire Basquine's ballsy approach.

"If they won't come out," the Captain said, "we'll just have to go in and get them! Okay?" The drumming fingers increased their tempo; then, without looking around, he barked: "Mr. Hardy, what the hell are you doing?"

Hardy's admiration evaporated. "Permission to go topside, sir."

"I don't know any other way I'm going to send that position report by twenty-two hundred hours. Move it!"

Hardy retreated awkwardly up the ladder.

He popped through the hatch into the black Pacific night and stared at the Great Empty. The whine of the submarine's diesels and the hiss of the sea—Hardy could communicate with these. His eyes slowly grew accustomed to the dark. He sucked in a lungful of the moist air, clearing his senses of the machine-oil smell of the sub. He snatched a life jacket from a corner locker and put it on. It cut the cold better than his foul-weather.

Behind him the lookouts were perched on the periscope shearwater, in the truncated crow's nest that was the highest vantage point on the *Candlefish.* Above them loomed the twin periscopes and the radio and radar antennae. And beyond that, only the heavens.

Hardy looked up in surprise when the first strands of mist rolled in. He watched patchy hunks of the stuff creep by, low to the water, hovering on top of the deck slatting below. While he still had a clear canopy of night sky above him, he hefted Cyclops and moved to starboard of the bridge. He craned his neck to pick out stars, then steadied himself and raised Cyclops.

He locked in on the North Star, timed it, and moved

the horizon glass. Adjusting the clamp screw, he found another star. Swinging his body, he picked up his third point. He jotted the positions down on his pad and then stopped.

The entire bridge shivered abruptly beneath his feet.

He looked around. The others on the bridge were reacting to the tremor: the lookouts; Stanhill, the Officer of the Deck; Lopez, the chief of the watch—they all gazed ahead, into the gathering fog, then to the sides. Had they struck something?

"Bridge—what the hell was that?"

Stanhill moved to the open hatch and looked down at the Skipper's red-illuminated, upturned face. "Nothing topside, sir."

Hardy joined Stanhill and ventured an opinion. "Maybe an underwater earthquake, sir?"

Basquine ignored him and turned to the sonar operator in the con. "Anything?" Collins adjusted his dials, listened, and shook his head. Then he whipped off the headset and offered it to Basquine.

And then the second tremor hit. It sounded even more like an earthquake.

The sub took another violent shimmy, and this time the men in the con could hear things below rattle and fall to the deck. Somebody swore.

On the bridge they heard Basquine's familiar "Now nobody get your bowels in an uproar" boom through the ship's comm line and up the open hatch. "Stanhill, sonar and radar don't have a thing. What's the sea like?"

Stanhill looked over the side. If anything, the water had grown calmer, more subdued. Hardy looked over too, and could make out glassy smoothness through the thick patches of fog. It felt as if the sub weren't moving at all . . . Yet she must be. The diesels were still going. He checked his watch. It was 2130.

Without warning, the sub took a rending shudder that whipped her stern sideways. Hardy's feet shot out from under him. He caromed off the TBT and slammed into Stanhill, cold-cocking him on the jaw with his elbow. Both men fell. Hardy's Cyclops made a lazy arc in the air and landed with a sickening clank on the cigarette deck aft. Hardy tried to sit up, but this time the shaking wouldn't stop; the sub was gripped by a series of tremors. Hardy reached out to protect Stanhill from the heaving deck plates. He wondered fleetingly what it was like below—

Basquine, in the well under the conning-tower hatch, managed to hang on. Bates was okay, but Jordan was down. He must have hit the chart table. The Captain took a fast nose count, then hollered up the well, "Bridge! Do you see any shell splashes?"

The sub took another shake and leaned starboard. Lopez's head filled the hatch. "Mr. Stanhill's out cold—Mr. Hardy's shaken up a bit—but nothing else, sir!"

Basquine lurched over to the intercom. "All compartments, report!"

The *Candlefish*'s superstructure took one quivering jolt after another, and Hardy heard responsive cursing from the con.

From the forward engine room came Walinsky's distraught bellow: "Skipper—we're getting screwy readings! I think we should shift to batteries!"

Hardy struggled to his feet when the diesels cut out. He grabbed the Target Bearing Transmitter as the sub heeled sharply to port, whipping and bucking like a long steel snake. The panic welling up inside him subsided as the boat righted herself in a shower of spray. He ducked instinctively, then straightened and looked forward. Swirling fog was closing in, drifting higher.

Then, as the bow disappeared in the mist, the *Candle-fish* bucked again. Hardy gaped at seas that he could barely glimpse around the boat. The glassy smoothness was gone, replaced by churning, frothing waters. A teeth-rattling crash and flying spray blurred his vision. The sub was trembling and twitching in the throes of some incomprehensible disease. Hardy's grip on the TBT loosened. He tried to shield his head as he fell. He got a fleeting glimpse of Lopez and the lookouts hanging on to the shearwaters. Stanhill was still down.

The next crunch slammed Basquine into the peri-scope shaft. Stunned and hanging on, he watched Jor-dan slide past him, his head bouncing off the back of Collins's seat. He was dimly aware of a cry of pain, then saw the quartermaster clutch his face and reel back, blood streaming through his hands.

"Bates! Get topside! Report!" Bates nodded to the Captain, then staggered to the ladder and started up. Water showered through the hatch and knocked him loose. Doggedly, trying to match his steps to the now constant spasms of the submarine, he started up again.

Hardy felt the next big shake coming—a flutter fast and hard, rippling through the boat, followed by a wrenching convulsion. The juggernaut churning through the *Candlefish* refused to stop. And then he heard a godawful metal-grinding screech coming from somewhere below—somewhere aft—

"Main engine number one just jumped its mount-ing—God, what a mess!" The voice boomed up through the con. Basquine cut him off and screamed something unintelligible through the mike.

The submarine took to plunging up and down, in ad-dition to its rapid sideward shakes. Two hands shot out of the dark, and Bates pulled himself up out of the conning-tower hatch. He looked into Hardy's surprised face. In the fog and darkness, they could barely make each other out. Basquine's bellows filtered up from below as he yelled instructions to the helmsman, trying to fight the starboard lean. Hardy and Bates lay face down on the twitching bridge. Bates used Hardy's body for support and lunged upward, grabbing the side of the bridge to survey the boat. Over the roar of a howling wind that had come up from nowhere and now whipped around them in concentric circles he could hear the *Candlefish*'s plates groaning, but he could not see any signs of attack.

"Where the hell did this storm come from?" he yelled at Hardy. He moved to the voice tube, but Hardy, also on his feet, went spinning into the Exec, almost knocking his teeth out on the lip of the voice tube.

"Dammit, Jack. Make yourself useful. Get Stanhill below!"

Hardy ducked as a wall of spray hit them. He looked for Stanhill, then thought of Cyclops. Where was the sextant? A heavier wall of spray hit the bridge, and the sub was caught in an epileptic seizure. Bates wedged his hands around the voice tube, closed his eyes against the salt spray, and hung on. But Hardy went down again. His fingers splayed out, trying to get purchase on the wet metal. He rolled past the con structure and kept going, past the after machine gun and out the cigarette deck. His hands shot out too late as the lower railing of the cigarette deck passed over him. He fell on the top deck and landed with a crunch on his right knee. His scream was lost as the rushing water carried him back, slamming him into the base of the huge deck gun. He snatched at the traversing gear and tried to stand. His right leg was like jelly; it went out from under him. He fell, still clutching the gear, conscious of acute pain and terror. The submarine's jolting tremors were even more severe on the deck than on the bridge. He held on tightly as the *Candlefish* shimmied and frothy waves formed high over his head and crashed down on top of him.

In the conning tower, Basquine grabbed the intercom mike and shouted, "Come to battle stations! All hands to battle stations! Secure all compartments!" He whipped around to the helmsman. "Maitless, what's our course?"

Maitless glanced at the compass as the alarm rang through the boat.

"Two-five-three, sir."

"Left full rudder. Come to two-zero-five."

Maitless strained at the wheel. It was frozen. "She won't answer, sir."

"Emergency helm!" Basquine shouted below.

Bates flipped up the cover of the voice tube and shouted over the howling wind, "Captain—there's nothing shooting at us. I'm positive!"

Basquine's voice crackled up: "Mr. Bates, stay on the bridge!"

Reports were pouring into the control room from all stations. Gauges and dials were getting so hot, the glass was shattering right out of them. Main diesel number one was still sliding around in the forward engine room. Shackles had snapped; a torpedo had rolled off its skid. The reports spelled pandemonium.

Basquine hit the diving alarm and yelled, "Clear the bridge! Dive! Dive!"

Hardy sloshed around on the afterdeck, still clinging weakly to the traversing gear of the deck gun. He heard the OOGA! OOGA! of the diving alarm and felt a rush of fear—they were going to submerge and leave him. He could just make out fog-shrouded silhouettes on the top of the conning tower, the lookouts rushing down from their perches and disappearing below. He was alone on the deck of a twisting, bucking sub, and she was going to drop right out from under him.

Bates, the last man down the ladder, watched Quartermaster Jenavin secure the hatch, his face still streaked with blood. The sub's trembling gathered momentum, and their teeth chattered in time to it.

"Bates! Where's Hardy?" bellowed the Captain.

"Didn't he get Stanhill below?" Looking around, Bates could see he hadn't. He leaped for the intercom, swearing out loud, "Shit! Hold the dive! Surface! Surface!"

Basquine hit the alarm—three blasts. Bates was already up the ladder again, opening the hatch. The pumps reversed, and he could hear the air-intake valves.

Hardy heard the rush of high-pressure air as the *Candlefish* forced out the water ballast she had so eagerly sought seconds before. He had already started to make his peace with God, desperately cried out for his wife, Elena, and Peter, the son he would never see. Through the mist and flying water and the awful trembling of the boat he made out a figure standing on the bridge, looking for him.

Yelling into the wind, he hailed, "Down here! By the deck gun!"

He saw the figure turn, homing in on his voice. His joy turned to horror as the entire superstructure of the *Candlefish* lit up in a blue-white display of electricity. Bates froze. Still crying out for help, Hardy dragged himself along the strakes. The roar of air and the extra shudder that ran through the boat told him that the *Candlefish* was getting ready to submerge again.

The sub took a bonebreaking spasm, and Hardy was ripped loose of his hold on the slatting. Water rushed up around him and flung him hard against the base of the conning tower. For a moment he was bathed

clearly in the blue-white light from the flickering St.
Elmo's fire on the antenna cables, and Bates flopped
down on the cigarette deck and flung out a hand to
grab him—too late. The decks went awash, and Hardy
was carried away on a wave. The bow dug in deeply;
Bates could feel the stern rising, the water cascading off
the afterdeck. He jumped to his feet and, with a last
glimpse at Hardy thrashing around in the sea, Lieutenant Bates struggled back to the hatch and rode the
lanyard down. He secured the hatch himself, avoiding
Basquine's gaze. He could hear men starting to yell
around him and below as the sub tilted forward. His
eyes met Basquine's, and he saw at once horror, anguish, and total, mind-bending fury.

"Not now!" Basquine let out a roar that reverberated
through the boat as he felt glory slipping through his
fingers. The deck canted, and somewhere forward
Bates heard a grinding noise.

The rending screech of metal cut through Hardy's
numbed senses. He watched through fog and heaving
waters as the stern of the *Candlefish* lifted high in the
air and loomed almost directly overhead, then slowly
slipped beneath the ocean surface.

After a few moments, silence descended. The sea
stopped churning. The fog wisped around him, and he
looked about for some trace of the submarine. It was
gone. The quickness of it all overwhelmed him. He let
his arms dangle around the life jacket, and his heart began to slow its powerful thumping. After a long time
just drifting around the little patch of sea, he began to
swim away . . .

PART II

CHAPTER 2

October 5, 1974

Ed Frank lay sound asleep on rumpled blue sheets. One of those hot, muggy Washington nights. Joanne was beside him on her back, her half of the sheet tossed carelessly away sometime during the night, her body splayed out over two thirds of the bed, long hair swept across her face and breast.

Frank's eyes fluttered open at twelve minutes past two. After a few moments of groggy consideration, he knew he wasn't going to sleep any more that night. He rubbed his scratchy chin and ran one hand through his stiff black hair.

He rolled over on one side and studied Joanne. One of her arms was crooked up at the elbow, the hand trailing over her bare midriff. Her mouth was open; he could hear her breathing. Her skin was burned red in all but a few strategic places, but Frank was tired of sympathizing. He couldn't even work up a convincing cluck; he had spent two hours last night covering her with ointment and listening to her plaintive cries and half-assed excuses. Sunburns are deserved, he had told her, the result of unforgiveable carelessness. And if Joanne possessed one serious character flaw, it was her consistent, mind-numbing, monumental carelessness.

During a recent disastrous evening at a posh night-club, the White Pelican, she had managed to demolish one wine glass, one tablecloth, and one waiter carrying a fully loaded tray. Frank's five-and-a-half-foot frame had shrunk into a corner, ten degrees right of embarrassed. He hadn't let her hear the end of it for three days.

He would flare up at Joanne, as he had with all his women, and say things he didn't mean, and go on saying them because once he was into it there was no way out. But at least she was able to take it calmly, without being intimidated.

And Joanne had other compensations. Frank sat up on one elbow and studied them: long legs, a tapering waist, a full, round bust, and a soft, heart-melting face. Perfect. Except that Frank thought she could do with a bit more in the way of brains: opinions on matters beyond TV, movies, shopping, and suntans. He would grow bored with Joanne, as he had with all the others. But he was determined to make the best of it while it lasted. At least she wasn't in love with him, sparing him those embarrassing complications. She loved sex—but she only *liked* him. He smiled broadly and scratched his leg. Then he scratched hers. She stirred, and he waited to see if she was going to wake up.

Joanne moved, just an inch, and Frank traced a finger across her flattened breast. Again she stirred, and he anticipated the bell signaling round three for tonight . . .

The phone rang.

"Jesus!"

Frank jumped out of bed and ran to the dresser to grab it before Joanne woke up. He snatched up the receiver, cupped his hand over it, and muttered, "Hello?" He looked back at the bed—she was still asleep.

"Ed? This is Ray Cook." The voice on the phone

waited for Frank to grumble back. "Hey, I'm sorry I woke you, but something's come up. You're needed right now."

"What for? I'm in the middle—" He didn't have to finish. Cook couldn't miss the implication.

"Ed, this is really urgent."

Frank sighed. "Where are you?"

"Guard desk, Pentagon."

Frank digested that, and his mind began to race.

"Okay, I'll be over in thirty minutes."

He hung up and frowned. Joanne still seemed fast asleep. Frank stumbled to the window and looked out across the capital. He could pick out landmarks silhouetted against the moonlit sky, streetlights bathing parked cars below.

Fifteen minutes to the Pentagon. Gotta shower and shave and get into uniform, the whole bit. He knew he would be late. He swore under his breath. The Navy calling at two in the morning. Wouldn't do that to a goddamned married officer, he growled to himself.

He padded over to the bed and looked down at Joanne. Suddenly he was hungry for her again. He fell on her and snuggled into her shoulder. Her eyes flew open, and her arms came around him hard.

Mystifying, he thought. They all mystify. That's how these things last . . .

One hour later, he pulled into his parking space at the Pentagon and locked up the Ford. Indian summer. The heat was stultifying. He strode wearily across the lot and nodded to the gaping guard.

"It's three fifteen, Commander."

"It's also Saturday, Charlie."

The outer lobby was deserted except for the security guard. Frank was admitted and then walked over to an ashtray to load his pipe. He looked out at the floodlit Pentagon grounds and waited while the security guard informed Lieutenant Cook of his arrival. Frank tamped the tobacco down deep into his pipe and lit it. He sucked the smoke and sniffed at the nutty aroma.

It was five minutes before Lieutenant Cook emerged from a long hallway in a crisp, fresh uniform, his heels clicking across the room, his blond hair and tall good looks contrasting sharply with Frank's own dark swarthiness and short frame.

"Hullo, Ed, did I tear you away from something good?" Cook's grin was infectious during working hours, but not before dawn on a Saturday.

"You better have a good reason," growled Frank.

"I do. We have a little submarine situation. Follow me." He led the way to the escalators, and they glided up to the third floor in silence.

Frank waited patiently. This was a little game they played: Cook in possession of vital national secrets and Frank obliged to pry them out of him like sardines from a can. Cook was young and sharp and assigned to the Naval Investigative Service because he had zeal, brains, and big ears. He was twenty-eight years old, quick, efficient, dedicated, and sometimes a downright pain in the ass.

Finally Frank broke the silence. "What submarine situation?"

"A sub surfaced in the Pacific a couple of hours ago about six hundred miles northwest of Pearl Harbor."

"So what?"

"She broached right in front of a Japanese freighter. Scared the hell out of her captain. He got on the line to his people, and they got on the line to ours, and then everybody got on the line to *us*."

"Who called you?"

"Somebody in the State Department."

"Anybody I know?"

"Somebody from Henry the K."

Frank grunted, then spread his hands. "What's so earthshaking about a submarine?"

They stepped off on the third floor and went on down the angular halls. "No identification," mumbled Cook.

"What are you talking about? Is she ours?"

"Yes. Seems to be one of our fleet types. But there are no markings."

"None at all?"

Cook shook his head. "That's what the telex said." They arrived at Room 3012, and Cook unlocked the door marked NAVAL INVESTIGATIVE SERVICE.

"Let me see the telex," demanded Frank.

Cook swung open the door and paused to pull a rumpled cable from his shirt pocket. Frank spread it open and turned on a wall switch. A large office sprang to life. Fluorescent tubes lit up reception desks, partitioned cubicles, and the telex.

COMSUBPAC
P050221Z OCT 24
FROM COMSUBPAC TO COMNIS WASH DC

CDR JAPANESE CLASS 5 FRTR SHIMUI MARU POSIT 34-56N 149-12W COURSE 084 SPEED 4 DEST SAN FRAN REPORTS UNIDENT SUB SURFACED 0124 HRS BEARING 000 POSIT ANGLE 90 STOP SUB HAILED NO RESPONSE STOP NO RADIO CONTACT STOP SUB UNCONFIRMED USN FLEET STOP ADVISED STATE DEPT AT REQ JAPANESE ADMIRALTY STOP SITUA-

TION VERY HOT ADVISE ACTION STOP

"This doesn't say anything about markings."

"No," said Cook, leading the way back toward their cubicles, "that must have been in the phone call."

"From Henry the K?"

"You betcha. And the one from DOD, and the one from SubPac, even."

"By George, you *have* been busy." If the Submarine Force was already involved—*and* the Department of Defense—who was going to listen to the NIS?

Cook opened one of the glass-partitioned cubicles and let Frank pass through first. "I've got a pot of coffee going, Ed. Maybe you'd like some."

"Yeah."

Cook went to an adjoining cubicle. Frank sat behind his desk and stared at the telex. An unidentified United States fleet boat pops up and scares the hell out of some Japs? Why no markings? Why no response to the radio?

"Cook!"

"Yessir?"

"What the hell is SubPac *doing* about that boat?"

Cook walked back in with two cups of coffee and sat down opposite Frank. "Defense Intelligence Command has scrambled a recon from Pearl. There's a carrier in the area, about a hundred miles away, and they're sending up a chopper to take pictures. Should be coming over the wire shortly. I called in our photo division and they're standing by downstairs. That's where I was when you came in."

"Have any units tried to make contact with this sub?"

"Every U.S. ship within two hundred miles." Cook sipped his coffee and made a face.

Frank frowned and glanced over at the framed picture of Joanne. She smiled back at him. "What about the Japanese freighter—the *Shimui Maru?* Is she still in the area?"

"They wanted to get the hell out real fast, but their own people told them to hang around. If the sub isn't doing anything—if she's just noodling—they figure it's better not to get a rise out of her. You know, sort of like standing real still on top of a coiled snake. No fast moves."

"Very sharp, the Japanese."

"Yes, sir. And mad. Jesus, they must have hauled half the State Department out of bed at two A.M. Thought we were getting even for Pearl Harbor all over again."

Frank smiled and drew a mental picture of a shipload of astonished Japanese officers and crewmen, gaping as a submarine swept up out of the water off their bow and settled down in their path . . . Whoever was skipper of that sub had better get his affairs in order. There was bound to be a Naval Court of Inquiry in his near future.

"Where's Diminsky?" asked Frank.

"Golf. The whole weekend."

Frank nodded absently. What did he expect? The exalted presence? Assistant Chief of the NIS striding purposefully through the door at three in the morning, setting his jaw, and barking, "What the fuck is going on?" Nope. Not Diminsky. Off to the links, old boy. Round of golf, eh what?

That left Ed Frank, the highest-ranking available Submarine Force Officer attached to the NIS at administrative level.

"Well, Lieutenant, seeing that I'm in charge of this mess, I guess I should delegate a little work, right?"

Cook's smile faded.

"Get hold of ComSubPac and have them run a complete check on all fleet boats in that area. I don't care if they can guarantee that sub isn't theirs. Have them check it through again. Then get back to Defense Intelligence Command. We want priority clearances and access to current fleet disposition—I want to know where every goddamned submarine in the entire fleet was sitting at exactly 0134 hours this morning. If this is somebody's idea of a joke . . ."

Cook nodded and got up quickly. He went into the next office, and Frank could hear his muffled voice on the phone. Frank sat back, sipped at the terrible coffee, and rolled the telex information over in his mind. An American submarine defies all general orders for patrol operation and surfaces directly in the path of foreign shipping in international waters. Not necessarily a threat—it *could* be only a joke. Poor timing, at the very least. But why? And what about the markings?

Thirty minutes later, an ensign walked in and stopped to announce that wirephotos had just arrived and were being processed, and would everybody please meet in the enlarging room on the second floor in fifteen minutes?

Frank was poised over a chart of the Pacific Ocean. He was studying in particular the area six hundred miles northwest of Pearl.

He went down to the second floor with Cook, who had managed to reach everybody by phone.

"ComSubPac will clear the information with DOD, and we can get it within two hours. But they've already double-checked. There are no fleet boats of any sort, not even nukes, in that general area. They are now contacting all boats on patrol, and they'll let us know if anybody's fibbing."

"What about sending out a boarding party?"

"Defense Command wants to deploy a few oceango-ing tugs, ATFs, and they're coordinating with SubPac."

"Let's insist."

"I did. And I used your name."

"You get smarter every minute, Cook."

"Yessir."

"But if I get transferred to the Sahara, you're going as my Exec."

"Be happy to, sir. I'm a big desert freak."

Frank enjoyed the banter. It always took him a while to warm up in the morning, but once he got go-ing he and Cook could toss barbs like footballs all day long.

Cook turned on his way out. "By the way, old Wal-ters wants a look at those photos. I told him to meet us there."

"Walters? The guy from the sub force records divi-sion? Who called him?"

"I did. Who knows? He might recognize the bloody thing."

Frank and Cook entered a paneled projection room. Another ensign was setting up the enlarging projector. A sixty-year-old Submarine Force officer sat in the front row, smoking a pipe. The old man turned around, waved, and smiled. Captain Walters was an anomaly in the NIS—just about the only officer happy about sailing a desk. He was a year away from retirement and couldn't stand the idea. He intended to die on the job.

Frank smiled back and sat down next to him. Wal-ters gripped Frank's forearm and patted it affection-ately.

"How are you, son?"

That always did it. Frank liked Walters, but when would he learn that a thirty-six-year-old Lieutenant Commander in the U.S. Navy was nobody's "son"?

"Fine, Pops."

Walters grinned. "What have you got to show me?"

"Just some snapshots. How Cook and I spent our summer vacation."

The lights went down and the ensign set up the first photo on the big screen. It was an aerial shot over a portion of the sea, and they could make out two fuzzy black spots in the distance. The second picture was closer, and now they could distinguish the shape of the submarine from that of the freighter. The next one was directly over the freighter, and they could make out a load of automobiles gleaming in the open cargo hold.

Finally, a clear view of the submarine. Definitely a fleet-type boat: conning tower, double periscopes, huge deck gun . . .

"One of ours," said Frank. "No mistake there."

Cook spoke quietly. "How many have we still got with the damned deck guns aboard?"

"I don't know." Frank glanced at Walters, whose warm smile was gone. He was frowning, a bit perplexed.

The next image was even closer, still high aerial but abeam of the sub. The boat was black, and the telex was apparently correct: no markings.

Walters rose, put on a pair of glasses, and went right up to the screen to inspect the image at close range.

"Fleet boat . . . early type. I'd say vintage World War Two."

"Vintage?" questioned Frank.

"Well, she's definitely not one of the updated models. Most of those still in operation have been converted. You know that—you've served on them."

"Sure, but there must be a few around unchanged."

"Of course." Walters rubbed his chin. "They've been sold to every foreign country on the planet or turned into floating museums. Besides, this boat looks in pretty good shape."

Frank turned to the ensign. "You got anything closer? Anything on the conning tower?"

The ensign fumbled through a short stack of photos, found one, and placed it in the enlarger.

Walters was still pacing around in front of the screen when the new image came on. It was a very close shot with the conning tower off to one side.

"Center it," said Frank, "and bring it up closer."

The ensign pulled the tower in to the center of the screen and then blew it up slowly.

"A little higher," said Walters, stepping up close. "Hold it."

The image froze. Frank could barely make out markings on the side of the conning tower.

"See those buttons? Those raised buttons, like rivets?" said Walters, getting excited. "They outlined the number in the old days. That's the way they used to do it. Just paint in the number when you want to be identified—right between the buttons. Paint it out when you want to be incognito."

Frank tapped the enlarger. "Make it bigger."

The ensign resumed enlarging the shot, and they all studied the buttons, barely visible on the fuzzy blowup.

Finally Walters turned and announced in triumph, "Two eighty-four!" Walters tapped the screen happily. "Have to check it out. But I think it's about a 1942 commission."

Cook nodded, but Frank slowly turned to granite. "Wait a minute," he said quietly. "Are you telling me this really *is* one of our World War Two subs?"

Walters's head bobbed up and down. "Yes. Sure. Positively."

Now even Cook froze. Frank got up and stared at

the fuzzy blowup and the raised buttons on the tower.
No wonder ComSubPac had no information on this
one.

Walters led the way back to his office in the records
division, his face alight with excitement.

Cook and Frank walked behind him, Frank carrying
copies of the photographs. Cook wanted to know if
they should tell SubPac to call off the dogs.

"No," said Frank, "let them stew. Maybe they'll
come up with the same information, and maybe they
can tell us why. Has to be an explanation for it.
They've probably got a few of the unconverted old
types left and they just don't want anybody to know."

Cook grinned. "Or maybe we sold this one to the
Brazilian Navy."

Walters barked back over his shoulder, "I think I
know that sub." He said no more, just picked up his
pace. Frank hurried to keep up.

"You know, you qualify as a spry old man."

Walters grinned back over his shoulder and did a
Cagney two-step.

His office was larger than Frank's, larger and far
more cluttered. The shelves were lined with dusty old
naval volumes. Walters rummaged through them and
invited Cook and Frank to sit down. He pulled out a
thick book and thumbed through it on the desk. He
flipped pages quickly, muttering to himself until his
searching finger slammed down on something.

"Here, look at this," he croaked.

Frank got up and came around the desk.

"Number Two eighty-four. The USS *Candlefish,* reported sunk around latitude thirty off the coast of
Japan—11 December 1944."

"Sunk?"

"Yes. And with no explanation. Nothing that would jell. I remember that damned thing. There were a couple like that on the Pacific patrols. December of '44, yessir."

"Thirty years ago?" said Cook in disbelief.

Frank stared at the photographs in his hand. "Hell. She looks like new."

Walters chuckled. "This is gonna cost you boys some time," he said. "Can't just file a report and forget it. Gonna have to account for it. Ha!"

Cook made a face. Frank was lost in thought. Something else had occurred to him. Latitude 30. That rang a bell.

At nine o'clock that morning, Cook and Frank were in the main coffee lounge, bent over trays of ham and eggs, coffee and toast, when Cook spotted a figure ambling past the other minor Pentagon officers stuck for Saturday duty.

"Diminsky," announced Cook, and Frank turned to see a short, graying admiral. He too was in uniform, and he didn't look very happy about it. Rear Admiral Lobell Diminsky was the Assistant Chief of the NIS, and wasn't even happy about that. He would rather be Chief Chief, and one day probably would make it—as soon as the civilians could be shoved aside.

"Boys." He smiled briefly.

They acknowledged the greeting, and Frank asked him how the golf was going. Diminsky gave him a hard look. "I got pulled off the second tee by the Secretary of State. I had to bloody *fly* back here, yet."

"No sense of priorities," clucked Frank.

"No sense of timing!" barked Diminsky. He hailed a passing busboy and ordered coffee. Then he eyed Cook's half-finished eggs and toast. Cook caught him looking and very generously pushed the tray toward the admiral. Diminsky grinned at him and nibbled at the toast.

"Next time order rye," he offered.

"He didn't know you were coming," said Frank.

"I gather we've got ourselves a submarine that nobody's seen for thirty years. Right?"

"Yessir," said Frank.

"Bring me up to date."

"ComSubPac firmly denies that it's one of the current fleet boats. It appears to be the USS *Candlefish,* sunk in the Rampo Depth, around latitude thirty in December of 1944. How she got where she is, nobody is even venturing a guess. We ordered DIC to scramble three tugs and some of their people to go out for a look. They may even attempt to board her."

"What about the Jap freighter? The Secretary was very concerned about their position."

"We've ordered DIC to send out a crew to calm them down and take their report. We're assuring them the sub meant no harm."

"You don't know that."

"Admiral"—Frank smiled—"a sub thirty years old?"

"Exactly! You don't know why it surfaced."

Frank sat back. "I think it's more a matter of *how.* I mean . . . there can't possibly be any crew left alive on her, unless she really wasn't sunk in '44 and somebody's been running around the ocean in a stolen submarine for thirty years."

Diminsky waved his coffee cup.

"What about those Japanese soldiers in the Philippines? Every year they turn up some joker who's still fighting for the Emperor. What if our side has a bunch of trigger-happy submariners whose radio got knocked out in '44 and who've been running around the Pacific for thirty years growing beards and afraid to show their faces?"

The look on Cook's face was enough to slow Admiral Diminsky to a crawl. He snatched up the rest of Cook's toast and ate it. "Okay," he growled, "just wanted you to see that any guesses on our part at this point are ridiculous. We cannot assume that boat is just a harmless old hulk until we *prove* it's a harmless old hulk!"

Frank sighed and finally nodded agreement. "I think we should be glad to have it back."

"Glad!" bellowed Diminsky. "I'm glad you're glad. And you'll be really tickled to know we've been ordered to remove that damned boat from the shipping lanes in one fat hurry."

"And then?"

"And then figure out how it got there."

Frank relaxed. Good. He was relieved. Sometimes the Navy had a tendency to ignore things that posed too many problems. Shove them into a hole they can't stick out of—that was the attitude. In the Navy—in all the services—the inexplicable was equated with the disagreeable. But to Ed Frank the inexplicable was of paramount interest. He loved intrigue and danger and the unknown—seized on it doggedly whenever he encountered it.

Diminsky rattled off orders about procedure. The next step would be to line up transportation to Hawaii and quarters at Pearl Harbor. Diminsky wanted to leave at 0800 the next morning.

Frank couldn't resist: "What time do you want to tee off, Admiral?"

Diminsky eyed him squarely. "I'll leave my clubs home if you'll leave your girl friend."

Frank spent the rest of the morning in his office,

pulling out the charts and notebooks of independent research he had been skulling out during the last few years. He got on the phone with Joanne at 1100 and apologized for leaving in the middle of the night. Then he had to apologize for waking her up at 11 in the morning. She complained about her sunburn, and he listened patiently and wondered if he could somehow sneak her over to Pearl Harbor. On second thought— she would only get sunburned again. The hell with that.

He hung up and leaned back in his chair. He studied her photograph: the frozen smile, the hair swept back, the delicate skin. Around him, the other cubicles were empty. Somewhere, from far across the room, came the sound of a typewriter. Another Saturday soldier. Frank sat up straight and looked over his notes again.

This whole project of his—the notes and charts he had put together for himself, the research he had done, the interviews—all looked now as if it might take on fresh purpose. The *Candlefish* could be the key. At last those little red dots he had spot-marked on the Pacific chart—the ones clustered around latitude 30°—might really provide the first concrete evidence that the Devil's Triangle off the southeastern coast of the United States was no myth; that, in fact, she had a sister.

CHAPTER 3

October 6, 1974

They flew cross-country in a Navy jet transport.

While they were crossing the Rockies, Cook accepted a call from ComSubPac and listened intently. "Could you hold a second, sir?" Cook covered the mouthpiece and leaned over to Frank. "ComSubPac. The ATFs report their people are unable to gain entrance to the submarine."

"What does that mean?"

"They sent over a boarding party—couldn't crack the hatches."

"Probably rusted shut." Frank thought a moment, then took the phone. "This is Commander Frank. Tell your people not to try any more. Just have them tow the damned thing into Pearl. Okay?"

The voice on the other end of the line murmured acknowledgment. Frank thanked him and hung up. "Ray . . . get hold of DIC. Tell them we'd like to have a conference with that boarding party when we get into Pearl. And tell SubPac that when the *Candlefish* gets in they should have Graves Registration standing by."

"Yessir." Cook got back on the phone and relayed the requests to Defense Intelligence Command.

Frank returned to his notebooks and spread out his chart, a standard Navy cartographic relief of the Pacific from the west coast of the U.S. to the east coast of

China. He had hand-painted nearly a hundred red dots on it, and over a few of them had added tiny black submarine caricatures. There were three American submarines, six Japanese, and one Brazilian. Frank had tagged each with a date copied from a separate list. All of them were centered around a single large area of sea off the coast of Japan. He lowered his pencil to the one U.S. sub tagged with the date 11 DEC 1944. He circled it.

He looked up to see Diminsky standing over his shoulder, watching him and sipping a Coke. "What the hell have you got there, Ed?"

"A little private research, Admiral."

"Yeah?" He sat down next to Frank and ogled the chart. "What exactly is it?"

"Maritime disasters. Unexplained disappearances. A little hobby of mine. There is one area in this part of the Pacific where more disappearances have occurred than anywhere else."

Frank swept a finger around an area roughly due east of Japan. "Right here—Latitude Thirty." The way he traced his circle, it formed an oblong blob exactly parallel to the tiny nation.

"The eastern edge of the Northwest Pacific Basin, right over the Japan Trench, stretching from Iwo Jima up east off Morioka by some four hundred miles. Roughly fifty percent of all the unexplained disasters in the North Pacific have occurred right in this circle."

"What's with all the little red dots . . . ?"

"Ships, planes, anything that disappeared or was found deserted over the last hundred fifty years."

"The last hundred fifty?"

Cook came over to have a look, and Frank turned the chart around so they could see better. He pointed out the red dots. "Each dot indicates the last recorded position of a specific ship or plane. In all cases they've simply vanished without any trace and to this day haven't been found. Crews and all—just phfft."

"And the little subs?" asked Cook.

"The three American subs, the *Candlefish* among them, disappeared during World War Two."

"Sunk by the Japs," barked Diminsky.

"No—these are the ones that *weren't* sunk by anyone. Granted, there are official explanations for each one—still, none are confirmed. It's just that the Navy—the Office of Naval Investigation in those days—said this is what happened and that's how it's going down in the record books. A bit arbitrary."

"Well, we don't operate that way today," Diminsky offered gruffly.

Both Cook and Frank became suddenly silent, but it failed to register on Diminsky. Finally Frank was prompted to make a comment. "Admiral, I hope you're right. Because I have a feeling there isn't going to be any *simple* explanation for the reappearance of the *Candlefish*. And I hope we're not going to assign one arbitrarily just because it *seems* to fit."

Diminsky displayed a look of pronounced displeasure. "This is no time to be advancing theories, Commander. First examine the sub—*then* figure out what you've got."

Diminsky rose. Frank looked up at him tightly. "What we've got is a submarine that has no business being where it is."

Diminsky shook his head. "This is going to be a very brief preliminary investigation, Ed. I have no intention of letting it get blown up out of proportion. We'll get in—we'll take a look—we'll make a determination. That's it."

* * *

They landed at the Ford Island Naval Air Station shortly after 1300 Pacific time, and all three of them were whisked across the Southeast Loch by launch to the submarine base and then driven right down to the pier.

A huge old gray submarine tender, the USS *Imperator,* was moored by itself, and a portion of the dock was being cleared for the arrival of the *Candlefish.* They checked aboard the tender and were escorted to their quarters above the main decks. Diminsky was given the Flag Quarters. Cook and Frank shared connecting offices. Cook checked with SubPac and learned it would be another three days before the *Candlefish* could be expected to arrive. Frank gave Cook an armful of orders covering the inspection of the submarine. He wanted a platoon of technicians present. He wanted explosives in case they had to blow the hatches. He wanted radio equipment, protective suits, gas masks, and complete authority to run the operation. Cook promised all but the latter. "That you'll have to arrange yourself." He smiled.

Frank took a car over to the base offices of Defense Intelligence Command. He was greeted by a tall, wild-looking man with a great shock of red hair, who introduced himself as Captain Melanoff, and then apologized for not having his boarding party back quickly enough.

"A chopper from that carrier is picking up one of my boys, and they'll wing him right back to you. Should be in tonight. Can I show you around, Commander?"

Frank demurred, but asked to be called the moment the DIC officer got in. He drove back to the pier and went up to his quarters aboard the *Imperator.*

He was lying on a hard vinyl sofa under an open

porthole, studying a cutaway of the fleet submarine, when his eyelids fluttered and he collapsed into slumber. Four hours later, Lieutenant Cook banged into the office and woke him up. "I did my bit," he announced. While Frank blinked himself awake, Cook plopped into the chair behind the single desk and rattled on about the arrangements he had made, until he too drifted off to sleep. Frank got up, went to the port, and looked out, sniffing the fresh sea air.

Across the water he could see the smooth black conning tower of the USS *George Washington,* one of the newer "nukes," or nuclear-drive submarines. Most of her was underwater, but what showed above was enormous, dwarfing the few converted fleet types nearby. Frank had never had the pleasure of serving aboard one of those floating hotels. He had spent his time tied to a desk or skulking the Tonkin Gulf in a cramped fleet boat. At least aboard the *Candlefish* he would be on home ground.

As he stared at the *Washington,* he thought of the USS *Scorpion*—a $40-million nuclear submarine that disappeared with a crew of 99 in May of 1968. Her wreckage was found strewn all over the Atlantic floor at a depth of 10,000 feet some 460 miles southwest of the Azores—directly over the mid-Atlantic ridge. And the Naval Court of Inquiry had concluded: "The certain cause of the loss of the *Scorpion* cannot be ascertained from any evidence now available."

Nothing but superstition? Frank smiled. Although there was a load of hogwash surrounding the Devil's Triangle, the facts couldn't be dismissed. Ships, planes, and subs—all sorts of craft—had disappeared with alarming frequency in the waters off the coast of Florida, in an area forming a rough triangle between Miami and points north of Bermuda and south of Barbados. And now, according to Frank's own research and the independent studies of others, the area off the coast of Japan, known as Latitude 30°, was emerging as a similar center of oceanographic terror.

He swung around and looked at Cook, asleep behind the desk. It was Diminsky he had to contend with—and all the little Diminskys—and the NIS, the Joint Chiefs. How in the world was he going to wake them all up? And why in the world did they always sleep through things like this? Pretend they don't exist and the problems will go away! What an attitude! What a goddamned maddening attitude—this rampant official *blindness!* Places like Bermuda and Latitude 30° would go on claiming their victims ad infinitum, and no one would ever make a move to prevent it. After all, how can you take action against something that "doesn't exist"?

The return of the USS *Candlefish,* after thirty years of dark, lurking oblivion, presented a matchless opportunity. Somewhere, on board or below her decks or in the path she had patrolled, there were answers. And Ed Frank was positive he was the only one willing to ask the right questions.

At 1730 hours Captain Melanoff called to say that his officer, a Lieutenant Harry Nails, had just arrived by helicopter with a full report on the attempted boarding and preliminary recon of the *Candlefish.* Frank arranged to meet him at the Officers' Club for dinner, then woke up Cook. They changed shirts and hurried across the sub base under a threatening afternoon sky.

The Officers' Club was crowded.

Lieutenant Nails had a Navy raincoat slung over his chair. He greeted them with a brisk handshake and invited them to join him.

"I've ordered steaks, Commander," he said to Frank. "Melanoff wants everything on his bill."

"Happy to oblige, Lieutenant." Frank sat down next to Nails and motioned Cook into the other chair. "Let's hear something about the *Candlefish*."

"Mint condition, sir. Not a spot of rust or a sign of rot. She's almost like new."

"Did you go aboard?"

"Yes, sir. I took a boarding party of four men, all technical ratings—they know their stuff."

"Okay," said Frank, "now backtrack and tell us exactly what happened."

"I got my first look at her from the Japanese freighter that reported the surfacing. The captain himself pointed her out to me. She was lying dead in the water about a half mile away, with no number visible on her con. I checked her over through the captain's binoculars, until he tugged at my sleeve and started talking. He was so frightened over the whole incident that he couldn't even tell me how she had surfaced— straight up, bow first, stern first. All he said was 'Submarine come up! Up!'"

Cook couldn't restrain a smile.

"Apparently he tried everything. Hailing, radio, Morse code, white flag . . . got some idea into his head that he had provoked an attack. His interpreter was very busy quoting me the unwritten law: Never surface in the path of friendly shipping, not even as a joke. In the radio message the captain sent out to his people . . ." Nails paused and dug in his briefcase for a notebook and opened it. "Here we are . . . he says, 'The submarine surfaced in an unfriendly manner.'"

Cook snorted. "That's why the State Department was in such an uproar yesterday."

Frank smiled. "That's okay. We thrive on panic."

"It turns out," said Nails, "this fellow has been in

the Japanese Navy some forty years. He's been a skipper on *Maru*-class freighters since before the Korean
War. As a seaman during World War Two, he had his
share of submarine encounters. On one convoy every
ship but his was sunk. So you can imagine how much
love he has for our boats. He got to smiling and joking
about it by the time I left, but I could tell he was still
upset."

Nails paused to devour part of his drink, wiped his
mouth, and then added: "And if you need it, I've got
the whole interview on tape."

The steaks had arrived, and they ate while Nails told
them about boarding the sub. "We approached from
three separate quarters and kept the radios going all
the time. I guess we were being understandably cautious. But she didn't do anything at all, just sort of sat
there, never responded to our signals. We even hailed
her with bullhorns. Nothing. So I ordered boarding
parties from two of the tugs, and I went with one of
them. There were five of us. We fanned out over the
boat and checked her out. I swear, Commander, she
looked like she hadn't been out to sea more than two
days from her last refit."

"Was there seaweed or silt or anything like that?"

"Sir, she was bone clean." Nails buttered a roll and
glanced at his report. "When we checked for ID, we
found the raised bolts on the side of the con and could
verify the number—Two eighty-four. But none of us
knew at the time what that meant. Then one of the
techs found the name lettered on the rescue buoy at the
top of the periscope shears. *Candlefish*." He paused
and chewed on a piece of steak. "That didn't ring a bell
either. Then we tried rapping on the sides of the con.
No response. So I ordered them to crack the hatches.
Well, sir, those guys were down on their knees, puffing

and straining—just couldn't get them open. Wouldn't budge. So we abandoned that and just made a tour of the deck to collect evidence."

Nails grew silent again and chewed his steak quickly. Frank and Cook ate and waited patiently. Nails finally wiped his lips with a napkin and bent over his briefcase. "Excuse me, sir, this thing is wedged in here kind of tight—"

He pulled a large object free and set it on the table. "Found this hooked on the afterdeck gun, sir."

Frank stared at the single binocular tube and the strange-looking sextant arrangement jerry-rigged on top of it.

"What is it?" asked Cook.

"Sextant," said Nails. "The captain of the ATF recognized it. They were rather common in World War Two, I'm told. A lot of the navigators used it. It's half a pair of binoculars—one lens—and the sextant. You can make very accurate sightings with it, even through light mist. But it seems they haven't been used *since* World War Two."

Frank stared at it. Here was proof—not photographs or reports or numbers in an old fleet catalog. Here was a relic of a war fought thirty years ago, and it looked almost new. More than ever, he found himself eager to be face to face with the *Candlefish*. He had the feeling that he would be confronting his future.

October 8, 1974

Frank tumbled into the sack at 2000 hours and couldn't drag himself out of bed until 0930 the next day. He had breakfast with Cook in the Officers' Mess and then went off to brief Admiral Diminsky.

Diminsky listened patiently to the tape of Lieutenant Nails's meeting with the Japanese skipper, but was not very impressed. He asked Frank to have a secretary cull out "only the facts" and submit them as the official briefing. Frank objected on the grounds that the Japanese captain's feelings and impressions were just as valid as his eyeball observations.

"No," said Diminsky, "we are not going to turn this into a Navy horror story. We don't need any of that stuff about the man's past history with the Imperial Navy. Keep it simple and to the point."

"Well, Admiral, I don't know how I'm going to make something simple out of *this*." Frank opened his briefcase and flipped the sextant-scope onto the admiral's desk.

Diminsky listened patiently to Frank's account of it, but looked as if someone had just dropped a two-day-old body at his feet.

He suggested listing the sextant under "artifacts."

Frank departed with the tape and the sextant and walked across the sub base alone, resolving from now on to use subtlety where the admiral was concerned. Let him discover everything for himself. Diminsky hated being upstaged, so if he could be made to feel that it was all his idea . . .

Frank stopped when he felt the first few drops tapping on his cap. Rain. He dashed for shelter as the clouds broke and he was drenched by the worst showers he had seen since the monsoons in Vietnam.

He stood under the porch of the DIC office and watched the rain but thought about the *Candlefish*. The circumstances of her sinking—that information must be available, but it was probably buried somewhere in the files in Washington. He would have them sent out.

When the time came to coordinate all the evidence,

reports, and coincidences, how should it all be presented? The wire services were sure to pick up some of the flak from the Japanese. Of course, the whole thing could be tossed off as a simple *incident*—an accidental surfacing of a fleet submarine—no mention at all of the various extenuating circumstances. But what if there was a leak . . . ? FLEET SUB MISSING THIRTY YEARS RETURNS—BIG SHOCK TO NAVY—GREATEST MYSTERY OF OUR TIME. Frank could see the headlines and the implications. A big thrust from the press might be all the impetus necessary for the Navy to launch a full-scale investigation.

Frank chewed it over a long time, until the rain slowed to a drizzle and he could make his way back to the tender. By the time he got there he was smiling, beginning to form a plan so that he could have it his way.

CHAPTER 4

October 10, 1974

At 1200 hours the pier was packed with Navy officers and technicians. Equipment was hauled from trucks and stacked in rows: radios, temperature gauges, crowbars, blowtorches, explosives, protective suits and helmets, and gas masks. Two ambulances came screaming up to the end of the dock, Graves Registration insignia on each of them. Ed Frank arrived with Admiral Diminsky. Cook opened the door for them.

"Morning, Admiral. Going to be a little late. They were reported off Koko Head ten minutes ago."

Diminsky grunted. Frank walked over to the technicians checking out the inspection gear.

Diminsky followed. He stopped behind Frank and, with his hands on his hips, regarded the equipment skeptically. "You need all this, Ed?"

Frank stood up and flashed him a smile. "We don't know what we're going to find, Admiral. Have to be prepared. No telling what could be running loose inside that big metal cigar. We can't just pop the hatches and stroll aboard."

"No," Diminsky muttered in reluctant agreement. He turned and went off to the edge of the pier.

Frank turned to the demolition experts approaching with their gear: two middle-aged submariners, one with a pipe and the other with a cigar.

"Tell you honestly, Commander," said the one with

the pipe, "we ain't defused any Mark 14s in eight years."

"Maybe we'll get lucky." Frank smiled. "Maybe the *Candlefish* fired all hers."

"I doubt it. She had a pretty slim war record."

At 1230 the first ATF steamed up the channel between the Waipio Peninsula and the Navy Yard and into Pearl Harbor. She drew up south of Ford Island as the submariners waited tensely for their first view of the *Candlefish*.

Binoculars rose as the second ATF steamed up the Southeast Loch, with the old sub in tow.

Despite expectations, she was not rotting at all. There didn't appear to be a barnacle or a spot of rust on her. She was sleek and black and murderous-looking. She seemed loaded and ready for action, a trim fighting ship whose day had hardly begun, much less passed into history thirty years before.

In submarine circles, the boat *is* the weapon, and this one was dark and formidable.

Frank found himself unable to restrain a swelling flood of fatherly pride. The prodigal daughter was returning home, and Frank was ready to take full possession. But as she glided softly in past the Magazine Loch, he wondered fleetingly if the world wouldn't be better off without her.

They had her moored by 1330. The ATFs dropped cables and departed. The men of the *Imperator* stood in the stern of their ship and stared down at the *Candlefish* until the duty officers began herding them back to work. There was no chance now of maintaining even a semblance of security. Stories would be flying all over Pearl by six that night. By tomorrow every newsman and journalist on the island would be clamoring for a base permit. Frank made a mental note to order an

"X" security condition at all entrances. If his plan was to work, he had to make an honest effort to quash publicity. He would leave it to Diminsky to come up with some sort of press release.

The technicians and demo experts were dismissed for mess and ordered back for work at 1430. Only Cook, Frank, and Diminsky were left on the dock, along with the people from Graves Registration. The three NIS officers walked the dock alongside the *Candlefish* and gave her an expert once-over.

A car came up, and Captain Melanoff and Lieutenant Nails of Defense Intelligence Command got out to view the boat. Melanoff's red hair shot every which way in the breeze as he took off his cap to wipe his forehead.

Nails pointed to the deck gun aft. "That's where I found that sextant. Just dangling from those gears."

Frank wondered why that sextant bothered him more than anything else about this business. He felt a nagging desire to know its story—as if in some way it was the key to the mystery of the *Candlefish*. He approached Diminsky.

"Admiral, what do you think?"

There was a long silence. "The Japanese never claimed her as a war kill, you said?"

"They did at first, but later they denied it."

Diminsky looked uncharacteristically perplexed. "Well . . . I don't understand it . . . she's in awfully good shape." He looked up at Frank, expecting an answer, an explanation. The old man just could not stomach the unknown.

At 1445 they were ready for boarding.

A technician named Lloyd introduced himself to Frank. "I'll be going down ahead of you, Commander. Just follow my light all the way. Don't veer off into any compartments. Do exactly as I do."

"Okay," Frank agreed, and the two of them were helped into protective suits by several technicians.

Cook explained to Diminsky the reason for all the precautions.

"If the compartments are flooded, there's a high probability that salt water has found its way into the cells or the closed circuits. We don't know what sort of life there may still be in those batteries. The entire atmosphere inside there may be chlorine gas."

"But you'd smell it right away."

"Not if it's localized, compartment by compartment. Frankly, Admiral, we don't know what the hell we're going to find down there."

Frank turned to Lloyd. "What about flooding?"

Lloyd shook his head. "She'd still be at the bottom. But then . . ." He hesitated.

"But then what?"

"*I* wouldn't depend on *anything,* Commander."

Both men were fitted with radio headsets and gas masks. Through the plastic eyepiece, Frank peered at the demolition experts descending the gangplank to the *Candlefish* top deck, carrying a hydraulic jack and an acetylene torch.

Frank reacted to a voice crackling in his ear. He turned and saw Cook grinning at him, clutching a microphone and carrying a portable radio. Cook was wearing a headset too. Frank gave him a Bronx cheer and then descended the plank after Lloyd.

They followed the demo experts over to the conning tower and waited below while the others swung up to the bridge alone to set up their hydraulic jack.

The demo men readied themselves over the conning-tower hatch.

"Better stand back, sir," one of them said, pitching

his cigar overboard. "No telling where the pieces are gonna fly."

Frank kept his head below bridge level and waited for the first teeth-rattling sounds of the jack. When they didn't come, he peeked over the edge. The other demo expert had a restraining hand on his partner's arm, and there was a whispered argument going on.

"What's up?" Frank asked.

His voice crackled over the speaker in Cook's hand and rang out across the boat. The reticent expert stepped over the hatch and spoke to Frank. "Well, sir, it just occurred to me—there's no rust or corrosion or anything—has anybody tried to open this thing by hand?" He got down on his knees in front of the hatch.

"Mister," called Frank, "it won't open. Lieutenant Nails tried it—" He stopped in mid-sentence as the demo expert ignored him and gave the dogging wheel a tug. It spun out of his hand, and the hatch popped open like a cork.

Frank stared at it.

The demo expert got up and wiped his hands on his trousers. "Like she was greased this morning," he said with a smile. His partner flung him the jack and swung off the bridge in disgust. He stood there and gazed down into the open black hole, curiosity taking over.

Frank was climbing up the bridge rail when he felt a sharp tug on his protective suit.

It was Lloyd. "Me first, sir. Everybody else off this boat."

The demo expert descended from the bridge. Frank stood aside and permitted Lloyd up the ladder first, then joined him on the bridge, where they both looked down into the access trunk hole. Lloyd switched on his light and aimed it below. In the dim light, they saw nothing but crisscrossed metal decking and a puddle of water.

"Let's go," said Lloyd and dropped down into the conning tower, Frank right behind him.

Frank landed in the puddle, and water splashed up over his rubber boots. He looked down to be sure it wasn't acid eating through the protective material. Lloyd played his light quickly around the con. Frank followed the sweep of the beam and picked out familiar instrumentation.

Frank lowered his light to search the deck. There were bits of broken glass, papers, litter. He held the light up to a bank of gauges: The glass had shattered on most of them.

"Come on," Lloyd said, and stepped into the well. Frank followed him down the control-room ladder. Their lights played around the bulkheads and picked out valves, levers, switches, and instruments—still intact. Litter covered the control-room deck: charts, books, pencils, ashtrays, a shirt . . .

But nowhere they looked was there evidence of rust or corrosion or anything that might even remotely betray the wear and tear of thirty years underwater. There was only the minor flooding in the bilges.

Lloyd's voice went out over the headset radio: "We're in the control room. She's tight as a drum. Kind of messy, but we don't see any bodies yet."

Frank shot another quick glance around the compartment. Lloyd was right. No sign of human remains at all. Everything pointed to recent human habitation, even to some sudden, unexpected mass exodus.

Lloyd tapped him on the shoulder, and Frank followed the technician through the open connecting hatch.

Holding the radio, Cook led Diminsky and Nails down the gangplank and aboard the sub, then up the ladder to the bridge. He stood over the conning-tower hatch and sniffed the air coming up from below. Then he lifted the mike: "Ed, this is Cook. I'm on the bridge. My nose tells me the air is okay. Have you found any sealed compartments?"

Lloyd's beam flashed around the next compartment and settled on the rows of green bunks stacked three deep down the length of the crew's quarters. Frank went down the opposite corridor and threw his light on the bunks on that side. They were looking for bodies.

"We're in the crew's quarters," Frank reported over the radio. "No problem getting in. All the watertight hatches are wide open. Bunks are empty, no bodies here. Lots of personal belongings all over the——"

He froze at the sound his foot made—a loud crunch. He whipped the light across the deck.

"What the fuck was that?" Lloyd mumbled across the way.

Frank moved and found the offending culprit. He had crushed a small framed photograph. He bent over and picked it up. "I just stepped on somebody's mother."

Lloyd chuckled and moved on, picking his way through debris. The deck was littered with the crew's personal belongings. Frank stopped again and picked up an old Gillette razor. He held it under the light: the edge was still sharp and gleaming.

"Son of a bitch!" Frank heard Lloyd snap from the next compartment. He was standing half through the next hatch. Frank lumbered across the darkness and followed him into the forward engine room.

They directed both lights at something in the aisle, blocking their way. It was main engine number one. "Got an engine jumped its mounting down here," Lloyd reported over the radio. "Damned thing's pulled away from the bulkhead, looks like it tried to drive through into the next compartment."

"Still no bodies," added Frank.

They picked their way delicately across the forward engine room, swearing as they lost their footing and slid around in a mess of hose and oil.

On the bridge, Diminsky and Cook listened to the comments coming from the radio and stared down into the gaping mouth of the conning tower.

Diminsky spoke softly, concerned for the first time: "Must have been some kind of accident. Crew abandoned ship. And here it is."

"Yes," said Cook wryly, "only thirty years later."

Diminsky looked at him sharply.

Lloyd led Frank back through the midship compartments. The engine rooms had proved too dangerous a quagmire to traverse without proper lighting. They returned past the control room and picked through officers' country. All they found were more belongings scattered on the decks and a few overturned bunks.

Eagerly Frank pressed on into the forward torpedo room. Lloyd caught up with him and warned: "Sorry, sir. Me first again."

Their lights picked out the old Mark 14 torpedoes, still racked in their bays, except for one lying peacefully on the deck against the bulkhead, as if it belonged there. Lloyd bent over the torpedoes and checked the warheads and the arming mechanisms. Frank stood out of the way in the darkness, until Lloyd straightened and mumbled, "Uh-huh."

Technicians had begun to file down the gangplank and aboard the forward deck, assembling their equipment. One of them gave a surprised grunt as the wheel started to turn on the forward hatch at his feet.

The hatch puffed back, and Lloyd stuck his head out. He threw off his gas mask and climbed out.

"We've got live fish below. Better get those two

demolition boys back here."

"What about the crew?" Cook called from the bridge.

"Tell Graves to take home the body bags. There's nothing. Not even a bone. Maybe they all escaped before she went down." Unzipping his protective suit, he looked up as he became conscious of everyone staring at him.

"Well, go see for yourselves," he said.

Slowly the technicians headed for the bridge.

Cook called out to Lloyd, "Where's Frank?"

"Said he'd meet you in the control room."

Cook nodded and set the radio down on the bridge. He dropped into the conning tower and stood in the darkness until the technicians followed him with lights. He borrowed one and looked around. Basically unfamiliar with submarines, he almost bumped into the periscope shaft. He played his light over it, then ran a finger along the tube. The grease was fresh.

A Navy photographer, carrying a big case of camera equipment, descended the control-room ladder ahead of Cook and went through the connecting hatch to officers' country. Cook waited in the control room, pressed against a bulkhead. He was there a full five minutes before Frank appeared, ducking through the hatch.

"Had to start that guy taking pictures," he said, pulling off his gas mask. "Let's have a look at those instruments."

They directed light across the instrument boards. Glass was broken down here too, but everything looked workable. A technician came through and played his light on Frank.

"Would you believe it? Forward battery's still holding a charge."

Frank stared at him, then turned back to the panel

and flipped a switch. Instantly the control room was flooded with light—the red combat lights. Frank stared at Cook's red glowing face. The technician flipped another switch and the radar scopes came on.

"She's alive," he said.

By the time Diminsky descended to the control room to join Frank and Cook, the room was filled with the hum of electronics and the pinging of sonar. Everything was working. Diminsky looked it all over in amazement, then gestured expansively.

"Well, what are we going to do with it?"

Frank straightened and wiped his hands on the protective suit. "Admiral, I'd like to handle this personally."

Diminsky looked at him suspiciously, then shrugged. "Okay. Take a week and figure out what happened."

"A week!"

"Ten days. If you need more—call me."

"I *will* need more."

"Mr. Frank"—Diminsky leveled a gaze at him—"you watch your step. If you come back to me with your wild stories, I'll throw you out with them and put somebody else on this case. The last thing we need is more confusion. Let's leave well enough alone and see if we can put this boat back into service." He turned and looked for the hatchway. "Now then, I'm going to have myself a tour."

He disappeared aft. Frank turned sharply to Cook. "You get me a list of names."

"What?"

"The crew of this boat. Get me a list of the men who served on her in 1944. Get the division reports, squadron reports, force reports, whatever you have to. They should still be here in Pearl. Get me all the yard reports—and get back to Walters for the stuff from his end. See if we can come up with *anything*."

"Like what?"

"Like a *survivor*."

October 11, 1974

The rest of the day was largely unprofitable. Frank was hung out to dry while Diminsky locked himself in his quarters with a secretary and a member of the Board of Inquiry in the USS *Catchewa* mutiny case.

But when Frank met Diminsky for breakfast late the next morning, he was at last prepared for the fight that lay ahead. He made his first move—

"You want to do what?" Diminsky bellowed.

"Take that boat out again. We'll refit, lay in stores, and go out to sea. We'll follow the same path she followed in 1944, on her last patrol."

"What the hell is that going to prove?"

"I don't know exactly. But I'm convinced it's the only way we can get even a glimmer of an idea what happened to her."

Diminsky glared at him a long time, then said, "You're convinced that something of a physical nature happened *to* the boat, right?" Frank nodded. "Suppose you're wrong? Suppose it's something else entirely? Suppose the men simply abandoned her when they found out she was breaking up inside? Suppose she was attacked—boarded? There are so many plausible explanations, why in hell do you pick the most *implausible?*"

"I'm not picking anything. I'm just telling you that no *simple* explanations will wash! Not for what happened thirty years ago, Admiral!"

Diminsky scowled and reached for the coffee. Frank pressed on: *"Candlefish* is a boat the Navy wrote off thirty years ago. At the very least, we have a chance to put her back into service. She's in great condition, needs a minimum refit—she could pass her sea trials with flying colors. As a bonus, we can *make use of her* to find out what happened."

"It's going to cost a fortune," said the admiral.

Frank shook his head. "We'll go out primarily with the original equipment."

"Hell, no! Navy wouldn't let you. Submarines are five hundred percent more sophisticated today."

"Only the nukes," said Frank. "The fleet types are essentially unchanged from World War Two."

"What are you talking about? They're all transistorized today. Improved radar and sonar, electronic countermeasure equipment—everything's been updated."

"But we're not going into a shooting war. Besides, radio is still radio—"

Diminsky scoffed at the simplification.

"Admiral, we don't need any improved equipment. What's on board, once it's checked out, will suffice. We have to be cost-conscious," Frank added, parroting one of Diminsky's favorite phrases.

The arguments bounced back and forth over ham and eggs, toast, and four cups of coffee each. And ended with them no closer in spirit. Finally, however, Admiral Diminsky succumbed to the sheer force of Frank's persistence. "All right . . . I'm returning to Washington tonight. I'll go to the head office tomorrow morning and present the plan to Smitty."

Frank gazed at him balefully. He knew what Diminsky would do: corner Smitty, give him the facts—and simplify everything. But it was better than nothing. Frank knew he had loused things up with the admiral through his own unrelenting abrasiveness.

Shortly before noon, Frank contacted Captain Walters himself, bypassing Cook.

Walters cackled over the phone, "God, I'd like to be there with her. To me, she's magic."

Frank had to give him a lengthy description of the *Candlefish* before he could ask, "Listen, Walters, we need that information now. The official reports on Two eighty-four. The investigations, Board of Inquiry findings . . . What's the holdup?"

"The Submarine people. They want to go over it first. Our people, Ed. They screen everything."

"Well, tell them it's going to *me*, Eyes Only."

There was a silence at the other end, and Frank knew he was pressing too hard. Walters was a good man, and if he had run up against a brick wall, it had to be a real brick wall. "Walters—just let me know immediately if I'm not going to get any of that stuff. And look, if you can, shoot it out to me before noon tomorrow. Diminsky's going back to Washington, and I don't want it to wait around until he looks at it, because that's another eight weeks."

"Okay, Ed."

Frank hung up. He couldn't let Diminsky put a clamp on the whole thing before he got enough information to justify his case. Fucking politics! Frank slammed out of his office and went back down to the dock.

He spent the rest of the afternoon walking the boat between the forward torpedo room and the aft section. The demolition experts were disarming the entire load of Mark 14 fish. The *Candlefish* had fired eight torpedoes her last time out.

Frank mulled that figure over. Not a very successful patrol, considering that the aim of any submarine venture was to expend all torpedoes before coming home—but then, her journey had been interrupted . . .

Frank joined a crew of technicians picking their way through the rubble in the forward engine room. All ship lights were on now; the batteries were charged and functioning fine.

One of the technicians picked up a length of twisted pipe and held it out for the others to see. "I don't get what happened here. These lines just expanded from heat until they blew. How could they get so hot?"

The men groped under machinery and in bunks for bits and pieces of wreckage. They slogged through the oily debris on deck and gathered around main engine number one, wedged up against the hatchway, trying to figure out how the thing had burst its mountings. Finally Frank pointed at it and said quietly, "We'll want to get that back into shape."

One of the men looked at him in amazement and croaked: "Why?"

"We might want to take her out for a little spin."

Frank headed for the pantry, which was located forward of officers' country. He found three men already there, poring through the piles of packaged and canned goods. Frank inspected the unfamiliar labels on the cans. Everything dated from World War II.

In the galley they found perishable foods, all of it fresh and new. One of the technicians held up a loaf of bread and, squeezing it, remarked: "Could've been baked last night."

Another man came up the ladder from the below-deck icebox, carrying frozen meats under his arm. "Most remarkable case of preservation I ever saw. Anybody care for a steak?"

Frank stepped in and gruffly ordered, "Get all that stuff out of here—all the perishables."

He went back to officers' country and peered into the wardroom. It was a shambles: books, records,

record player, charts, cups, pencils, clipboards, everything flung about as if someone had had a violent tan-
trum.

He opened the door to the captain's tiny cabin. It
resembled a dozen others he had seen, including the one
he had lived in when he took over command of the
Prang for a month in 1969. It held a double bunk, the
lower one tucked out of sight behind an overhanging
curtain. There were two chairs, a stainless steel wash-
basin, and a desk, the last two on piano hinges that
could drop from the bulkhead. Frank opened the desk
and found it crammed with stacks of papers, a few
books, and other litter. Either the captain of the *Candlefish* had been a very disorganized man or someone
had worked his desk over in a cocktail shaker. Frank
paused over the signature flamboyantly displayed on a
ship's order dated 20 NOV 1944:

LT. COMDR. BILLY G. BASQUINE, U.S.N.

The name was a mouthful. Something slipped out of a
cubbyhole, and Frank caught it before it crashed to the
floor: a black-and-white portrait of the Captain, with
his arms around his wife and two young children.
Frank stared at it a long time, trying to measure
strength and resolve in the man's features. But something lurked behind the stiff smile, and for the moment
Frank couldn't decipher what it was.

He turned and saw the low filing cabinet across the
tiny cabin. He sat down on the bunk and opened the
drawers: They were thick with manila folders containing dossiers, fitness reports, promotion recommendations, a ship's-organization pamphlet, copies of the
watch bills, diving bills, emergency bills—a wealth of
information. Good. He would have Cook remove all
this material to his office right away.

He got up, and as he turned to close the desk the log caught his eye. It was not the official ship's log; that was kept in the control room by a quartermaster. This was the captain's day-to-day log, his personal account of all events aboard the boat that ran counter to the Ship's Daily Orders. In it there should be records of every dive, every attack, every gun action, every course change or order change enacted by the *Candlefish* during her last patrol. Immensely valuable. The book was open, face down, buried under a stack of papers. He flipped it over and gazed at the open entry, the top of the page ribboned with the Captain's hasty scrawl.

The date was November 21, 1944. The entry began: "*0800. Underway from Pearl, proceeding under orders to general area Kuriles, Pacific.*"

That was all. Nothing more on that page or the one opposite. Frank flipped back and found entries running back to January. He flipped to November 22, 1944.

His hand froze, and he stared at the page.

It was blank.

He went on. November 23rd, 24th . . . right on through to December . . . up to December 11th, the day the *Candlefish* was reported lost.

Nothing. Blank and fresh, not even the mark of an eraser.

How could that be? The sub had left Pearl; that much was certain. They had fired eight torpedoes. SubPac had records of their kills on that last patrol. Had Basquine failed to keep his log? Frank stared at the blank pages until he was interrupted by a tapping on the door. He closed the log and tucked it under his arm.

"Come in."

Cook opened the door and grinned at Frank. "Found a survivor."

CHAPTER 5

October 11, 1974

Frank was angry. Cook had obviously taken time to read all the material before he even told Frank he had it. Cook turned red in the face and apologized profusely. The notes *had* come in that morning; he *had* read them through himself; he wanted to be able to brief Frank. "And I mean brief," he added, and indicated the crammed manila folder under his arm.

They walked back up the dock together, heading for the *Imperator*. Cook gave Frank a résumé, occasionally referring to the file.

"He came aboard the *Candlefish* in January of '44 as a lieutenant and served eleven months as navigation officer. He was the only known survivor of the sinking, and it's largely his report that makes up the history of the incident."

"What happened to him? How did he get off the boat?"

"Washed off the bridge and busted up his knee just before she sank, picked up by a Japanese fishing boat within two hours, then delivered over to their Navy. He was put in with the surviving crew of an American destroyer, and they were all taken to the copper mines in Ashio. He worked there till the end of the war. They never took care of his knee, so all the time he spent in the mines the pain was so intense he could hardly walk."

Cook and Frank went to their quarters aboard the *Imperator* and closed the door.

"Did he file reports on the sinking?" asked Frank.

"Yes. He was repatriated August of '45 and taken to a hospital at Pearl. Must have been there four months while they worked over his knee. He was questioned repeatedly by SubPac and the Office of Naval Investigation, all preparatory to the Board of Inquiry. But on the subject of his competence as a witness, everybody wrote a different opinion."

"Oh?"

"His story seemed to change a lot. He was unsure of the sequence of events and, in some cases, the events themselves."

"What information did you get on the sub?"

"She went down at about 2130 on the night of 11 December '44. The approximate position was thirty degrees forty-nine minutes north and one hundred forty-six degrees thirty-eight minutes east. That's based on her last reported position, speed, and direction. From all weather reports—ours and the Japanese— they were surrounded by calm seas and clear skies. But according to Hardy there was fog, thick as soup, and some kind of inexplicable heavy sea action."

"Inexplicable?"

Cook skipped some papers in the folder and came to one and read: " 'Asked if the *Candlefish* came under attack on December eleventh, Lieutenant Hardy said, "No—no—no. She simply started shaking herself to pieces." When asked what in his opinion had caused this, Hardy had no explanation.' " He closed the paper and looked up. "The first few go-rounds, that's the way all the interrogations went. They kept throwing suggestions at him, possible explanations, and he kept fielding them, insisting that there was rough sea and some kind of electrical thing going on."

"Electrical?"

"Yeah, he reported that the antenna cables were all lit up like Fourth of July sparklers."

"That doesn't sound like anything to do with rough seas."

"I know. That's what I mean when I say his story doesn't jibe. He jumps around from detail to detail, and you put all of them together—well, they just don't make sense. It really sounds as if he had a bit of a trauma and afterwards couldn't remember things properly." Cook opened the folder again, pulling out another letter. "A supervising officer from ONI writes the following: 'Further questioning led us to suspect Lieutenant Hardy had suffered delusions—either at the time the submarine was lost or later as a result of his treatment in the POW camp.' "

"Well, that's just an opinion," Frank said.

"Yeah, but everything from Hardy comes out as conjecture." Cook flipped the page and read on: " 'On the fourteenth day of questioning, Lieutenant Hardy ventured a new theory and, when pressed, insisted on its validity. He theorized that the Japanese had developed an electromagnetic weapon powerful enough to pull a boat apart.' "

This time, even Frank frowned skeptically.

Cook skipped a few more pages in the file and continued: " 'During the Board of Inquiry, Lieutenant Hardy brought up this and other theories and, as he could not substantiate any of them, they were regarded as inadmissible evidence. In view of Hardy's apparent unreliability, no further effort was made to investigate the matter.' "

Cook folded the file on his lap and waved a hand. "The *Candlefish* was chalked up as missing in action, and that was the end of it."

"I see. And how did they chalk up Hardy?"

"They didn't. They just ignored him." Cook thumbed to the back of the folder and drew out papers, handing them one by one across to Frank. "Here. Fitness reports, qualification exams and reports, summaries by ComSubPac. Here's his whole history since he was discharged in 1946—everything relating to the Navy."

Frank hefted the pile of papers. "What do you mean? He had more contact with the Navy?"

"Yeah. Lieutenant Jack Hardy is now Dr. Jack Hardy of the Scripps Institution of Oceanography. He's been in the field for twenty-odd years. Very well thought of, in fact."

"That's a pretty responsible position . . ."

"You mean for a guy who shows such an apparent lack of it?" Cook again closed the folder.

Frank said nothing. He picked up one of Basquine's dossier files with Hardy's name penciled on the lip. He glanced through it quickly while Cook sat in silence. Suddenly Frank sat up in surprise. "Listen to this! This is the Captain's report, dated August 14, 1944." He read through Basquine's account of an incident involving Hardy and the performance of a routine slug test in which Hardy made a gross error of mechanics, resulting in heavy damage to the sub and the loss of a torpedoman's life. Basquine's account was heavily laced with terms like "gross negligence."

Cook frowned his concern. Frank placed the report on the desk and pointed out the words: "The Executive Officer, Lt. Bates, recommends Lt. Hardy for immediate transfer to shore duty upon our return to Pearl, pending investigation for court-martial. In my judgment, justice will be better served by full disclosure of the facts to a Board of Inquiry, no transfer acceptable even if requested by Lt. Hardy himself, and no recommendation for court-martial."

The meaning was abundantly clear to both Frank and Cook. In effect, Hardy was being "sent to Coventry." Basquine was recommending that he be forced to remain aboard a submarine with eighty-three men who were probably all convinced he was a monumental fuckup.

"Pretty stiff," said Cook. "I wonder if Lieutenant Hardy knew he was being shafted."

"I wonder . . . if he didn't deserve it." Frank dropped the report. "And he ends up in *oceanography?*"

Frank got up, stuffed his hands in his pockets, and moved to the porthole. He gazed out at the *Candlefish* and ran the name "Hardy" over in his mind. Hardy—and oceanography. Cook saw the smile.

"What's so funny?"

"I'm suddenly very impressed with our good fortune." He ignored Cook's puzzled look and slapped a hand down on Hardy's dossier. "We can *use* this guy."

The first newsmen began calling at mid-afternoon, interrupting Diminsky's last-minute packing. He played dumb with the first man, annoyed with the second, and outraged with the third. Then he stopped answering the calls. When he stepped off the *Imperator* after a fruitless search for Frank, he ran smack into the first crew of cameramen from the local Hawaiian TV station. They hurried past him to set up cameras alongside the *Candlefish* and get some footage before they lost the sun. Diminsky stood on the dock and fumed.

He found the base commander in his quarters and demanded to know who had authorized the break in security around the *Candlefish*.

"I did."

Diminsky sat back in defeat. Admirals don't outrank admirals, and the man across the desk looked ready to argue the point. He explained quite calmly that his brother-in-law was a vice-president of the same local TV station and had asked for permission—

"How did he get wind of it?" Diminsky stuck a finger on the base commander's desk. He was rewarded with a cold silence.

"Somebody leaked the information!" Diminsky snarled.

"I don't know that, Admiral, but if you would like to hold an inquisition, I'll provide you with the implements of torture."

Diminsky left the base commander's office without getting satisfaction. Once he had calmed down and sorted everything out, he realized the admiral hadn't withheld anything. He had only been miffed.

Diminsky stood on the dock as the TV crew were wrapping up and suspected the fine hand of Ed Frank. But he had no proof. And, as yet, no motive.

For the rest of the afternoon, he couldn't find Ed Frank anywhere.

Diminsky left for Washington on a 9 P.M. flight, unaware that the information from Captain Walters had arrived earlier aboard the same plane. Frank was very pleased with his tactics so far. He had the publicity he wanted—he watched it on TV at 6 P.M.—he had Diminsky out of his hair for a few days, and he had managed to spend the day hiding in Captain Melanoff's office, poring through the mountain of documents sent by Walters.

Frank set to work consolidating the papers and notes. By late evening, after a supper of sandwiches, Frank had decided that Hardy could be approached, though he would have to be handled with kid gloves:

He appeared to be an extremely sensitive man. It would take maneuvering to get him to help out on this project. But Frank would do whatever had to be done; he felt that Jack Hardy's assistance was crucial.

Frank sat back and went over his notes, sipping soda water and sucking on his pipe.

Over the years, that last night of December 11, 1944, must have become the most baffling riddle in Jack Hardy's life. Was that riddle directly responsible for his entry into the field of oceanography? It seemed likely that he would have felt a strong urge to become involved in the one field of study that might provide answers to the mystery of the *Candlefish*.

Frank rummaged for Cook's folder and flipped through the records on the Board of Inquiry. No one on the Board had ever openly cast doubt on Hardy's story, but the evidence seemed to suggest they had managed to get him so rattled and insecure that after a few days he was no longer sure *what* he believed. They never pieced together a story that satisfied Hardy, but what they settled on seemed to satisfy *them*.

So Hardy had found his way into oceanography—perhaps in an attempt to justify himself, to prove his theories right. He had taken advantage of the GI Bill after the war to put himself through Scripps School of Oceanography, which in those days was little more than fledgling. He got into the field on the ground floor. He studied marine biology, marine geology, marine geography, and aided in the development of early programs for research submersibles.

Over the years he had tried to associate himself with study projects involving marine phenomena similar to what he suspected had occurred December 11th, 1944. But nothing ever panned out. His one venture out to the infamous Bermuda Triangle, aboard the support ship *Estefette* in 1955, proved an abortion. He had assembled a project on the magnetic index of cross-currents and was trying to prove the existence of powerful electromagnetic field centers in that area. It was a dismal failure. The equipment refused to respond. The other scientists insisted that the instruments failed simply because there were no such electromagnetic forces. But Hardy was convinced the instrumentation had been affected by the very forces he was seeking—only he couldn't prove it. And no one was very much interested in spending more time or money on it.

So he had returned to Scripps and concentrated on research and the preparation of other men's programs. His heyday was in the 1950s, when he nearly made the project team on board the *Trieste,* one of the first and most important of the research submersibles. The records showed that he had placed applications, had been seriously considered by the project team, but the minute the Navy got into it, Hardy was dropped.

Frank searched further in his notes. Every time the Navy got involved in a submersible project that meant an opportunity for Hardy, somehow the opportunity disappeared. Did the Navy keep a copy of his *Candlefish* testimony in front of them at all times?

The material covering the incident in 1965 was terribly skimpy—just brief references to a submersible called *Neptune 4000* and Hardy's leadership of the expedition, his nervous breakdown, and the cancelation of the entire project.

It was probably his greatest opportunity, and for some reason he had blown it. Frank wanted to know more, but the information simply wasn't here. What so intrigued him was the fact that Hardy had designed the project himself with a syndicate of builders and backers—and the expedition was to have centered around latitude 30° southeast off Japan!

Even today, Hardy was still employed at Scripps. Frank had his home address, an office, and the phone numbers of several close associates. One in particular—Dr. Edward Felanco, a vice-chairman of the Board at Scripps—was presently working with Hardy outfitting the submersible AGSS-555 *Dolphin* for a special project.

Frank polished off his soda water and went up on deck to find Lieutenant Cook.

The next morning he caught a plane for San Diego.

CHAPTER 6

October 12, 1974

Frank landed at the Naval Air Station on Coronado at 1030 Saturday. He was escorted to the west-side wharf and boarded a launch that took him across the bay to Point Loma, where a car met him to cover the short distance to the submarine base.

He was driven past a sign that read SUBDEVGRU ONE, and then down to the docks. A support craft was moored along the same finger-pier as AGSS-555 *Dolphin*. Frank got out of the car, and the driver went to find Dr. Edward Felanco. Frank walked to the end of the dock and looked the *Dolphin* over. She was a smaller version of the *Candlefish*. In fact, of all the research submersibles built over the last twenty years, she bore the closest resemblance to the old fleet-type warboats.

"What do you think of her?"

Frank looked around to find a silver-haired man, short and powerful-looking, smiling at him from the afterdeck of the support craft.

"Are you Ed Frank?" the man asked.

"Dr. Felanco?"

"Yes."

Felanco hurried down the deck of the support ship and shook Frank's hand. Together they walked down the dock to the *Dolphin*. "She was launched in 1968," said Felanco. "She's owned and operated by SUB-

DEVGRU ONE for the Navy. She's one hundred sixty-five feet—half the length of your mysterious fleet boat . . ."

Felanco's eyes made a quick run at Frank's face. Frank smiled. "I see you've guessed why I'm here."

"Wasn't too difficult. You wanted to meet Hardy. I'm the one who told him about the reappearance of the *Candlefish*. I never had much trouble putting two and two together."

Frank stood looking at the *Dolphin* while Felanco told about his current ills with the project: The research trip had been pushed back four times already for mechanical failures aboard the sub.

"Is Hardy going with you?"

Felanco looked at him quizzically. "No. I assume you know some things about Jack Hardy."

"Some."

"For instance, he will never again go on a submarine voyage of any kind."

Frank lost his smile. "What do you mean?"

"He refuses. Oh, he'll plan the research for these jobs, outline the projects, and help to fit the boats, but once we head out to sea, we go without him."

"This goes back to his days aboard the *Candlefish?*"

"Hell no. Goes back to 1965, I think . . ."

"The *Neptune 4000?*"

Felanco nodded.

"I want to hear all about that one. It may have some bearing on my meeting with Hardy."

They went aboard the little support ship and sat down in the officers' wardroom. Felanco ordered coffee and began to tell the story of Hardy's last sea voyage.

"Jack got involved with a team from Woods Hole Oceanographic Institution and a company of builders. They developed the *Neptune 4000,* an advanced deep-submergence research ship. Hardy assembled the project for traversing the Mindanao Depth in the east Pacific—"

Frank interrupted him. "Wait a minute. I understood he set this thing up to examine Latitude Thirty and the Ramapo Depth."

"Not quite. He wanted that, eventually. That was to have been the second voyage. He submitted a lot of plans on it to the Navy. I think part of his idea was to conduct a search for the remains of the *Candlefish* . . . He had very heavy communication with the Navy about it. They turned him down flat."

Frank's eyes narrowed. The 1944 business seemed to haunt Hardy wherever he went. "What happened with the *Neptune 4000*?"

"They were on a shakedown cruise off Pearl. They had been underwater about three hours, at a depth of twelve hundred feet . . . when Jack just seemed to go berserk. Two scientists with him called it acute claustrophobia. Whatever it was, they had to surface. Eventually they canceled the whole project."

"Why?"

"Jack's was the mind behind it, and he had a nervous breakdown. Put him out of commission for quite a while. His son, Peter, came down from law school in Seattle and stayed with him for three months."

Frank folded his arms and sat back. "He's an unstable character, isn't he?"

"Not any more. He's fifty-six years old, and I think he's resigned himself to sailing a desk. When he came back to Scripps in the winter of '66, he said to me, 'Eddie, I am never again going out on a submarine, a submersible, or any other undersea vehicle. I've had it.' He wasn't kidding, Commander."

Frank took it under advisement.

"You said that you were the one who informed him about the *Candlefish* reappearing. How did he take it?"

"Stunned . . . Jack is a very well-tanned old boy, and I could swear he turned white. He didn't believe it at first, and he asked a lot of questions. I told him what was making the rounds on the base. I think the shocker was the fact that there was no evidence of the crew. No bodies. He just looked at me a long time, then he turned around and hobbled away. I haven't spoken to him about it since."

Frank began to feel itchy. He wanted to cut this short and get up to Scripps right away to see Hardy. He rose and thanked Felanco for his coffee and his time.

"No trouble. I'm sure you'll find Jack in his office . . . on Monday."

"Monday?"

"Yes. He flies up to Seattle every third weekend to see his boy. Quite proud of him, you know?"

"Are you sure that's where he is?"

"Oh, yes. Positive. My secretary arranges his flights. He picked up the ticket this morning. So—have you got a place to stay over the weekend?"

Frank left Felanco on the wharf and went off to a pay phone. He dialed Hardy's office number and let it ring until he was sure no one was going to answer.

October 14, 1974

Ed Frank remained in San Diego over the weekend, borrowing a Navy staff car from the base at Coronado and setting out to see the sights. He spent the rest of Saturday in Balboa Park, visiting the aerospace museum and the Reuben H. Fleet Space Center, fight-

ing hordes of kids into the planetarium show, and then
enjoying it as much as they did. Sunday he went to the
San Diego Zoo and stood in front of the gorilla's cage,
peering at a big ape who bore a remarkable resemblance to Diminsky.

Monday morning, bright and early, he swept onto
the San Diego Freeway and raced up to La Jolla, then
took the coast road to Scripps. He pulled onto the cam-
pus and stopped the car simply to admire the morning
beauty of a cluster of buildings overlooking the Pacific.
The landscape was colorful and manicured; trees
swayed in the ocean breeze and brushed against each
other. There was a romance about this place. Working
here within a stone's throw of the sea . . . Frank fully
expected to find Jack Hardy standing on the edge of a
wind-swept cliff, long strands of white hair flapping in
the breeze, a chart in one hand and a compass in the
other, every inch the ancient mariner.

Instead, he found Hardy tucked away in his office on
the third floor, behind a door lettered JACK N. HARDY,
PH.D., PROFESSOR OF OCEANOGRAPHY.

Ed Frank knocked, heard a muffled reply from
within, and opened the door. A gentle sea breeze
wafted in through large, open windows. In the center of
a room filled with papers, books, charts, globes, sex-
tants, and stacks of Xeroxed reports was a big old
carved oak desk. Behind it a figure rose awkwardly to
full height. He was tall and lanky, with a bristling gray
beard, his skin thick, tanned, and grained like leather.
He had the look and the frame of a Nantucket whaler.
Frank had examined Jack Hardy's wartime photos
closely, and he recognized the big blue eyes, the
turned-up corners of the lips, giving him a near-per-
manent look of innocent friendliness. The hair had

gone thin and was speckled with gray, and now he had that twisting, curly gray beard. But Frank looked past the open smile to the eyes: They betrayed a softness and vulnerability that was evident nowhere else in his make-up.

Hardy smiled and came around the desk, favoring his right leg, hand outstretched. In the thirty years since his short-lived career aboard the old fleet boats, he had changed from a gawky boy to a weatherbeaten old coot. Frank looked up at him—Hardy was a good six inches taller—and shook his hand.

"Professor, I'm Lieutenant Commander Ed Frank. I'm with the Naval Investigative Service."

"I was wondering when I would hear from you people," Hardy spoke firmly. He motioned Frank to a chair. "Come on in. Have a seat."

Frank kept smiling, doing his best to put Hardy at ease, but once the big man was safe behind his desk again, he fell into a cool restraint. He intended to maintain his distance; Frank could see that clearly.

Frank gestured at the clutter around him. "Quite a setup."

"Yeah, it's taken me ten years to get it this messy. They wouldn't dare fire me."

"No," chuckled Frank, "they'd better just burn it and start over." He paused, grinning, until Hardy responded with a smile. "Professor, let me get right to the point. We have ourselves a hot potato."

"After thirty years? I'd say she's had time to cool off."

Frank smiled tolerantly. "Maybe you haven't heard, but the *Candlefish* is still in running condition."

Hardy stopped smiling. He went cold. "That wasn't on the news."

"There's a certain amount of internal damage, causes unknown. We suspect it has to do with—well, with what you put in your original reports. Anyway, she's seaworthy."

Hardy was very quiet, eyes boring into Frank. "I don't see how."

"She surfaced about six hundred miles northwest of Pearl Harbor. We've had her towed back to the sub base and we've opened her up and checked her out. There is no sign whatever of the crew." He watched Hardy's features tighten. "No bodies, no bones, no trace."

Hardy slid back in his chair very slowly, eyeing Frank. His face was a mask.

"I thought maybe you might come out to Pearl and have a look at her."

It must have been a full thirty seconds before Hardy said, "No." And Frank made him repeat it.

"The Navy will certainly pay your way—"

Hardy waved it off. "That's old business, Commander. *Old* business."

"It's new to me," Frank said stiffly. And then he smiled again, still trying to find the warm side of this man. "I've been going through your reports to SubPac and the Board of Inquiry. Your ideas on what might have happened? I find them intriguing."

"Nobody believed me then—why should they believe me now?"

"I see," said Frank, and got up to pace around. He felt his patience going. "I guess we'll just have to park the *Candlefish* in a used-submarine lot somewhere and hope we can find a buyer who wants to turn her into a floating museum. Or maybe we can put her back into service—a refit, a bit of conversion here and there—brand new!"

Frank spun around quickly and growled at Hardy, "I'll tell you, Professor, that thing has been in my hair nine days now, and everywhere I go I find people who range from uncooperative to downright ignorant! My own superiors would just as soon sweep the whole boat under a rug and pretend it never even existed. It's a thorn in everyone's hide, and nobody wants to take the responsibility for doing any more than *removing it!* Well, I want more! I want to find out *how* that bloody boat came back! And I need help!"

Hardy shifted uncomfortably. "What do you want with me?"

"I want you to come out to Pearl."

Hardy shook his head, *No.* Frank closed in on him. "As a scientist! You're a survivor and an oceanographer. You know the boat and you know the sea!"

"No."

Frank scowled and realized he must appear comical to the old man—all loud and eager foolishness. "Professor, in 1965 you were writing letters to the Navy outlining your plan for investigating Latitude Thirty." Frank saw Hardy's body stiffen. "That spot off the coast of Japan is renowned for the disappearance of ships and planes, for crews turning up dead or vanishing without a trace . . ."

Hardy's arms folded across his chest; he looked as if he were preparing to retreat into himself.

Frank pressed on. "It's an area uncomfortably similar to that goddamned Devil's Triangle off the coast of Florida. Only this one is in the Pacific!"

Hardy tried to remain unconcerned. "So?"

Frank's next announcement was delivered with quiet but deadly conviction. "Professor, the *Candlefish* is the first one of those things that has *ever come back!*"

An unmistakable swell of fear crossed Hardy's face, and Frank didn't know whether he had secured him or lost him. It was to be several days before he would know for sure.

CHAPTER 7

October 15, 1974

Joanne came home from work early and found Frank changing uniforms in a stumbling hurry. She let out a shriek of joy and leaped all over him. He laughed and hugged her tightly.

"I missed you. I missed you!" she purred in his hair.

"Did you miss me?"

"No—" She pulled away with a smile and fixed his tie.

"What sort of trouble have you been getting into?" He played with the buttons on her blouse.

"Oh, I shacked up with two sailors from the Mexican Navy. We survived eight days on beans and tacos."

"Sure. And what are you doing home at two thirty in the afternoon?"

She padded away in calculated nonchalance. "There was a fire in my wastebasket."

Frank blinked in surprise. He followed her into the bathroom and watched her run cold water over her face. She made a ceremony of the ablutions, until finally she glanced up at him out of the corner of her eye and said, "Yes, I started it, but don't ask."

He burst out laughing and grabbed her around the waist. Her face was dripping wet when he pulled her around for a kiss. He never saw her hand come up over his head, but the rush of water down his neck made him leap a foot in the air. She jumped back, the wash-cloth still clutched tightly in her hand.

"Son of a bitch," he growled, and ripped off the clean shirt.

After a moment, she came up to him in a warm slink.

"Isn't it lucky I came home early?"

Two hours later, Frank was convinced that Lady Luck certainly had played a big part in his afternoon. In fact, she'd made his day. He drove over to the Pentagon at six o'clock and met Admiral Diminsky in the coffee lounge. It was hot, and the admiral was wearing short-sleeved suntans. He was busy dictating to his secretary, and would hardly even look at Frank while they waited for John Allen Smith, the civilian chief of the NIS, to appear.

Smitty came in at six thirty and crossed over to them with a big smile. The rest of him was even bigger. Smitty was a huge, forty-seven-year-old Mormon; he neither drank nor smoked, and didn't approve when others indulged. So Frank, who had brought his pipe kit from the apartment, had to refrain from smoking through the entire meeting. It was a trial.

"Ed, how are you?" Smitty's voice boomed across the lounge. He shook Frank's hand and sat down. He ordered a club sandwich and a pitcher of iced tea. "Down to business. The admiral has filled me in on your efforts to date, and he has acquainted me with certain details of your plan. Namely, the expected cost."

The old knife-in-the-back routine, thought Frank. No wonder Diminsky wouldn't look him square in the eye.

"Sir, I am as aware of cost as the admiral is. But I am convinced that an opportunity like this cannot be allowed to—"

"I am not convinced," said Smitty flatly. "I don't see what you are out to prove."

"I'll lay it out as simply as I can, sir. We all know the popular myth, the incidents that are supposed to have occurred in the so-called Devil's Triangle. We are aware that somewhat related incidents have occurred in latitude thirty degrees off the coast of Japan as well. If we can prove to some degree of satisfaction that Latitude Thirty is actually another Devil's Triangle, we will go a long way toward scientific acceptance of what has been up until now a purely conjectural phenomenon."

"In English, please, Commander," mumbled Smitty.

"Yes, sir. The point is that scientists do not take this business seriously. And if they are ever going to, we have to provide them with evidence that they can use as a basis for further investigation. We have to prove that the *Candlefish* was a victim of forces unknown, that her sinking was not of natural cause, but clearly *unnatural*. The fact that she is here is almost enough to prove it—but not quite. There may be a scientific explanation for how she was preserved so well over a thirty-year period. And if we dumped her into the hands of scientists tomorrow morning, I'm sure they would come up with one. But it's not the preservation we're concerned with. It's what got her in the first place—what got the crew—and how she came back."

Diminsky sipped a Coke. "What evidence do you expect to turn up?"

Frank leaned forward and thought very carefully before he spoke, not wanting to commit himself too much, but wanting to tantalize as much as possible. "I feel that in this instance, as in many others taking place in the Devil's Triangle, we are dealing with *time* more than with any other physical factors."

"Go on," said Smitty, attacking his sandwich and washing it down with giant swallows of iced tea.

"Time slip, time warp, time barrier. I don't know what. It sounds like third-rate science fiction, I know, but I'm convinced these things must be taken into consideration."

"Just a second." Smitty dabbed his lips.

Diminsky sipped more Coke and let a little contemptuous smile creep over his face. He was happily watching Frank make an ass of himself.

"Commander, are you going to try to prove that the *Candlefish* was snatched out of 1944 and *dumped* into 1974?"

"Sir, I don't know. Basically I am only interested in opening up areas of investigation for other, more qualified people. You have to remember, our Navy and Air Force and those of a lot of other countries have lost several hundred planes and vessels in this area. That's costly. And if we have a line on how to stop it, we goddamned well better follow it."

"How?" Smitty eyed Frank intently.

"If we can retrace that last patrol of the *Candlefish* and come to some conclusions about what happened to her, based purely on eyeball observations, we will be able to go before the Senate Appropriations Committee and solicit funds for a much more thorough research job, perhaps for the creation of a specific project under Naval auspices."

"Christ Almighty, Ed"—Smitty rolled back in his chair—"the Navy can barely scrape enough money together to build up its own fleet! What makes you think they'll spring for something like this?"

"Smitty, far wilder ventures have been attempted."

Diminsky took offense. "What do you mean, wilder?"

"October, 1943. The Philadelphia Navy Yard. The secret application of a force field to a Navy warship which promptly disappeared from its dock and reappeared a few moments later at another dock in Norfolk." He gazed sharply at Diminsky. "Remember that one?"

Diminsky squirmed. "If it happened."

Smitty cut in, "That was wartime. A specific project with a specific application."

"So is this. Let's *save* the Navy some money. Avoid more incidents."

"And what about the crew? The men who were aboard the *Candlefish* in 1944. They seem to have missed the return trip. Somewhere in those thirty years they got lost."

"Yes, they did. We want to find out why. Did they get off the boat? Did they die? Did they disintegrate?"

"What?"

"Sir, these are just possibilities. All I'm requesting is the authorization to begin at the beginning, to follow that boat's last course, to recreate as closely as possible the events that led to her disappearance."

Diminsky volunteered information. "Mr. Frank has found a survivor of that last patrol, Smitty. Fellow happens to be an oceanographer. I would suggest his views might settle the matter."

Frank cut in sharply. "I've seen him. I doubt whether we will ever *get* his views. He's had the *Candlefish* up to here." He tapped his neck. "Besides, his testimony was taken after the war. Nothing he said was conclusive. At best he could only offer opinions."

"Those opinions are more valid than your conjecture," snapped Diminsky.

"Look, the man is a scientist. Somewhere along the way, his natural curiosity will get the better of him. I can have him when I need him."

"Boys," interrupted Smitty, "we're getting in over our heads anyway, so let's keep it simple. This is all over the newspapers now. The Navy's got people breathing down its neck: Gold-Star Mothers of World War Two, American Legion, Veterans of Foreign Wars —they all want to know what happened to their relatives who served on that boat in 1944. We're going to be *obliged* to give an answer."

Diminsky looked pointedly at Frank. "We wouldn't be if somebody hadn't taken a *leak*."

"Over a hundred men saw that sub towed into Pearl, Admiral," purred Frank. "There was no leak necessary."

"Stick to the essentials," said Smitty. "The submarine people are not too pleased. They would like to avoid any unnecessary attention. They want us to wrap this up quietly."

"That's what *we* want, too." Diminsky nodded vigorously.

"I just hope the admiral is exercising the royal *we*," said Frank.

He watched Smitty for a reaction, but the big Mormon got very busy pouring iced tea.

"Listen, Commander Frank," Diminsky blustered, "we are not running an investigative service for the pet projects of our own agents. We are in business to take orders, and if you cannot control your impulses, I may be tempted to give you one!"

Smitty smiled tolerantly at both Navy men. "I can't tell you how relieved I am to know that I am not among those shackled by the Chain of Command. I have a free hand with this job, and that's the way I like it. However, I am bound by certain responsibilities—

one of them a cardinal rule: Do not piss away the Navy's money."

Frank felt a rock sinking into his gut.

"I am not convinced by your arguments, Commander Frank, but I am not turned off, either. I think you have a point. We are faced with a hazard to navigation—not the *Candlefish,* but the area in which she was lost. On that basis I might be able to coax some funds out of Appropriations to finance your expedition. But I doubt it. I will, however, make an attempt."

Diminsky stared at Smitty, helplessly enraged.

Frank sat back and felt the little rivers of sweat pour down his inner arms. He ordered more iced tea all around.

October 19, 1974

The morning sun bounced off the water, bathing the *Candlefish* in its warming rays and causing great aggravation to the pain of Ed Frank's hangover. He screwed up his face and took another gulp from the steaming mug he was holding in an unsteady hand. As the warmth flowed through him, he thought back over the last three days since the Diminsky-Smith meeting and declared, "Jesus. What a mess."

The frigidity that had solidified between Diminsky and himself had coincided with the sudden arrival of fall in Washington. Cold rain driven by gusting winds had blanketed the city, an effective damper on everything and everybody. And the fight with Joanne had been the capper. He winced just thinking about it.

They had both said stupid, hurtful things. He had given her hell about her constant clumsiness, and she had read him the riot act over what she called his "egotistical self-sufficiency." He had left the apartment for the flight back to Pearl, feeling about as tractable as a bull moose at the height of the rutting season.

A breeze flapped the canvas tarp that shielded the dockside desk from the tropical sun. Frank drained his mug; the "bottom of the birdcage" taste had left his mouth. Another cup, maybe a try at breakfast, and he could face the day. But first the coffee.

Thank God for the Navy, he thought, they always have enough money for coffee. He was definitely on the mend. He wouldn't pull a dumb stunt like this again; getting blind smashed out of frustration was certainly not the answer. For the first time since he had made his way from the *Imperator* to the *Candlefish* this morning, he watched the activity with some semblance of interest.

The working party was bringing up the last of the enlisted men's personal gear. The old blue sea bags with the white-stenciled names and serial numbers were being loaded onto a truck, sealed, and tagged. The sailors read the names off quietly. Cook and a quartermaster, both with clipboards, checked them against the 1944 roster. Frank became aware of the hush that had fallen over the pier. Looking back toward the *Imperator,* he saw the groups of men lining the rails of her upper decks. They too were quiet. Watching.

The sound of the tailgate locking into place signaled the end of the impromptu ceremony. The clusters of men drifted away, returning to their normal duties. The truck moved off, heading for the warehouse which held everything recently removed from the sub except her explosives.

Frank eased himself into the chair behind the desk and slid open the middle drawer. He removed the pictures from the folder and studied them. They were all that remained of the thirty-year-old calamity. Compartment by compartment, the mess that had been his first view of *Candlefish's* interior stared back at him. Now it was almost a bare boat.

The head of the maintenance team, Chief McClusky, popped through the aft hatch, bounced up the gangplank, headed toward him, and came right to the point.

"The mountings are all in and seated, sir, but I'm still worried about moving that Fairbanks-Morse."

Frank reached for the blueprints, rolled them open, and studied the layout. "What does engineering say, Mac?"

McClusky snorted and rubbed an oil-streaked hand over his face. "They think it's a cakewalk, sir. We can jack the mother up, move it forward on rollers okay—but I'm worried about the hoists. We're cutting some down to size, but . . ."

"But what?"

"Commander—if those hoists break, I'm liable to put one hell of a hole in your boat."

Frank looked at the blueprints. Cook approached the desk and, without being asked, put his clipboard down on one corner of the breeze-whipped paper. "What's our alternative?" asked Frank.

McClusky's finger jabbed at the blue paper. "Let me cut through the overhead plating, sir. I can run a crane down here and have that engine dropped into place and snugged up in a sec."

Frank did not want to rip the deck off; there had to be another way.

The desk phone rang. Cook picked it up, listened, then shoved it under Frank's nose. Frank barked a greeting into the phone.

"When? Eleven hundred? Thanks!" He handed the phone back to Cook, a surge of adrenalin shooting through him. He stood up. "Mac, try it with the hoists. If that doesn't work, we'll skull out something else."

The Chief gave him a dubious look, then turned and

made his way back aboard. Frank had already dismissed the matter. Good news was in short supply, and some had just arrived over the telephone. He savored the moment.

"Ray, guess who's coming for a visit?"

Cook glanced up from the papers on his clipboard. He was wary. "Bob Hope?"

Frank spit out a laugh. It wasn't just the last vestiges of his hangover; he knew a break when he saw one. "Jack N. Hardy, late of the *Candlefish*. Be here in less than three hours."

"Congratulations."

Frank acknowledged the slight bow that Cook tossed him, but his mind was already racing over details. VIP treatment all the way. The launch, to bring Hardy from Ford Island to the sub. A car and driver from the Base Motor Pool. And a room at the BOQ. "Make that on the first floor, Cook. The Professor's got a bad leg."

He left Cook and hustled down the forward gangplank, headed for the hatch, and zipped down the ladder. The stone that had been sitting in his gut ever since Washington was gone.

Below decks, the changes were astonishing. What had been a disaster area ten short days ago was now neat and shipshape. He looked at the empty torpedo bays on either side of him. Aft, through the hatch, he saw some movement in the officers' quarters. That was where he wanted to go.

Alone inside Basquine's cabin, he brainstormed, going over his options for handling Hardy. Without the man's cooperation, Frank was a dead duck. The trick was to get it.

Cook found him twenty minutes later and reported that everything was set up.

"Now what?" said Cook.

Frank smiled, eased himself out of the chair, and

checked his watch. Hardy's jet would be landing in a little over two hours. They both had a lot to do, but first he had to get Cook on his side.

"Hardy's quarters are still intact, right?"

Cook nodded. "As per your instructions."

"Okay, here's what we're going to do."

Cook listened, a look of distaste spreading over his handsome features. "Sextant, pictures, gear from the warehouse . . . You're setting him up! Salting this boat like a phony gold mine."

"That's right. I want to put a hook so deep into this guy that he'll *beg* to go along."

"Why?"

"I need him. Badly."

Cook didn't like it at all.

"Now, I want you to make one more phone call. Cohen and Slater. By fastest transportation possible, I want them here and set up at 0800 tomorrow morning."

Cook's distaste turned to outright horror. "The Gold-Dust Twins? Are we going to do a little mind-bending?"

"Not bending, Lieutenant. Just peeling. Now make the call and get that sextant up to the dock."

Cook nodded coldly and turned toward the door. He stopped and directed a blast at Frank. "You know, it's strange. Hardy's coming back after thirty years, and he's still getting shafted . . . by the Navy."

Frank and Cook watched the launch glide up to the pier. One of the crewmen held her fast with a boathook as Hardy prepared to disembark. Frank reacted to Hardy's hopping steps. He hadn't realized the man limped as badly as that. Christ! All he needed was for the good professor to fall down a hatch. Then what?

"Welcome to Pearl, Dr. Hardy. I'm very glad you

came." Hardy stood at the foot of the gangplank to remove his jacket and loosen his tie. He smiled up to them.

"I forgot just how hot it gets out here, Commander."

Frank introduced Cook, who hurried down the plank to take Hardy's suitcase.

"Well, want to see her?" Frank asked. Hardy nodded, and Frank led them to the opposite side of the dock. He stood aside to let Hardy view the *Candlefish*.

The professor lifted his sunglasses and studied the low, sleek hull. He stood quite still, his eyes traveling the length of her back and forth several times in succession.

"How does she look to you?"

Hardy lowered his glasses, saying nothing. He turned and asked about a hotel.

"You'll be in the Bachelor Officers' Quarters right on the base. Everything is set."

Hardy nodded and slowly turned back to the sub. His eyes riveted on it. Tiny beads of perspiration broke out on his weather-beaten face.

"Come on," said Frank, and led him toward the dockside desk. He glanced back as they walked, and was pleasantly surprised. Bad leg and all, Hardy moved well enough.

The sun, now almost directly overhead, beat down on the three men and cast shadows on the steel-sheathed sides of the submarine. Frank walked around the desk and slipped his hand under the tarp. He found the strange-looking sextant buried under the blueprints. He stood behind Hardy a long time, watching the old man scrutinize the submarine's bridge superstructure.

Hardy stared at the raised bolts on the conning tower which spelled out the sub's number.

"Two eighty-four," Hardy muttered hoarsely.

"Professor?"

Hardy turned slowly, and his eyes locked onto the strange device that Frank was holding out for him to see.

"Cyclops," he said, in a low, strained voice. "Where did you find it?"

"Wedged just forward of the breach lock on the deck gun." Frank handed it to him. "You recognize it?"

"It's mine," Hardy mumbled. "Or it *was* mine. Thirty years ago." He cradled the sextant, his fingers turning it, feeling the metal. The muscle in his left cheek started to pulsate. The vein on his forehead stood away, the blue line clear beneath the tanned skin.

Alarmed, Cook moved to his side. Hardy took off his sunglasses and wiped his eyes. His breathing returned to normal.

Frank was stunned. "Are you all right?"

Hardy nodded and rubbed his temples, regaining his composure. "I've been bracing myself for this ever since you left my office at Scripps. Guess I just wound myself up a bit too much."

"Look, why don't we get you settled into quarters? We can go aboard later."

Hardy refused and stepped toward the gangplank. He got on and limped down to the deck, holding the rail tightly. Frank returned the sextant to the desk and opened the drawer. He grabbed the manila folder containing the photographs and approached Cook.

"Did you get everything I asked for?"

"And then some."

"What the hell does that mean?" Frank tried to read Cook's expression. "Hey, no surprises, Ray. Not now."

"Just some things to sweeten the pot." He added quietly: "Go easy on him."

Frank went aboard the boat. What the hell did Cook think he was going to do? Take a rubber hose and beat the man?

Hardy was on deck just aft of the cigarette bridge, his head craned upward. He ignored Frank and stepped back a few feet, his eyes dropping to the wooden strakes covering the deck. He was measuring.

"I must have hit—right about here." He stomped the deck with his good leg, then tapped his bad one. "That's how I got this." Frank followed his gaze, measuring the distance, getting a mental picture of this man, thirty years younger, trying to keep himself from being swept from the protection of the bridge in a rush of raging water.

Hardy moved to starboard of the sail and looked up again at the raised bolts—at the number 284. That was the evidence. That made it true, made it fact. This was the USS *Candlefish*. No doubt about it. Frank saw the old man's cheek muscle start to throb again.

"We can go below by the forward hatch, Professor."

Hardy smiled tightly. "Don't let my leg fool you, Commander. I still move pretty well"—he grabbed the metal ladder and hoisted himself up to the bridge, his powerful arms compensating for the right leg—"even for a man of my *superior* years." He stood on the bridge and beamed down at Frank, daring him to do better. Frank smiled, impressed. He clamped the manila folder between his teeth and shot up the ladder.

Hardy's head slipped from view as he dropped down the conning-tower hatch. Frank scooted down the ladder after him.

Hardy scanned the tight quarters and sniffed the air, wrinkling his nose at the familiar odor of machine oil. He moved toward the helmsman's seat, his eyes climbing over the instruments. "What happened to the glass on the gauges?"

"Shattered. All through the boat." Frank watched the look of puzzlement on the Professor's features, then saw it disappear as he was distracted by something in the corner.

The first plant. Hardy picked up a military pamphlet and weighed it in his hand. He mouthed a name and held the book a moment, reflecting. Then he dropped it. "Hell of a guy— Jenavin," he said. "Breaking his ass to get into OCS." He fell silent and stood in the center of the conning tower a moment. Frank could almost sense the memories swarming in on the old man.

Hardy turned abruptly into the well and dropped down the ladder to the control room. Frank followed, and halfway down saw the Professor jump as a series of metallic thumps, followed by a muffled stream of profanity, reached the control room from somewhere aft.

"That's just the crew in the forward engine room, Professor," Frank said quickly. He moved to the plotting table, opened his manila folder, and spread the pictures out. Hardy's attention was drawn to the source of the sounds. Frank had to tug on his sleeve. "I think you should look at these."

Hardy slowly drifted back to reality and studied the black-and-white stills. Revealing the chaos compartment by compartment, they were far more eloquent than anything Frank could have said. Hardy stared at them and asked, "Was it like this everywhere?"

"All through the boat. Without exception. We've cleaned her up since these were taken. Most of the personal gear has been removed and stored, but your quarters haven't been touched. Would you care to have a look?"

Hardy shook his head. "Not yet. Let me get used to this . . ."

Heading aft, they passed through the galley and into the crew's mess. This compartment was devoid of personal gear—no deliberate plants or anything.

They stepped through the bulkhead into the crew's quarters. All the bunks were folded back snug against the inner walls of the hull. Clanking sounds again drew Hardy aft, and he went to the next connecting bulkhead. He stared in surprise at main engine number one, still thrust out at an angle, blocking the entrance to the forward engine room.

McClusky, obviously frustrated with his task, cut loose with a blast of invective directed toward the Navy in particular and the world in general. Hardy smiled.

"At least *that* hasn't changed in thirty years."

Frank relaxed. Hardy was loosening up; his defenses were dropping. In the crew's quarters, his roaming eyes caught the Ann Sheridan pinup posted on one of the lockers. "We had one guy . . . I can't remember his name, but he was nuts about Ann Sheridan."

"That was Jones," said Frank. "We found two scrapbooks loaded with pictures."

"Right! Corky Jones. Hey—what about Walinsky's pipes?"

Frank was puzzled a moment; then he remembered the carved shelf. "You mean that rack over main engine number two? Still there." He pointed back toward the forward engine room.

Hardy muttered the name of his friend. "Chief Walinsky. Anton. The pipes—they were . . ." He stopped, drifting off, remembering the off-duty hours he used to spend with the Chief, chatting while he shined up those bloody pipes. Once in a great while he would even smoke one.

Frank smiled; at least Hardy's memories were pleasant. This was the time to steer him to his old quarters.

Favoring his leg as they walked forward, Hardy kept

up a steady stream of chatter. Passing back through the control room, he stopped to examine a duty roster posted on the bulkhead. Silently he mouthed the names, reaching deep within his memory to match them up to faces. His eyes did a tour of the bulkheads, searching, listening for voices he hadn't heard in thirty years.

In officers' country Hardy stuck his head into the wardroom and glanced at the silhouette charts of the various classes of Japanese shipping displayed on the bulkheads. He pointed out the old 78-rpm record player on the overhead shelf. Another of Cook's contributions. "We had about the best collection of Glenn Miller records in the entire fleet."

"Yes, sir. They've been removed and stored."

Hardy ignored him. "Stanhill," he murmured, "that's all he ever played. Glenn Miller. Remember 'Moonlight Serenade'?" Frank gave him a patronizing smile.

With a last look, Hardy moved down the corridor. Frank watched him step into the officers' stateroom, then followed and stood by the door while he explored the curtained sections inside. Frank waited until Hardy slid back the curtain covering his own berth, then stepped in and came up behind.

"Small, isn't it?" Hardy's smile did not match his voice. He was hurting—a deep, long-ago hurt. Frank refrained from comment; he was doing a little soul-searching of his own. Maybe Cook was right. This was like calling the cadence for Hardy's march through hell. He waited, sensing the anguish building inside the old man.

Hardy was staring at the pillow at the head of his bunk. Slowly, as if in a trance, his hand crept under the pillow and felt around.

"It's in your locker, sir," Frank said quietly. "We

didn't know quite where you kept it."

Hardy looked up at him and examined the younger man's face, then turned and opened the locker. He took out a framed photograph. The Elena of many years ago smiled at him. Frank watched him struggle to keep the tears back.

"Your wife?"

"Yes. I lost her in 1963."

The two men stood in silence. Even McClusky's gang had stopped their frantic activity aft. Hardy sighed, his emotions finally in check. "May I take this with me?"

"Everything in here belongs to you, Professor."

"Not quite." Hardy put the picture on his bunk and reached back into the locker. "I never had enough money for two of these." He pulled out one of two officer's caps hanging on hooks and tried it on. Frank smiled at the obvious misfit. Hardy slipped it off and flipped it over to look at the inner plastic lining. There was a fleeting look of anger and distaste.

He handed the cap over, and Frank read the name stenciled on the lining: BATES, W.

Frank silently cursed the stupidity of whoever it was on the cleanup crew who had stowed Bates's cap in Hardy's locker.

"How about the forward torpedo room, Professor?"

Hardy simply shook his head. "I've had enough for one day."

Cook and Frank walked the Professor to a waiting car. Hardy accepted Frank's invitation to dinner, then sat back in the seat and stared at his wife's picture as the car drove off.

Cook finally relaxed. "Must have been pretty rough down there."

Frank shot him a dirty look and handed him Bates's

cap. Cook was effusive in his apology. "Jesus! Talk about mixing oil and water . . ."

Frank nodded. A stupid mistake like this could have set Hardy off like a skyrocket. This time they were lucky. Next time . . . He felt drained. The tour of the boat was not enough. It was going to take a hell of a lot more to get Jack Hardy involved.

Frank and Hardy took an early dinner at the Officers' Club. Just the two of them. As if by mutual agreement, neither mentioned the *Candlefish,* so the conversation was light, at times bantering.

Halfway through dessert, it dawned on Frank: The wrong man was doing all the talking. In the course of an hour plus, Hardy had managed to pump out of Ed Frank nearly his entire background, from the six-year-old boy who learned of his father's death at Omaha Beach on D-Day, to the early years at the Academy, through Submarine School and then sea duty. A little alarm went off just before Frank started to recount his posting to NIS. What amazed and amused him was Jack Hardy's deftness. He could have been a natural interrogator. His questions were direct without putting Frank on his guard. Hardy gave the impression that he really cared. He was a great listener. For the first time since his return from Washington, Frank was completely relaxed. He pushed away his coffee cup and refused a second refill.

Hardy, polishing off a dish of chocolate ice cream, was busy watching the room fill up with officers and their women. He grew reflective again. "I'll make a purely scientific observation, Commander."

"What?"

"The ladies are getting prettier. Maybe it's the setting, or maybe I'm starting to slip into senility, but they're definitely prettier."

"Whatever you say, sir . . . but since we could do without those distractions, what do you say we go off to a place where we don't have so many of the fairer sex?" He called for the check and hustled Hardy out into a balmy Hawaiian evening.

Hardy sat quietly, as Frank slowly toured the car through the base. Hardy smiled now and then as he saw something he remembered from the past. Frank didn't intrude. Let the man come down off his high, he thought. The fun and games were over. Business was about to begin. The car rolled to a stop, and Hardy chuckled when he saw where they were. "The Clean Sweep, huh? Very subtle, Commander."

"If you'd rather not—"

Hardy waved it aside. He got out and waited while Frank retrieved his attaché case from the trunk.

In the wartime parlance of the Submarine Service, "clean sweep" meant a successful return from a war patrol: all torpedoes expended and, hopefully, all targets sunk. A broom lashed to the periscope of a sub slipping back into home base was a signal to others that the boat had "swept the seas clean" of enemy shipping.

The bar was a favorite haunt of SubPac officers. Its walls bore a collage of photographs of the great sub skippers: Lockwood, Grenfell, Morton, O'Kane. From lofty perches they looked down on a new generation. There were photos of crews, old supply ships, and exotic stations, along with other memorabilia. Equipment used by submariners was scattered throughout the bar. It almost qualified as a museum—an ongoing tribute to the thousands of men who wore the Golden Dolphins.

Frank listened as Hardy slid back into recollections. But the Professor was still shutting out the *Candlefish*.

Frank decided on a new tack. "What made you get into submarines, Professor?"

Hardy, a cagey look on his face, cocked an eyebrow at Frank. "You just said it."

"What?"

"The movie *Submarine,* with Jack Holt and Ralph Graves."

Frank, who had never heard of either *Submarine* or Jack Holt, nodded as if he understood perfectly.

Hardy saw through him. "I guess I better explain."

He told Frank about growing up in Connecticut, on Long Island Sound; how he had developed a love for boats, all boats. When he became old enough, he went sailing every chance he could get—mostly with friends whose fathers had sloops, yawls, or ketches that put out from West Haven every weekend. His own parents ran a small dockside market which, during the spring and summer, did landslide business when the weekend sailors came up from Manhattan and Long Island to race and drink beer. Jack's knowledge of the local waters, plus his ability to handle his share of the work, made him a welcome addition to the crew of many a fine boat. His parents, sensing his enjoyment, never tried to tie him down to the store. Besides, he was great public relations for their business.

In 1929, as an eleven-year-old boy, he saw his first submarine movie. For an hour and a half he sat motionless, and when the film was over he knew where his life was headed. But, just to make sure, he sat through the next performance.

The Great Depression made a big gouge in his sailing time. Men who had once owned boats suddenly found themselves hard-pressed to keep jobs. His parents barely eked out a living during those hard times, and he was obliged to spend his spare hours helping in the store. Still, the dream persisted. And still he sailed—when he could.

In 1936, just before he graduated high school, he be-

gan to pay attention to the fact that the Navy's Submarine School was at New London, Connecticut—
barely thirty miles from his home. But he decided it
would be better to become a Navy officer first, then
later volunteer for submarine training. So he applied to
the U.S. Naval Academy. His appointment came about
through the help of one of the families who still sailed
during the season. He then promptly failed the entrance exams.

Humiliated, frustrated, but refusing to give up, Jack
Hardy finagled himself into a prep school for a year,
took the exams again, and finally entered Annapolis in
the fall of 1938.

"And then?"

Hardy became interested in a toothpick. He held it
out in front of him, studying it. Finally he looked at
Frank. "I imagine your department has a pretty good
fix on what I've been doing since 1938, Commander.
Not everything, but . . . we all have our little secrets."

"Care to elaborate?"

"No. I don't think I would."

Their attention was diverted by a group of young officers apparently celebrating the last night of bachelor-
hood for one of their number. Shouts of condolence
and advice reverberated around the room. After much
milling about, it was decided that they would all go to a
certain house off the base. Amidst much confusion, the
party left.

Hardy, who had been enjoying the scene, turned
back to Frank. "Why is it that men who are about to
get married feel obliged to go out and tie one on? That
never changes."

It was a piece of cognac philosophy, and Frank
neatly dovetailed it into what he wanted to be the topic
of the evening. "I'll tell you something else that hasn't

changed, sir." Hardy looked up woozily. *"Candlefish*. After thirty years, still the same. No age, no rust, no crew. Any ideas?"

Hardy pushed his brandy snifter away. "I don't know why . . . but I have some theories on the how," he ventured. "But then, I don't think they'd do you any good. You're not a scientist."

"Try me."

Hardy leaned back in his chair and, steepling his hands, tapped his index fingers together. "Suppose the boat was sealed up tight. Complete hull integrity. No leakage."

"All right."

"That could account for the lack of deterioration."

Frank recalled Nails's description of the bridge when he had boarded her at sea. The hatches had been dogged tight. "Go on," he said.

"Some of the subs carried nitrogen flasks. I forget what they were for, but suppose one of them popped loose, broke, causing a nitrogen atmosphere to fill the boat. Suppose? Okay, it would act as a preservative— everything aboard would be pickled—if there was a vacuum. If all the air had been sucked out, the interior of the sub could have remained *intact*."

"What about the outside hull?"

"If she'd sunk to the bottom . . ." He started to wave his hands. "If she'd been buried up to her bridge in silt all these years, given the coldness of the waters in those latitudes, she *could* have survived without any sea growth at all."

"That's not bad, Professor. In fact, it's damned good."

"It's just a lot of *ifs,* Commander."

"Granted, but it sure sounds better than some mysterious Japanese secret weapon." He regretted his words as soon as they were out. Hardy looked at him through a half smile; he wasn't angry, just a little hurt.

"That's what you get for my twenty-five years in oceanography." He paused, tapped his glass, and added, "Anyway . . . we never carried any nitrogen."

There was silence for a few moments, while Hardy ordered another round from the waitress and refused to talk until it arrived.

Frank tried to regain lost ground. "What about the crew?"

"Well . . . if they rode out the final dive, they could have tried to escape later. The fishing boat that picked me up had a radio. I could hear them sending, but it was obvious they never even sighted the *Candlefish*." He paused and took a big swallow of cognac. "Did you check the ship's log? See if there were any entries after December eleventh?"

"We haven't been able to find it, Professor. It's missing."

"Well, Basquine kept his own day-to-day log."

Frank reached down and opened his attaché case. He pulled out Basquine's logbook and handed it to Hardy.

"You check it," he said.

Hardy gingerly flipped it open and thumbed through to the date he remembered. "Let's see . . . we left Pearl on the twenty-first of November . . . Here." He read from the top of the page: " *'0800. Underway from Pearl, proceeding under orders to general area Kuriles, Pacific.'* " He lapsed into silence.

He stared at the rest of the blank page.

Frank concentrated on Hardy's reaction as he turned to the next page and surprise grew on his face, turning quickly to incredulity. He thumbed the next page and the next. Finally he closed the book and sat very still for a long time, before handing it back to Frank.

"That's right, Professor. They're all blank. After the first day—nothing!"

"But Basquine never missed. I tell you, he was a fanatic! There must be a mistake."

Frank returned the log to his case and snapped it shut. He knew Hardy felt uncomfortable, unsure of himself.

"You don't believe me."

"Yes, I do. Your theories are just as valid as anyone else's, but this log—it says more where it says nothing. Do you see what I mean? The *Candlefish,* Professor, is one hell of a puzzle."

"What are you going to do with her?"

Frank paused, choosing his words carefully. "I'm going to refit the boat and reshape a crew. Then I'm going to retrace the last patrol—from start to finish."

Hardy was astonished. "You can't do that."

"If I get the authorization, Professor, I can and I will."

"For what reason?"

Frank sat up and looked him in the eye. "Because after thirty years, *it came back!* And it's just aching to tell us what happened. You're not only a scientist but you served aboard her! Don't you want to know?"

Hardy didn't answer, but *No* was written all over his face. "What do you want from me?"

"I want you to complete the missing twenty days in Basquine's log."

Hardy laughed; he couldn't believe it. "I'm flattered, but . . . you said it yourself, Commander: after thirty years . . . ?" His voice trailed off, waiting for Frank's reply.

"I've thought of that, sir. Two men that I have sent for will meet you tomorrow morning. They'll help you."

"To do what?"

"To remember." He saw the fleeting look of pain. "Just the portions that I need to fill out the log. Nothing else."

"How? Do they use drugs?"

"I'm going to have to depend on you for that answer," Frank smiled. "I don't even know. But I know they get results, and that's what we want."

The harsh, official tone went out of his voice, and he became softer, more pleading. "It's what we *need,* sir."

Five minutes later, he paid the bill and they left the Clean Sweep. Hardy was quiet during the drive back to the BOQ. Frank kept the car idling while Hardy lurched up to the building, a slightly plastered list to port compensating for the limp.

During the drive back to the *Imperator,* Frank said a silent prayer. Cohen and Slater had better come through. Hardy was right: Thirty years was a long time.

October 22, 1974

At 1230, Frank headed for the *Candlefish.*

Cook met him at the foot of the gangplank. "Just coming to get you. Mac passed the word. Number one is in, seated and hooked up to the main shaft."

They went down the after hatch and swung through to the forward engine room. They hovered over McClusky. "Gimme another half-hour or so, Commander, and you can fire her up. But keep everything crossed."

Frank's eyes surveyed the huge engine. The once oil-spattered Fairbanks-Morse, now wiped clean, was receiving last-minute adjustments. Frank went off to inspect the damaged bulkhead. In a few moments he was satisfied that those repairs would be minimal.

Moving forward, he checked Basquine's cabin. Pads and pencils were neatly laid out on the desk. The aroma of fresh coffee attracted him to the wardroom. Sure enough, a pot was brewing. He helped himself to a cup and sat quietly on the leatherette couch. He was on his second cup when Hardy found him. There was a quizzical look on the Professor's face, as if he had just been through a confusing experience.

"How did it go, Professor?"

"Oh, fine . . ."

Frank couldn't tell if the reply was dipped in sarcasm or— "Did you have lunch, sir?"

Hardy took a cup from the rack and poured from the pot. "Look. If we're going to be working together, there'll have to be some changes."

"Such as?"

"No more Professor or Doctor or sir. My name is Jack."

"I'm Ed." Frank reached across for the extended hand, expecting a sudden rush of warmth and openness. But not so. Hardy simply wanted to get the point across. It seemed he would forever be holding something of himself in check.

Frank rose. "C'mon, you'll be working in Basquine's cabin. It's all set up."

"Why not here in the wardroom?"

"There's going to be a lot of traffic through here in the next few days. You don't need distractions."

Hardy finished his coffee and followed Frank across the corridor. Frank held the door open for him and pointed out the pads and pencils. As he settled into the chair, Frank inquired about his session with Cohen and Slater.

"Can't tell you. They made me promise."

"Okay, but if you hit a dry spell, relax. Get up and take a stroll through the boat. Let it jog your memory.

You know where the coffee is. Meals—I'll come and get you. If you need me this afternoon, I'll be aft."

Hardy sat still for a long time after Frank left. He looked around the small space that once held the man who had made his life miserable. And his thoughts kept going back to his morning meeting with Cohen and Slater.

His first reaction to them was resentment. Those two total strangers somehow knew almost everything there was to know about Jack Hardy. But they were so smooth that once he got over his anger, he was filled with admiration. They had dissected him, but in such a way that he had found himself helping them, filling in blank spaces, enlarging on a comment and, what's more, enjoying it. The last half-hour was spent in going over facts he had long since forgotten.

Finally Slater explained what they were doing. "We're isolating the last patrol. We've dispensed with all the other areas. Now you can just concentrate on key points. Push everything else out of your mind, and the log will practically write itself."

Now Hardy picked up a pencil and opened one of the pads. He started to write. He forced his mind to follow Slater's instructions. He felt awed by his fresh powers. He could and would write the log, and, what's more, he would do it in Basquine's cabin.

Frank hung up the phone. Slater had been cautiously optimistic. "Hardy wasn't all that complex. And he responded well." Frank put a seventy-two-hour hold on them and hotfooted it back down to the forward engine room. For now, Hardy would do his best work alone. More important things were going to be happening aft.

McClusky's men were ready, gathered around main

engine number one like a gang of expectant fathers. The Chief was at the engine stand with Cook. Frank came up the aisle and asked, "Ready?"

"Just in time to give the order, sir."

Frank crossed fingers on both hands and held them up high. "Fire away, Mac."

McClusky's stubby finger punched the starter button. The engine roared to life, filling the compartment with its power. Eyes checked gauges and experienced hands made adjustments. McClusky, a smile splitting his face, gave Frank the thumbs-up sign. Frank grinned back, letting the noise and the rising heat blanket him. Another plateau had been reached.

He felt great.

Hardy didn't.

The sound of the starting diesel coursed through the boat and went through him. Was he imagining it or did he hear the diving alarm? Images crowded in on him. A blur of movement as men raced to battle stations. Periscope sliding down the well. He felt a tight dry feeling in his mouth, the one he always got bracing himself for an imminent depth-charging. The fear of showing fear. He struggled for control, forcing the dark impressions out, and he won. The cabin, which had seemed to be pressing in on him, lost its threatening crush. The vibrations faded away to nothing. He wiped his sweaty palms, picked up the pencil, and started to write, gathering momentum, driven by something deep within him. Something he didn't understand.

CHAPTER 8

October 23, 1974

Frank had determined the date of departure would be November 21st, to coincide with the original 1944 patrol. As each day passed, he became increasingly upset with the slow grinding of government wheels. He and Cook were virtually buried under a blizzard of paperwork. There were requests every morning from Smitty's office for more detailed briefs on the intention, the procedure, the requirements of Frank's project. An inter-office memo that Frank was sure had originated with Diminsky requested a study on backup safety measures for the voyage, to be submitted through regular channels at his convenience.

"Regular channels!" Frank screamed. "The bastard is trying to bury us!"

He threw the memo to Cook, ordering him to work up the information. "And then just hand it over to me."

"In triplicate?" asked Cook.

"In *twenty-four hours!*" Frank roared.

Frank avoided Jack Hardy as much as possible, reluctant to let him see the strain taking its toll.

Cook reappeared the next afternoon, grinning unnaturally. He tossed a fresh manila folder on the desk and said. "Escort."

"Escort?"

"We can't cram any safety devices into that boat—

we'd have to remove too much existing equipment. Plus the time necessary to install it. Instead, we have all the Boy Scout stuff aboard *another ship*." Frank gaped at his shit-eating grin. Cook went on: "I had Walters check into that memo. It *did* originate with Diminsky. He figures he can hold us up at least a month. By that time he could get Smitty to change his mind. Stall tactics. *Candlefish* disappears from the headlines: no pressure—no project. An escort will get us around the whole problem. With a support vessel tailing you, we eliminate the risk."

Frank chewed on his pipe and studied Cook with a gleam growing in his eye. Cook couldn't get rid of the grin. "And guess who's volunteered to be on the escort?"

Frank was very quiet a long time, until he set down the pipe and admonished, "Didn't your daddy tell you never volunteer for *anything?*"

Cook waited while Frank made a conference call to Smitty and Diminsky, catching them both at home just before bedtime. In excited tones, he explained Cook's idea about the escort, played humble by apologizing for not coming up with it earlier, and generally made it sound as if it were the greatest idea since Saran Wrap. Smitty wasn't sure. Frank pointed out the time factor and the lack of space aboard *Candlefish* for installing modern safety equipment. A fully equipped escort would be considerably less costly. Besides, any modern devices placed aboard the sub could be only temporary.

Smitty let Frank go on at length, once he began pointing out how everything related to cost.

Then Frank did some listening. Five minutes of it.

He hung up, sat back in relief, and answered Cook's unasked question: "Smitty will present it to the Committee tomorrow. Regular channels, my ass . . ."

"How did Diminsky take it?"
"I think I added ten strokes to his golf game."

October 25, 1974

An orderly from Captain Melanoff's office charged up the gangplank of the *Imperator* and a moment later pounded on the door to Frank's cabin.

"Telex for you, sir."

It was from Smitty's office in Washington.

COMNIS
R251038Z OCT 74
FROM COMNIS TO COMDEFINCO PEARL

ADVISE CMDR FRANK SENATE AP-
PROVAL CANDLEFISH MISSION SECURED
STOP AUTHORIZATION PROCEED REFIT
BOAT ASSEMBLE CREW AND ESCORT
AWAIT FULL ORDERS COMSUBPAC
STOP NAVAL APPROVAL ACTIVATE JACK
HARDY COMMISSION ONLY AS LAST
RESORT STOP PREFER VOLUNTEER CIT-
IZEN STOP GOOD LUCK STOP

Frank stared at it a long time, then let out a whoop that carried all the way to the crew's mess.

He put on fresh suntans and hurried over to Melanoff's office at Defense Intelligence Command. Melanoff greeted him with a vigorous handshake and offered a bit of liquid celebration. Frank accepted the beer and guzzled it. He was pacing up and down, muttering "Boy oh boy oh boy . . ."

Melanoff laughed and popped another can of beer.

"What if she sinks before you reach Latitude Thirty?"

"She won't do that," Frank said, going to the window and looking out to make sure she hadn't already. "She wouldn't dare."

The phone rang with a call for Frank from Washington. It was Diminsky, and he was eating crow. "Well, Commander, you pulled it off. I sure haven't got the foggiest idea what convinced them—"

"I realize that, Admiral." Frank couldn't resist the barb.

"We'll have to review this in the office, Frank. You know there are a great many important cases pending, and perhaps this little effort doesn't require the services of a full Lieutenant Commander—"

"Then demote me, Admiral, because I'm going."

Diminsky blustered some more and finally, grudgingly, wished him good luck.

Frank accepted graciously and then said, "Look, if we go out there and sink all over again, you can tell everybody 'I told you so.' "

The real test of his powers still lay ahead: convincing Jack Hardy that he should become a part of this expedition. The telex had pointed out one way to have him assigned to it—simply activate his commission. But that would make him an unwilling participant. Frank wanted him not only willing but eager.

As he hurried back down the dock clutching a bag of sandwiches and a six-pack of beer, he considered the best way of breaking the good news to someone who wouldn't appreciate it. When he drew abreast of the *Candlefish,* it was twelve noon and the technicians were just clearing out for lunch. Hardy himself was coming up the conning-tower hatch, and Frank hailed him from the pier.

"Hold it! Wait right there! I got sandwiches!"

He held up the bag. Hardy stood still on the bridge and waited for Frank to come aboard and scamper up the bridge ladder. Frank passed him the sandwiches.

"I'm not going below, if it's all the same to you. I've got to get off this tub *sometime*," Hardy grumbled.

"Sure, sure. How about aft?"

Frank didn't even wait for an answer. He led the way around the conning tower. There were several crates on the cigarette deck; they sat down there and had lunch.

Frank munched a corned-beef sandwich and looked the submarine over happily, measuring what was to become his new domain. He glanced at Hardy. The man was staring at the deck, somberly chewing on a ham-and-Swiss.

"Hey, how's it coming?" asked Frank.

"The log? I was right. Thirty years *is* a long time."

"Yes, it is."

"And I happen to be digging back into some unpleasant history."

"Such as?"

"Well . . . Basquine. He may have been the Navy's idea of a good CO, but not mine. And Bates, the Exec . . . hated my guts."

"Why?"

Hardy slowed down and stared at his sandwich. "I made a mistake. They never forgave me."

Frank waved a hand and spoke with his mouth full. "You mean the slug test?" Hardy looked up slowly, in surprise. "Basquine kept a file. I read it."

"I don't expect it was very complimentary."

Frank looked at Hardy and sensed rather than heard the bitterness. "Why don't you tell me about it? I mean, from the beginning. From the time you came aboard the *Candlefish*."

Hardy was silent a long time; then he asked for an-

other beer. He cracked it open and drank a third of it,
then settled back and started to talk.

"January of '44. That's when the tough part started.
I guess up till then I was very young and idealistic. And
I was very dependent on my wife, Elena. She was my
crutch. You remember that picture under my pillow? I
kept it there all the time, and I wrote letters constantly.
I'd save them until we got back to port, then I'd post
them all in a packet." He paused and rolled the beer
can in his palms. "Anyway . . . in January I got a wire
from her. She'd had the baby, and she was naming him
Peter, after my father. Peter . . . I went out on a toot.
I had five of the best days of my life. The best days
since I had married Elena. For the first time, I really
felt like a man. I felt there really was a . . . a *me*."

Hardy clasped his hands behind his head and rocked
back. "Did you know we had two weddings?"

Frank blinked in surprise. Hardy grinned. "Yes, sir.
Probably the most daring stunt I've pulled in my whole
life. In the summer of 1940, just before I started my
junior year at the Naval Academy, we decided we
couldn't wait any longer. But the Academy had a rule
that midshipmen couldn't be married. So we did it in
secret. No one knew about it—I mean no one. We had
to live apart for quite a while. It was a trial; it was
tough, but I think we were stronger for all of it.

"And when the war broke out, the whole thing became ten times more difficult," Hardy continued. "But
having her there, even in the background, seemed awfully important." Hardy looked at Frank and smiled.
"Here comes the good part. I got into the Submarine
School in 1942 and immediately after went to the base
commander for permission to marry. I hounded that
son of a bitch for weeks until he gave in. I brought
Elena out in the spring of '43 and we did it again. This
time it was a military wedding. I swear to you, nobody

ever figured out what we were laughing about!"

Hardy broke into a long chuckle. Frank grinned broadly. "It wasn't so easy after that," Hardy went on, sobering. "I got transferred to Fleet Sonar School in San Diego. Elena was pregnant, so we rented a house. The war had gotten worse, and I guess I began to worry about the decision I had made, about my career. We all heard the reports. Submarines were making a dent in Japanese shipping, but they had started making a dent in our fleet. Finally I got posted to Pearl, and we knew this was it." Hardy's face clouded over. "Elena couldn't make the trip. Too pregnant; besides, no wives allowed. I spent the rest of '43 as a junior officer, floating from one sub assignment to another. It wasn't until the first of February, 1944, that I was assigned to the *Candlefish*. Then I met Basquine . . . and Bates— the toughest sons of bitches in the entire submarine fleet. They never gave an inch—to anybody for anything. They were a matched set. It was like sailing on the *Pequod* with Captain Ahab."

Hardy grunted. "Captain Ahab, that's Basquine. But he could be a charmer. And *that's* why the crew let him get away with it. He used to deliver the greatest pep talks. But everything he did or said was directed for one purpose: war. He was . . . he was like a psychologist with an ulterior motive. And the Exec, Bates, backed him up. I made the mistake of thinking I was qualified when I stepped aboard this boat. Bates cut me down to size. In my first five days he had me up for oral exams three times. He walked me through the boat with all the lower ranks watching and made me peg every valve, every gauge, and line. I passed those exams, but I'll tell you, I contracted a whopping case of insecurity."

Frank was impressed. The old oceanographer had a pretty good understanding of himself.

"Then we had our first patrol in late February. Bates had me researching engineering problems one on top of the other. Understand: That wasn't unusual—we always had controlled problems to work out. But he had me doing them *all* the time. Anyway, I moved around in rotation until they sort of settled on me as navigation officer. That worked out fine. I spent more time on the bridge and got a chance to see Basquine at work." Hardy looked directly at Frank and spoke tightly: "Commander—that bastard tried to sink *everything*. He was out for blood, and everybody knew it. In 1944 he was the least cautious skipper at sea. And with Bates as his yes-man, and me working the charts, he began to form his grand plan."

"What was that?"

"A top-secret, lone-wolf attack on Tokyo Bay. Even SubPac didn't know about it."

Frank felt a chill. It was true. He hadn't found any mention at all in the records about any such plan.

"It was maniacal," said Hardy. "A complete lack of regard for the safety of the crew and the boat. It's one thing to sneak up on enemy shipping, fire a few fish, then run like hell. But this was crazy—placing ourselves squarely in a closed ball park. I think he really was a bit of an Ahab. A self-destructive monster."

"Did you try to stop him?" asked Frank.

"Yes. Yes, I tried to talk him out of it. I got three days of orals from Bates. They took me off the plan and put in Jordan, the gunnery officer. He thought the plan was 'workable.'"

"Did you ever think, Professor, that maybe you just weren't suited for war?"

"I *know* I wasn't. But I wasn't crazy, either."

Hardy stopped talking for a while. He leaned back and rocked against the plates of the conning tower. He unbuttoned his shirt and took sun on his chest.

"What about the last patrol? What was he like then?"

"Well, you know, for all Basquine's rootie-tooting about how great we were, we still had a comparatively lousy record. In the first six months I served with him, we sank only two Japanese freighters. He took after a couple of fishing boats one day when he was feeling particularly ornery. Outside of that, nothing."

"Was there a reason?"

"Yeah. I think we missed a lot of targets because of bad attack planning, faulty torpedoes—those Mark 14s were not the most reliable—and rotten weather. So, by August of '44, when we set out on our third patrol, he was riding the crew pretty hard, trying to make up for his own failures. He drilled everyone right up to and beyond effective preparedness."

"What about you?"

"I was a nervous wreck."

Behind those stiff gray whiskers, Hardy fell silent. His lips became a thin red line slashed across the curls.

"Want to tell me about that slug test?"

"My side of it?" A wry smile crept through Hardy's whiskers. "You've already got it from the horse's mouth."

"I'd like to hear it from yours."

"No." Hardy got up. "Enough is enough, Mr. Frank. You really don't need to know any of this. It has no bearing on what you want to do, and it's a big pain in the ass for me."

He waited for a reply, challenging. Frank was certain that if he could get Hardy to tell the rest of his story, it would turn out that in all the years since the incident with the torpedoman Hardy had vigorously sought but never found redemption.

Frank got up and patted the dust from the seat of his pants. He pulled together the trash from their lunch and stuffed it into the paper bag, then asked rather casually: "How *is* that log coming?"

Hardy looked at him a long time. "I think I'm getting the navigational points down straight. The charts are a big help."

"I thought so." Frank smiled. "I've always found that mental recall works better if you try to remember things in the order in which they occurred." Hardy grunted and turned to go below. Frank stopped him. "Just a minute. In your opinion, Professor—how good a navigator were you?"

"I was okay."

Frank looked him right in the eye. "Think you could get us there again?"

Hardy blinked. "Again?" He almost choked on it. "You're not suggesting—!"

"I sure am."

Hardy swung around on him, threatening, fire burning under those hefty gray brows. "Now, look! I said I'd come out here to have a peek! And then I said I'd work on that log—but that's as far as I go!"

Frank pulled the telex from his pocket. "Read this."

Hardy took it and skimmed it once—then again, slowly. His mouth opened.

"Smitty came through. The funds are approved. The project is *Go*." Frank put out a hand for the cable, and Hardy returned it with a muttered growl of disapproval.

"At least admit it's an accomplishment." Frank smiled.

"It's a mistake!" Hardy barked. "This boat has no business being here, and you have no business being on it. It should have stayed at the bottom of the ocean!"

"Will you come along?"

Hardy grew cold and tight. "I'll finish that log! But when you *sail*, I'll be on the dock waving aloha!"

Hardy turned on his heel and stumbled as fast as he could around the bridge. He tumbled down the hatch, apparently wanting to escape Frank before the matter could be pressed further.

Frank felt anger building inside. After all the coaxing he had done, the man was proving more difficult than ever.

Lieutenant Cook came bounding down the dock, waving a copy of the telex and whooping at the top of his lungs. He spotted Frank on the cigarette deck and bounded aft. He waved the telex up at Frank and literally blubbered with happiness.

"We did it! Here's the good news!"

"I've seen it," growled Frank. "Get me an appointment with SubPac. We want to find a CO with fleet-boat experience. Then we'll have to line up a crew. You start arranging provisions, fuel—line up that escort—and do it all pronto!"

Cook swallowed his smile. Frank was in no mood for trifling. The lieutenant turned right around with a snappy "Yes, sir!" and dashed off the boat.

Frank walked around the bridge and gazed down the open hatch, wondering what he was going to do about Hardy. It seemed so obvious—so essential—that he come along. What if the log he wrote was not right? What if details were missing? Certainly he couldn't be expected to remember *everything*. If he were along, the constant prodding of events would stimulate his memory and gradually he would fill in the gaps.

Jack Hardy had to be volunteered, bought, or shanghaied onto the *Candlefish*. And there were only twenty-seven days left to accomplish it.

CHAPTER 9

October 28, 1974

On the morning of October 28th, Frank met with Vice-Admiral P. G. Begelman, Jr., Commander, Submarine Force, Pacific Fleet: ComSubPac. Frank appeared in his office at 0900 with a list of possible submarine COs provided by Diminsky.

Begelman, a burly, suntanned warrior of fifty-odd years, with a reputation for being tough but fair, took the list and went through it quickly, removing his glasses as soon as he had finished.

"Uh . . . this one. Byrnes. Commander Louis F. Byrnes. Most reliable CO I've ever met."

Frank came around the admiral's desk and peered at the list.

"Yes, sir. Do you know him well?" asked Frank.

"Very well. He's by-the-book, right down the line."

Frank stepped around the desk. By-the-book? He wondered if that was what he needed. Wouldn't he be better off with someone flexible—someone young and daring?

As if reading his mind, Begelman came back with an explanation. "You're not going to find any younger men who've got CO experience aboard this type of fleet boat. Except perhaps yourself. I understand you skippered one in 'Nam a few years back."

"Yes, sir. That's true. The *Prang*. For one month."

"Well, the Navy would prefer someone senior with

extensive experience, someone who will have the interests of the boat at heart, while you handle the investigative aspect of the mission."

"I see." It made sense, from the Navy point of view. But Frank could sense the hand of Diminsky at work. "Well, Byrnes sounds fine to me. Is he available, sir?"

"Yes. His own boat is in for a three-month refit. Installing some new technical equipment. We can have him here Wednesday, the thirtieth."

Frank thought about it a moment, then nodded. What could he do? He was cornered. But the thought of having to contend with a stiff, inflexible Navy CO type—on top of his problems with Jack Hardy—made him queasy.

On the same morning, Lieutenant Cook met with two officers from the Bureau of Naval Personnel. He handed them copies of his request and watched two sets of eyebrows lift almost in unison.

"Eighty-three men?" said one of them.

"All volunteers? Where the hell are we gonna dig them up? And all with fleet-boat experience? Holy ranchero, Lieutenant! Give us a break."

"My boss will break your necks if you don't come up with them," said Cook.

The two BuPer officers relaxed. Intimidation almost always provoked the same response: "In that case, do it yourself."

Cook grinned, and the two BuPer men began to relax.

"All right, Lieutenant, what do you need to know?"

"First—who is still in the Navy who's been assigned to that kind of boat?"

"We'll have to work up a list," said one of the officers.

"Fine. Second—which guys are in the Pearl Harbor area?"

"No problem. That'll take a day."

"Third—which ones are the bums and which ones the good guys?"

One of the officers did a slow burn and then came back with a wry smile. "Which kind do you want?"

"Very funny," replied Cook, and stood up. "Soon as we've figured out who the best guys are, we'll go ask them to volunteer."

"You want us to give them a choice?"

Cook blinked. "What sort of choice?"

"Service aboard the *Candlefish* or assignment to the South Pole."

Cook snorted. Both BuPer officers laughed. Evidently this was a routine gag with them. Cook was impressed with their limited repertoire. "On the matter of officers," he said, "don't look for any regular line officers. Try to pick up some Limited Duty Officers—guys who are old enough to have served on those boats. That's the main criterion."

"You want LDOs—they're probably crawling all over the tenders. Take your pick."

"I want a list. We'll present everything to the incoming CO and let him select the guys he knows first."

"We've got a lot of ex-enlisted people who are officers now. We can draw from them."

"Great," said Cook. "And the yardbirds. Anybody who *is* Navy or who's *been* Navy. Just get me a list."

October 30, 1974

At noon on Wednesday, October 30th, Ed Frank walked up the companionway from his quarters aboard the *Imperator*. He buttoned his uniform blouse and squared his cap. He went across the deck to the gang-plank and gazed off up the pier. A Navy staff car rolled down the road from the BOQ. Two men got out and approached the tender. Frank could make out Lieu-tenant Cook's confident lope; he was being paced by a tight, stern-looking officer.

Frank stepped back and took up a position to greet the new arrival. Commander Louis F. Byrnes stamped up the gangway and stepped aboard, Cook at his heels. Frank saluted and introduced himself.

"Ed Frank."

"Louis Byrnes. Glad to meet you."

Byrnes was somewhere in his early forties, with a face full of angular crags. They shook hands, and Cook muffled a smile to Frank as Byrnes looked slowly around the tender.

"When do you intend to sail, Commander Frank?"

"November twenty-first, 0800," Frank returned quickly.

Byrnes shot him an interested glance. "That's very precise."

"I've been told you appreciate precision."

"Close. I thrive on it."

Frank managed a weak smile and wondered briefly what the hell he was going to be put through once this man got them out to sea.

Byrnes loosened up, sensing the uneasiness, and smiled. He clasped his hands behind his back and toured around the tender, making his way aft.

"I would like a crew of seventy-five, including of-ficers," he called out over his shoulder.

"We'll be eighty-four," Frank flung back. "I want to match the wartime crew man for man."

Byrnes accepted that impassively. Frank watched his

back: His shoulders rippled as he walked. They came astern, and Byrnes stopped to look down on the *Candlefish* at the end of the pier.

"She looks fit."

"Deceptive," said Frank.

Byrnes smiled at him and said, "Pee-culiar."

They took a tour through the sub after lunch. Byrnes found it much to his liking: It appeared to be in better shape than 90 percent of the boats he had served on. The yard crews had repaired most of the internal damage, so Byrnes was deprived of the sight of broken instruments, strewn personal effects, main engine number one thrust up out of her mountings, and torpedoes flung against the bulkheads.

Frank felt it best to play down the more mysterious aspects of the sub's condition, figuring that Byrnes would find out anyway; why take a chance on ruffling that cool, rigid composure? The man needed to know only as much as it took to get the submarine to sea with a full crew. Frank had decided very early on that the investigation—the nature of the mission—should not be a subject of too much conversation until they were well on their way. Accordingly, he let slip only minor details of the sub's history now, doing everything possible to keep Byrnes's mind on the task at hand.

Byrnes peered into the captain's cabin and stared at Jack Hardy, engrossed in writing his log. Hardy looked up and then stood up. Frank introduced them. The fact that Hardy had served aboard this boat thirty years ago provided the first ripple in the new skipper's icy exterior. But what sort of reaction did Byrnes elicit from Hardy? And what would happen if the two men ever sailed together?

Late that afternoon, Frank and Byrnes sat down for

drinks in Frank's quarters aboard the *Imperator*. Frank handed him stack after stack of papers on the *Candlefish:* charts, fitness reports, equipment checklists, supply manifests, blueprints, and a fat hundred-page ship's-organization book, the SOP for the *Candlefish,* as prepared by Basquine and Bates in November of 1943. Watch bills, crew assignments, material cognizance, emergency bills, engineering instructions—the ship's-organization book was a gold mine of information.

Byrnes wanted to rewrite the entire book to his own predilections.

Frank was insistent. "No. We haven't got time for that. Besides, we want to run this patrol the same way they ran the one in '44. Same watch bills, same orders, same engineering procedures. We can make this work —it worked fine thirty years ago."

"The sub sank, didn't it?"

"Yes, and we want to find out why. That's the whole purpose of this."

Byrnes gazed at him with cold determination. "Fine. But we don't want it to happen again." Frank fell silent, so he added, "Do we?"

"No. Of course not."

"My first concern, Mr. Frank, is with the boat and the safety of the crew. Your assignment is your own business. It has nothing to do with me unless it conflicts with my duty. I was given to understand that the action of the patrol will be your responsibility, except when it encroaches upon mine. Are we agreed?"

"Yes." It was a blow to Frank's ever-broadening conceit, and he had to roll with it. Basically, Byrnes spoke the truth. Every operation needed a counterbalance. If Frank were permitted total free rein, he would probably run the sub into what could be construed as dangerous circumstances.

October 31, 1974

At 2000 hours on Hallowe'en, Ed Frank and Byrnes were still closeted with three officers from SubPac in an immense briefing room on the base at Pearl, trying to lay out potential crew for the *Candlefish*. Lieutenant Cook stood at a window, watching outside as a long line of cars drew up to the Officers' Club for the Hallowe'en Ball. He smirked as two officers arrived at the same time in the same bunny suit. Cook picked at his uniform and wished for the days when he too wore a costume and made-believe . . .

In the front of the briefing room, three blackboards were filled with lists of the different watch organizations aboard the *Candlefish*. Byrnes was chalking up names for crew assignments as fast as the SubPac officers approved them.

"Now then," said Byrnes, "the engines. I want a machinist to serve as chief engineer, a floating jack-of-all-trades. And I want a man who knows *this* submarine."

"Have you got someone in mind?" asked Frank.

"As a matter of fact, I do. There's a yardbird up at Mare Island. Cassidy."

One of the SubPac officers cleared his throat. "I know him. Little guy. About sixty. Been there forever. But he's civil service now."

"He *was* Navy," said Byrnes.

"Do we want civil service?" asked one of the other officers.

"I want *him*," Byrnes insisted.

Everyone shifted in discomfort. Frank said nothing. "Then it's settled," Byrnes announced. "Let's turn to officers."

Frank stood up and went to the blackboard with a

piece of chalk and wrote in a name opposite the post *Navigation*. "As long as we're picking favorites—our navigation officer will be Jack Hardy." The SubPac officers, Byrnes, Cook, all stared at him. "And keep it under your hat, because he's playing hard to get."

Byrnes gave Frank one of his frigid glares, then said quietly, "I want another qualified navigator aboard."

The SubPac officers agreed immediately. Frank felt himself losing ground. He gave in, irked that he now found himself in competition with the new captain.

November 4, 1974

The first of the new crew began arriving early that morning. Most of the machinists, engineers, oilers, and throttlemen had been culled from the ranks of available submariners and reservists at Pearl—on a volunteer basis. Each man was told the same story: The *Candlefish* was a World War II vintage submarine in mint condition and a crew was being assembled for a special sea trial across the Pacific. No reference was made to any of the more mysterious circumstances surrounding the mission.

Hardy came to Frank's quarters aboard the *Imperator* just before noon and dropped a hefty notebook on his desk.

"That's it," he said cryptically, and flopped down on the vinyl couch. He was tired, drained. "I spent all last night finishing it."

Frank opened the book and skimmed through page after page of readable longhand. Dates, names, places, long descriptions of events: Hardy had remembered a great deal. Frank could not restrain an excited smile. "Pretty good work," he said.

"As long as you've got what you want."

"This looks incredibly thorough."

Hardy nodded, relieved.

Then Frank took a daring shot in the dark. "Well, that wraps it up for you. I can get you out of here within three hours and we'll take over. If we have any questions, can we reach you at Scripps?"

Hardy thought it over a long time, then said quietly, "I'd like to hang around for a few days. I might have made some mistakes in the log."

"Suit yourself." Frank rose with a straight face. "I have to go down and check out some of the crew. Want to come along?"

"Yeah."

Hardy stood out of the way on the dock while Frank shook hands with a steady stream of new arrivals coming in by truck. The crew seemed roughly divided between boisterous old-timers—reuniting with mates they hadn't seen in years—and enthusiastic twenty-year-old volunteers. Frank greeted each one, asked a few personal questions, then turned them over to Byrnes, whose smile was as warm as he could manage. Hardy watched them tossing their gear down the after hatch and jumping in after it. When Frank came up, he could see the nostalgia warming Hardy's eyes.

"What do you think?" he asked.

"There's a lot of kids."

"Qualified kids."

A jeep screeched around the corner at the inland end of the dock, then roared up to the end of the pier. The second it stopped, out jumped a small, skinny, craggy, sixty-year-old seaman. He hoisted his worn duffel bag over one shoulder, then padded to the edge of the dock and regarded the submarine with an amused gleam. Hardy stared at him, thoroughly taken with the man's cocksure attitude. Frank leaned over and muttered, "Old enough for you?"

"Christ, he looks like he built this boat."

"He did."

Hardy glanced at Frank in surprise, then was distracted as the man jumped to the gangplank with a resounding grunt. He swaggered down to the deck and flung down his duffel. Walter "Hopalong" Cassidy tucked his thumbs into his belt loops. He stamped a foot on the deck slats and was amazed at the resilience of the wood. He marched over to the conning tower and pushed and poked at the plating, then kicked it. It rang with a solid metal thud. Pleased and surprised, he strolled back and picked up his gear, glancing over his shoulder at the conning tower. He made his way aft and tumbled down the hatch.

On the dock, Frank gave Hardy a sidelong look. The oceanographer was smiling, one hand stroking his beard.

Cassidy padded forward through the engine rooms, running his hands along the diesel shells with a professional touch. He stopped in the forward engine room and stared at main engine number one. A few technicians were still working on it, fitting new bolts into place, painting the shell, rewiring the engine stand. Cassidy flung his gear into a bunk over main engine number two on the port side, then made his way forward.

The bunks in the crew's quarters were beginning to fill up with gear. Cassidy paused at the forward bulkhead and stared at the Ann Sheridan pinup pasted at eye level. Cassidy grinned in fond memory until a torpedoman named Clampett bumped into him.

" 'Scuse me, Pop."

Cassidy blinked. He was brought down to reality—

hard. Cassidy arrived in the control room just as Hardy and Frank came down the ladder.

Byrnes saw him first and managed another one of his almost friendly grins. "You've aged a bit, Hopalong."

Cassidy grinned and showed well-used teeth. "You ain't getting any younger yourself, sir."

Hardy pressed forward, eager to be introduced. Byrnes stood aside and motioned everyone together. "Walter Cassidy, this is Ed Frank . . . and Jack Hardy."

They all shook hands. Then Frank announced, "Hardy served on the *Candlefish* during World War Two."

Cassidy lit up like a hundred-watt bulb. "You *served* on her? Son of a bitch! For how long?"

"Eleven months."

"You lasted eleven months with Basquine? I can't believe that."

"It's true."

"You know, when he came to Mare Island to pick up the boat in '42, I could have sworn the guy was psychotic."

Hardy smiled but remained silent.

"And that's a goddamned conservative estimate. He couldn't wait to take her out and sink Japs. It's all he talked about." He turned to Byrnes. "You never knew him, did you?"

Byrnes chuckled. "Afraid I was a little too young."

"Well, he was something." Cassidy shook his head sagely. Then he looked up sharply at Hardy. "But for all that, you guys were never any blazing success."

"What do you mean? What about our last patrol?"

Cassidy waved it off. "Okay—for three weeks you got lucky."

"Lucky!"

Frank watched in amazement. Something had put Hardy on the defensive. He began telling Cassidy about the log he had just completed.

"I'd like to read it."

Frank promised to have Hardy's log typed and circulated among this little group.

Then, unexpectedly, Cassidy shoved in the stinger. "Hey, I'll bet you can't wait to get out there and relive the whole thing."

Hardy's mouth was open and stayed open. He didn't know what to say. Frank replied for him. "Actually, Dr. Hardy doesn't plan to go along."

Cassidy was stunned. "No shit?" he said, and stared at Hardy as if he'd just been introduced to a plague.

There was nothing else Hardy could do. He shook his head meekly, smiled at Cassidy, mumbled something about "Nice to meet you," and went up the control-room ladder. Cassidy watched him go, puzzled.

Byrnes straightened in supreme satisfaction. "Mr. Frank, I have a standby navigation officer due to report in Friday. You better get with it."

Byrnes shook hands with Cassidy again, muttered, "Great to have you aboard," and went aft. Frank and Cassidy were alone in the control room.

"Coffee?" offered Frank.

"Sure."

They moved into the galley and took coffee from a ready percolator, then moved to the officers' wardroom.

Cassidy was hesitant. "I'm not exactly an officer."

"You're not exactly in the Navy either, but you're assigned as chief engineer. That's an officer's post with an officer's privileges. So sit down."

Cassidy shrugged and sat. "Okay . . . but if it's all the same to you, I'll bunk with the engines."

Frank chuckled. They sipped coffee in silence. Frank

pulled out his pipe kit and assembled a smoke.

"Byrnes tell you what this is all about?"

"Yeah."

"Do you think we're nuts?"

"Hell no." Cassidy looked at him seriously. "I've been around submariners forty years, Commander. They are the most rock-headed baboons in the service. They'll tackle anything."

"But this is a big risk. We don't know what we're going to find. And I don't think anybody coming aboard has the slightest idea that this might turn out to be dangerous."

"Look," said Cassidy, "we both know submariners have a lousy insurance rating. Anybody who's going to allow himself to be sealed up at sea in this tin cigar for any length of time is living with one foot in the grave. And they're all aware of it. Risks are nothing to them. If you told them they might not be coming back, there's no way in the world they'd believe you. They can't. They just learn to live with that possibility—and they live with it by ignoring it."

He got up, drained his coffee, and thought a moment, then said, "There's only one thing. They might be just a little superstitious. But everything's okay on that score." He fished in his pocket and produced a long, hairy rabbit's foot. He grinned broadly. Frank grinned back.

November 15, 1974

The long yellow and green torpedoes were guided across from the tender and slowly lowered into the forward loading hatch.

Frank descended the hatch and dropped into the forward torpedo room. Lieutenant Cook was there with a full complement of submarine officers, Byrnes's staff. He was conducting a tour of the boat. Hardy hovered in the rear of the little party.

Cook waited for the noise of the torpedoes rolling into the port and starboard bays to abate, then indicated one of them. "In order to follow the pattern that Dr. Hardy has laid out for you, you will have to fire these at designated times during the voyage. We have equipped you with Mark 14 practice torpedoes; the warheads are non-functioning dummies. Since they will not explode on contact, you don't have to have any reservations about firing them. That's it for the torpedo room. Shall we move aft?"

The officers turned and started shuffling out. Cook led them. Byrnes hung back with Frank, and they both watched Jack Hardy limp to the connecting hatch and step through.

"We're all set to go," Byrnes said. "What about your navigation officer?"

"He'll be there. What about yours?"

"Mine has already plotted our course," Byrnes said with silky satisfaction.

"From a log written by mine." Frank smiled back. He was beginning to get the hang of dealing with the captain. "Incidentally, I have decided that you'll also have two executive officers aboard." He watched Byrnes stiffen. "One qualified and one nose-grabber. I'm the nose-grabber."

Byrnes looked at him a long time, then smiled back. "Fine. I'm the *captain*."

Byrnes raised a hand, and Frank edged back; he thought the skipper was going to tweak his nose to make his point. But Byrnes merely straightened his cap and went through the hatch.

Frank was left alone to reflect on the fact that bluff

carries only so far. And he still didn't have Jack Hardy. But he felt he was close.

November 19, 1974

They were two days away from sailing. Frank and Cook had finished all preparations for the voyage: All stores were aboard, the crew was complete, the boat had been pronounced fit by yard inspectors. There were only two things remaining: the trim dive—which would be conducted on their first day out, in deference to Hardy's log—and the posting of Hardy as navigation officer.

For several days Frank had been waiting for the other shoe to drop, and it finally did.

Cook arrived with a memo from Smitty. The timing was perfect: It was too late to fight back. Smitty was notifying Captain Byrnes, with a copy to Ed Frank, that his escort would be the USS *Frankland,* a special-duty destroyer which had recently been used in a series of *Glomar*-type tests. The *Frankland* was already equipped with numerous undersea research devices which would be working ahead of the *Candlefish,* sensing changes in ocean currents, electromagnetic fields, and anything else that could put the submarine into jeopardy. Byrnes's instructions were short and simple: At the first sign of unusual ocean behavior, he was to fall back on the *Frankland.* He was in no way to place the crew of the *Candlefish* in danger.

"Clipped your wings," said Cook.

"I smell Diminsky again." Frank held the memo a long time, then crumpled it. "The hell with it. I can work with this. What do they think we're gonna do—go out and sink this thing? Let them carry any gizmos they want, as long as it makes *them* feel better."

Cook smiled. "Sure beats a cancelation."

"Yeah," said Frank, and grinned back.

After dinner Frank put on a light sweater, lit his pipe, and took a stroll over to Bachelor Officers' Quarters. He opened the door and walked down the hall of the first floor toward Hardy's room. Seeing the door ajar and light splashing across the floor, he slowed and approached cautiously. He peered into the little room and stood watching a long time.

Hardy was hunched over the desk by the window, his eyes buried in one of the typed copies of the log he had written for *Candlefish*. The framed photo of his wife and son was on the edge of the desk, right under the lamp.

Frank rapped gently on the door and waited for Hardy to look up. The bearded face turned slowly and fixed glassy eyes on him.

"Professor? Mind a visitor?"

Hardy's lips formed a "No." His voice was lost in a throaty mutter. Frank came in and sat on the bed, leaned back, and relit his pipe. Hardy looked at him, his finger holding the page he had been reading.

"I've always believed that a man recalls best those things in life that he'd rather forget. The bad times are much more vivid," said Frank.

"You're probably right."

"You did a hell of a job."

"Yes."

"It's going to prove very useful to us."

"Yes."

Hardy watched him with impassive, liquid eyes.

For once Frank was not smiling. He deliberately dropped all pretense at diplomacy. "Professor . . . tell me about Mud Kenyon."

There was a long, long moment during which Hardy never changed expression. Then his eyes lowered and his shoulders sagged.

"Have you ever fired a torpedo, Commander?"

"Sure."

"You open the outboard door, flood the tube with sea water, charge up the impulse tank, then press the firing key. Four easy steps."

"Right."

"Ever fired a water slug?"

Frank nodded.

"The torpedo stays in place in the tube. The outboard door is shut, the inner door opened, safety interlocks are tripped, then the tube is fired. The fish stays where it is and the tube is blasted clean. Water and air are expelled back into the compartment. Again—easy. Routine."

Frank waved his pipe, and there was a pause.

"On August 14th, 1944, Torpedoman Second Class Mud Kenyon and I were assigned night detail in the aft torpedo room. We had fired slugs on tubes seven and eight and were preparing tube nine. Kenyon opened the inner door and charged up the impulse tank. I lifted the safety interlock, and Kenyon nodded he was ready. I pressed the firing key. Nothing would have happened if Kenyon and I had been operating the same tubes. I lifted the lock and fired number ten instead of number nine. There was a terrible blast; the boat took a whacking from one end to the other. The inner door on tube ten sprang open, and Kenyon took it full across his face. He was thrown across the deck and collided with me. We both went down, and were immediately drenched by a flood of sea water. I heard the alarm go off and men behind us hollering. They sealed up the compartment and then stumbled around us, trying to reach the tube to stop the propeller on the tail of

the torpedo in tube ten. It was a surface-ready tube—
its impulse tank had been charged earlier, and both
doors were shut. The blast had sent the torpedo bash-
ing into the outboard door and then blew out the inner
door, making a shambles of the tube. It took them forever to stop the propeller—and if they hadn't, the
whole boat would have gone up.

"When I finally managed to get to my feet, there was
Kenyon's body sloshing around in the bilges. He was
face down, his head a mass of smashed bone and
bloody pulp. I watched him . . . a long time. Somebody dropped beside him and poked him, but it was no
use . . . he was dead."

Hardy looked up. "I was responsible." The words
came in a throaty quaver.

Frank felt a chill. For a moment he was not certain
whether it was produced by the words or the breeze
from the window, but he knew one thing for certain:
He now had the key to the man.

"The burial at sea—the four days that followed—I
endured all of it. First the sympathy, then the open
hatred from Kenyon's crewmates. The story got
around. On a little three-hundred-foot steel island, everything gets around. But it wasn't until Bates and
Basquine offered their feelings that the crew began to
take sides on the issue. Bates demanded a Board of Inquiry, a court-martial, or, at the very least, my transfer
from the boat the moment we returned to Pearl for repairs. We were in the Skipper's cabin. I think Basquine
left the door open deliberately, so Bates's voice would
carry through half the boat—what didn't carry would
be picked up and passed on by the men. Bates finally
ended his harangue and sat down. Then Basquine took
over. He spoke quietly at first, and I remember his
eyes—cold with contempt. He told me that my dog

days aboard the *Candlefish* were all over. And he refused to transfer me off the boat. He said, 'Because that's just too goddamned easy. I want you here, where I can see you, where every day you spend in my sight will remind you of what you've done. I'm going to make you remember this the rest of your career, Lieutenant. I'm going to teach you what it means to be responsible for another man's life!'

"And I became the scapegoat—the one they could blame for all our troubles aboard the *Candlefish*—all our months of failure."

If Lieutenant Commander Billy G. Basquine had been a witch, he could not have handed down a more effective curse.

Frank watched Hardy fall silent, sag a bit in his chair, and at last lose his place in the log as his hand dropped away from it. His eyes came up slowly and met Frank's.

"I know why you're here," he said, and Frank stiffened. "You've been trying for days. You think you've just got to have me along."

Frank tapped out his pipe on the windowsill. "I suppose I'm a little obvious."

Hardy's voice rose, "Don't you understand? I was *responsible!* A man *died* on that boat because of me!"

"According to that log, you and the rest of that crew were responsible for a lot of lives on that last patrol. *Enemy lives.*"

"Not the same."

"Yes it is. There are casualties on both sides in any war. Individuals aren't responsible. The war is."

"This was different. They *made me* responsible."

"They couldn't make you *anything*. You made yourself!"

"Mr. Frank, that boat went down and *I'm* the only one left!"

Frank stood up and pointed the pipe at him. "Don't try to tell me you're responsible for *that!*"

Hardy's gaze dropped.

"Look, Professor, I've met a lot of submarine officers in my life, but I've never even heard of a skipper as tough as Basquine. If you're telling the truth—and I'm sure you are—if he gave you a thirty-year guilt complex—then Basquine was the last man in the Navy qualified to be the captain of a submarine. Either he became that way without drawing the attention of the review boards, or—"

"Or what?"

"Or you have one hell of a subjective imagination."

Hardy stood up, and Frank had the sinking feeling that once again his mouth had done him in.

"As it turns out, Professor, I believe you. It would seem you've had more than your share of anguish over the whole thing. I can't force you to come along. And I won't have you if you don't want to be there."

He turned and went to the door, then looked back at the old man silhouetted in the window. "Only one point bothers me now: If you were responsible then— for that crew—you're even more responsible now, for this one."

"Why?"

Frank pointed at the log on the desk. "Those are *your* words, Hardy. We need *you* to back them up. If something goes wrong—if you forgot to put something down on paper—how are we going to know? If something happens to this crew because of *that*"—his finger stabbed at the log—*"then* what are you going to feel?"

Hardy never moved.

Finally Frank turned and walked out. He strode quickly down the hall, clutching the pipe, disgusted with himself. But he had done what had to be done.

November 20, 1974

At 0800 the morning before they were to set sail, Byrnes and Frank held a final briefing for the entire crew, in which they spelled out the history of the *Candlefish,* the purpose of the voyage, and the dangers they might encounter. They were immediately met with a barrage of questions about what they hoped to accomplish.

"Is it possible that when we get back to where *Candlefish* went down before, it could happen again?"

"Anything is possible," granted Frank, "but it's highly improbable."

"What's to prevent it?"

"Look—in 1944 there was a shooting war going on. We don't have that situation today. What we do have is an escort sitting on our tail. If it ever gets rough, we just jump off." There was a short silence, followed by much grumbling. Frank added, "How come you're expecting trouble? The Navy sees this as a normal, run-of-the-mill submarine patrol, otherwise they wouldn't have authorized it. We're looking for *clues,* we're not expecting catastrophe."

It was another thirty minutes before Frank managed to shift the topic of conversation. He was busy reading off the watch bills when he saw the back door open and Jack Hardy step quietly in. He stood there a moment, looking for a seat, then walked straight down the aisle to a chair in the front row, next to Lieutenant Cook.

Frank hurried through the watch bills, then turned the meeting over to Lieutenant Dorriss, the qualified executive officer. Frank sat down on the other side of Cook and leaned forward to look at Hardy. Their eyes met across Cook.

Finally Hardy whispered, "I'm going with you."

PART III

CHAPTER 10

November 21, 1974

0345 hours.

Watery darkness lapped at the hull. Night blended with the fresh coat of gray-black paint on the conning tower and the upper decks. Men were busy detaching the guard rails that ringed the perimeter of the forward deck. The men on watch detail shifted around silently on the bridge. The only sound came from the Officer of the Deck, sipping coffee.

Two figures came down the pier at a fast clip, carrying zip-cases and clipboards: Ed Frank and Ray Cook. They stopped at the gangplank and exchanged a few last words, then shook hands and parted. Frank went aboard the submarine; Cook hurried away to board the destroyer escort, USS *Frankland,* along with Captain Melanoff of Defense Intelligence Command and one Admiral Lionel Kellogg, assigned to supervise by ComSubPac.

Ed Frank pushed his gear into a locker in the large stateroom he would share with most of the other officers. Hardy had quarters in the chief petty officers' stateroom, just forward of the control room; he had refused his old bunk.

In the forward engine room, Hopalong Cassidy, stripped down to overalls and undershirt, was already covered with diesel oil though they hadn't even started the engines yet. He double-checked all the dials and gauges on the engine stand, then went back to inspect the aft engine room and the maneuvering room. He was followed by two old cronies dressed in similar outfits, two aging machinist's mates Cassidy had unearthed from his own little black book: Googles was the throttleman and Brownhaver the oiler.

At 0430 Cassidy got on the horn to Roybell in the control room: "Tell the skipper engine rooms are secure, ready to answer bells."

Roybell hollered the information up to the conning tower, and Byrnes got on the intercom and ordered quietly: "All stations at ease. We will rig the maneuvering watch at 0730. Underway at 0800."

The crew relaxed. There was little to do now but prepare personal kit for getting underway.

Ed Frank went aft. He found Cassidy at work in the forward engine room, washing down the diesels, polishing them with big, heavy cloths. Cassidy stopped and dabbed at the oil on his arms, then went aft to the crew's washroom. Frank followed and waited until the old yardbird came out of the can.

"Hey, Hopalong, how well do you know the skipper?"

Cassidy threw a questioning glance over his shoulder. He shrugged. "I'd say I've known him off and on almost eighteen years."

"What's he like?"

"A real stickler. Anything goes wrong with his boats, he finagles them back to the yard for a refit right away. Most conscientious skipper I know, when it comes to the Navy's property."

Frank nodded and began to stroll down the aisle.

"Mind if I ask you a question, sir? About the Professor."

"Shoot."

"Do you think it was such a good idea—bringing that old man along?"

"He's at least five years younger than you."

"Yeah—but he doesn't want to be here. It could get sticky."

"Cassidy, I'll make a bet with you. Within forty-eight hours, Jack Hardy will be the happiest man aboard."

Cassidy grunted. "That could get sickening."

Frank laughed. It was the only response he could openly allow himself. More than anyone else aboard, he had to maintain the conviction that Hardy's presence was absolutely essential.

He strolled back through the boat, stopping in the crew's quarters to see what the men were doing. Most were catching sack time before the call to duty. Some of the old-timers were already telling stories to the kids.

Frank stepped into the control room and joined a small group around the plotting table, examining a chart. Hardy was there, plotting their departure course from his log and from copies of the wartime charts they had found aboard. Lieutenant Dorriss and the communications officer, Lieutenant Stigwood, were offering help and suggestions.

Byrnes came down the ladder and peered over their shoulders; he seemed to be regarding Hardy with great curiosity.

At 0730 Byrnes passed the word to station the maneuvering watch. Then he ascended to the bridge with Frank and Hardy. Stigwood came up to the conning tower as conning officer.

At 0750 Byrnes gave the order to cast off. The deck crewmen slipped the lines and flung them to the dock. Lieutenant Dorriss got readiness reports from all compartments. Then Byrnes looked up at the aloha committee crowded into the stern of the *Imperator* and ordered:

"Start all main engines!"

The controllermen in the maneuvering room moved their levers to ALL BACK ONE-THIRD. In the conning tower, the helmsman felt the wheel respond and pulled it steady.

Slowly the *Candlefish* moved away from the pier and into the Southeast Loch. Her horns were answered by loud blatts from the *Frankland*. She came around to port, ALL AHEAD ONE-THIRD, and quietly began to churn up the bay toward Ford Island.

Frank and Hardy climbed off the bridge and walked down the forward deck toward the bow. They stood letting the morning sea breeze brush back their hair and whip their suntan khakis. The *Frankland* maneuvered into their wake seven hundred yards astern.

Blue skies rose out of a diamond-blue sea until they met blinding white clusters of puffy clouds. Frank saw Hardy regarding the great Hawaiian backdrop—the mountains ringing the city which ringed the bay—and knew that neither of them had taken advantage of the beauty at hand in the last few weeks. The smooth sands of beaches, the rough edges of the mountains, the shining glitter of the sea—somehow the magic of this whole garden island had escaped them. They had been preoccupied with the problems of a man-made machine, the details of a carefully plotted sea voyage, and the dangers of an undetermined goal. In the six and a half weeks he had spent here, Frank had lost nearly all connection with the outside world. Just as Hawaii had slipped through his fingers, so had his personal life in Washington. Joanne! My God, he hadn't even called her to say good-bye. Six weeks from now he would be hard-pressed for explanations—if she was still there to hear them.

Frank and Hardy walked farther out to the bow of the sub and let the spray shoot past them. The *Candlefish* was holding her own extremely well—a solid deck under their feet, with no unexpected motion to port or starboard. Frank saw Hardy staring at something ahead and looked to see what it was.

They were coming abreast of the USS *Arizona* memorial, a long white modern concrete structure on the waters at the northern end of Ford Island, entombing the remains of 1100 men slain on December 7th, 1941, when a Japanese bomb was dropped down one of the *Arizona's* stacks, resulting in the biggest loss of life ever suffered by this country in one wartime blow.

Thirty years ago Jack Hardy had stood on the *Candlefish* as it slid quietly past the gutted wreckage of the *Arizona,* not yet covered and converted into this white mausoleum. Now Frank saw the old man do something he wouldn't have expected, given the circumstances of his Navy experience. Hardy's hand went up shakily, and he pulled off his cap. He stood bareheaded, staring at the concrete island in silence, as the sub swept on past. Then he slammed his cap back on his head, shoved his hands into his back pockets, and closed his eyes, letting the breeze and the spray whip and wet his whiskers.

They sailed into the East Loch and began the swing around Ford Island that would take them out to the Pearl Harbor channel. Soon they would be at sea. Frank turned back to stare down the length of the sub. His own ship—in a sense, his own command—and the most important one of his life. How had he allowed the Navy to shape so much of his career? This time he had taken the bull by the horns and insisted. And it had paid off. If it weren't for Ed Frank, there would be no voyage. This submarine would be taken out of service and either cut up for scrap or sold to a museum. He felt proud, and justified. And a little smug.

Within an hour they had sailed out of Mamala Bay
and into the ocean. They were due to spend most of
the day on a northwest swing around the islands.
Somewhere north of Kauai, they would attempt their
trim dive. The USS *Frankland* slipped farther astern
until she was trailing by a full mile. She would remain
at that position for the rest of the voyage . . . unless
she was needed.

Frank went into the radio room and had Giroux call
Lieutenant Cook, who reported that everything was going smoothly aboard the *Frankland* and then added,
admitting his envy of every man on the sub, "Send me
a postcard—wish I was there."

Hardy checked out their course with Lieutenant
Dorriss in the control room. Byrnes remained on the
bridge. Then Hardy wandered back to the engine
rooms and found Cassidy tinkering with the control
stand. Hardy kept silent at first, then ventured some
advice:

"I just thought you might like to know—number two
engine had a tendency to buck a little at high speed.
Something funny with the cylinders."

Cassidy nodded.

"We used to get fresh water leaks, too." Hardy went
on, warming up, "And then the oil cooling channels—"

Cassidy interrupted. "Shit. I could've fixed all those
things thirty years ago. Why didn't you send her back
to the yard?"

"We were a little busy."

"Doing what?"

"W-A-R. War."

Cassidy smirked. His opinion of the *Candlefish*'s war
record had been made clear to Hardy already. Cassidy
walked around and checked the pipes, feeling for leaks

and overheating. He stopped abruptly, and was startled when Hardy bumped into him.

Hardy grinned sheepishly. "I just want to feel useful."

Cassidy shook his head. "Professor—we're busy."

Hardy nodded, gave a quick smile to Brownhaver and Googles, and limped out of the engine room.

Back in the control room, Byrnes had come down to check Hardy's log, to make sure they were following it as closely as possible. Frank had followed him into the control room.

Byrnes closed the log with a snap: "I see it's time for the first trim dive."

Cassidy stepped through the hatch in time to hear that. He slapped his hands together broadly and winked. "Hope she don't leak!"

No one else laughed. Leaning on the bulkhead, Frank spoke drily. "If she does, what are you going to do about it?"

Cassidy whipped the gum out of his mouth and displayed it. "I'm ready."

"Clear the bridge! Dive! Dive!"

Byrnes's voice rang through the communications system to all stations. The klaxon went off, two resounding OOGA-OOGAS! On the bridge, the deck watch tumbled down the hatch—first the lookouts, then Dorriss, then Stigwood. The lookouts piled down to the control room and took up positions as bow and stern planesmen. Stigwood stopped at the foot of the control room ladder and became the diving officer.

The men on watch in each compartment had checked their areas thoroughly for hull integrity. Torpedo tubes were secured shut, negative tanks were flooded, fuel ballast tank flood valves were locked, and three of the air banks were connected to the high pressure air distribution manifold.

Stigwood closed the conning-tower hatch and dogged it down. In the control room, Chief Roybell went to the hydraulic manifold and opened the vents on all tanks. He riveted his eyes on the "Christmas tree," the light board advising him of hull integrity. He called to the two lookouts, "Rig out the bow planes." Then he closed the main induction valve and checked that all lights on the board were green. He called out, "Green board!"

In the engine rooms, Cassidy ordered, "Stop all engines!" on the second blast of the diving alarm. Then he started the commands to his throttlemen.

In the maneuvering room, the controllermen hit their switches and relayed the word to the conning tower, "All main engines stopped, sir."

In the conning tower, the helmsman rang up "BATTERY MOTOR" on the Motor Order Telegraph and put the rudder amidships. The controllermen threw levers and then called back to the conning tower, "Ahead standard on battery, sir."

In the control room, Lieutenant Stigwood took over, supervising as the planesmen started up their motors and put the planes on a twenty-degree dive angle.

And throughout the boat, the men waited in deepening silence and apprehension to find out whether they were going to level off to a trim or sink like a stone.

The boat took a drop into utter silence. One by one, the men looked around at the bulkheads for telltale signs of leaks, droplets of water, condensation, tiny jets from holes no more than a pinprick wide . . . There was nothing. The hull seemed secure.

Hardy stood in the conning tower, studying his wristwatch, waiting for the command to level off, counting the seconds since the alarm had sounded. Frank stood below, out of Stigwood's way. Stigwood watched the barometer of the high pressure air manifold, a bank of valves which controlled compressed air blown to the tanks. When it reached an acceptable level, he called out, "Pressure in the boat, sir!"

His call rang through the nearby compartments, and men within earshot traded relieved glances.

Byrnes moved from the helmsman to the ladder well and called down, "Make your depth sixty feet!"

Roybell glued his eyes to the depth gauge. "Sixty feet! Aye, sir!"

Stigwood barked, "Shut negative flood! Blow negative to the mark!"

"Flood shut. Negative blown to the mark. Permission to vent negative inboard," the auxiliaryman called back.

"Vent negative inboard."

In the maneuvering room, the controllermen watched as the MB system rang up the signal, AHEAD ONE-THIRD. The senior man pulled the telegraph around and called, "Engines secured. Ahead one-third."

Everyone aboard heard that one. And in every compartment, color drained back into faces and bodies relaxed in relief.

In the conning tower, Jack Hardy turned to Byrnes and tapped his watch. "Thirty seconds. Bates used to get us down in fifteen."

Byrnes snorted and gave Hardy a cool look. "What's the rush? At least we're submerged. And, according to your log, we're right on schedule."

Frank came up the ladder all smiles. "Thank you very much," he said, and shook Byrnes's hand vigorously.

"You're welcome. It was nothing. A submarine is supposed to go down."

"Just as long as she comes back up." Frank grinned.

"We will. At about twenty hundred."

Uninvited, Hardy piped up, "Exactly twenty hundred."

Byrnes hesitated. "I think a little leeway won't hurt."

Hardy looked at him oddly a long moment, and Frank could sense a sort of blankness washing over the man, as if for a fraction of an instant he wasn't even there. Then Hardy shrugged, and that was the end of it.

Byrnes turned to the intercom and opened the line to all compartments. "This is the Captain. For your information, we are submerged." He waited for the cheer of approval. "That is not to say *permanently*. We would like to turn this into a successful trim dive, so we ask that you all stand at your stations while we check out the trim manifold function as thoroughly as possible. I would suggest you tie down loose gear, as we will probably do a bit of rolling around. Thank you."

Frank and Hardy made a tour through the boat, checking for signs of flooding. There was nothing in the bilges, not a sign of sea water. They reached the crew's mess and found a small contingent of youngsters and old-timers taking coffee and trying to make light of what they had just undergone.

"Glad to see everybody's taking this so easily," said Frank, pretending not to notice the sweat stains of tension under their armpits.

The torpedoman, Clampett, sat back, thumbs hooked in his belt loops. "What the hell is there to worry about, sir? If I've ever drawn easier duty in my life, I wouldn't know it. Hell, this is nothing. We're just gonna ride around in this old whale's belly for a while and then go home."

Frank slung a leg up on a bench. "A little more to it

than that. You guys were sure worried the other day."

"Well, we got together—most of us—and talked it out. Witzgall here has been on subs for twenty-two years, mostly these old fleet boats." Witzgall nodded through a scraggly peppered beard and lifted his coffee with gnarled fingers. "He points out the one thing none of us should lose sight of."

"What's that?" asked Frank.

"Whatever happened to this boat thirty years ago ain't going to happen again. Everybody knows the same thing can't happen twice."

The men around him smiled with him and nodded their agreement.

Frank thought it over, and he too nodded. Only Jack Hardy was noncommittal. And a couple of the men looked to him for support.

"How about you, Professor?" probed Clampett.

"I . . . agree," said Hardy with some deliberate hesitation. "The same thing probably won't happen again. In which case, Mr. Frank will be the only one disappointed. But as I see it, the special equipment the *Frankland* is carrying will forestall any trouble we might . . ."

The men waited for Hardy to continue, but he had stopped himself. He turned with a little uncertain smile and moved forward, toward the galley. Frank followed and caught up with him just outside the radio room, and asked him what else he was going to say.

"Just one thing. Even if the trip to Latitude Thirty doesn't sink us, other things could happen."

"What other things?"

"I don't know . . . Can't you sense it? Feel it? This boat—you become part of it . . ."

"I think you're talking about yourself, not the rest of us." Frank hoped they weren't headed for a repeat of

Hardy's nightmarish breakdown aboard the *Neptune 4000*.

"I'm talking about all of us. You may not feel it now. But you will after a few days. This boat . . . takes over. You can bend it to your will, because it is only a machine. But as long as it operates, we serve *it*—not the other way around."

Frank did not feel like arguing with him. He suggested that Hardy get some sack time before his watch, and the Professor obediently took off down the corridor.

Frank ducked into the radio room and had Giroux raise Lieutenant Cook aboard the *Frankland* via "Gertrude," the underwater telephone.

"All in all, Ray, it's smooth as silk. No problems so far. We'll stay on our present course, so advise your people out there, and radio Diminsky—send a cable— tell him everything is okay and we are *Go*. Over."

"Okay," Cook's voice crackled over the receiver, "you guys realize you're going to miss Thanksgiving? Over."

"Nuts, I don't think we even packed a turkey. Over."

"Ham sandwiches will do. Talk to you later. Out."

Frank clicked off and handed the mike back to Giroux.

Close to 2000, Frank took the handles of the periscope from Byrnes and pressed his eyes to the rubber shade. The tip of the scope was just above the waves and angled aft. He could see its wake feathering the water and, far in the distance, the lights and the shadowy bulk of the escort destroyer. Frank watched for a while, gradually becoming conscious of his isolation aboard the sub. Stranded with eighty-four other sweaty bodies on a submerged island. The smells were already beginning to permeate the boat. The men, the diesel oil, cooking, coffee . . . And outside, up above, the clean cool darkness of night—the Pacific Ocean and her smells.

Hardy popped up the ladder and regarded the clock impatiently. It was 2002—two minutes past eight o'clock. He approached Byrnes quietly. "Running a little late. We should be surfaced."

Byrnes smiled genially. "We will. Just take it easy."

Hardy watched the Captain bent over the charts with Lieutenant Dorriss. They were comparing plastic overlays to see if they had varied at all from the 1944 course. Frank stepped away from the scope and let Hardy take a look. Hardy put his eyes to it, but he was itchy. He kept looking over his shoulder at Byrnes and the clock. By 2008 Hardy had backed up to the bulkhead and stood flat against it, arms folded across his chest, an unpleasant cast on his face.

Frank regarded him curiously. What was so important about—

"Okay—take her up!"

Byrnes hollered below and Stigwood flew into action, shouting commands at the auxiliarymen and the trim manifold operators. The red combat lights went on, and two lookouts prepared themselves at the foot of the control-room ladder. All vents were shut, and Byrnes ordered, "Slow to one-third." The surfacing alarm went off—three blasts on the horn. Main ballast tanks were blown, bow buoyancy was blown. They rose to forty feet, and Roybell started the low-pressure blower.

The *Candlefish* broached the surface evenly, water cascading off the bridge and out the side vents. She leveled off.

Byrnes ordered the hatch cracked. The Officer of the

Deck shot up the ladder first and spun the dogging wheel. He flung the hatch back and went up, followed by the two lookouts.

In the control room, Stigwood called out, "Rig in the bow planes, open main induction, get ready on main engines."

In the conning tower, Hardy waited until Byrnes went up the ladder, then grabbed Frank's arm and beseeched him. "If you're going to do this, you ought to go by the book—my book."

Frank went up the ladder, amused by Hardy's concern for following the log exactly. After all, Frank had spent several weeks drilling the importance of it into Hardy's head. Now it appeared Hardy was going to hang it around his neck like an albatross.

They gathered on the bridge and scanned the sea. Byrnes gave the order to charge all batteries and maintain present speed and course on two engines.

Frank and Hardy walked around to the cigarette deck and gazed aft. They could see the lights of the destroyer steady in the distance. Frank watched for ten minutes, then went below.

Hardy didn't come down until 0100.

CHAPTER 11

November 26, 1974

After five full days at sea, the *Candlefish* had settled into a routine. Lieutenant Cook received reports from Frank every eight hours and relayed them in briefing sessions to Captain Melanoff and Admiral Kellogg. Aboard the sub, Byrnes conducted briefings in the wardroom at mealtimes. They would dine, have coffee and smoke, and then exchange complete reports on the sub's operation, hull integrity, problems, and plans for the next few hours.

Hardy kept himself busy with navigation, making rounds in the control room, the conning tower, and the bridge, even during off-duty hours, to check the ship's course against his charts and log. In the control room, the quartermaster of the watch kept the official log, and as soon as the captain signed it Hardy checked it against his own records, letting out a grunt if it seemed acceptable. Once in a while he came across what he felt were odd coincidences, mishaps that were common to both the log he had created and the one they were currently keeping: valve leakage here, a broken gasket there. They puzzled him.

Once he drew one of them to Frank's attention. Frank shrugged it off, but took to standing over Hardy while he compared logs. On the morning of the 26th he saw Hardy freeze for a moment, and asked what seemed to be wrong. Hardy showed him a report concerning the failure of forward battery connector cable number 81 at 0734 the previous morning, then pointed to his own notation in the 1944 log: A similar cable had failed on the same date thirty years ago. Obviously, it was nothing remarkable, because battery connector cables were frequently wearing out, and Frank was able to point out a dozen more instances where the factor of coincidence simply did not apply. Hardy grudgingly accepted the reality. Frank began to suspect that the Professor would spend a great deal of time on this voyage looking for anomalies.

During Frank's frequent tours of the boat, he found ample evidence of growing camaraderie among the crew. They were sorting themselves into those who joked and those who were joked about. There were pranks; there were mascots. Even among the officers there was a pecking order. The junior officers, Danby and Adler, were constantly leaving themselves open for ribbing, and they would get it from officers and lower ratings alike.

But everyone kept out of the Captain's way. He was a stern, imposing figure, and they were all appropriately respectful of him. And Byrnes obviously preferred it that way.

He was a stickler for cleanliness, making daily inspections of all cooking and health facilities, combing the galley, the pantry, the below-decks storage freezer, the washrooms, showers . . . and the latrines.

He wanted the latrines to shine, and he made no bones about it. The second day out, he found a spot of crusted cleansing powder wedged under the rim of the toilet seat. He warned the entire crew that if such inattention to detail occurred again, he would forbid the use of the after head, and the crew would have to fend for themselves at night, surfaced, from ass-to-the-wind positions in the stern of the boat.

The next two days Byrnes made careful inspections of the after head, actually sticking his head inside the bowl to check under the rim. Satisfied each time, he straightened up, nodded to the duty officer, and walked out, all smiles for the men. Some of them described it as "a regular shit-eating grin, like he knew he was getting our goats . . ."

Then, on the morning of the 26th, Byrnes was making his usual rounds. Dankworth, the pharmacist's mate, had been assigned latrine duty and had decided to put an end to the Captain Bligh treatment. He took a jar of peanut butter from the cook's pantry, hurried back to the after head, and cleaned and scrubbed the toilet until it was spotless; then he wiped a small dab of the peanut butter into the ledge under the rim. He rushed the peanut butter back to the cook and raced back to his post, managing to get there only one compartment ahead of Byrnes. He stood at attention outside the washroom until the Captain approached.

"Ready for inspection, sir."

Byrnes acknowledged the salute and entered the washroom. Ed Frank stood behind Dorriss, who carried a clipboard with the duty assignments. They watched Byrnes inspect the shower, the floors, the washstand, then the toilet . . . He got down on his hands and knees and thrust his head inside the gleaming white bowl, and his eyes traveled around the rim. He stopped abruptly, and for a long moment seemed not to believe what he was seeing.

"Mr. Dankworth."

"Yes, sir?"

"What is this?"

Dankworth grew a superb blank look. "What is what, sir?"

"This—here!" Byrnes stood up, the blood draining into his face. His finger was inside the bowl, pointing.

Dankworth got down on his hands and knees and put his head inside the bowl. He could hardly restrain a smile. The little dab of peanut butter stood out clearly.

He straightened and, as dutifully as possible, said, "Looks like shit, sir."

Byrnes blinked in surprise. Dorriss and Frank were stunned. "It does, does it?" asked Byrnes.

Dankworth shrugged, bent over, whipped a finger under the rim, came up with a dab of the stuff, and ran it into his mouth.

"*Tastes* like shit, sir."

Grins spread across Frank's face and Dorriss's. The Captain froze. Suddenly he knew he was being had. Very deliberately, he too ran a finger under the rim of the bowl and delicately licked at the brown goo. He eyed Dankworth grimly. Dankworth didn't bat an eye.

"You're right," said Byrnes. "And since you're so good at it . . ."

Dankworth slowly turned pale.

". . . I'm appointing you official shit-taster for the rest of this trip. And mind you, not just during inspections, Dankworth, but immediately following all meals aboard this boat, you will inspect all heads in the manner to which you have become accustomed." Byrnes pantomimed running his finger under the rim. Dankworth stood very still. The Captain thanked him for the inspection, then departed.

For the rest of the day, after every meal, it was a race to the after head—with the crew in a dead heat against Dankworth. Dankworth figured if he could get to the can before they did, he could take a run at it and have done with it, but if they beat him to it and lined up—God help him.

From that moment on, things were lighter all around. Byrnes became a "regular guy" in the eyes of the crew, so in a sense the hapless pharmacist's mate had accomplished his purpose. And the men—all of them—were now more firmly convinced than ever that they had drawn the best duty in the Navy.

November 28, 1974

The *Candlefish* slipped quietly through calm Pacific waters at periscope depth for most of the day. They were supposed to be within visual range of Wake Island, and Byrnes wanted to confirm the first sighting of land since Hawaii. He was idly swinging the scope around when something made him stop: a black object looming to starboard, traveling at an angle parallel to the sub. He turned the scope on high power and examined it. It was a medium-sized Japanese freighter with a brilliant blue hull and letters emblazoned ten feet high the full length of her: DATSUN. She was returning from the States after delivering a cargo of automobiles. Byrnes turned and mentioned it to Frank. Frank took a look and couldn't restrain a smile. "What if we took her picture through the scope and sent it to her with a note: *What a swell target you'd make—*"

"*—on a dark night!*" Byrnes finished for him, and they hooted in laughter. Even Hardy stood by and smiled; he had loosened up over the Dankworth incident, and ever since that morning had attacked his tasks with relish rather than with his usual suspicious gloom.

Byrnes reclaimed the scope and resumed his scan of the horizon. Again he stopped. There was a smaller dot in the distance. Magnifying it, he brought up the image of a long, low piece of land. He breathed easier.

"Wake Island," he announced, and turned the scope over to Hardy, who eagerly took the position and recorded it on his chart. Next to a little dot identified as

"Wake I." he wrote the notation: 26 NOV 1530.

Hardy stood up, tucked his pencil into a pocket, folded the chart, and went below. Frank exchanged looks with Byrnes.

"He's shaping up," the Captain admitted.

"He's having fun," said Frank.

Byrnes had decided Frank needed a refresher course in submarine operation, so Frank was stationed in the control room, required to make hourly inspections of all forward compartments, including the forward battery and the pump room below decks.

Frank ducked below at 1700 and walked through the pump room. The engines were quiet. The sub was running submerged on battery power. But diesel oil was all over everything, and Frank was becoming as filthy as everyone else aboard; his clothes were covered with oil spots, and he smelled to high heaven. He went above and trotted into officers' country, popped the forward battery hatch, and lowered the top half of his body through. He played a battle lantern over the tops of the enormous battery cells, looking for water leaks, rust, corrosion, bubbling acid. There was nothing. Everything was in order. He lay on the deck longer than he had to, staring at the batteries, thinking back to the time he had spent aboard these subs during the Vietnam War—of the million and one thankless little jobs that had to be done aboard a sub, of the constant surveillance on all operable equipment, the attention to detail . . . Now he knew why he had been grateful for the desk job with NIS. It had meant relief from *this*. Yet here he was back again—just like Jack Hardy. He clicked off the lantern.

At 2000 Byrnes brought the sub to surface, not a second off schedule, which pleased Hardy immensely. He felt a great sense of relief every time his log was

followed to the letter. Frank went off duty and passed
through the galley to pick up a dinner tray. He
brought it back to the wardroom and settled in with his
briefcase. He spread papers and notebooks out on the
table as he ate. He had brought along all his research
on the Devil's Triangle: all his charts and reports and
his Maritime Disasters notebook. He pulled the world
globe down from its shelf over the phonograph and set
it too on the table, twirling it absently, settling first on
the Florida vortex, then spinning it around to the
Japanese area . . .

Jack Hardy strolled in with a dish of ice cream and
smiled at Frank. "Cookie made fresh ice cream this afternoon. That old freezer still works like a charm. You
better hurry. It's going fast."

"No, thanks."

Hardy sat down and watched Frank study the globe.
Then Frank pushed his dinner aside and sipped at his
coffee while he began poring through his notebook.

It was a solid five minutes before Hardy asked what
he was doing.

"I'm preparing a lecture on what we're going to be
up against. Thought I'd better bone up."

Hardy reached for one of the notebooks and asked,
"May I?"

He spent the rest of the evening and all his off-duty
hours the next morning studying Frank's material, poking around the globe, and frowning to himself. He
never uttered a word to Frank.

November 29, 1974

At Frank's request, Byrnes relieved all of the officers
except the juniors at 1600 the next afternoon and or-

dered everyone to assemble in the wardroom for coffee and a briefing.

The officers slid in around the big table. Frank positioned himself at the head; he had already spread out his maps, charts and notes, and had planted his globe within easy reach. Hardy pulled up a chair and sat near the entrance. Cassidy ducked in at the last minute and removed his cap, taking a deferential stand against the far bulkhead. He had still not gotten used to sitting in the same room with officers.

Frank scratched his chest, then lit his pipe. He gazed around at the friendly, chatting faces: Byrnes, Dorriss, Stigwood, Roybell, Hardy, Cassidy . . . Only Hardy had some idea of what was going to be discussed.

The mess steward circulated cups. As soon as the men were quiet, Frank began.

He pulled the globe closer and picked up a red felt marker. He drew a neat red oblong around the area off the coast of Florida, then turned it around for all to see.

"Gentlemen, the Devil's Triangle."

Everyone fell silent. No sailor in any modern navy is unaware of that infamous vortex. Though many do not believe in it, most have at least a genuine respect for the stories.

"I have to warn you before we begin, gentlemen," said Frank, "that we are going to be dealing with an area of discussion that some authorities consider myth, superstition, or just plain folly. But whether you believe in these mysteries makes no difference to us today. At this very moment, we are standing aboard such a mystery. This submarine is our central focus on the inexplicable. And it is my feeling—my personal feeling —that her story is directly related to *this*." Again he pointed out the circled blob, the Devil's Triangle.

"Ships and planes and submarines have been known

to enter this area and vanish. Not all ships and planes, mind you, but enough to rate the descriptive term: an alarming number. I'm alarmed. The Navy is alarmed, but only, it seems, when a fresh ship or plane or sub disappears. Then, for a short time, all hell breaks loose. There are searches and theories, some recriminations, and finally: obscurity. No one in the Navy wants to believe that unnatural acts are possible in our precious oceans. They are not only possible, they are a *fait accompli*."

Some of the faces shifted. Eyes looked away.

"There are many theories about what happens in the so-called Devil's Triangle. I'm sure Professor Hardy is well aware of most of them. But what isn't so well known is that there appears to be more than one Devil's Triangle."

He spun the globe around and drew another red oblong: "Here—off the coast of Japan. Two hundred fifty miles south of Honshu, between latitude thirty to forty degrees north, and centered around one hundred forty to one hundred fifty degrees east longitude." He paused to let this little bombshell have its effect. Roybell and Stigwood were staring at the red circle, agog. Frank added quietly, "Gentlemen, the *Candlefish* went down in this very area in 1944."

There was some mumbling. Byrnes looked at Frank, his eyes reflecting displeasure. He was not the sort of man who appreciated this brand of science fiction.

Neither did Hardy. He sat with arms folded across his chest under his beard, impassively eyeing the charts spread on the table.

Cassidy fidgeted with his machinist's bandanna.

"According to the original reports, she sank in the Ramapo Depth at about latitude thirty degrees north and longitude one hundred forty-six degrees east. That's smack in the middle of this particular . . . shall we say, anomaly?" He moved the globe aside and eyed his captive audience. He picked up his coffee and sipped it.

"Let's go back to the original Devil's Triangle, the one off the coast of Florida, the most popular one. To be a bit more exact, it isn't a triangle at all—it's more in the shape of an oblong sphere, a football with round-ed ends—and it's doubtful that the Devil is much in-volved. Roughly, it is bordered at three points: Ber-muda, central Florida, Puerto Rico. It extends from thirty to forty degrees north latitude, and fifty-five to eighty-five degrees west longitude. It sits right over the Sargasso Sea, another of history's more unpleasant mythical centers. The Sargasso Sea is a surface of ocean literally matted with seaweed. For a few centuries dur-ing the early explorations to the Americas, the Sargasso was rumored to have caught and tangled dozens of ships, ensnaring them until the crews would desert or die or the boats would rot and sink. And considering that most of the monster legends grew out of this strange section of sea, it's very possible that what sailors took to be sea serpents were no more than long strands of seaweed pushed up and curling in the moon-light—or perhaps they were fish, eels, or squid, caught in a surface patch while trying to feed. There certainly are some reasonable explanations for such bizarre events. But legends have a way of perpetuating them-selves, and the superstitions of early sailors have un-doubtedly contributed to the aura of myth surrounding this . . . triangle today."

From the faces around him, Frank knew he had found the right approach: Temper the bizarre with the real, feed the fantasies with documented evidence.

"Vincent Gaddis coined the phrase 'Bermuda Trian-gle' in a magazine article he wrote in 1964, document-ing the more infamous incidents that have occurred over the last hundred years in this area. John Wallace Spencer has written a book titled *Limbo of the Lost,* a list and description of all the major known vanishings that have occurred in the triangle.

"Of course, we have to realize that some of the things that have happened here can occur over land as well. Planes have disappeared over our own United States, over dry land, without a trace. Nevertheless, there does not seem to be a pattern for those incidents. They never seem to occur twice in the same place.

"The triangle is different. Every strange thing that could happen to a ship or a plane has happened here. The most famous single incident took place on December 5, 1945, when five U.S. Navy Avengers, TBM torpedo bombers, took off from Fort Lauderdale Naval Air Station in Florida. They were on patrol, each with three-man crews. The day was perfect: sunny with no clouds. They were on a two-hour flight out over the Atlantic, and they had been airborne only an hour and a half when they radioed back——" Frank picked up a folder and read from a report: " 'We seem to be off course . . . we cannot see land . . . Can't be sure just where we are . . . We seem to be lost . . . Even the ocean doesn't look right . . .' "

He put down the folder and carried on without it. "Air-to-ground chatter continued for another hour, and all of it amounted to the same thing. The pilots were confused and panicky. The air, the ocean——nothing was familiar. And then they simply disappeared. A rescue plane was scrambled, a Martin Mariner Flying Boat, and it took off toward the last known position of the TBMs. Within fifteen minutes the Martin Mariner and its crew of thirteen had also disappeared. Nothing was ever found of any of the planes, despite an immediate massive sea and air search, in which, thankfully, no more planes were lost. But this is not the first nor the last mysterious occurrence. I have here a list of ships and planes that have disappeared over the last hundred years."

Frank pulled copies from his folder and passed them around. It was a detailed list, compiled from many different sources, and accounting for a vast number of missing planes and ships that had purportedly sunk, disappeared, or turned up adrift without crews.

Frank watched Hardy glance at it quickly, then turn it over in front of him. Cassidy stood staring at it, a tight frown stretching his features. Byrnes had a hand to his mouth, covering it so that no one could see his skeptical expression.

Frank resumed. "As you see, there have been many different types of incidents, and that emphasizes the strangest fact of all concerning the triangle: It would seem to be responsible for a lot of apparently unrelated phenomena. What ties all of them together is the fact that so *many* unusual disasters have occurred in the *same* area."

He then produced another list and passed it around. It wasn't quite so well-detailed as the first one, and he explained that was due to lack of proper investigation on the part of authorities. But it was still a substantial collection of dates and facts about a great number of similar disasters that had occurred off the coast of Japan.

And opposite the date December 11, 1944, was the notation: "USS *Candlefish*, American submarine lost on wartime patrol. No satisfactory explanation. One survivor."

"We are headed for this area because we want to see what physical and natural phenomena are indigenous to it, and what interaction this submarine might have with them. We don't know how the *Candlefish* got back after thirty years; we want to find out. It would seem that she hit some sort of physical hole in space—disappeared just like the five TBMs. Maybe it's some sort of time warp: She got caught in it and reappeared in 1974."

Byrnes groaned aloud.

"All right," said Frank, "I'm sure no one wants to believe anything like that. I'm not asking you to. We are sailing to Latitude Thirty to find some evidence of what really did happen to the *Candlefish*. At the moment, our theories don't matter. Maybe these areas act like air pockets in which hot and cold currents collide and interact, creating violent electrical disturbances. Maybe there are similar forces clashing beneath the sea, creating underwater storms, whirlpools, whatever it takes to suck a plane out of the sky or pluck a ship off the ocean surface. Who knows what could happen under such circumstances?

"We don't know how this relates to the *Candlefish*, but it's part of our job to find out. And if the physical characteristics of latitude thirty degrees off the coast of Japan are the same as those of latitude thirty degrees south of Bermuda, then we can report back to the Navy for a *fact* that there are *two* Devil's Triangles!"

Frank paused to pour himself more coffee. He was sweating. He almost did not hear Hardy's gravelly tones. "There *are* two. In fact, there are *ten*."

Frank froze, the cup halfway to his lips.

Hardy scratched at his beard and eyed the officers around the table. "Is that steward still here?"

"More coffee?" asked Byrnes, and signaled the steward standing in the corridor. He stuck his head in, and Hardy touched his sleeve.

"Would you go to the galley? Get me a large butcher knife and all the skewers you can find."

The steward blinked in surprise and looked to Byrnes for confirmation.

"Go ahead," said Byrnes, and sat back to survey Hardy with growing suspicion.

Hardy was studying Frank's globe. Finally he looked up. "Let's go over some of the points you've raised, Commander Frank. I will admit the scientific elements interest me more than the mythical aspects of this business. But then, I have been directly involved in scientific projects closely related to some of the explanations you have so neatly given us. I have to say I don't care much for your methods; they're so damned obvious. You want to excite us, frighten us, and impress us. And in the end, what do you really think you're going to accomplish?"

Frank's eyes widened. He could see his own humiliation rippling around the compartment. He opened his mouth.

"I would rather you didn't answer," Hardy cut in immediately. "I may have some startling facts of my own to present in this matter, and you may find some of them in direct support of your purpose. I'll ask that you hear me out."

Frank sat down. "Go ahead," he muttered.

"Thank you." Hardy smiled and stood up. He scratched his beard again, smoothing it down over his open collar while staring at the table full of charts.

"The point you made about legends perpetuating themselves. I hate to be nasty about it, but you are yourself a contributor to that irresponsibility. It is very difficult to talk of the things that go on in the Devil's Triangle without sounding like the worst sort of crackpot, even if you do your best to dress it up with scientific explanations. But I should like to point out certain factors common to the so-called Bermuda Triangle and the Japanese area and . . . all the others."

He picked up Frank's list and waved it. "First of all, if this business is ever going to be investigated in a

thoroughly scientific manner, we have got to differenti-
ate between outright vanishings and more natural
disasters such as sinkings, wreckings, piracy, founder-
ings, etc. To do the investigating, a project will have to
be created on a Federal level. People will have to collect the records of international navies and air forces,
of commercial shipping lines and air carriers, and of
maritime insurance agencies. These records, once assembled and examined, may eliminate half of what appears on this list. As for the rest, we might be able to
find common circumstances in all of them, leading us
to one or another satisfactory explanation. The word
'satisfactory' is tricky. I don't mean satisfactory in the
sense that we can all rest easy . . ."

Frank sat back and relit his pipe, his initial shock
and displeasure fading as he began to sense Hardy's
drift.

"I mean that we may confirm once and for all that,
yes, these disappearances are due to natural phenomena, or unnatural phenomena—that they are due to
extraterrestrial kidnapping, or a colossal time warp, or
a very large hungry fish."

That drew a laugh from Roybell, and ripples of it
went around the table.

Hardy smiled. "If we could pinpoint to our satisfaction that it is all due to one or another of these utterly
fantastic explanations, then we *should*. And *live with
it.*"

Hardy leaned back against the bulkhead and looked
down at the table as he spoke. "Let's go back to what I
call *my* involvement. During the late 1960s, I was connected with the National Center for Atmospheric
Research in Colorado. We were a large team of ocean-
ographers brought together to set up experiments
dealing with deep-water ocean storms. My specialty
was electromagnetic forces in what we have come to

call deep-water eddies. Our concern was to find out how the ocean deeps move—what drives them. We know what moves the surface of the ocean: atmospheric conditions, winds, storms, etc. But the ocean's surface is a relatively impotent force in comparison to the energy created in the great deeps. We found abundant evidence that the lower layers of ocean move in directions opposite to the surface, and at first glance they seem to be driven by temperature differences. As Commander Frank brought up briefly, in some ocean areas currents of vastly different temperatures meet, collide, or interact. Let's say, a freezing polar current meets a warm tropical flow. They don't simply blend and change temperature, as when your half-full cup of hot coffee is suddenly filled with cold water. When these vast movements of ocean meet, they do so as layers sliding over each other, each one carried by the force of millions of tons of moving water. What occurs is a deep-ocean storm, much like an atmospheric storm, a disruption in the even flow of energy. A sizable electromagnetic reaction takes place. Just how powerful it is, we have not yet been able to measure. Nor how far-ranging are its effects—that too is still a mystery.

"What we were looking for in our project was the answer to a question: What makes weather in the seas? What exactly *are* the undersea forces that are *similar* to atmospheric forces? Where do these undersea storms take place? The major test area, explored by the research ship *Glomar Challenger,* was directly over the Bermuda Triangle. The second project center was to have been in the Ramapo Depth off the coast of Japan. I was to have headed it, and we had built a new deep-submergence vessel, the *Neptune 4000.* Unfortunately, that project was blown. But I think I know the answers we would have received, because if you know anything about science at all, you know that a scientist conducts his business in a manner quite similar to a military court-martial. He designs his experiment around all the known factors leading to a certain unavoidable conclusion. He must be convinced of the outcome before he commits to the project. I was convinced that by testing the currents in the Latitude Thirty area from a submersible, I might be able to prove that what gripped the *Candlefish* on the night of December 11, 1944, was a thoroughly natural phenomenon, the nature of which we simply knew nothing about up to that time."

"Just a minute," said Frank. "What happened with the Bermuda Triangle experiment?"

"Well, it never really was a Triangle experiment, per se," admitted Hardy. "It was a strictly limited research program into deep-water eddies."

"So the results were inconclusive?"

"Not at all. We proved the existence of eddies. You have to understand the tremendous pressures and forces at work in an eddy. A deep-ocean storm uses and dispels more energy than an electrical thunderstorm, and it lasts more than a hundred times longer. A hurricane that starts this week off the coast of Florida may burn itself out within a month. An eddy might last for years! And the movement, compared to an atmospheric storm, is incredibly slow."

He waved a hand in the air to indicate the gentle sweep of an undersea storm. "It may seem to inch along, but it is the most relentless force on the face of the earth, backed up by the weight of an entire ocean."

He stopped for a moment, and the tension in the room subsided.

Frank said quietly, "Your tools are here."

Hardy turned around. The steward was standing in the doorway, clutching a large butcher knife and a handful of skewers. His eyes were wide open. How long had he been standing there? Hardy thanked him and placed all the kitchen implements on the table. Cassidy leaned over his shoulder to examine what had arrived. Roybell sat back in the vinyl sofa and folded his arms over his chest.

"All right," Hardy said, "what we are coming round to is the fact that in both of these areas"—he tapped the two circled spots on the globe—"and in most of the others I will point out, we have some of the strongest ocean forces in the world. In both areas we have known evidence of colliding surface currents, and now, thanks to the *Glomar* research, every indication of ongoing underwater eddies as well. Here, off Florida, and off Japan, we have hot surface currents streaming up out of the tropics and colder waters coming down from the polar and subpolar areas. They meet on the surface and they swirl"—he made a swirling motion with his hands—"clockwise. And right here in these two most legendary areas, the swirls make their tightest spiraling turns. For these are geographical areas of extreme temperature variation, centers of hurricanes, whirlpools, oceanic and atmospheric disturbances. And undersea eddies."

Hardy stopped for a moment to suck the rest of the coffee from his cup. He pulled the globe closer and picked up the red felt marker that Frank had used. "Commander Frank has done twenty percent of the work on this globe. Now, let's see if we can do the rest. So far, we have two distinct mystery areas. From this point on, let's refer to them as geomagnetic anomalies. For short—GMA."

There seemed to be no objection, so Hardy continued, "GMA number one is the original . . . the Bermuda Triangle." He lettered a "1" inside the center of the oblong circle off the coast of Florida. "We're going to call Japan our GMA number four."

"Why four?" asked Frank.

"Because there are more than two, as I said, and we will pinpoint them clockwise around the globe. Meanwhile, we may notice some immediate similarities between GMA-1 and GMA-4. For instance, both of them lie based on the same latitude: thirty degrees north. Both are oblong blobs tilted at—oh, I'd say forty-five degrees to the right. And both lie just off a continental shelf—to the right of a continent, to be precise. And if you will study your sea charts, I think you will find that both GMAs are centers of swirling currents. In fact, using that as a basis, let's look for our next GMA."

Hardy leaned over the charts and appeared to be sniffing around, but Frank was well aware that the old man was planning every word he uttered.

"Ah!" Hardy barked. "Here we are. The northern Pacific, northwest of the Hawaiian Islands . . . This would be right over the Murray Fracture Zone, another area of extreme temperature variation. In fact, this appears to be where the northern Pacific currents are swept around against themselves by the subarctic currents flowing south. Again we have a GMA based on latitude thirty degrees north, from about one hundred sixty to one hundred forty degrees west longitude. We'll call this GMA number five."

Hardy paused. "Notice anything peculiar about this one?"

Byrnes was first. "Yeah. It's nowhere near a continent."

"True," agreed Hardy. "But you're missing the most important detail."

"What is it?" cut in Frank.

Hardy took the felt-tip pen and, selecting a longitude and latitude in the center of GMA-5, made a small red dot. "Thirty-four degrees north, one hundred forty-nine degrees west. Recognize that, Mr. Frank?"

Frank shook his head, puzzled.

"That is where the *Candlefish* came *up*."

For a full twenty seconds, the only sound in the wardroom was the gentle press of the air-conditioning. Then Hardy turned the globe again and resumed.

"The next two GMAs do not lie entirely over oceans. GMA-2 in fact falls over the western end of the Mediterranean, covering parts of Morocco, Algeria, and Gibraltar. Again, it is based on latitude thirty degrees north, and lies between ten and zero degrees west longitude. GMA-3 emerges from latitude thirty degrees and is entirely over land, right smack over Pakistan and Afghanistan, between sixty-five and eighty degrees east."

Hardy drew another neat oblong circle around the two eastern countries; then he stood back and spun the globe slowly, pinpointing each of the five GMAs he had identified.

The officers seemed to lean forward in unison, examining each circled section of the globe as it turned before them.

"They all seem to be the same distance apart," noted Byrnes.

"That's true." Hardy smiled. "About seventy-two degrees from center to center."

"They're all in the northern hemisphere," Frank blurted out. "And there are only five. You said ten."

"Glad you brought that up. Five are in the northern hemisphere and five in the southern." He proceeded to draw, very quickly, five more oblongs, one each off the eastern coasts of South America, South Africa, and Australia, plus one in the South Pacific and one in the mid-Indian Ocean.

As he made his circles, Hardy called out the longitudes and latitudes and pertinent details to Frank, who wrote them down and, when Hardy was all finished, passed the notes around. All five lay with their northern tips right on latitude 30° south:

GMA-6
East of Brazil, centered over Trindade, around 30° W. longitude, latitude 30° S. in the Brazil Basin, north of the Horse latitudes.

GMA-7
South Africa—east of the Malagasy Republic and Madagascar, between 50°-80° E., and latitude 30°-40° S. Center of the equatorial currents. Very sparsely traveled ocean.

GMA-8
Middle of the Indian Ocean—north of the Diamantina Fracture Zone, west of Australian coast, south of the great Wharton Basin. 90°-110° E. Based at 30° S. Area of enormous depths, bad weather, rarely sailed.

GMA-9
East of Australia—lat. 30° S., between 180° E. and 170° W. Centered over Kermadec Trench, north of New Zealand.

GMA-10
South Pacific—the Challenger Deep—30° S. lat., between 120°-100° W. Right over the East Pacific Ridge—Center directly over Easter Island—2500 miles west of Chile.

Byrnes held the list longest of all. He examined it dourly, an unpleasant look settling into his usually impassive features. When he looked up, Hardy was slowly turning the globe, pointing out the funny configuration between each set of GMAs. "Five of these things lie directly to the right of a continent: Bermuda, Australia, South America, South Africa, and Japan. In all five areas we get those swirls we've been speaking about, opposing currents clashing on the surface as well as in the deeps. Every meteorological phenomenon you can think of happens regularly in these places. And in case you haven't noticed, there are direct correlations between the northern GMAs and the southern ones. Each GMA is located the same distance from the equator, whether above or below it—that's the latitude-thirty-degrees factor. Each GMA in the north has a southern brother shifted almost exactly thirty to forty degrees to the right. Ten GMAs, ringing the earth in two belts, five in the north and five in the south. And each one centered about seventy-two degrees from the next in line. All lie completely over water, except for the one in the Mediterranean and the one over Pakistan. Each is centered over a section of the earth's core with an extraordinary concentration of magnetic pull. And each of them has a documented history of disappearing acts."

Hardy lifted one of the skewers. "Now then, let's see if we can find some sort of mystical correlation among all ten. Mr. Frank, you'd better kiss your globe good-bye."

Hardy didn't even look at Frank as he placed the skewers along the table like surgical instruments. Delicately he pointed the first skewer into the center of GMA-1 and pushed it through. He leaned over the top of the globe and seemed to fish around for a while until he decided his aim was right, then gave the skewer a shove. It came out on the opposite side of the globe, in the southern hemisphere, directly through the center of GMA-8, in the Indian Ocean. He picked up the next skewer and placed it through GMA-2, coming out in GMA-9, diametrically linking the Mediterranean to Australia. One by one, he went around the globe until five skewers had gone in the northern centers and come out through the southern centers, until the globe resembled a giant's pincushion.

Hardy stopped and spun the globe slowly on its axis so that everyone could see where the skewers went in and where they emerged. "As you can see, gentlemen, there is an alignment here which we may as well call mystical, for want of a better word. Each of these blobs is linked to each of the others. We have discussed nearly all the various correlations—physical, magnetic, geographical, meteorological, and mystical. Now, I would like to show you the strangest reciprocal effect of all . . ."

He picked up the knife and turned the globe over on its side. Carefully inserting the blade at the equator, he proceeded to slice it around, like a watermelon. Frank's features drew into a tight frown. Byrnes sat up slowly. Cassidy was sweating, clutching his bandanna to his neck. Hardy worked with deft surgical hands. The globe was composed of a hard plastic shell, and the cutting was not easy. At last he came the full 360 degrees, and the two halves popped apart by a half-inch. Hardy put the knife down and pried the pieces farther apart with his hands. They were held together by the five crossed skewers. The metal rods relented, and the two halves of the globe gave away like the ends of an accordion. When they were a full four inches apart, Hardy put the globe upright on its stand and pushed it to the center of the table. The officers peered into the opening, and one by one reacted in stunned silence.

The split halves revealed the skewers forming an al-most geometrically perfect criss-crossed path, each of them cutting right through the exact center of the earth.

Ed Frank's lips parted. He stared at the globe in disbelief for a long moment, then regarded Hardy with awe.

Hardy displayed a self-satisfied smile and met Frank's gaze. "My students just love this one," he said. He waited for the officers to finish poking around inside the globe. They were on their feet now, huddled around it, pointing at the various circled blobs, muttering to each other.

"A little scientific hocus-pocus, gentlemen," said Hardy, getting their attention back. "But, as I said before, it's easy to perpetuate legends, myth, and superstition. Personally, I don't want to have anything to do with that. And furthermore, I insist that none of this applies to the *Candlefish*."

Again he was met with silence. Frank was getting tired of these bombshells. "What do you mean, none of it?" he asked.

"What I have given you is fifty percent fact and fifty percent supportable conjecture. But only a small percent of it has anything at all to do with this submarine."

"You've taken us this far; now you better explain."

"All right. It is quite possible that the *Candlefish* fell victim to peculiar electromagnetic forces in GMA-4, off the coast of Japan in 1944. It is possible that she is one of those legendary vanishings that have been known to occur in that area. But that just doesn't answer all the questions. What Mr. Frank is failing to see is the selectivity that goes on in these GMAs. In some instances ships and crews disappear completely. In others only the crews disappear. In others planes are thrown off course, or lose altitude in a split second, or suddenly find themselves missing ten or fifteen minutes of time. With all these different things happening—how the hell can *one explanation suffice?* All we can say at best is that these areas have one thing in common—*weird things happen here!* A lot of weird things. And we can say that these happenings may all be related to electromagnetics. After all, our bodies are electromagnetic devices. We are held together by the same forces of energy that bind our entire planet together. Scientists are just beginning to get away from particle theories of the binding source—and they are taking off in a new area. Energy. What exactly is it? What is the force that makes particles revolve around a nucleus? What is the force that holds a body together? What holds the earth's core together, the crust, the seas? It would seem to me that some sort of natural balancing act is at work in what we know as energy. Now along comes man and sticks his little fingers in and starts reproducing the energy for his own use—creating more energy, upsetting the balance. He disrupts what is already there. And if he starts monkeying around with an unstable environment, such as our Geomagnetic Anomalies One through Ten, the consequences could be severe. We don't know how sensitive the instability really is! Suppose—just suppose—that the *Candlefish* somehow struck an unstable energy environment, triggering a disruptive effect which resulted in complete energy chaos. Suppose the submarine itself—bound together by rapid forces of energy, forces strong enough to be solid, such as steel and wood, forces that do not utilize energy except on a superficial binding level—suppose the sub was shot intact through a time warp and propelled into the future in a single catastrophic instant!"

He fell silent a moment, waiting for reaction, but everyone was quiet again. He had the floor.

Frank cut in. "What about the crew?"

"Different forms of energy! Man is not as solid as steel. As a matter of fact, his mind is an extraordinary propagator of electromagnetic waves. Picture a crew of eighty-four men, undergoing a mental trauma as this submarine went down on December 11th, 1944. Eighty-four minds, thrown suddenly in or out of phase with whatever energy force was causing the sub to go down. Perhaps these men were literally blown apart—disintegrated—sent off to a sudden oblivion—without any trace at all."

Hardy looked around. Every face was beaded in sweat. "Look," he said, "we have learned how to play with electricity. We have seen how phasing can work in experiments. Divert energy from one frequency to another, until you have a lot of frequencies in combination, interacting in phase, and what happens? They either cancel each other out or they create a new, separate impulse. Suppose the forces in GMA-4 went into phase with the energy in the minds of those eighty-four men, creating a terrible power imbalance—you might call it a mental backfiring. Minds suddenly running amok could have thrown a whole tremendous complex of power consumption out of phase. Something on board, an electronic device or a human mind, may have locked in on a frequency over which we were sailing. That frequency may have belonged to some underwater force, or to the interaction between a cool lower air fog and a hot sea surface—there *was* fog, you know, thick fog, and the surface was churning—and the interaction may have triggered the shaking that caused all the damage, and then eventually the time-snap."

He was speaking faster now, sorting through his own mind the points he had wanted to make all these years.

"And yet, however remarkable the explanation for what happened thirty years ago may be—however much we may be able to support or prove on this voyage—I have to insist that it still doesn't apply."

"Why?" asked Frank.

"The *Candlefish* disappeared like all the others in all these places, for whatever physical reason there may be, but—as you pointed out, Mr. Frank—she came back! She came back after thirty years, and that is the one factor that sets her apart. Nothing ever came back before! So even if we do find out how she went down, it isn't going to mean a thing! What we have to know is *why* she came back!"

"You mean how."

"That's exactly what I *don't* mean! I mean *why!* There has to be a *reason*—not just a satisfactory explanation! There is some kind of logic to this—something beyond the physical!" He waved a hand over the charts and reports and the wreckage of the globe, and then snapped: "And all of *this* has nothing to do with it!"

Hardy subsided into silence, then turned suddenly and stumbled out of the wardroom.

Frank stood up in embarrassment. He didn't know what to say; Hardy had drilled a hole in his self-assurance. Byrnes stood up and adjourned the meeting, ordering everyone back to stations.

As the officers filed out, Cassidy paused to stare at the demolished globe, then stepped quickly out of the compartment. Frank looked down at the shambles on the table and began to clean it up.

Byrnes was the only one left. He was unbuttoning a sweaty shirt and pushing the empty coffee cups together for the steward.

"What did you think?" Frank asked.

"I think there is no question as to who is the better lecturer," he said without expression. "I just wish he had kept his mouth shut."

"So do I," said Frank, and was immediately surprised at himself. But Frank was growing very sick of interference. Ever since this business had begun, he had been getting it from Diminsky, from Smitty, from Byrnes, and from Hardy himself. Now Frank was more determined than ever to follow this thing through to its conclusion, no matter how dangerous it became. He wondered how cooperative the rest of the crew would be, once the substance of today's meeting made the rounds of the boat. It could be dealt with. Most submariners are far from superstitious; they are too busy contending with reality. The stories might make great conversation, but he doubted they would become a fixation. Frank mentally kicked himself for bringing the matter up at all. He had never even stopped to consider his own motives. What had he tried to do today? Create paranoia? He hoped this wasn't going to mean that eighty-four other men were going to spend their off-duty hours on deck looking for devils and triangles . . .

What *would* they be looking for? And, come to think of it, what was *he* looking for? Really looking for?

Repetition?

CHAPTER 12

December 1, 1974

The *Frankland* knifed cleanly through the long Pacific swells, her bow skimming the gray-green water, leaving a phosphorescent wake that shimmered in the early darkness. Ray Cook stood at the stern rail and studied the churning water displaced by her surging engines. He burrowed deeper into his jacket, warding off the cold bite of the night air. Normally this noble panorama of vast, empty ocean would stimulate him, but tonight he had other things on his mind. Something had gone sour aboard the *Candlefish*. That he was sure of . . . but what?

Cook snorted to himself. Over the years Cook had perfected an intricate mental alarm system which, for the most part, accurately gauged the moods of people he knew or simply met for the first time. Face to face, over a telephone or, in this case, on a speaker monitor in the *Frankland's* radio room, all the indications were there. Frank himself was probably unaware of them: the flatness in his voice, the hint of suppressed anger, the deliberate restraint. Something or somebody had disturbed Ed Frank and he was trying to cover it up. Why? What was he trying to hide?

Cook had attempted to relay his suspicions, but Captain Melanoff refused to act without concrete evidence.

"How in the hell can I convince anyone that something is wrong purely on the strength of *vocal inflections?"* he had demanded.

So Cook was left to wrestle with the problem alone. As he tried to deal with it in the stern of the destroyer, the first tendrils of fog drifted past him and off into the wake. He turned and watched as the *Frankland* entered a massive fog bank. Her superstructure lost its crisp lines, and the running lights diffused in a cloying dampness. Cook frowned and began to plod forward, hoping that Frank could handle the problem himself— whatever it was.

A mile ahead of the *Frankland* and sixty feet beneath the surface, the *Candlefish* slithered through the water, her sleek hull offering a minimum of resistance in the familiar liquid world. Whatever the weather was topside, it could not impede her progress in this element.

It was quiet in the conning tower. Frank rolled his shoulders, stretching his back muscles, grateful for the opportunity to sort out his thoughts.

Hardy's wardroom lecture, as carried aft by the steward, had exploded among the crew like a bomb. What had been until then a tightly knit boat now was showing signs of coming apart at the seams. Hushed conversations in the crew's mess and quarters, conversations that trailed off whenever an officer passed through, were the rule rather than the exception. Frank had felt the undercurrents of tension and reported them to Byrnes. The Captain had seemed unconcerned, dismissing Frank's warning with a laugh and some remark about "superstitious."

Frank had taken it upon himself to form a flying squad with Dorriss, Cassidy, and Roybell, to talk to the men, to assure them that what Hardy had expressed was a theory and nothing more. He had even tried to enlist the Professor's help—but Hardy had refused. So a coolness had developed between them. The old man just would not listen to reason.

It had taken them the better part of a day to calm everyone down. Frank was determined to avoid making Hardy the scapegoat. He did not want to be responsible for recreating that aspect of the 1944 patrol.

By midwatch December 1st, nearly everyone had forgotten the lecture and its implications. But Frank was worried by his own attitude toward Hardy: Was it the fact that the Professor had punched as many holes in his theories as he had into that skewered globe? Was it jealousy he was feeling?

Lieutenant Danby came up the ladder to relieve Frank as conning officer. "We'll be surfacing soon, Mr. Frank. Skipper wants you below."

As Frank dropped into the control room, the bridge lookouts, wearing red night goggles, were already standing by to surface. Byrnes and Dorriss were at the plotting table, deep in conversation. Hardy was behind them, his face puckered, as if he didn't like what he was hearing. Frank moved forward, well past the hatch ladder, and waited. With the barest hint of a smile, Byrnes stepped away from Dorriss and shouted up the hatch, "Mr. Danby, take a look!"

Over the whine of the other motors, Frank heard the hiss of the periscope hoist lifting the tube out of the well.

"All clear, sir," Danby replied, "but we're in fog."

Byrnes grunted something as he stepped to the center of the control room. Then he gave the order, "Prepare to surface."

The red combat lights went on as Stigwood readied the boat. He gave the orders quietly.

"Slow to one-third."

The talker passed the order back, and Byrnes waited for the change in rhythm. He glanced at the clock. It was 1952. He snapped, "Take her up, Mr. Stigwood."

Dorriss punched the button, and the blare of the surfacing alarm rang through the boat. Frank shifted his balance to compensate for the lifting sensation that would come when the main ballast tanks were blown free of water.

"Blow all main ballast," called Stigwood.

Roybell timed his move with the third blast of the klaxon. His hand closed over the high-pressure-air manifold valve wheel. He strained, trying to turn it. He gave it a tremendous yank, but the wheel would not budge.

"Sir," he said, "pressure manifolds are not responding."

Stigwood was caught off guard. "Try it again."

Byrnes turned a steady gaze on Roybell. The Chief wrapped both hands on the valve wheel . . . nothing.

"No response, sir. It's frozen."

Stigwood barked the next order: "Pump trim tanks to sea!"

The trim manifold operator tried his best. "Nothing, sir. I can't even move the trim pump switches."

Byrnes kept his voice quiet as he ordered, "Blow the bow buoyancy tanks," and got the same results.

Frank slipped between the men to check the barometer and the depth gauge. "We've still got pressure," he announced. "Holding steady at periscope depth."

The boat was holding where it was, refusing to respond. Examining all the options, Byrnes made up his mind quickly. Turning toward the radio room, he shouted, "Giroux!"

The radio operator stuck his head out of his cubicle. "Yes, sir?"

"Contact the *Frankland!* Tell them we are having problems surfacing and request them to stand by." As Giroux ducked back, Byrnes gave a string of instructions to the control-room talker. He wanted watch commanders to check all compartments and Cassidy to take some men to check the air-bank hull stop valves.

Frank felt no threat of immediate danger, but he noted, with some satisfaction, that most of the men in the control room showed signs of a tension that he did not feel at all.

Giroux approached Byrnes with the reply from the *Frankland*. "She'll stand by until we're surfaced, sir. She wants us to remain surfaced until everything checks out."

Frank saw the smirk on Byrnes's face and knew why it was there. Byrnes would not even consider submerging again until he had found out what had prevented them from coming up. Safety. Safety first. Frank continued his appraisal of the control room. His eyes rested on Hardy. The Professor was rooted where he stood, stroking his beard and, for want of a better description, looking pleased . . . Frank blinked in surprise, wondering what *he* had to be tickled about. He followed Hardy's gaze to the clock on the forward bulkhead. The time was 1959.

Byrnes's movement to the air-manifold operator's station distracted him. The Captain grabbed the valve wheels and tried them himself. After three tries, and just as he threatened to become violent, one of the wheels responded. Roybell stared at him, incredulous.

"Why you and not me?" he asked.

Byrnes triumphantly moved the other valve wheels. Frank was still staring at Hardy when the whoosh of compressed air brought him around. Byrnes stepped back from the panel, satisfied.

The general surprise lasted all of four seconds. Stigwood took over and controlled the *Candlefish's* rise to the surface. Whatever tension had been building in the control room vanished as the sub's low-pressure blowers kicked in. And Hardy watched the clock tick off the seconds past the hour of 2000.

Frank gazed at the depth gauge and called out, "Zero feet!" He heard Danby in the conning tower giving the order to crack the hatch, then open it. This time nobody minded the change of pressure as the sea air washed over them, replacing the staler air that they breathed while running submerged. What was normally considered an uncomfortable transition was greeted with enormous relief as fresh air circulated through the boat.

"Lookouts to the bridge!" came Danby's voice over the intercom. The lookouts scampered past Byrnes and up the ladders to the bridge. The Captain took one sweep around the control room, then followed. Hardy limped over, swung in behind him, and horsed himself up the metal rungs.

Byrnes ordered, "Ready main engines!", then checked the dense fog that all but obliterated the top decks of the sub.

"Anybody pick up the escort?" He tried to pierce the white blanket that shrouded them. "Sound the foghorn," he ordered.

The deep blasts seemed to get swallowed up. And no one picked up any answering sounds. He hit the intercom button. "Scopes! This is the Captain. Where's the *Frankland?*"

Frank's eyes moved up to the high triple towers over the scope shearwater and the slowly turning radar dish.

"I've got them at range thirty-two hundred yards astern and bearing one-seven-three starboard, sir."

Byrnes gave the order to charge all batteries on two engines, ahead one-third. He rested his hands on the TBT and stared straight ahead.

Frank stepped closer. "What do you think went wrong?"

Byrnes glanced at him and started to answer.

He was interrupted by Hardy. "It wasn't twenty hundred."

Byrnes glanced over the other shoulder quizzically and muttered, "What?"

"It wasn't twenty hundred hours," Hardy repeated. "If the area was clear, we *always* surfaced at twenty hundred. I told you that. Check my log."

Byrnes made an effort to control himself. He spoke thinly. "Just what the hell has that got to do with when *I* want to surface?"

If Hardy was aware of Byrnes's anger, he chose to ignore it. "We got away with it once, but from now on," he continued, "if you want the boat to cooperate . . . I would follow that log." His smile was lost on the Captain.

Frank was flabbergasted. He spoke across Byrnes's back. "That's a little farfetched, Professor, don't you think?"

Hardy turned and gazed off into the fog.

Byrnes was disgusted. He jabbed the intercom switch and bellowed: "Cassidy! Get up a work party and check out the electrical system. From stem to stern! I want an explanation!" Then, for Hardy's benefit, he added, "A believable one!"

He released the switch and turned his back on both Frank and Hardy, gazing down the forward deck, which was completely obscured by fog. And in Frank's opinion, for the first time, so was Hardy's head.

Hopalong Cassidy was stretched out on his stomach, checking the last of the stop valves, when the Captain's order came over the speaker. "Chief engineer, chief engineer," he grumbled. "Always the Chief—never the Indians." He got up and went looking for Witzgall. When Cassidy found him, the old electrician's mate had already assembled a small group of troubleshooters. Quickly they split the boat up into sectors. Witzgall started forward, but Cassidy grabbed him. He suspected that if the trouble were to be found, it would be found aft.

The two old men zipped through the forward engine room, heading for the battery cage in the maneuvering compartment—the large junction box containing all of the boat's circuit-breakers. There were enough volts in the cage to burn a bungler to a crisp.

Witzgall grabbed a battle lantern and opened the gate. Carefully they eased themselves inside and scanned the banks of electrical contacts. Working from memory, Cassidy isolated the sections that activated the ballast tanks. "Okay—we'll start here," he said.

Witzgall played his light beam on the contacts. Both men hoped that what they were looking for would be visible. They had no desire to do too much digging—not in here. After several strained minutes, Cassidy released a disappointed sigh. Everything looked to be in order. He reached for the lantern, then turned to Witzgall. "Do me a favor," he said. "Pass the word not to make any sudden course changes."

Witzgall grunted and went forward to relay the order.

Cassidy stooped over and placed the battle lantern on the deck. Gingerly he started to check the cables.

Just hold her steady, he thought, just hold her steady
. . . He stopped to wipe the sweat from his hands,
then hunched over again. There was so little space in
the cage, so little air—and the darkness. His hands felt
along the bunched wires for the connectors. He tested
each wire for firmness, each contact for solid coupling.
He was on the next to last line when he found the
problem. Cautiously he tugged on the heavily insulated
wires and felt them give.

"Son of a bitch."

The main air-bank connector contact was gone. A
few exposed bits of copper causing all that trouble? He
could hardly believe it. And he could see the outcome
of all this. Byrnes would skin Danby, the electrical officer; then Danby would let a few electricians have a
jolt—Witzgall included. Cassidy whipped out his
bandanna and wrapped it around the defective wir-
ing as a signal.

He picked up the battle lantern and backed out of
the cage just as Witzgall returned. Cassidy played the
light beam on his kerchief and said curtly, "There's the
problem. Fix it."

Witzgall took one look at it and cursed, turning a
pursed lip on Cassidy, who shrugged. They both knew
it was Witzgall's fault. The cage was the senior mate's
responsibility. Witzgall snatched the lantern and went
inside.

The tension on the bridge was almost as thick as the
fog. There was none of the usual small talk; even the
lookouts were quiet. Frank stood over the TBT, one
hand on his binoculars, his vision obscured by the mist,
his brain clouded by thoughts. Hardy's outburst could
have been enough to trigger renewed doubts in
Byrnes's mind, start him building a case for scrapping
the voyage.

"Found your problem, sir." Frank turned and saw Cassidy half out of the bridge hatch, facing Byrnes on the cigarette deck.

"What was it?" asked the Captain.

"Play in the main air-bank circuit contacts. You could hardly notice, but they weren't making a clean connection. Witzgall's shimming them in right now."

"You're sure?"

"Yes, sir."

Byrnes didn't even try to mask his triumph. He looked at Hardy with a flinty smile, then thanked Cassidy.

Cassidy's head disappeared down the hatch. The Captain, still pleased, rocked back and forth on his heels, then turned, pursed his lips, and fixed Hardy with iron-hard eyes. "So much for your twenty-hundred-hour theory, Professor. You may know all there is to know about Devil's Triangles, geomagnetic anomalies, and other things we mere mortals aren't privy to. But you can leave the running of the *Candlefish* to me. I don't want to hear any more about when I should or should not surface. Is that understood?"

Hardy seemed to wilt. Without a word, he moved to the hatch and went below.

Frank had mixed emotions: He was glad to see Hardy chewed out, but he did not want to turn the man off and lose his cooperation. He moved alongside Byrnes. "Captain," he said, "it took work to get him out here. Hard work. Don't chase him away."

Byrnes looked straight ahead. "*Your* hard work, Mr. Frank. This whole lashup boils down to *your* hard work. Do you realize we could have lost this submarine tonight?" he shouted. "As long as we can operate safely, we'll go on. But I'll be damned if I'm going to jeopardize this crew just to verify your hare-brained theories—and *his!* Understood?"

Frank could only nod.

"Get below and contact the *Frankland*," Byrnes ordered in a burst of authority. "Tell them we've located the problem and we're secure. We'll submerge at 0400. If we get a visual contact with them before then, fine. If not, we'll see them tomorrow night."

Still shaking with anger, Frank stood by as Giroux raised the *Frankland.*

Cook informed Frank that they had gone to general quarters as soon as they had heard about the problem.

"It's good to know someone's thinking straight," Frank replied, ignoring Giroux's startled look. But when Cook asked, hesitantly, whether Frank had considered calling the whole thing off, Frank had no hesitation at all about snapping back a quick "No!"

He signed off before Cook could apologize and start a campaign of rationalization. He did not want to hear any of it.

Jack Hardy slipped into the wardroom. It was empty, and he needed solitude and quiet, time to examine his feelings. Maybe the Captain was right—he could be pressing too hard. But this was supposed to be a scientific experiment. The only official reason for his presence was to make certain that his log was accurate. Accepted scientific procedures should be followed. To deviate would do nothing but hinder the experiment. Why couldn't Byrnes and the others see that? Hardy frowned at his reflection in the coffee cup.

His mood failed to brighten when Cassidy entered.

Hopalong helped himself to coffee. "Christ, it was thick up there." He eased himself into the booth, balancing the cup and saucer.

Hardy bristled. "What does that mean?"

The chief engineer looked up from his cup, surprised at Hardy's tone. "The fog. Or didn't you notice?" His spoon clinked, stirring the coffee.

Hardy felt foolish. He was convinced that Cassidy didn't like him, but Cassidy was being oddly sociable now.

"Tell me something," Hopalong said. "This business tonight—did the same thing happen on your original patrol?"

"You mean failing to surface? No. Why?"

Cassidy sipped his coffee and considered it. "Well, Professor, if you had those foul-ups then . . . Mind you, I'm not superstitious, but forewarned is forearmed and all that shit . . ." Cassidy's face was friendly, but the question in his eyes gave him away.

Hardy relaxed. Maybe his impression of the yardbird was wrong. "The only thing I left out of the log," he said, deciding to trust Cassidy, "was the plan that Basquine came up with."

"What plan?"

Hardy hesitated. "You were pretty close to the truth when you called him psychotic."

"I was just mouthing off. What plan?"

Hardy snorted, then spoke into his beard. "Billy G. Basquine was the nearest thing to a certified nut that I've ever come across. Just before the boat went down, he was going to come off station, *assigned station,* and take the *Candlefish* into Tokyo Bay."

Cassidy was a moment in reacting; then he said, "Well, isn't that initiative?"

"Initiative!" Hardy spluttered and pushed his coffee away. "Goddamned lunacy is what that was!"

Calming down, he outlined Basquine's lone-wolf plan, meant to be the absolute, complete, final moment of glory for the USS *Candlefish*.

Cassidy listened, a look of amazement growing on his craggy features. "But that was December, 1944. The war was almost over—we just about *had* the Pacific. Why take such a risk then?"

"Tonnage! He wanted to chalk up a record . . . make a name for himself and the boat, join the ranks of the heroes. He was so hungry for targets, I think he would have sunk anything—including our own ships! And Bates, the Exec—" Hardy struggled to keep the hard edge of remembered rancor out of his voice. "If anything, he encouraged Basquine."

Cassidy shook his head in disbelief. "All alone? No diversion? No air cover?" Hardy shook his head too. "They *were* nuts," Cassidy said, "both of them. Basquine *and* Bates." He drained his cup and rose. "One other thing I gotta ask you. That talk you gave in the wardroom—with the skewers and the globe. For my own satisfaction, is there anything *to* that?"

Hardy smiled at Cassidy's candor. "Just a theory, Hopalong," he said. "Nothing more, nothing less."

"Then you don't expect any trouble when we get to this Latitude Thirty?"

"None whatsoever. Why?"

"I've been calming down the crews. Now maybe I can feel like an honest man." He got up and headed out, turning at the door. "Hey, Professor, if you've got a sweet tooth, check out the galley in about twenty minutes."

The submarine plowed steadily on, still wrapped in the depths of the massive fog bank, the muffled throb of her engines the only evidence of her presence. The lookouts had given up on their binoculars; they huddled on their perches, safe in the knowledge that the ship's radar could and would pierce the all-pervading grayness and warn them of anything in their path. The strident hoot of the *Frankland*'s fog horn, deadened by the mist, was their only contact with the outside world as the *Candlefish,* fog curling and licking at her sides, inched through the Pacific night in a cloak of complete isolation.

Ed Frank came off watch at 2400, dropped into the conning tower, and gave the quartermaster details to record in the ship's log. While he waited for Lang to complete the notations, he finished sorting out all his options in silence. The Captain was his problem at the moment. Byrnes, with his safety-first policy, still could not scrub the cruise without damned good cause. If Byrnes was considering termination, he would need something more substantial than minor equipment failure to get Melanoff and Kellogg to agree. Of one thing Frank was positive: Louis F. Byrnes would not do anything that would adversely reflect on his service profile. Cutting the cruise short without ample reason, with the attendant Board of Inquiry, could become a nasty blemish on his spotless record.

Hardy left the comfort of the wardroom and headed for the galley. Byrnes was not in the control room; he must have turned in for the night. The men in control were relaxed but bundled up. The open conning-tower hatch and the ladder-well formed a natural funnel, and cold, moist air chilled the compartment.

Hardy stepped into the galley. Cookie and one of his mates were hard at work in the tiny space that served as food-preparation center for the sub. Just aft, in the crew's mess, several small groups were clustered around tables—some reading, some writing—and there was a furious game of acey-deucy in progress.

"What can I do for you, Professor?" Cookie looked up with his customary surly expression.

"Something smells good, and I heard a rumor."

Cookie snorted. "Did it start with the stomach that walks like a man?"

That was Cookie's somewhat affectionate name for Cassidy. In the eleven days since leaving Pearl, a feud had developed between them. Cassidy needled Cookie about the quality of his food, and Cookie bitched about Cassidy's bottomless pit.

Hardy smiled and held out a pleading hand.

Cookie wilted. "Only one," he said, with mother-hen firmness.

"Right." Hardy nodded.

Cookie placed a fragrant hot apple popover on a plate and handed it over. He watched Hardy's mouth close over it and the look of enjoyment spread on his face. Then he turned proudly back to his lasagne.

"Hey, Cookie! Any more of this stuff?"

Hardy glanced up as the pharmacist's mate, Dankworth, came in waving a jar in his outstretched paw.

"Jesus H. Christ! What is it with you, Dankworth?"

Dankworth grinned sheepishly. "Can't help it. I got a *craving*."

Hardy froze in mid-bite. Dankworth was waving an empty peanut butter jar. Cookie reluctantly handed him a fresh one. Dankworth unscrewed the cap and quickly smeared some crackers, which he tossed on a plate. He secured the lid, returned the jar to Cookie, and headed for the mess, happily munching.

Hardy slid his plate to the counter, mumbled thanks, then looked into the mess. Dankworth was seated facing away, but Hardy could tell from his movements that the crackers were steadily disappearing. He was not only eating, he was *concentrating* on eating.

Rattled, Hardy headed forward, disturbed with himself. He was struggling, trying to keep the image of Slugger out of his mind . . . Albert P. Daley, "Slugger" from the crew of the *Candlefish*—1944.

Frank, who had made it his business to look up Cassidy after coming off watch, to recheck the battery cage, also had a glimpse of Dankworth diving into his peanut butter. Coming through the crew's quarters, he had a head-on view as the pharmacist's mate flopped onto Clampett's bunk and demolished his third load of goodies. Frank was even more surprised than Hardy, but for a different reason.

Human nature being what it was, Dankworth should have been the last man on board to have a craving for that stuff. With that latrine-cleaning episode only days old, it seemed unlikely Dankworth would be seen within three hundred feet of any peanut butter. But there he was, filling his face and obviously enjoying it.

"Well," thought Frank, "there are better things to do than watch a man make a pig of himself."

But he did look back from the hatch. It *was* strange.

CHAPTER 13

December 2, 1974

Frank got to sleep around 0130, after lying in silence with his arms clasped behind his head for an hour, staring at the upper bunk.

He didn't want to think about the host of unsettling things that kept cropping up. Hardy's insistent adherence to his own precious words, the failure of the boat to respond . . . The important thing was to keep the purpose in focus, never lose sight of the original goal, no matter what peculiarities became manifest. Not that he expected more incidents, but he was determined to hold to his method for dealing with everything. The method was simple: Don't let Ed Frank lose control of the situation for even one minute. If that meant bucking Byrnes and Hardy, and everyone else, then so be it. Frank pulled his arms under the covers and relaxed. Once he was satisfied that his grasp on events could not be loosened, he felt able to rest and so let himself drift off to sleep.

At 0300 he was awakened by an urgent hand on his shoulder. He endured it for a moment, then suddenly flipped over and stared into Byrnes's worried face.

"I'm sorry," the Captain said. "Can you give me a minute?"

Frank nodded and rubbed his eyes. He sat up and watched Byrnes pacing the stateroom. Dorriss was cocooned on an upper bunk.

"What's the matter?" asked Frank.

Byrnes kept pacing, his jaws working. "I've been in the radio room—in and out of it and up to the bridge like a goddamned monkey, non-stop for the last two hours. We've lost radio contact."

"What?"

"With the escort." Frank's incredulous expression made Byrnes snap back. "I can't raise the *Frankland!* First visual, now radio."

Frank let it sink in, then stared at the deck. He watched the Captain's shiny black shoes pass back and forth three times before anything more was said.

"What about radar?" Frank asked.

"Still got them on the scopes," Byrnes admitted. "But how reliable is that?"

"Perfectly."

"Oh?" Byrnes said nothing more, just gave Frank a quick, skeptical glance. Then he stepped to the center of the compartment and thrust his hands into his pockets.

"Not a word out of them. I can't believe it."

"You think they've had a malfunction?"

"I *hope* so. I just hope."

"Well, that's probably what it is. We couldn't lose contact. We might not be able to see them in this fog, but we *do* have them on radar."

"What if that's not the *Frankland?*" Byrnes looked Frank in the eye. "What if it's just a piece of debris, a large patch of seaweed, or a Russian trawler?"

Frank swung his legs over the side of the bunk and kept his head low so he wouldn't bump it on the upper.

"All right," he said. "What if?"

"Well, we can't go on like this. Our orders require constant radio and visual contact with the escort. That's security procedure. Without the presence of the

Frankland, this mission is jeopardized. And it's getting close to 0400," said Byrnes quietly. "Time to submerge." He turned suddenly. "Look, Frank, do we have to follow that log?"

Well, well, thought Frank. Why in the world didn't he just say "Fuck you, Ed, but we're going home"? "That's what we set out to do."

"I know. But the circumstances are changing."

"What do you want to do?"

"Keep this boat dead in the water until we reestablish radio and visual contact with the *Frankland.*"

He stopped and waited for Frank's reply.

Frank stood up. His answer was a firm "No. Captain, we *have* to follow that log or, as far as I'm concerned, the whole project is blown."

"Maybe it is already."

"That's an assumption."

Byrnes pulled one hand out of his pocket and worried his chin with it. "It's up to me, Commander, not up to you. I want to make that point now, so that if and when I order a course change, you know the reason why. I don't want any fights about it."

Frank stuck his jaw out. "There's no reason to act like a dictator."

They were interrupted by a booming voice over the intercom: *"Captain to the bridge. Captain to the bridge."*

Byrnes hesitated only a second, then charged out of the compartment. Frank grabbed his pants and rushed after him.

Byrnes stopped in the control room, one hand on the ladder, the other on the radar operator's shoulder. "What is it, Scopes?"

"Don't know, sir. Something about planes . . ."

In the red light of the conning tower, Frank could

feel the cold seeping down from the bridge. He asked the quartermaster for a jacket. On the bridge they found Jack Hardy, wearing a jacket slick with mist, sweeping the shrouded horizon with a pair of binoculars. An Arctic sea smoke roiled up off the rippling waves, adding to the overhead blanket of gray. The only sound was the plunge of diesel exhaust and the sea lapping against the bows. Frank zipped up the borrowed jacket.

"All right, what is it?" asked Byrnes.

"Planes," said Hardy. "Two or three of them. Not jets. Prop jobs."

"What?"

"I heard them."

Byrnes turned to the lookouts on the periscope shears. They shrugged. One of them responded, "Captain, I'm sorry. I don't know *what* I heard."

"I heard them," snapped Hardy. "They were prop jobs. I'm sure of it."

Byrnes flipped on the bridge phone. "Radar, did you pick up any planes?"

"No, sir. Nothing at all. Still trying, sir."

Byrnes gave Hardy a sidelong look. "Probably our own," he mumbled.

Hardy turned sharply. "With props?"

"This far out at sea? I don't think so. Do you?" Byrnes was smiling; he didn't believe Hardy at all.

"I heard them," the Professor said tightly.

"Congratulations. Next time, let me know when you *see* them." He pressed the phone again. "Radar, you still have the escort on that scope?"

"Aye, aye, sir. Bearing one seventy degrees off the starboard bow. Range, six thousand yards."

"Thanks."

Byrnes turned and watched Hardy scan the fog a

moment longer, still looking for his planes. Then he turned and faced Frank. Frank read disgust in the Captain's eyes and knew what he was thinking: Hardy was an old, incompetent fool and neither he nor his goddamned log could be trusted. Frank frowned unpleasantly. Why in hell couldn't Hardy have just stayed out of the way?

Over the transmission sounds of diesels pumping, a voice came in loud and strident: "Captain, this is the forward torpedo room. We've got two fish loaded and ready—"

Byrnes whirled in surprise and grabbed the mouthpiece. "This is the Captain. You've got what!"

"Tubes one and two ready for firing, sir. Just like it says in the log. Fire a pair of torpedoes at around 0415 on December second, sir."

"Well, you just hold on to those two fish, Mr. Vogel! Don't let them go anywhere!" He released the speaker button and swore. Another voice came on:

"Captain, this is control. It's nearing 0400, sir. Time to submerge."

Byrnes's eyes widened first in exasperation, then in anger. Again he jabbed the button and hollered below: "This is the Captain. That is a negative. We will remain on the surface. That is all!"

Hardy lowered his binoculars and turned in silent appeal to Frank. Frank faced Byrnes. "What good is that going to do?"

"I told you before. We will hold our position and wait for the escort to catch up." He spoke into the phone again. "This is the Captain. All stop."

The muffled pumping of the diesels slowed and came to a halt. The submarine drifted into the next wave and then sat quietly, shrouded in fog.

Byrnes started to pace the bridge. Twice he called

below to Radar and asked for positions on the escort. The first time he was advised 5800 yards. The second time, 5700 yards. The escort was making slow progress. Too slow for Byrnes. He ordered Giroux to make another attempt at radio contact. Giroux reported back two minutes later.

"Sorry, Captain. The *Frankland* still doesn't respond."

Frank checked his watch. It was one minute to 0400. "Captain?" He waited for Byrnes to give him full attention. "What about a compromise? Let's submerge now, fire those torpedoes on schedule, *then* surface and wait for the escort."

Byrnes scowled at first, then appeared to give the idea some serious consideration.

Frank pressed his advantage. "At least let's *try* to keep this project going."

Hardy was watching anxiously. Byrnes glanced at him and finally nodded. He was not too pleased about it, but it was easier than just waiting.

"Very well. We'll go down."

"And the torpedoes?"

"We'll see. I want to get a fix on that escort with the sonar." He hollered out: "Lookouts below!" The lookouts slid down the shears and dropped through the hatch. "Stand by to dive. Clear the bridge!"

Byrnes hit the klaxon. Frank and Hardy followed the lookouts below. Byrnes yelled over the battle phone, "Dive! Dive!" Then he dropped into the conning tower and pulled the hatch lanyard after him. The quartermaster dogged the hatch shut, and Byrnes went below to the control room, spouting orders: "Take her down to seventy-five feet. Rig out the sonar!"

"Aye, aye, sir." Roybell went for the valves.

The sonar operator, Nadel, switched on his gear and fitted his headphones. He turned up the speaker, and in a second the compartment was echoing with *pings*. Hardy and Frank came below from the conning tower and listened.

Byrnes tapped the radar operator. "What was the last range on that escort, Scopes?"

"Fifty-two hundred yards, sir."

Nadel piped up, "Got something, Captain. High-speed screws approaching. Range, three thousand. Bearing zero-four-nine. Closing on our bow."

Byrnes blinked. "What the hell is that?"

"The escort?" said Frank.

Byrnes turned sharply to Scopes, who shrugged and insisted, "Couldn't be. They're astern! I made them at fifty-two hundred yards, bearing one-seven-zero. I'm positive."

Byrnes swung a finger at Nadel. "Then what the hell has *he* got?"

Hardy took a step forward. He was mouthing something—the numbers zero-four-nine—the position on the sonar target. His brow was furrowed; he seemed to be trying to work something out in his mind.

Byrnes waved a hand at Scopes. "You were wrong. No wonder we couldn't see them. They're running ahead of us!"

Hardy spoke quietly. "Are you sure this is the escort?" He laid a hand on the sonar gear, and they all listened to the churning sound.

"Has to be!"

Nadel spoke, hesitant. "Not so sure, sir. Running kind of low in the water." He clasped the phones to his head. "And her screws—they don't sound familiar."

"What do you mean, familiar?" barked Byrnes.

"She just doesn't *sound* like the *Frankland*."

There was a long silence while Byrnes carefully listened to the *pings* and the interspersed churning of distant, approaching screws.

"It's another submarine."

Everybody turned at Hardy's remark. He stood stockstill in the center of the control room, listening just as intently as everyone else.

Byrnes straightened slowly. "Mr. Hardy, if you please—"

"Captain, I think you should check my log—"

Byrnes's eyes flashed. "This isn't the time for that."

Nadel clutched his headset in white fingers, a frightened look in his eye. "Sir? Excuse me, sir. I think Mr. Hardy's right. That does sound like a submarine."

Frank felt the confidence draining from his middle.

"That's impossible," said Byrnes hoarsely. "It has to be the escort!"

"No, sir." Nadel was firm now. "She's riding much too low in the water. It's another sub, all right."

"It can't be," Byrnes muttered, then turned to Frank. "Mr. Frank, should we encounter any other subs in this area?"

"No. We're supposed to be running in clear lanes."

None of them was aware of just how quiet it had become in the control room until they were all startled by the sudden clatter from above. Byrnes shifted to the hatchwell and looked up into the conning tower. Stigwood's face appeared at the ladder, ashen.

"Captain—"

"What's going on up there?"

"Captain, it's the TDC. It's acting up—"

"Acting? What are you—"

Stigwood looked sideways, then back down at Byrnes. He spat it out. "It's computing a setup!"

Frank blinked. Hardy had turned and was looking up past Byrnes's shoulder. The TDC—Torpedo Data

Computer. Computing a setup? By itself? A setup on what? Frank's lips parted.

Byrnes flew to the intercom. "Forward torpedo room. This is the Captain. What's going on down there, Vogel?"

The torpedo officer's voice rang out, "Sir, we're standing by. Outer doors open on tubes one and two."

"The TDC is sending down data. Are you receiving?"

"Yes, sir."

The Captain's eyes widened. He shouted, "Well, don't do anything! Don't fire! Stand by to unload!"

"Aye, aye, sir. Standing by."

Frank shoved past Hardy and shot up the ladder. In the conning tower he sidestepped Stigwood and the quartermaster, who were staring incredulously at the TDC. Frank leaned over it and studied the position. How in the world could the thing set itself up? And what target had it set up? He checked the coordinates on the metal plates. Bearing 000 dead on. A bow shot. The bloody thing had set up a bow shot on that—that—whatever it was that was swinging in ahead of them. Was it another sub? Or was it really the escort? Frank felt a chill of fear.

"Captain, that sub is still closing." Nadel's voice drifted up from below, along with the sound of slashing screws and increasing *pings*. "Bearing zero-three-eight relative."

Zero-three-eight! The target was coming about to approach head on—their sonar must have already locked onto the *Candlefish!* Frank stared at the crazy little machine. It had computed a down-the-throat shot on an undetermined target, transmitted the information to the torpedo gyros in tubes one and two, and now—

He heard Hardy speaking his own thoughts. "She's drawing a bead on us!"

"Hardy—shut up!" said Byrnes.

Frank dropped down the ladder. "Captain, you better do *something*. He may be right!"

Byrnes was sweating. Terror was creeping all over his face.

Frank pressed home. "We've got a bow shot set up by the TDC. We can wait until they're in position and then fire—"

"We're not firing on a fucking thing! What in hell do you think I am? Crazy?"

Nadel barked over his shoulder, "Range, fifteen hundred!"

"That might be one of our *own* submarines!" yelled Byrnes. "I can't shoot at it!"

"You can't do any damage. We're carrying torpedoes with dummy loads, remember? Fire one off as a warning—and then *run!*"

Byrnes snapped up. He saw sense in that. "Fifteen-degree angle—take her deep." Levers clattered as the planesmen switched from power to manual control on the bow and stern planes. "Rig for silent running! Take her down to two twenty-five!"

"Aye, sir," said Roybell. "Flood negative—hard dive on planes."

"Shut off all machinery—no unnecessary movement or talking!" barked the Captain.

An auxiliaryman turned off the air conditioners, shut off the whining motor generators that ran the lighting system, and switched on the red combat lights.

The MB registered ALL STOP at 225 feet.

In the control room, Byrnes edged closer to Nadel and asked quietly: "Sound?"

"Still coming, Captain. Bearing zero-two-four relative. Range, thirteen hundred yards."

"Switch off our beacons."

Smart, thought Frank. Now the guy is starting to act like a fighting skipper. Sit here in silence and wait. They'll never find us. They'll pass right over us. Whoever they are . . . He wondered briefly if Byrnes shouldn't call down to the forward torpedo room and be sure they unload . . . No, of course not. Don't break silence.

The only *pings* coming over the sonar now were the beacons from the other craft. A steady rhythm, alternating loud and soft. Hardy spoke quietly. "They're still scanning—haven't locked on us."

"Bearing zero-one-seven," whispered Nadel. "Range, eleven hundred yards."

Everyone was mouse-quiet, listening as the screws churned up the sea ahead of them and grew in volume.

"Bearing zero-zero-nine. She's swinging dead on—"

They felt rather than heard the thumps.

The sub shook, and everyone froze until Vogel's voice bellowed over the intercom: "Shit! We just fired two fish!"

Byrnes, the master of disbelief, shouted back, "You did *what?*"

"We didn't *do* it—it just happened!"

They could hear the twin *pfushes* over their own sonar gear and the sound of the torpedo propellers churning away toward the approaching lower-pitched screws of the unknown ship.

"It's all right," muttered Frank hopefully. "They're dummies."

But they all jumped when Cassidy came swinging through the open watertight door from aft on his way to the forward torpedo room.

Byrnes jumped to the tracking indicators.

"High-speed moving away," reported Nadel. Evidently the target had also picked up the sound of the torpedoes firing and was backpedaling to safety. "Bearing zero-zero-four relative."

Too late. The other ship would never get out of range. Hardy tensed and listened along with everyone else.

Suddenly the steady gassy noise of the fleeing propellers stopped. Over the sonar's speaker they heard a twin pair of thunks. And then—explosions.

Everyone stared at the speaker as sound bellowed from it. Metallic crumpling. Rumbles. A rush of bubbles.

A direct hit.

The shock wave hit the *Candlefish,* and she took a roll to port. The collision alarm went off. Everyone hung on and, when they were leveled again, Byrnes swung up to the conning tower. "Emergency surface!" he called. "Secure from silent running. Secure from collision! Take her up!"

The *Candlefish* surfaced at a sharp angle, cutting a big hole in the dense fog bank lying on the water's surface. As Byrnes, Hardy, and Frank broke through to the bridge, an eerie red glow spread from the east: Dawn broke through the mist. They leaned over the bridge coaming and gazed down at the sea. After a few moments the mist spread to port and starboard, and they saw the bow pierce a widening oil slick dotted with debris. Jagged pieces of wood, metal, instruments—

"What the hell did we hit?" muttered Byrnes.

Hardy stared at the debris but hardly saw it. He was seeing something else, a dim memory jogging to the surface. "It's in the log," he said. "On December 2nd, 1944, the *Candlefish* tracked and sank a Japanese sub."

Byrnes turned slowly and stared so hard at him that his jaw began to quiver.

Frank was also speechless, but only for a moment. Then he gripped Hardy's shoulder and turned him around.

"Hardy—this is *1974.*"

The old man reacted slowly, drawn agonizingly out of his reverie. Then the simple fact of what Frank was saying registered, as if it had eluded him until just this moment. He scowled in confusion.

Byrnes hit the bridge phone and called below. "Radar, this is the Captain. Give me a position on the escort!"

There was a pause. Too long, Frank thought. And he was right.

"I'm trying, sir . . ." the voice came back.

"What do you mean, trying?" barked the Captain.

"Well, sir, it looks like we've lost them."

Byrnes was very still. They were all looking at the same thing, the debris in the waters around them. The *Frankland* . . . ?

"Radar, are you certain?"

"Captain . . . I'm sorry, we've lost all contact."

"When?"

There was another pause.

"Sir, I'm not sure. I rigged out the set as soon as we surfaced. They weren't there. I've been trying . . . Sorry, sir."

Scopes choked on his last words. Evidently he was convinced of what the men on the bridge only suspected. Frank voiced it: "My God, have we sunk our own escort?"

"No!" croaked Hardy. He shook his head as he looked at each of them. He seemed positive, but Frank could see how little that meant to Byrnes.

The voice echoed across the submarine from the

bridge phone: "Bridge, this is Cassidy. Captain to the forward torpedo room, right away."

Byrnes was halfway down the hatch when he paused to look up at Hardy one more time.

Hardy glanced up at the lookouts, then again out to sea, at the drifting wreckage bumping the hull and slipping past into the spreading dawn. He knew Byrnes thought he was an idiot. He wondered if the captain wasn't right.

As Byrnes dropped into the control room, he exchanged a look with Scopes. "Keep trying" was all Byrnes could bring himself to say. Then he swung around to the radio room and told Giroux the same thing. Giroux shrugged in hopeless indifference. As far as *he* was concerned, they had lost the escort when *his* equipment had lost it.

With Frank right behind him, Byrnes swung through to the forward torpedo room and saw Cassidy hovering over one of the torpedo bays. Vogel, the torpedo officer, came forward immediately, effusive in his apologies. "Captain, I just don't know how it happened. I swear nobody touched anything. She—she fired all by herself."

Byrnes took a deep breath and muttered generously, "I know—I know—"

He and Frank moved to join Cassidy at the forward end of the skids. The old yardbird was staring at the arming mechanisms on the torpedoes.

"Hopalong?" said Byrnes.

Cassidy looked up at him, at Frank, at Hardy slipping through the connecting hatch and joining them. He tapped the huge green-and-yellow fish. "We loaded Mark 14s with dummy warheads at Pearl, didn't we?"

"Yes," said Byrnes.

"These aren't dummies."

He pointed to the exploder nipple protruding from

the tip of the warhead. Byrnes leaned over to inspect it. He stared hard for a moment; then his fingers moved in and touched. He straightened and walked down the skid to the ass-end of the fish, stopping to check the inspection plate.

"These are live," he said.

"Yeah, they all are," said Cassidy.

Hardy moved around the skid to the other bays, passed down the torpedoes, checking each of them with no more than normal curiosity. Frank watched him; his brow furrowed; why wasn't Hardy more concerned? Harmless ballast had turned into deadly bullets, each containing 668 pounds of volatile torpex. From a scientific-research ship, they had turned into a malignant hazard on the seas. If this crazy ship could shoot off its fish whenever it wanted to—

"Who's responsible for this?" Byrnes snapped sharply, his voice cutting across the compartment.

Frank saw what was happening; Byrnes couldn't accept the facts as they were. How could he be expected to? But to accuse . . . ?

"Well, somebody did it! Somebody switched these things. Now who?"

Hardy was passing down the other side of the center skid. Frank saw something dark in his eyes . . . the Professor didn't seem to be himself.

Byrnes suddenly snaked an arm across the nearest torpedo and grabbed Hardy's shoulder. "Was it you?" he growled.

Hardy stared at him a long time before he answered, not so much choosing his words as measuring the accuser. "No, it wasn't me. But it's a good thing."

"What?"

"Otherwise . . . that debris on the surface would be *us*."

Byrnes released him. He looked around at the

frightened faces of the crewmen. He straightened and rubbed his sweating face. Then he looked from Hardy to Frank.

"I want to see you two in my quarters. Right away."

CHAPTER 14

December 2, 1974

Hopalong Cassidy questioned every torpedoman forward and aft and was convinced that no man aboard had deliberately or otherwise tampered with the big fish. The only explanation seemed to be that someone in the Pearl Harbor armament detail had loaded the wrong torpedoes. Vogel protested vigorously. He was positive they had left Pearl with regulation practice torpedoes. Cassidy nodded and accepted the answer, but knew from forty years' experience that far stranger mistakes had been made. As for Hardy, how could Byrnes point the finger at him? To accuse the Professor didn't make any sense at all.

No matter how, they were now carrying a full load of lethal weapons. And for the time being it wouldn't be wise to attempt to deactivate them. No one on board was qualified as a demolitions expert; they had left those fellows ashore. But then, hundreds of crews had sailed aboard fleet boats with armed fish—that was part of the nature of submarine duty. After all, the *Candlefish* was no fishing trawler, was she? Then what bothered him? Why did he keep asking himself these stupid, nagging questions as he made his way back to his station in the forward engine room? If submariners were accustomed to eating, sleeping, and sailing in the company of high explosives, what made *him* so bloody

nervous? The fact that he was a yardbird and in reality
not a submariner at all? No, for he saw the same nervous, worried expression on other faces. He wasn't
alone in his fear. Was it really fear? He stopped in the
aft engine room and leaned against the bulkhead, listening to the murmuring whine coming from his own
diesels just through the next hatch.

The *Candlefish* wasn't supposed to be armed. And
yet somehow the temptation had been placed in their
hands. Temptation? He wondered about that. Cassidy
did not believe in fate or the occult or the extraordinary—or anything except cold steel and greasy engines.
Yet he couldn't deny the rush of excitement he had felt
when those two fish had blown clear of tubes one and
two. And then the strikes! The explosion! The sudden
flurry of submarine war action. He had been a yardbird
all his life; he had taken boats out only on their initial
trial runs; he had never seen action before. Now he had
gotten his first taste of excitement, and was strangely
anxious for more.

Grabbing the hatch lip with both hands, he propelled
his body through, landing on both feet and immediately
padding over to his engine stand. He checked the
gauges and whistled at Googles and Brownhaver. Both
of them threw him the thumbs-up gesture, and he
leaned back, satisfied that at least his little corner of
the world was in fine shape. He eyed the carved mahogany pipe cabinet secured to the bulkhead over main
engine number two, the cabinet with the name etched
into the wood beneath the little hinged doors: WALIN-
SKY—HIS PIPES. Cassidy smiled. Every engineer he had
ever known was the same. Incurable grease monkeys,
yet they all had to have their little bit of class. Pipe
cabinet—that had been Walinsky's grasp on dignity.
Cassidy opened the cabinet doors and admired the

clean felt lining, the carved Larsens, Charatans, Dunhills, a Barling, and a pair that must have been handmade by a loving amateur—probably Walinsky himself. Lovely things. Cassidy inspected the bowls, looking for carbon deposits. The lack of ash buildup surprised him. What the hell had Walinsky done with these pipes? Just shined them?

They looked a little dusty. He rubbed one. It needed wax. There were pipe tools, rags, wax, cleaners, and nails in a small rack to one side. He pulled down one pipe after another and polished them to a high gloss, working as if they had always belonged to him, as if he knew all there was to know about pipe care.

And while he worked, he thought about Jack Hardy. The problem.

Hardy and Frank spent a most unpleasant forty-five minutes in the Captain's cabin.

Byrnes sat in his desk chair, straddling it backward, and kept leafing through Hardy's log, at Hardy's prodding.

"Detail for detail," the Professor insisted, "we're duplicating the 1944 patrol, Captain. It's more than what's covered in that log. There are things happening that I couldn't possibly be expected to remember, yet when they happen, I do remember them! Clearly!"

"*Déjà vu*," muttered Byrnes.

"No! I'm not imagining these things. I *have* been there before. They're happening again. That submarine we sank—"

Byrnes interrupted, "That unknown vessel!"

"Whatever it was—the same thing happened thirty years ago to the day, to the hour! I remember it. And there it is in the log!"

Byrnes slapped the log shut. "I don't give a damn

what you wrote. That was *then*—this is *now*."

"Right! And what's happening *now* is what happened *then!*"

The muscles tensed in the Captain's neck. "What in hell do you want me to do, Professor?"

"We have to react the way our crew would have reacted thirty years ago. If a target appears—if it fulfills the log—then we have to act as the log tells us to act. That's why we're here! Ask Frank! Whatever is going on is giving us the perfect opportunity to recreate the 1944 patrol!"

Byrnes snapped back, "You're so busy recreating things—you're imagining planes in the middle of the Pacific."

"Nobody imagined that oil slick."

Frank smiled. Hardy had a point. They had sunk *something*. The fact that no one knew precisely what it was did not diminish the coincidence—they had fulfilled that moment in the log.

"Look, I've heard enough nonsense about Devil's Triangles and geomagnetic anomalies and disappearing ships and recreating bullshit!"

Frank held up a hand, appointing himself instant referee. "Let's think this out logically for a moment."

Byrnes jumped up and shouted, "No more logic! Just orders. You forget, both of you, that we have lost contact with our escort and all that special equipment! That is a large enough catastrophe to put an end to this mission, as far as I'm concerned. The experiment is over! I'm keeping this tub on the surface. We're going to sit right where we are until that escort shows up. I'm going to radio Pearl right now and inform them that we will return to base as soon as possible!"

Frank's jaw slackened. Hardy opened his mouth to protest.

Byrnes pointed a shaking finger at the Professor. "As for you, don't give me a hard time. I'm responsible for eighty-four other lives! I won't have one *nut* putting the rest of them in jeopardy!"

Frank spoke in as controlled a voice as he could muster. "That's a bit rough, Captain. I don't see any reason for pinning anything on Hardy. He's certainly not responsible for—"

"He confuses the issue! And so do you—and I don't want another word out of you."

Frank stood up, and the two men faced each other across the tiny cabin, as if for a fist fight. But then Jack Hardy made it clear the battle hadn't even begun yet.

"About the radio," said Hardy. "I wouldn't advertise our position if I were you."

Byrnes was caught by surprise. "To who?"

"The enemy."

Byrnes couldn't believe it, and neither could Frank. Byrnes once again pointed at Hardy, but this time to say, "You're relieved as navigation officer."

Hardy sat still a moment, staring at Byrnes, not understanding what he had done wrong. Then he rose and silently left the cabin.

Frank was stunned and speechless as Byrnes turned to him. "From now on, you will act as full-time Exec. I'll need Dorriss at navigation. That should keep you out of trouble. And I'm holding you responsible for what Hardy does and says. I don't want him alarming the crew."

Frank couldn't hold back the contempt in his voice. "Well, if they're like me, they're already sufficiently alarmed. And as for returning to Pearl—I've got a hunch it isn't going to be that easy."

Frank stepped out quickly, before Byrnes could muster a comeback. But the thud and slam were unmistakable as the Captain kicked his door shut. Frank hurried aft to the galley to pick up a cup of coffee. His nerves needed calming.

Cookie was a small, heavily bearded pug from Brooklyn with all the mouth of a Manhattan cabbie. He tolerated no criticism. Frank found him carrying on a one-sided argument with an electrician who had found a matchbook in his stew.

"You're lucky it wasn't my toenail clippings!" Cookie raged.

"I already ate those! They were in yesterday's pudding."

Cookie waved a greasy ladle at him. "Then you're gonna *love* today's ice cream!"

The two continued shouting while Frank poured himself coffee, snatched a fresh doughnut, and shoved past them. He slipped into the crew's mess and spotted Cassidy with his two cronies, Brownhaver and Googles, at a corner table. Cassidy was sporting a queer-looking pipe clamped tightly between his teeth. Frank couldn't remember having seen him smoke before.

Brownhaver appeared to be dominating the conversation.

"I'm tellin' ya, the Japanese don't have no long-range submarines today. Haven't had 'em since the end of the war. That was part of the settlement. They couldn't maintain a navy. If we sank a submarine, it sure wasn't Japanese!"

Googles shook his head, confused, and turned to Cassidy. "What do you think?"

Cassidy rolled the pipe across his mouth, then pulled it out and spoke sagely. "We sank *something*. And somebody's bound to complain."

Frank sipped his coffee and thought about it. Of course, if they sank a domestic ship there was bound to be something about it broadcast on the radio. He must remember to tell Giroux to monitor the civilian bands. Of course, if it really was their own escort . . . One thing seemed ruled out. If Brownhaver was right, and Frank was certain he was, it could not have been a Japanese submarine. If there *weren't* any . . . well, one wouldn't just *appear* to fulfill their purpose, would it? He wondered if Byrnes wasn't right: Maybe Jack Hardy was deranged. But Byrnes's panic, his inability to keep cool under pressure, was just as dangerous. Byrnes seemed to be slipping his anchor. In fact, maybe he posed more of a threat than the Professor. Hardy had no desire to be responsible for anyone else's life. Byrnes was responsible for eighty-five of them, including his own.

Frank's concern was the expedition. The experiment. Proving himself right.

Cookie and the electrician were still at it when Frank strolled past the galley and flung the empty cup at them. Cookie fumbled to catch it and stared after him.

Frank found Hardy sitting alone in the wardroom, working on a cup of tea. His arms were flat on the table, and he was staring at the globe he had ripped apart only a few days earlier.

Frank sat down a few feet from the Professor and pulled out his pipe kit. He loaded, tamped down, and lit, then puffed in silence for a few moments.

"Byrnes has a very short fuse," Frank offered. Hardy looked up slowly, as if coming out of an absorbing personal reverie. "He jumps off the handle—and always a little early."

"Mr. Frank . . . I hope *you* realize . . . we sank a *real* submarine."

Frank lowered his eyes and tamped down the pipe. "Apart from that—"

"*Nothing* is apart from that!"

Frank saw that Hardy was going to maintain his position to the last. That wasn't going to help matters at all. He relit the pipe, then looked Hardy in the eye.

"Isn't it possible that you are recreating for yourself what you wrote in that log?"

The Professor's eyes bored angrily into him, and Frank felt the trust slipping away. "I didn't create that oil slick" was all he said. He got up, left his teacup, and went to the door. He turned at the last moment and half smiled. "Tell you one thing, Commander. You wanted to find out what happened in 1944—I think you're going to find out firsthand."

"Not if Byrnes turns us around."

"Don't think he'll find *that* too easy."

Hardy departed, his limp echoing down the deck. Frank was conscious that the older man had echoed his own words to Byrnes. Perhaps they both suspected the same thing: The *Candlefish* was in the grip of some force bent on fulfilling their project. Or . . . or could they themselves be in the grip of the submarine . . . ?

Frank didn't want to believe that the submarine was acting independently, but if he accepted Hardy's explanations and theories, it all fell into place.

But that was impossible.

The project was directed at finding out *how* the submarine had come back. Hardy insisted on knowing *why*—not how. Byrnes wanted to fall back on the tactics of Basquine and Bates: find a scapegoat; blame everything on him. That was the ignorant approach.

Yet there was the reality of it—these things *were* happening! Nobody was imagining them.

As Cassidy had said: "We sank *something*."

Well, what?

Frank rose and headed toward his quarters, intending to reread Jack Hardy's log. Carefully.

* * *

Frank spent most of his eight off-duty hours stretched out on his bunk with the curtain pulled closed, reading and rereading Hardy's log by flashlight. On every page he found something to disturb him anew. For there was no way around it: Down to incredibly tiny details, they were duplicating the patrol of 1944. He recalled vividly Hardy's actions on those last days in November, when he had been carefully checking the quartermaster's log against his own, remarking on the similarities: leaking valves, busted gaskets, the battery connector cables . . . Things that he had shrugged off when Hardy had first brought them to his attention now seemed to take on more meaning. Then there was the airplane sighting—or "hearing"— last night. That certainly jibed with the log. It had happened exactly the same way thirty years ago, and it was Hardy who heard it then, too. Of course, that could be explained: Both times he was hearing things. The lookouts didn't support him, did they?

". . . Sorry, I don't know *what* I heard . . ."

But then there was December 2nd, 1944 and 1974. The sinking of a suspected Japanese submarine. They had been able to verify the kill thirty years ago, but they never knew exactly what they had killed. And the same thing had happened this morning. Too close. Too much of a coincidence.

It couldn't be explained away. They were caught in something, and they were going to have to find a way of dealing with it. Frank put the log down and lay still.

He raised his arms over his head and stretched, becoming conscious of the sweat soaking his blouse. He felt sticky and uncomfortable. Funny—he had always felt that way reading Hardy's log. There was something inherently creepy about it. Now, he could understand why—they were living it.

He swung his legs off the bunk and listened to the

sounds from the sub's interior. The motors ran silent; they were still cruising at periscope depth. He could hear the *ping* of the sonar: Byrnes must be keeping Nadel glued to that headset. Then there was Byrnes's voice, coming from his cabin a few feet up the corridor, growling at the mess steward bringing him his supper. Frank checked his watch: It was 1730.

He got up and went to his locker, pulling off his shirt and rolling it into a ball. He swung the locker open and threw the shirt in, reaching for his only fresh one. He smoothed out the starch and struggled into the sleeves, gazing at the worn Xerox copy of Hardy's original log, the handwritten copy the Professor had first turned over to him. He pulled it out and thumbed through it, checking December 2nd to be sure that the information was the same. It was; no one had made a typo. He couldn't attribute these hair-raising similarities to the overworked imagination of some irresponsible Navy secretary. It was all there in Hardy's precise handwriting. He tossed the log back into the locker and buttoned the shirt as he gazed at Captain Basquine's original day-to-day log, which he had brought along for . . . for what? Comfort? What good was it? Bloody thing was as blank as a dead man's face. He pulled it out and thumbed through it in disgust—and he was immediately sorry that he had. The two pages he was looking at were full of Basquine's hasty scrawl. And the date? His eyes went to the top of the page.

November 29th, 1944.

That wasn't right. It couldn't be. He remembered clearly the first time he had opened the log, the morning he had found it stashed away in the Captain's desk. And how he had shown it to Hardy the night they had drinks in the Clean Sweep. The blank pages had run from the opening notation on November 21st to the

date of the submarine's loss, December 11th. Blank—
all blank.

And now? He turned the pages, one after another.
They were all filled solid. Scratchy blue ink—Captain
Basquine's uncooperative old fountain pen, his familiar
chicken-track scrawl, from November 21st on . . .

Even the date of sailing itself. The first date, November 21st, had carried only the notation *"0800. Underway from Pearl, proceeding under orders to general
area Kuriles, Pacific."* Now the entire page was filled in
with details that matched every move Frank remembered from that first day when the sub had left Pearl
under Byrnes's command. There wasn't a single point
missing! Only those little things that a captain wouldn't
bother to record. But Basquine was meticulous—hadn't
Hardy said so?

Basquine? What was he thinking? How could
Basquine have filled in this log?

He went further, page after page, standing in front
of the open locker, more sweat pouring from his armpits, soiling his only other fresh shirt. He stared at the
details as they cropped up: December 1st—yesterday—the sub had refused to surface until exactly
twenty hundred hours—that was Hardy's view. And
here in the Captain's log? No mention of any problem
at all. Just the notation: *"Surfaced 2000. Heavy fog.
Proceeding on course 272 at one-third speed."* That
seemed to match last night as Frank remembered it.
But wasn't something missing?

Of course!

The escort. There was no mention of the escort. He
thumbed back to November 21st and checked it
through day by day, incredulity growing by the second.
He swallowed hard. There was no mention of an escort

destroyer anywhere in these pages. In these new, fresh pages.

December 2nd. Early in the morning before submerging time. *"Lt. Hardy reported hearing planes off to the north. Lookouts unable to confirm. No visual, due to heavy concentration of fog."*

It was an accurate record of the 1944 patrol. Up to date. It wasn't their patrol at all—not today's—not 1974's. It was the Captain's version of exactly how it really was back then. He turned the page—and stopped.

December 2nd was the last entry. Frank stared at the next blank page and felt nausea threatening him. It was up to date, all right. Exactly up to date and no more. Up to the minute was more like it. Basquine's writing accurately described the sonar tracking of an unidentified target, presumed to be a Japanese submarine, the careful cat-and-mouse game, the setting up of the shot from two hundred feet below the surface, firing—the direct hit! Surfacing in a sea of debris and oil, the inability to determine precisely what they had hit, but the satisfaction that whatever had been sneaking around up there had deserved it. And Frank sensed meaning between the lines: Basquine's personal contentment over the kill. He knew why, too. It was the first kill of the patrol. The first in months. It must have overjoyed him. Quite a contrast to Louis F. Byrnes and his nervous panic.

That was the end of the log for the moment. He stared at the rest of the blank page and wondered when it would be filled in, and who was doing it. He began to suspect Hardy. His thumb brushed the ink on the entry under December 2nd as he was closing the book, and some of it came off on his skin. He stared at his blue thumb, and this time felt a quiver of terror course through his body. He flung the page open again and rubbed his fingers over it.

He couldn't believe it. The ink smeared. It was fresh, as fresh as if it had just been set down. Impossible. The book had been in his locker all day, buried under his underwear and shirt and Hardy's handwritten log. No one even knew it was there. And he had been lying on his bunk all day. The curtain had been closed, but he could swear no one had been in or out of the stateroom—except perhaps Stigwood . . .

And Stigwood was buried under the covers right now, in the bunk above Frank's, fast asleep. Frank had heard him come in, open his locker, hang up his clothes, slam the locker, then swing up to the bunk. It wasn't Stigwood. It couldn't have been. Besides, he didn't have the brains . . .

Frank pulled Hardy's log out and took two quick steps to his bunk. He spread both logs out on the covers and opened them to November 21. Then he went through, page by page, comparing details and wording, and handwriting . . . Nothing was the same. Hardy's words were the words of a scholar, remembering things as they came back to him, and setting them down as neatly as he could. Basquine wrote in captain's lingo, short and to the point, almost cryptic. And the handwriting was so different—Hardy's precise penmanship against Basquine's ugly scrawl. And Hardy had written in pencil. Of course, that meant nothing. Somewhere he might have gotten hold of Basquine's fountain pen. But when could he have done the writing? And why? It didn't make sense.

Frank had another stroke of curiosity. He flung the pages back to the days prior to November 21st, to Basquine's record of events in port. It was the same handwriting—definitely Basquine's. Whoever was imi-

tating him—presuming someone was—had his handwriting and his word style down pat.

Frank leaned back and stared at the two open logs.
What about the other logs—the ones they were keeping
on this cruise? The quartermaster's log was okay; he
and Hardy had been checking it daily. But Byrnes's
day-to-day log—he wondered what he would find in
that. Again he became conscious of the sweat under his
arms. He felt a need to visit the head. He closed both
logs and wondered what to do. Who should he tell?
Hardy? He didn't feel like confiding in the old man any
more. The only one to tell was Byrnes. And Byrnes
would act to protect the sub. He felt little knives stab-
bing at him, twisting and turning, pulling his guts out.
He was not in control any more, and he resented it,
feared it, and generally could not cope with it. Who
was in control?

Whoever had written those entries in the log, obviously.

There was only one solution, and Frank knew it
even as he got up and stashed both logs carefully in the
bottom of his locker, under his shorts, his socks, his
Devil's Triangle maps and charts and reports, his dirty
shirt . . . He pulled down the padlock he hadn't found
necessary before and opened it. He closed the locker
and snapped the lock shut, then put both keys on his
key ring and snapped that to a belt loop. From now on
he would jingle when he walked, but he would feel better.

That should put an end to the mysterious self-writing
log. He smiled. He felt the pain in his groin again, and
knew he had only seconds to reach the toilet. He
snatched up the Xerox copy of Hardy's log that he had
been reading all day, and took it to the head with him.
As he stood poised over the urinal, he read ahead. De-

cember 3rd. It looked to be quite an eventful day, if everything went according to the account. Also looked to
be dangerous. Something unexpected, if they weren't
prepared for it. He decided from this point on to keep
his mouth shut and let events take their course. They
probably would anyway. So why interfere? The only
way to stay on top of this thing was to ride it out and
see where it would take him. He stared at the green
bulkhead and made a silent announcement to it, a
smile playing across his lips: "Bring it on, sport. All
of it. I'm with you."

CHAPTER 15

December 2, 1974

2200 hours.

The gray-black hull of the *Candlefish* plunged through the sea, the whine of her diesels shattering the stillness of the Pacific night. An occasional wave, larger than the rest, rolled over her bow and raced the length of her forward deck, splashing against the base of the conning tower, only to fall back and pour through the strakes, then cascade down the flanks of her hull, back into the ocean. The submarine glistened with a just-washed sheen. Clusters of foam, trapped in the ridges of her soaked planking, reflected the weak light of a waning moon.

Ed Frank huddled deeper in his jacket, trying to ward off the damp, numbing chill that only oceans can bring. His sinuses were acting up. He slipped a hand out of his pocket and gently explored his face. The pain was a dull, throbbing ache under his cheekbones. He blew into a cupped palm and was grateful for the momentary warmth. He thought about finding Dankworth when he came off watch; the pharmacist's mate would have some pills. He looked up. The wind, which had made everyone on the bridge uncomfortable, was finally dying down.

The scrape of shoe leather on metal, from one of the lookouts up on the periscope shearwater, reminded him of the five other men who were suffering with him. He glanced at Byrnes out of the corner of his eye. The Captain, aware of his movement, lowered his binoculars and turned to the men perched above him.

"Anything on the escort?"

Three mumbled "No, sirs" answered his question. For the umpteenth time since they had come to the surface, he depressed the intercom switch and listened as Scopes reported, "Still no contact, sir."

His face a blank mask, Byrnes released the switch, but the metallic click had the sound of finality about it.

On the starboard side of the bridge, Hardy's elbows were hooked over the top of the coaming, giving his binoculars a rock-solid support. He had held that position for quite a while, staring off to the northwest, and now his muscles were crying out for relief. Grudgingly he dropped his arms, stretched, and rolled his head, shaking the cramped feeling out of his upper body. His bad leg throbbed with pain.

His eyes met Frank's, and he shivered. "Cold," he said.

Frank nodded. "And then some."

"I think we can change that." Byrnes smiled thinly at both of them. "We're going to head for warmer waters, Mr. Frank." He was still smiling as he continued, "The party's over. I have decided to terminate— as of right now. We're going back to Pearl."

Frank knew he had to stall Byrnes until the attack. Just one look at those planes blitzing in on their first pass would be enough to convince even Byrnes that a turnaround at this point was sheer folly.

"Mr. Frank, did you hear me? Do you have an opinion?"

As if he cared, thought Frank, but he ventured it anyway. "It's only a matter of time until we catch up with the *Frankland,* sir, or vice versa." He was fighting for time.

"Oh, really?" Byrnes was way ahead of Frank. "Well, we'll see if we can find them—on our way back to Pearl. Do I make myself clear?"

Frank looked to Hardy for some support, but the Professor was once again draped over the starboard coaming, scanning the northwest skies and oblivious to the tension building behind him.

"Bridge, this is radar. Aircraft contact, bearing zero-three-five relative. Thirteen thousand yards and closing fast."

The voice, coming through the bridge speaker, was flat and emotionless. Byrnes, along with everyone else, swung his glasses up, then hesitated. Angrily he jabbed at the intercom. "Did you say aircraft, Scopes?"

"Confirming, sir," the radar man called back. "Two of 'em. Still closing. Range now twelve thousand yards."

Frank felt his adrenalin pumping as his eyes tried to pierce the night sky. He sensed Hardy's excitement too. Then he noticed that they were looking in the same general area Hardy had been watching all along.

"You'll see only one come in on the first run." Frank barely heard the Professor's mumbled statement.

"What was that?"

Hardy straightened out of his crouched position and brushed past Frank. "We'd better get under, Captain."

Byrnes ignored him for a moment, his eyes glued to his binoculars, trying to find whatever Scopes had picked up. Slowly he lowered his glasses and looked at Hardy. "Do what?" he said.

"I said, I think we better dive. And fast!"

Byrnes opened his mouth to deliver a scorching reply, then stopped. He cocked his head, listening. Over the whine of the diesels they heard the faint droning of motors.

"Seven thousand yards and still closing." At least Scopes knew where they were.

Six pairs of binoculars searched the night sky, trying to pick up the planes. The droning sound had changed pitch, becoming more of a snarl as the unseen aircraft bore down on them.

"They sure don't sound like jets . . ." It was one of the lookouts voicing an opinion.

Frank's glasses picked up the moving blue-white flicker that could be the exhaust flame of a piston-driven aircraft. He tracked it curving in toward them, lining up on the bow of the submarine. The powerful beat of the straining engine seemed to be directly over-head.

The flare lit up the submarine with the brightness of a noonday sun. Everyone was blinded by the dazzling glare. Shielding his eyes, Frank recovered first. He looked up, careful not to stare at the slowly settling, swinging light.

"What the hell—" Starkly outlined in the unnatural illumination, Byrnes was braced against the TBT.

"This time you'll *have* to believe me!" Hardy snarled, his beard glinting silvery-white.

Frank gave up trying to locate the high plane, the one that had dropped the flare. The other one was rac-ing toward them, low to the water and head-on. The main pontoon and the two smaller ones, one on the tip of each wing, were clearly visible. As he watched, the leading edge of both wings twinkled. Geyser spouts erupted in the water just forward of the sub's bow.

"Down!" Hardy roared, tackling Byrnes away from the TBT and flinging him to the deck.

In the brief second before Frank ducked, he saw the

line of geysers walk up to the bow. A terrific weight slammed into him, and he found himself being pressed against the deck plates in a tangle of arms and legs. The lookouts had leaped from their perches. One of them was all over Frank, swearing a blue streak. Over the yammering stutter of the guns Frank heard a series of metallic clunks, like hail pelting a roof. Chipped paint flew as a row of jagged holes blossomed on the after part of the bridge. Frank forced himself to his knees and got a glimpse as the plane flashed by. It was brownish-green with a bright red circle on the fuselage.

"Japs! They're Japs!" he hollered. His eyes were riveted on the plane as it slewed around for another pass.

"Watch out for the other one!" Hardy struggled to his feet and desperately searched the sky. The twin blasts of the diving alarm were almost lost in the pounding scream as the second plane started its attack.

"Clear the bridge! Dive! Dive!" Byrnes, his face contorted with pain, tried to stand. His right leg wouldn't support him. His trouser leg was turning red, the stain moving downward to pool around his shoe.

Frank lunged for the Captain, pushing Hardy back toward the hatch. The lookouts were already clear of the bridge. As the sound of the diesels stopped, Frank waved Hardy below and grabbed Byrnes under the arms, attempting to drag him. It was going to be close; the plane was boring in, growing larger by the second. When he sensed Hardy had cleared the hatch, he jerked the wounded Skipper upright. The boat shuddered—he knew what that was. Below they were opening the vents, taking in the water that would get them away from the death rocketing in for the kill.

Byrnes, trying to get his balance, staggered and lunged for the hatch lid, throwing Frank off-balance.

Frank hit the side of the bridge and slid to the deck.
The hammering started again. Byrnes, clutching the
hatch, was lifted and thrown, spinning violently. His
body slammed into the side of the bridge, slid all the
way aft to the cigarette deck, and crumpled to a stop
against the railing. Frank scrambled to his feet and
came around, then stopped, horrified. Blood welled up
out of three fist-sized holes in the Captain's back.

The flare, almost down to the water, illuminated the
plane as it roared by; the cockpit canopy glistened in
the fading light. Frank recognized the plane; he
remembered pictures of it: the Japanese float-zero.
With a last fleeting look at the Captain's body, he
dropped down the hatch into the conning tower.

Roybell, at the hydraulic manifold in the control
room, watched the indicator light change from red to
green as the hatch was closed. "Green board!" he reported. Quickly he opened the bow buoyancy tank and
the negative flood. The boat, heavy with water, slipped
below the surface, seeking the safety of the deep. The
operator on the high-pressure air manifold signaled
Stigwood, who called up the well, "Pressure in the
boat!"

Standing at the foot of the bridge ladder, Frank
heard Stigwood's voice from below. He became aware
of the men in the conning tower staring at him: Dorriss, Adler, Colby the talker, the helmsman, Hardy
. . . . Their faces were colorless, drawn taut by tension.

"Take us down fast," he called out. "Level off at two
hundred feet."

Stigwood's "Two hundred feet, aye" resounded up
the hatchwell.

Frank punched all the keys on the battle phone. "All
compartments report damage."

Colby spoke into his mouthpiece, and the various reports filtered in. No casualties, only small leaks caused by armor-piercing shells, and these were already being plugged up. Any other damage would have to wait for a closer inspection.

"Where's the Skipper?" Adler, standing alongside Hardy, had trouble masking the quiver in his voice.

"He's dead." Frank was surprised at his own composure. In the silence he heard a series of muted orders from the control room. The tilt of the deck changed as the submarine leveled off. No one in the conning tower spoke.

"Two hundred feet, sir."

Frank stared down at Stigwood's upturned face, sensing the unasked questions racing through the diving officer's mind. "Very well," he said. Slowly the enormity of what was happening sank in. The calmness he had felt started to slip away. He watched dumbly as Stigwood climbed the ladder and scanned the silent, crowded compartment.

"What the hell's going on?"

Frank ignored Stigwood. Something wet had hit his hand. His eyes traveled to the inner gasket of the conning-tower hatch. In the half light he could just make out three red streaks. Blood. He watched another drop detach itself and fall to the deck. Everyone was gazing up at the hatch. Hardy brushed past Adler's frozen form and stood in the center of the conning tower, glancing up to see for himself.

The words were spoken quietly, but the effect was electric.

"Welcome to World War Two," Hardy said.

PART IV

CHAPTER 16

December 2

They wasted about a half-hour submerged at two hundred feet, rigged for silent running, sitting motionless with all engines off. Confusion rippled through the boat. Crewmen waited anxiously at their posts for some word from the Captain. What was it all about? Were they under attack? No one had ordered battle stations—there was no diversive action taken. They just sat. Silent.

In the conning tower, Ed Frank stood with his back against the port bulkhead, his eyes fixed on the closed hatch. The blood on the steel decking had long since been diluted and washed away.

Hardy stood near the hatchwell, his hand clutching the overhead lanyard. He watched Frank, a grim expression etched into his face, his beard still dripping from the spray chopped up by the zeroes' machine-gun fire. In the first few minutes after the *Candlefish* had made her crash dive, Frank had turned to Hardy and asked quietly, "If they were so busy with machine guns, that would mean they weren't armed with bombs, right?"

Hardy had been slow to respond. "You never assume anything like that."

"I'm going to have to. We've got a skipper up there. We can't leave him."

Hardy didn't say another word, because he knew they were safe. According to the log and his memory, the zeroes would only make three sweeps with cannon-fire, then depart. They could sit here in safety all day if they wanted, but that wasn't what the log called for. He remembered the attack in 1944: Basquine caught completely by surprise on the bridge—they hadn't even heard the planes until it was too late. Then the sputter of the guns. But not one bullet had hit the sub; Basquine had crash-dived in seconds and hauled the submarine off to the south in one fat hurry.

That's where 1944 and the present parted company. Thirty years ago there had been no casualties. Hardy felt a fluttering commotion behind his rib cage, and then a cold sweat broke out on his forehead. No casualties thirty years ago—then why had they suffered one today?

And what might happen if they stayed here where their position was known? Would someone else come to get them? More planes? Destroyers? They should probably get out of the area, but he wasn't about to broach the subject with Frank. If Frank wanted to surface again, to search for Byrnes, let him.

Frank was concerned about the possibility of the planes having radioed their position to waiting destroyers—assuming that Hardy really was correct and they were smack in the middle of the war in the Pacific. If that were true, then it was stupid to stand around and wait. He would give it another half-hour and no more; then they would surface and find out what had happened to Byrnes.

"Stand by to surface!"

Throughout the boat the crew reacted to the unfamiliar voice, raising themselves at their posts slowly, looking at each other. Clampett was the first to voice the confusion: "Was that the skipper?"

The voice rang out again, firm and harsh. This time the men sprang into action.

They broached at a fifteen-degree angle. Hardy broke the conning-tower hatch and scrambled to the bridge. Frank was right behind him. There was no sign of Byrnes. They both hustled to the afterdeck and combed the entire superstructure with their eyes, hearts pounding, hoping for some sign. Frank grabbed a pair of binoculars from Lieutenant Dorriss and searched the seas for a bobbing bundle that might be the Skipper. There was nothing.

"Lookouts!" Dorriss yelled.

The lookouts combed the water from their upper perches and, one by one, shook their heads. Frank walked heavily around the conning tower, pausing for a moment to stare at the neat pattern of bullet holes cutting a slash right through the *Candlefish*'s number, 284, as if crossing it off.

More holes were found in the steel plate decking. Even the strakes, the wood planking forward and aft, were torn up. But nowhere, not anywhere, was there a trace of what had become of Louis Byrnes. Not a scrap of clothing, not a spot of blood.

It was as if he had never existed.

Frank and Hardy both risked as much time as they could inspecting the damage, not for the sake of repairs but to let reality sink in. Here they were in the middle of the Pacific, in the middle of a shooting war, virtually defenseless. Or were they? They had the torpedoes, armed and ready. They carried armament, the standard equipment on all fleet boats of the time: the big deck gun aft of the cigarette deck, the machine guns stored below, pistols and grenades in the control-room weapons locker. And they had a crew! They weren't defenseless at all—just out of time and out of place.

Frank walked to the bridge rail and looked over into the forward machine-gun position, at the gunner's chair and the feeder's stirrups. Could this crew fight, if it became necessary? If! Christ, who was he kidding? It was mandatory! They were going to fight. They had no choice in the matter. Unless . . . unless he turned the boat around and took them home. Could he do that—now? He wondered if it was still possible. He looked at his hands—did he have any control at all over this boat? Or was it really on a set pattern?

Frank turned slowly and looked at Dorriss, who had retrieved his binoculars and was sweeping the seas with them. Dorriss, the captain's hand-picked Exec, competent and efficient, just like Byrnes himself, but without Byrnes's air of authority. Still, his quiet intensity and reputation for fairness had put him on a decent footing with the crew. He had been Byrnes's buffer. Byrnes had maintained the stiff and formal aloofness; Dorriss had been warm and pleasant with everyone. A good combination. Frank began to wonder how he could make it work for himself. He was already positive of one thing: He was about to assume undisputed command of the *Candlefish*.

He caught Jack Hardy looking at him, frowning. Hardy met the look and asked, "What are you going to do?"

There it was—even Hardy was throwing it to him, laying it right in his lap.

Frank straightened and watched all eyes turn to him, following the Professor's lead. "Dive," he said, and hit the alarm.

They scrambled below, and within one minute they had dropped down to periscope depth. Frank had Dorriss pull out the charts and show him their position and course. He thought for a moment about attempting to turn back, then shook his head at no one in particular. "Keep her on this heading."

"Are you taking over, sir?" asked Dorriss.

"Yes."

"Hadn't you better make some announcement to the crew, sir?"

Frank nodded. He reached for the intercom. "This is Lieutenant Commander Frank. We have had an accident. I am sorry to report that Captain Byrnes has been lost. And we have been unable to recover his body. I am assuming command of the *Candlefish*."

His hand left the switch. Hardy grabbed his arm. "You better tell them the rest. How it happened."

Frank looked at him grimly. "I'm not out to scare them."

"You've already done that."

Frank sighed. Reluctantly he punched the switch again, and his voice echoed in every compartment of the boat. "It's not going to be easy for most of you to understand what I am about to tell you. Those of you who do understand it will not want to accept it. But it will be for the general good if you receive what I say with calm, controlled objectivity." He paused and glanced at Hardy. "At twenty-two hundred hours tonight, the *Candlefish* came under surprise air attack. We took heavy machine-gun fire on two successive sweeps from a pair of planes that looked to be Japanese float-zeroes of World War Two vintage."

The listeners fore and aft had stopped what they were doing. All eyes were fixed on the crackling loud-speakers.

"We are not sure who was responsible for the attack or why. Guesswork on the part of any member of this crew will not be appreciated." He stopped and waited.

In the crew's mess, Cookie wiped his hands on his apron and pressed the intercom. "Sir . . . what happened to Captain Byrnes?"

Frank replied quickly. "Captain Byrnes was on the bridge. He was hit by a burst of fire and went down. He did not make it to the hatch in time for the dive. We have searched the area and there is no trace of his body. That is all." He choked on the last words, and knew he could not go on.

He closed the switch again and looked up at Hardy. The old man's face was closer now, still burning with insistence.

"Now what?"

"Tell them all the facts," said Hardy.

"I just did."

"No. All of them."

Frank knew what he meant. Hardy wanted him to level with the crew, bring them in on the whole incredible story. It was just what Byrnes had tried to stop him from doing. "You're responsible," he had said, "I don't want him alarming the crew." Well, it was too late now. And maybe the moment called for complete candor.

Again he pressed the intercom. "There are a few more facts you should all be aware of. This voyage appears to have taken a turn that no one expected or could have foreseen. We are in some kind of situation that for the moment is unclear. When we get it sorted out, we will probably head for home." Frank paused—that should calm everyone. "We are alone out here. I mean alone. We have lost all contact with our escort. We don't know why, we don't know how, we don't know what it all means. It's going to require patience and trust. I'm asking you for that."

He paused again and looked at Hardy. The Professor nodded agreement. Frank went on, "There will be a meeting of all officers in the wardroom at twenty-three fifteen hours. That is all."

He turned immediately, not giving Hardy the chance for another objection. "Mr. Dorriss."

"Yes, sir?"

"You will resume your duties as executive officer. Mr. Hardy, you will resume duties as navigation officer." He stepped to the well and called below, "Mr. Stigwood!"

"Yes, sir!"

"You will take over the con!" Stigwood shot up the ladder. "Maintain course three-five-zero until further notice. Quartermaster!"

"Yes, sir?"

"Detail someone to clean out the Captain's cabin. I'll have to move in there tonight."

The quartermaster paused. Everyone was silent. Then the quartermaster nodded. "Aye, aye, sir."

Hardy caught him at the well, as he was halfway down the ladder. The old man bent over and looked him right in the eye. "You know, we're down to eighty-four men now."

"So?"

"We match the original crew."

Frank said nothing, just studied the grim smile on Hardy's face and wondered if the old man was enjoying this. He dropped into the control room and looked over his new domain.

The men around Cassidy stood motionless as the hiss from the overhead speakers was abruptly silenced. They stared into space, unaware of what stood in their direct line of sight.

To Cassidy they were blank faces; he had no idea what was going on behind any of them. He watched Brownhaver sit down on the engine casing and shake his head in disbelief.

If this was any indication of how the rest of the crew was taking the news, then it looked to Cassidy as if the dog days were definitely over.

Cassidy came out of the after head wiping his hands on a paper towel. He chucked it into a refuse can and stepped into the crew's quarters, smoothing down his hair, checking his watch to see how much time he had before the officers' meeting. He wanted to get back to his station to pick up a pipe. He paused at the hatch as his ears picked up a comment from Nadel, the sonar operator, who was off duty, sacked out on his bunk.

"Personally, I'd like to go back and give those fuckers hell."

Cassidy stared at the face of the pudgy little man. Nadel was not usually a vindictive man, at least he hadn't proven to be so on this patrol. Cassidy automatically made a long sweep around the bunks and saw the same resentment and indignation in other eyes. It seemed logical: Their Captain had just been cut down by the enemy and they wanted revenge. But who was the enemy? Cassidy shook his head, as if he could rattle the cobwebs loose. He just wasn't sure . . . of anything. Except the meeting. He had to get to the meeting.

Cassidy stopped at main engine number two and opened his pipe cabinet. He drew out the Barling and filled it. Googles and Brownhaver appeared at his side.

"Listen, Hopalong," said Googles, "just how much do you trust this guy Frank?"

"What?"

"Does he know what he's doing?"

Cassidy clamped the pipe between his teeth and fumbled for a match.

Googles went on, "I hope he does, 'cause none of us have any inclination to die out here."

"Nobody's going to die," said Cassidy. Brownhaver passed him a match. Cassidy eyed them both through the smoke. "Nobody. Is my word good enough for you?"

"Tell it to the captain we just lost," said Brownhaver.

Both men turned and went back to their business. Frank was going to have to become one hell of a diplomat, and Cassidy had not yet seen anything in his nature that would qualify him for that title.

He went all the way forward and entered officers' country, still feeling far out of place, and stepped into the wardroom. They were all there, ranged around the table, working on steaming mugs of coffee: Dorriss, Stigwood, the two juniors Danby and Adler, Vogel, Roybell, Hardy, and Ed Frank. Cassidy took the one empty seat and scrutinized the new captain. The same short body with the same elongated features, the same dark hair brushed back, but something new . . . a look of firm determination cemented into the eyes.

Frank studied the faces before him. They all seemed to reflect the same fearful uncertainty. He and Jack Hardy were the only ones who had any definite idea of where they were going and what they would encounter. And the Professor was sitting on his right, very still, arms folded across his chest, his chin sunk down and his beard flattened out. Damn him! thought Frank. He's hoping I'll break, so he can take over. And what would he do? Turn us around?

The eyes of his officers were unsure, questioning. There was no visible sign of inner terror, but he felt it pervading the room. And, strangely, it filled him with a sense of power. At last he had what he had wanted all along: complete control.

He caught the tiny smile etched across Jack Hardy's beard, the slash in that gray thatch of fur, and the eyes boring into his. He squirmed. How the hell did Hardy know what was going through his head?

"Gentlemen," he began, and stopped. Their faces swung up in unison, and he saw immediately what they were expecting him to say: "This has gone too far. We're going home now, before anyone else gets killed." If he said that, they would probably clap him on the back, splice the main brace, and start to sing! But he couldn't do it; there was too much at stake. He warmed up every tactful bone in his body and began again.

"It's very tough losing a captain. Even one we— Probably none of us knew him that well. We didn't serve enough time under him . . . but I think we all recognize a competent officer when we see one . . ." Frank found it hard to drag the words out, because he had found Byrnes so difficult. "He was a conscientious seaman, and he did what he felt was best . . . for all of us."

He looked around to see if he was coming across. The faces had gone blank.

"We all know the hazards of submarine duty. This one was unforeseen."

He swallowed on the last word and knew immediately it was a lie. It wasn't unforeseen at all. He had read the log. He had known all along what was coming, and he hadn't given poor Byrnes sufficient warning. Of course, Byrnes knew the log too; the difference was, he had never believed it. Besides, there was nothing in the log about a casualty. Frank's mind raced. It came to him after a moment of utter silence. He was the

Captain now, the focus of attention. He couldn't wait for them to feel; he had to show them *what* to feel.

But the truth was, he felt nothing. Nothing for Louis Byrnes and nothing for these men. He cared only about one thing: the expedition and what it could accomplish.

He was suddenly terribly frightened. Could they see through him? Were they sharp enough to sense when he was lying, when he was glossing things over? He began to see the tactics he would have to use. Toughness, firmness, conviction. If necessary, he had to make these men fear him—at least enough to follow him.

"Byrnes is gone," he said simply, "and we're going to pick up the pieces. We all know the mission and what has to be done to make it come off. We have to press on."

He saw Dorriss fidget in his seat. If anyone had been a close friend to Byrnes on this voyage, it was Dorriss, the executive officer. Frank addressed himself to the skinny lieutenant:

"Look, we've been through a lot already but there's more to come. Things were getting rough a few days ago and Byrnes wanted to turn back; I insisted we press on. I still do! I don't believe it is in the best interests of the Navy to abandon it now—not when we have a chance to go through something no one before us has ever gone through."

"Excuse me, sir," said Dorriss, "that's all fine for you. But maybe we don't feel the same way."

The most junior officer, Adler, stood up and clutched the edge of the table. "You know as well as we do, sir, we should turn back."

"I wish it were that easy. Even if we turn back, we don't know what we're going to be up against. We have to face the fact that we are no longer in 1974."

He drew silent stares.

"There really is no way out of this except to see it through to the end. I'm going to need your help for that. You're going to have to work *with* me, not against me."

He saw eyes lowering, men thinking it out, realizing he probably spoke the truth. Frank licked his lips.

"I know you're all loyal," he said, "to the Navy, to whatever ship and whatever captain you serve. I am not going to make excessive demands on that loyalty. But I'm asking for your help."

Dorriss stood up. "May I suggest, sir, that we radio Pearl for instructions?"

Heads turned. That seemed to be a rational and constructive idea. Frank shot it down abruptly. "What message would we send? *'Candlefish* is in trouble—caught in a possible time-warp'?"

"Why not?" asked Dorriss.

"If this is no longer 1974, who is going to receive it?"

"ComSubPac."

"If it's 1944 where we are, it's probably 1944 there as well," said Frank.

"We should try."

"Well, what are you going to say? We lost Captain Byrnes? They'll signal right back, 'Who the hell is Byrnes? Who are you?' "

"Not if we sign it with the other guy's—what's his name?"

"Basquine," Hardy offered helpfully.

"Right!" said Dorriss triumphantly.

Frank glared at Hardy, then jumped on Dorriss. "Tell me what you're going to put in the message."

"Ask for an escort back to port. Specify unusual circumstances."

Frank shook his head. "Impossible."

"Why?" Dorriss demanded, his eyes flashing.

"Because if there is anything suspect about that message, they are liable to think it was sent by the enemy. They will know our position, and they'll come after us with everything they've got. Or they'll ignore us . . . completely. The answer is no. We better maintain radio silence."

Hardy unfolded his arms and spoke up. "That leaves us with only one course of action. The present one. Right?" Frank nodded. "Then what about tomorrow night?"

"What about it?"

"Well . . ." He stood up. "According to my log, on the night of December third we intercepted a Japanese convoy at about twenty-one hundred hours. What are we going to do about that?"

Slowly, one by one, the men leaned back and let that one sink in.

Frank thought it over a while and then snapped out, "Attack 'em." Everyone looked up, so he qualified it. "If we have to."

There was no response.

Frank looked straight at Vogel, the forward torpedo officer. "What about that?"

"Well, sir." Vogel cleared his throat. "We're sure armed for it."

"What do you think about it?"

Vogel worked hard to get the frog out of his throat. "I think . . . it might be a fine way of . . . getting even for Captain Byrnes, sir."

It was probably the wisest remark made all day, and it had a revitalizing effect. Frank sensed the tension easing in the room. Now they had a scapegoat. The reasoning was a little off-center, but it seemed to click with everybody. Adler and Danby mumbled something to each other and nodded. Dorriss sat back and reflected deeply. Stigwood lit a cigarette and gazed into the smoke. Roybell sat back and nodded to himself.

Hardy's eyes rose grimly and locked onto Cassidy's across the table. Cassidy was worried.

"All right, then," said Frank, "if we're going to be called upon to fight, we better get ready. I want every watch to drill battle alert. I want it constant and relentless. Let every man aboard know we are in a potentially dangerous situation."

"Potentially, hell," said Cassidy.

"We're sitting on a powder keg, then!" Frank folded his notes and stuffed them into a back pocket. He felt in control again. "Anybody gives you any questions about where we're going or what we're doing or why—tell them we're at war! Tell them the truth. We don't know how we got here, but we're stuck, and from now on they're to concentrate on manning battle stations. Keep it on their *minds!*"

Hardy stood up and eyed him suspiciously. "Do you really mean to attack?"

"I mean to do whatever I have to."

"To accomplish what?"

"To follow your goddamned log."

Hardy went away without offering any reassurance, and that left Frank momentarily in doubt again. As usual, Hardy was providing no support.

Cassidy was last to leave. He turned in the doorway, relit his Barling, and cast an uncertain smile at Frank. "If it'll help, sir, I'll sort of pass the word to the crew."

"What word?"

"That maybe you do know what you're doing. I think they'd like to feel that. They'll sleep easier. Even if it isn't true."

Frank smiled. "Cassidy, you're pretty perceptive for a fucking yardbird."

"To the crack of doom, Skipper."

Cassidy whirled and hustled off. Frank blinked at the last remark and decided to take it in the light vein in which it was delivered. Relief surged through him. There was an extra bounce in his step as he went through control and up to the conning tower.

December 3

Frank spent several hours personally conducting dive drills from the bridge, attempting to reduce the amount of time it would take to get the sub under and attack-ready. It didn't seem to do much good. One day of training wasn't enough; the best he could get was nineteen seconds from sounding the alarm to shears awash. He didn't want to worry anyone, so he gave a short pep talk over the intercom. He expressed the hope that the "enemy" was operating on the same time clock, that the convoy would make its appearance at exactly 2100 hours, so they would be ready for it. He told them, "We have the advantage. We know what to expect, thanks to Hardy's log; we can predict what's going to happen. We won't be taken by surprise again."

Of course, the same problem kept nagging at him. If they followed the log and arrived safely at Latitude 30° on the 11th of December, just how safe would they be? There the log ended. Would this cruise end there too? His mind raced for an answer while he read portions of the log to the crew, letting them know exactly what they were in for. He finished with a carefully worded statement: "We will reach our objective with an eye-opening war record behind us. When we get there, let's *keep* our eyes open. We must make this work to our advantage—if we're to come through it alive."

No slipups—that was the important thing. He ordered the duty officer of each watch to familiarize himself with the log for the current day, make notes, and delegate men to follow prescribed courses of action.

By 1800, the men were breathing easier, gradually breaking out of their melancholy and shifting into a state of excitement. They were beginning to see the whole voyage from the positive points of view: getting even for Byrnes, living through World War Two, something to tell their kids when they got home. Frank was gratified.

The new Captain returned to his old quarters just after supper and went to clean out his locker. He keyed open the padlock and withdrew clothes, shirt and pants, socks and underwear, and piled them into the arms of the steward.

His hand froze when he touched Basquine's log. It had remained locked up in here since last night. Now he would have to take it with him.

As soon as his gear was stashed in the locker in the captain's cabin, Frank found himself opening the log. December 2nd was there, and December 3rd, complete up to the minute. But something in the description of the strafing bothered him. Something was missing. The time of the attack was right, the number of planes, description of the armament, of the damage, the two quick passes before *Candlefish* dived, the rush to get under, surfacing again to inspect the damage. Yet something was missing.

He opened Hardy's log again. The same facts, the same time, planes, number of passes, bullet holes. No casualties, of course. The crew had survived without a single fatality. He felt fine again. It was all there. He closed Hardy's log and consigned it to a cubbyhole. He placed the Captain's day-to-day log in the front of the hinged desk and tipped it shut.

Then he stretched out on the bunk and drifted off to sleep.

"No casualties," he mumbled, and clucked himself a round of congratulations.

At 2000 the *Candlefish* surfaced into the western Pacific twilight. Frank stood with Hardy on the bridge, sweeping the horizon with Byrnes's binoculars. Frank checked his watch and then spoke softly.

"Professor, only forty-five minutes to go."

"I know."

"How does it feel?"

"What?"

"Living through it again."

"Mr. Frank, I think if we sight that convoy we should run like hell."

Frank was silent, measuring Hardy with growing mistrust. "One minute you say 'Follow my log.' The next you say 'Skip it.' Make up your mind, Professor."

Hardy turned and pressed his elbow back on the bridge coaming. "I'm just not sure."

"Well, I am. We're here and we have to make the best of it. We're not going to run like hell. We're going to *shoot* like hell."

"Why?"

Hardy never got an answer. Frank was called below to control by the tracking party so they could plan what was to be done when the convoy showed up.

Hardy went below too, and stepped into the crew's mess with a cup of coffee. The relaxed faces were sporting beards in various stages of growth. There must have been a contest afoot among the men.

Then he noticed other changes in the crew. The men had taken to wearing their t-shirts on duty, instead of their blue Navy fatigues. And the haircuts . . .

Witzgall's sideburns and the curls around Googles's neck were gone. What was going on? The men were starting to look like throwbacks. Maybe the Navy does it to you, he thought. He had crossed to the hatch on his way to the forward engine room when someone in the opposite corner caught his eye. He was tucked into a bench, engrossed in what looked to be one of Jena-vin's old OCS manuals. It was one of the quartermas-ters . . . Lang was his name. Lang? So Lang wanted to get into OCS?

Hardy felt a brief chill but continued aft, curiosity drawing him on. He was conscious of music piped in over the intercom, but he couldn't tell what it was until he entered the crew's quarters, where they had it turned up.

The strains of Glenn Miller's "Moonlight Serenade" filtered over to him, and Hardy thought for a moment someone had found old Rah-Rah Stanhill's record col-lection and had piped it through from the record player in the crew's mess. But no—he heard the sounds of sta-tic and then the shuffle of hash as Giroux sought a bet-ter station. It was the radio. And they were playing Glenn Miller. Nostalgia time at home. Giroux settled on a louder signal, and the men started to hum along to the Harry James version of "You Made Me Love You." More '40s nostalgia. Amazing that these guys knew the songs so well.

The bunks were ranged with off-duty crewmen, asleep, reading, telling jokes, griping. A couple were playing checkers. Hardy's gaze came around to Clam-pett, the torpedoman, the fresh youngster with the natural disdain for anyone over thirty. Yet he was mouthing the words of the song while standing in front of the Ann Sheridan poster with his arms folded across his chest. His pose was terribly familiar. Hardy backed away in shock, positive that he was staring at the reincarnation of Corky Jones. He turned and fled the crew's quarters, stumbling back through the engine room until he found Cassidy.

The Chief was tucked into his bunk over main engine number two. He was fast asleep, a foul-smelling pipe clutched in his gnarled palm. Hardy shook him awake. Cassidy opened one eye, saw who it was, made a face, and closed the eye again.

"Cassidy!" Hardy hissed in his ear.

"Go away." Hardy shook him again. The eye opened, and Cassidy growled. "Wake me when it's World War Three."

He turned over and pulled the covers over his head. Hardy stepped back, confused, unsure what to do, who to tell.

Brownhaver turned up the radio so it drowned out the whine of the two diesels, and Hardy heard Giroux shifting stations again—garbled static, then a faraway transmission caught for a moment, long enough for him to determine exactly what it was. Christmas music—a choir singing "Silent Night." Momentarily relieved, Hardy sank back against the engine stand.

Then the final irony. The voices on the radio—the sweet sacred tones:

> Silent night,
> Holy night.
> All is calm; all is bright.
> Round yon Virgin Mother and Child—

The voices were Japanese, singing in English!

Then another voice cut in, the r's and l's of his speech hopelessly transposed: "Melly Chlistmas, Yanks! It's the rast one you ever see!"

Threats over the radio had never scared Hardy, not even in 1944. So this one didn't frighten him now. But

Brownhaver's response scared him out of his wits. The old oiler looked up at the intercom speaker and let out a Bronx cheer that drowned out the engines, the radio, and the chorus of "Fuck you's!" that came in from the crew's quarters.

Hardy lunged off the bulkhead and blasted through the engine room, swung through the hatch to the crew's quarters, paused to take in the defiant laughing faces, then raced forward.

He had to find Frank.

He burst into the control room, and Stigwood saw his wild look. "Captain's on the bridge . . ."

Hardy shot up the ladder and through the con to the bridge. He whirled and grabbed Frank's arm. "Frank . . . my God, there's something going on here. The crew—"

"What the hell is eating you now?"

Hardy was surprised at Frank's unpleasantness, but he went on. "The crew. They're acting funny. They were listening to the radio, and we got this Japanese broadcast and it was like it didn't even matter to them—they were—"

"Hardy." Frank groaned in exasperation. "What are you talking about?"

"They were acting . . . the way we used to . . . thirty years ago."

"Don't give me that bullshit," Frank snapped, "I've got enough on my mind without you adding to it!"

Hardy dropped Frank's arm, stunned. It was like listening to Byrnes all over again. Was Frank picking up where Byrnes had left off?

It was almost 2100, and the sky had grown terribly dark. If the convoy ever showed, they were going to have a devil of a time spotting it. Have to use infrared on the scopes, Hardy was thinking, letting himself forget the crew for a moment. He had to—they were faced with the imminent appearance of a target—

Scopes's voice came over the speaker, calm and controlled:

"Radar to bridge. Captain . . . we have radar contact, bearing zero-one-one degrees true, zero-eight-one relative. Range, eighty-five hundred yards."

"Captain—smoke on the horizon," a lookout called softly.

Frank stood stiffly, frozen to the spot. He didn't respond. Hardy came around him, stared at his face. It had become colorless and beaded with sweat. Hardy shook him angrily. "Come on, Frank—you've got your goddamned convoy!"

Slowly Frank came to his senses and turned, raising his binoculars. He focused on a roll of black smoke in the distance, dimly visible in the sparse moonlight.

"Be smart for once," Hardy said. "Let's get out of here. Don't tempt it."

Hardy turned and went for the hatch; he was stopped by a cold voice.

"Not so fast."

Hardy looked up at the tight face. But Frank never even got the chance to give his order. They were both thrown off-balance as the submarine picked up speed with a wrenching jerk.

And turned to confront the approaching target.

CHAPTER 17

December 3

The helmsman felt a sudden tug on the wheel. He fought to haul it back and found that he couldn't. It kept pulling hard starboard. Abruptly it popped out of his grasp and steadied itself. "Son of a bitch!" he yelped, and stepped back.

"This is the Captain. What's going on down there?" Frank's voice came over the battle phone.

Dorriss flew to the compass and checked their heading. The sub was coming about to course 030.

"Got a problem, sir," he called up to the bridge.

The senior controllerman in the maneuvering room looked up sharply as the motor-order telegraph rang up ALL AHEAD FULL without a command relayed by the talker.

"I didn't hear an order," said the junior.

"Go wake Hopalong."

On the bridge, Hardy was peering at the first column of black smoke through the vanes of the TBT, the Target Bearing Transmitter. "There's more than one," he said.

Radar called up, "Second radar contact, sir. Bearing twelve degrees true, zero-eight-two relative. Range, eighty-three hundred yards. Both contacts possible *Maru* tankers."

Frank stared off at the horizon and saw more columns of black smoke, one behind another. The convoy was on a southeast heading, spread out flank to flank and staggered. Where were the escorts?

"Captain, this is the conning officer." It was Dorriss, trying to restrain his excitement. "We've changed course; we're on a heading to intercept the radar contacts, sir."

They could feel the engines revving up to top speed. Hardy looked back at the stern vanes: They were churning up a wake as long as a football field, froth-white and glistening in the sparse moonlight. The sub was sure to be spotted. They hit a hard trough; the bow shot up out of the water and crashed down the steep side of the wave. Spray shot up over the forward deck. Every rivet strained in vibration as the *Candlefish* built up surface speed.

Hardy jumped to the phone. "Engine room—what speed are you making down there?"

Cassidy dashed to the maneuvering room in time to see the levers manipulating themselves, then hurried back to his station. He arrived in time for Hardy's call. He checked the indicators, and his eyes shot open. "Bridge, this is Cassidy. I make it eighteen knots."

In control, Roybell whirled to the pit log and watched it climb: 18 . . . 19 . . . 19½ . . .

"We're gonna break the fuckin' speed records!" he yelled up to the bridge.

Hardy turned to see what Frank had decided. But Frank was standing rooted to the spot, staring at the targets hull-down on the horizon, shielding his eyes from the spray. They were making headway in a worsening sea. In a few moments the contacts would creep into open view—and so would the *Candlefish*.

"Frank! What are you gonna do?"

Frank didn't answer. Hardy was suddenly frightened that it might all fall to him. And then the klaxon went off—three resounding blasts.

The lookouts nearly jumped out of their skins.

In the conning tower, the helmsman swore again as the wheel jumped out of his hand. And Dorriss stared up at the bridge and muttered a question: "Dive?"

In the control room, Stigwood instinctively ducked a shoulder as he felt a lever at his side move. When he looked up he saw the diving-plane levers moving free of any guiding hands. He grabbed them and tried to hold them in position.

"Holy shit!" he heard one of the auxiliarymen mutter, and looked around to see other instruments and dials acting independently of any control. Roybell pointed at the Christmas tree as red lights became green, one after another—

Dorriss yelled up the bridge well: "Captain—we're submerging!"

On the bridge, Hardy wasted no more time waiting for Frank. "Lookouts below! Clear the bridge!" As the bows went under, he grabbed Ed Frank and shoved him to the hatch.

Frank stumbled and looked up at Hardy in the moonlight. Everything was going wrong. He was supposed to be in control. Instead, he felt a desperate uncertainty.

Frank dropped below and Hardy followed, pulling the lanyard after him. He reached up to dog the hatch—the wheel spun itself.

The lookouts jumped off the control room ladder and relieved Stigwood and Roybell, who were trying to hold the diving planes. One of the lookouts stared in surprise: "Hey! Let it go—don't you want to go down?"

"Hell no!" yelled Stigwood. "Who hit the diving alarm?"

Roybell looked up at the Christmas tree and called out, "Green board!"

"Jesus!" muttered Stigwood as he saw the main induction valves close.

Frank and Hardy ducked out of the way as the attack scope slid up unassisted. The scope made a slow sweep around the conning tower. Frank moved with it, not knowing whether to grab and take over or just let it . . . He jumped. Behind him the TDC motors were starting to grind away in the little compartment. The scope had settled on a target. An unheard voice was relaying information to an invisible TDC operator— and the machine was responding.

Frank suddenly found himself clutching the handles of the scope. He was conscious only of the sensation, not sure what he would do next. A voice called from below, "Periscope depth, Captain. Shit, she's leveling off. Would you believe it?"

Frank put his eyes to the scope and peered at the infrared image. It was up to 1500x power. The black smoke he had seen before had become a group of *Maru* tankers—maybe a dozen of them—and now he could see the destroyer escorts coming up on the flanks, plowing through heavy swells.

"It's the convoy," he muttered quietly.

Hardy watched him grimly. His eyes moved around the conning tower, waiting for word from the loudspeaker. It came. Vogel's voice, quivering with fright:

"Captain, this is forward torpedo. We're all loaded, tubes one through six. Do you want me to—" He couldn't finish. He choked aloud. And down in the forward torpedo room, Clampett stood hot and sweaty by tube number one, his ear almost on top of the massive brass door. That was how he happened to hear the small click of the arming device switching on. He imagined he heard the gyro and depth mechanisms setting themselves on cue from the Torpedo Data Computer. He hoped he imagined it.

From the side bays a pair of restraining chains rattled irritably. A torpedo stored in the aft end of the center bays dropped onto the skid, freed itself of the chains, and slid all the way down to the loading rack.

Vogel grabbed the battle telephone and buzzed the conning tower.

"What the hell is going on here!" he screamed.

Frank ignored him. He was staring into the scope glass and admiring the perfect lineup on the lead tanker when he heard Hardy's urgent voice in his ear, whispering, "Steady . . ."

Clampett slipped and fell into the below-deck loading platform and landed with his head up against the door of tube number six. He saw Vogel race toward the torpedo tubes from the battle phone and stare at the dials and gauges. Then there was the unmistakable whoosh of compressed air as four impulse tanks charged up simultaneously. Another set of snaps as the safety interlocks were tripped.

Frank pressed his forehead grimly into the rubber facepiece of the scope and mouthed the words without uttering a sound. *Stand by forward tubes. Fire one and two!*

Clampett thought he heard a voice echoing down the forward torpedo room, *Fire one and two!* He did hear the *pfush* of escaping air and water and the thump as the two fish left their tubes. The boat shuddered unmistakably. Vogel stumbled back and yelled a protest.

Frank kept his face glued to the periscope, his mouth working silently, urging the torpedoes on. The twin white trails snaked out from the bow and inclined on the correction angle toward the distant targets. The scope jerked around, and his hands went with it. It reset itself, his fingers turning unwillingly on the handles as they deepened the magnification. He glanced at Hardy. The Professor was watching the

TDC, following the new information cranking into it.

There were two more loud thumps! The boat shook again.

Another pair of white trails—two more fish off toward the convoy.

The scope handles folded without warning. Frank jumped back. The scope slid down into the well.

The helmsman grunted and then complained, "She's going left full rudder, sir!"

Frank stared at the greased tube of the periscope shaft. Hardy moved behind him and leaned over the hatchwell.

"Turn up the listening gear!"

"Aye, aye."

In the sonar cubicle, Nadel twisted up the level knob and pressed his headset tighter. His eyes worked rapidly back and forth as he listened to the rush of faraway screws, the high-speed propellers of the four torpedoes. Nadel was a veteran of twelve years aboard submarines, twelve years as a qualified sonar operator. He let the words come out, shattering the stillness: "Torpedoes running hot, straight, and normal, Skipper."

No one answered. Not even Frank. Hardy shifted position to be closer to the overhead speaker. Frank stood by the periscope, his eyes closing, concentrating. In the forward engine room, Cassidy strained to hear over the sound of the motors.

A pair of distant *thunks!* Nadel looked up. Then everyone reacted to the rumble of twin explosions—followed by an eruption of hissing that drowned out the first blast completely.

The tanker must have gone up in a single burst of volcanic ferocity.

Nadel strained to hear the second set of torpedoes.

After an eternity, there was another twin pair of *thunks,* followed by a frenzied detonation, a savage underwater turbulence.

Nadel ripped off his headset and stared at the officers. "Christ Almighty—four fucking hits!"

In the conning tower, Frank turned a dazed look on Jack Hardy and asked, "What next?"

"Go deep. Find a thermal layer. You're about to be depth-charged."

The sub had already changed course, ninety degrees to port, so Frank ordered a hard dive to two hundred feet and all ahead full.

The boat responded to the crew.

The helmsman clutched his wheel tightly and refused Frank's offer to have him relieved. "I've got her back, sir. It's okay now, I've got her back."

Nadel called up to the conning tower, "High-speed screws approaching, starboard ninety degrees relative. Possible . . . hell, definite destroyer!"

Hardy suggested silent running.

Frank rebutted, "Let's make speed for a few minutes. We can always—"

Hardy grabbed him fiercely. "Do it my way, damnit!"

They heard Nadel calling: "She's coming fast! I make her about twenty-eight knots!"

Frank pulled free and ordered, "All engines stop! Rig for silent running!"

The talker, Colby, passed the word on the battle telephone. In a moment the sub was shut down and holding at 250 feet.

"Picking up splashes," muttered Nadel. Frank came down the ladder quickly and stood by him. "Depth charges coming down, sir."

They heard the first explosion over the speaker. First

the destroyer's propellers approaching, then a click as
the charge armed, then a body-jarring concussion as the
blast wave reached the sub and rolled her to starboard,
then the rush of water filling the empty space where
the burst had gone off.

There was no damage on the first charge.

On the second blast the sounds came closer together.
Some of the older hands looked up anxiously; they
knew the destroyer was closing in.

In the control room, Frank clutched the plotting
table and stared straight ahead. Hardy came tumbling
down the ladder as the third blast went off somewhere
south of them—closer yet. Light bulbs shattered; a big
chunk of paint popped off the after bulkhead. One of
the auxiliarymen let out a yell and grabbed his neck.

"You okay?" barked Stigwood.

"Yeah. Whiplash."

"So get the license number," growled Roybell.

A car smackup—that was precisely the feeling of the
fourth blast. It was so close that all the sounds blended
into one horrible bang that seemed to lift the boat ver-
tically by the stern.

Hardy jumped to the battle telephone and called:
"Aft torpedo—report damage!"

"No damage here, sir. All sec—"

The fifth blast was just off the starboard beam. They
felt it hardest in the control room. Frank was thrown
against Roybell. The planesmen fell on their instruments, and the submarine began to lose depth control.
Stigwood jumped to take their place, but one of the
planesmen got to his feet and said quietly, "Lemme at
it, sir."

His powerful arms moved in and eased the lever
back into place. The only complaint came from the
cook, who announced that dinner had just been
served—to the deck.

"It's a lucky thing I swabbed it, then!" bellowed Dankworth over the line from his battle station.

The laughter that shook the boat was drowned out by the sixth blast, the worst of all. Off the port quarter, it rumbled through the forward torpedo room. Vogel thought he heard a chain snap. He pulled all his men to the tubes and ordered the watertight door shut. Then he explored for damage.

The next blast lifted the main induction valve and knocked out the lights in the control room. Nadel screeched something about water in his shoes. When they switched on the emergency lights, Hardy saw several bolts loose on the deck, but couldn't see where the water was coming from. Frank ordered the hatches shut, the compartment secured. Hardy stood up straight and concentrated until it came to him: "The flood valve!"

Stigwood checked it and found the leak. Within two minutes it was fixed.

The crew thought they were safe now; the destroyer had made its pass, and that should have been the end of it. They were sweltering in the heat building up from the lack of air conditioning, and everyone wanted to get back to normal.

Frank stood by the periscope well and hung on to the plotting table, saying nothing. Waiting, because he knew there was more to come, just as Jack Hardy did.

It came within three minutes. The destroyer had swung around for a second pass, just to be sure. The depth-charging started all over again. One blast after another—relentless, teeth-rattling horrors.

In the forward engine room, Cassidy looked at his men. In the lull before each explosion, they were looking up and muttering curses.

"Sneaking rats . . . dropping rice balls, the fuckers . . . Pack of yellow pigs . . ."

Googles was right by Cassidy's shoulder when he muttered, "I'd say they're straining diplomatic relations. Wouldn't you?"

One of the motor machinist's mates clasped his hands in prayer and spoke to the heavens. "Bless us, oh Lord, for that which we hope we don't receive."

In the control room, Hardy got up from the deck where Stigwood and the auxiliarymen were finishing the repairs. Hardy's trousers were soaked, his beard sticky with sweat. He gazed at Ed Frank, who had an arm wrapped around the periscope well and was muttering angrily to himself. Hardy felt sorry for him; he believed the man was blaming himself for getting them into this situation.

He couldn't have been more wrong. Under his breath, Ed Frank was spewing curses at the Japanese, inflamed to a pledge of vengeance.

The deadly splashes stopped around 2320, but they maintained silence and sat dead in the water for another forty minutes. Nadel's sweat was starting to eat through the foam in his headset, he was clutching it so tightly. Over the loudspeaker they heard the screws of the destroyer slipping away, but still no one said anything; there was always the chance it would stop engines and lie in wait for the *Candlefish* to start engines and attempt a run.

Hardy knew it wouldn't happen. God, how he remembered this night thirty years ago. And he remembered that then too they had waited until exactly midnight before relaxing. He checked the big Navy chronometer on the bulkhead over Roybell's hot, sweaty face. 2400 hours. He eased himself away from his perch and faced Frank.

"That's all, Captain," he said.

Frank slowly turned a measuring eye on Hardy, then swiveled back to Nadel. "How about it, Sound?"

Nadel listened one more intense second, then yanked off the headset and grinned. "They've lost us."

Stigwood breathed an audible sigh of relief and turned to the ladder, calling up to the conning tower, "All clear."

Hardy picked up the battle telephone on the scope well over the plotting table. He opened all circuits, and his voice echoed through the boat. "Secure from silent running. Secure from battle stations. Secure from depth charge attack. All ahead one-third. Light the smoking lamp. Gentlemen, you can take a break. The Captain just sank two Japanese tankers."

Hardy gave Frank a big smile, counting on that little piece of flattery to open things up between them, to relieve the tension. Frank looked surprised, then pleased. Congratulations went round the compartment like a brush fire, whipped by the rush of fresh air through the vents. Somewhere in all the noise, Frank mumbled quietly, "Nothing to get our bowels in an uproar about . . ."

The sub broached at exactly 0011.

After a half-hour on the bridge, studying the smudge of black smoke several miles astern—all that remained of the two Japanese tankers—Frank dropped back into the conning tower. He stopped Lang, the quartermaster. "Fill out your log. When you're done, I'll sign it."

"Aye, aye, sir."

Lang went below to pull the ship's log and make the appropriate entries. Frank remained in the conning tower, alone except for the helmsman. Frank looked around the tiny con in silence. He straightened up, proud, immensely pleased with himself. He smiled and took a short tour around the tower. He reached up and drummed his fingers along the overhead. The helmsman glanced around, saw who it was, and gave him a big confident smile. Frank smiled back.

December 4

Frank was in his quarters by 0051. He sat on the bunk and sipped a cup of consommé, contemplating the peculiar feeling in his gut. The door was closed; his cabin was quiet. He could hear the far-off whine of two diesels and the hum of the air conditioners, but he wasn't interested in sounds. He wanted to know why he felt psychological discomfort in addition to physical queasiness. He reached over and pulled down the hinged desk. He studied the collection of papers, pencils, books, and reports. He made a mental note to start files on the crew: personnel reports, recommendations, the usual. He wanted to sleep, just lie back on the bunk and let it all drift away: the *Candlefish,* Latitude 30°, Jack Hardy, Basquine, Byrnes . . .

Everything seemed mixed up. He tried to sort out all the faces and found himself running unfamiliar names across his lips. Corky Jones, Slugger, Bates, Walinsky . . . who were these people?

Frank's head began to ache, as if somebody were clutching it in a vise, pressing into it things he didn't want to know or think about.

He stood up slowly, sensitive to a shift in his center of gravity. He placed his hands on the desk and threw his weight on them. His eyes fell on the day-to-day log, in the center of the largest cubbyhole. He pulled it out and opened it, pulling pages. November 30th, December 1st, 2nd, 3rd . . . There was no entry on December 3rd.

Damn! Still had that to do. And he remembered something else. He had to get back to control and sign the official log. But this one . . . There was something about this log that wasn't right. Entries that he hadn't written. That was it. He looked at the handwriting, and his brow furrowed deeply. Again he felt a wave of nausea washing over a wave of confusion.

Hardy.

Only Jack Hardy could have made unauthorized entries in the log.

He reached for the intercom. "Mr. Hardy to the Captain's cabin on the double."

Frank met Hardy at the door to the cabin and motioned him to sit on the bunk. Frank sat on the single chair, pulling it around so he could fold his arms on the backrest.

"You remember there were no entries after November twenty-first in the Captain's log?" He lifted the log from his desk and held it under Hardy's nose.

Hardy nodded. "Then look," said Frank.

Hardy opened the book. Frank reached a hand over and flipped the pages to December 2nd, pointing to the center of the inked account. Hardy looked blank a moment, then flipped pages back, one after another, seeing that every entry back to November 21st was inscribed in full. His eyes came up and locked onto Frank's.

"Have you been filling it in?" he asked.

"I was going to ask you that."

They looked at each other.

"Where have you been keeping it?" Hardy asked.

"High and dry in my locker until yesterday, then locked in this desk. Somebody's been filling it in."

"It's Basquine's handwriting," said Hardy.

"It's not yours?"

"You say it's been locked up. How could it be mine?"

"How could it be Basquine's?"

"It's not mine."

"Maybe you're imitating him."

"Maybe *you* are." Hardy met his accusing glare with one of his own.

"Why would I do that?" Frank's question was genuine. The thought had never occurred to him.

"You've been prancing around just like him since the meeting yesterday morning."

Frank sat up straight. "That's not true."

Hardy shrugged. "Maybe it's just something that comes over submarine skippers when they take command. Maybe they're all essentially alike."

Frank's arms came off the back of the chair and dropped between his legs. He stared down at the deck and felt suddenly cold. "What's going to happen to us?" he asked in a quiet voice, the chill rippling up his back and causing a pain in his jaw. "What if we start spraying torpedoes all over the Pacific?"

"We won't," said Hardy. "We're just going to follow my log."

"And what if we don't?" Frank asked. "What if we go off on a tangent, do something unexpected?"

"I don't expect that."

"Did you expect what happened to Byrnes?"

Hardy was silent, thinking a moment. "It got the crew down to eighty-four. I told you that. Look— you're the one who wanted to find out what happened thirty years ago. Well, the *Candlefish* is going to *show* you."

It was an expression of certainty, and Frank couldn't understand how Hardy could be so calm about such an incredible thing.

"I want to live to tell about it," he said hoarsely.

Hardy looked at him a long time and then shrugged.
It was no answer. He got up and reached for the door.

Frank grabbed him. "Well?" he said. "How does it
end?"

"I don't know . . . Captain."

Hardy pulled open the door and walked out. Frank
got up and looked down the corridor after him,
watching him move—and realized something that he
hadn't seen before.

Hardy's limp, once so pronounced, was now dis-
tinctly absent.

In the forward engine room, Googles reached up to
the intercom speaker and turned up the music Giroux
was piping through. A slinky female voice cut in:

"You are listening to the voice you call Tokyo Rose,
telling you of a war that is almost over. And you have
lost. Courtesy of the Japanese Imperial Navy—a big
hello to the crewmen of the American submarine *Candlefish* . . ."

Googles dropped his tools with a resounding clang
and barked, "Screw you with a wet torpedo, baby!"

Witzgall rose to conduct the engine-room orchestra.
"By the numbers!" he shouted. One by one, each man
down the line raised his arm and gave the Italian elbow
salute, accompanied by a chorus of Bronx cheers. Cassidy stared at them; they were acting like a pack of ref-
ugees from a John Wayne movie. He didn't understand the sudden surge of morale, but he felt glad to be
a part of it.

Jack Hardy came through with coffee and sat down
with him. They sipped quietly and listened to the
music.

"Maybe things are going to be all right after all.
What do you think, Lieutenant?"

Hardy arched an eyebrow and studied Cassidy. The gnarled old Chief with his religiously polished pipes, his fatherly smile, and his honest sympathy . . . In spite of their differences earlier, Hardy had grown to like him. Why? Hardy's brow furrowed, and he gazed deep into Cassidy's face.

Walinsky. Cassidy was just like Walinsky. Just *like* him? Or . . .

Hardy closed his eyes. He didn't want to think about it. He could accept the other things—the fact that they were somehow back in World War II, that they were fighting a shooting war, that they were actually duplicating the last patrol of the *Candlefish*—but the changes in the crew? That was too much. It amounted to one thing: He didn't *want* them back.

But did he have anything to say about it?

It was 0145 when Ed Frank woke up, something nagging at him, something he had forgotten to do. He rose like an automaton, sat down at his desk, reached for the Captain's log, and opened it to December 3rd. The blank page stared back at him. Was he looking for yesterday's report? Was that why he had opened the book? Was there some detail he wasn't sure of?

No. Of course, the blank page! *He* had to *make* the report. He looked around for his pen. His fingers shot over the clutter of pencils and the single ballpoint he had brought with him on the voyage. He was looking for something else. Rummaging in the cubbyholes, he found it. A fountain pen. Always used a fountain pen in the log—it looked better. He took the pen between the fingers of his right hand and began to scribble notes on the day's events. He wrote quickly, creating a page full of choppy scrawl. He didn't stop until the entry was complete. Then he blotted the ink, stared at it a moment . . .

He flipped back to December 2nd and compared. He wanted to be sure that his wording was the same, that his position notations and attack descriptions were consistent. He compared and grunted in satisfaction.

Everything matched perfectly. He flipped back to December 3rd and signed the log with a flourish.

Lights were down in the crew's quarters, but Torpedoman 1st Class Clampett stood with his arms folded at the forward bulkhead, grinning happily at the Ann Sheridan poster. He stood quite silent for a long time, then whispered for her ears only, "Hey, baby, everything's lookin' grand . . ."

CHAPTER 18

December 5

The squall line stretched to the horizon, obliterating the wintry afternoon sun in a jumbled mass of black clouds and sheeted rain.

The mist-shrouded destroyer, her outline softened by the water streaming off her decks, sliced sharply through the tortured seas.

The periscope slid smoothly above the sea. Ed Frank watched the destroyer plod on its tormented course. *Fubuki* class, he decided. His scalp tingled with excitement. He folded the handles and announced, "Destroyer! Sound battle stations! Right full rudder—all ahead full!"

The clang of the bell rang through the *Candlefish*. Frank wiped sweaty palms on his trousers and stood back while the fire-control party formed in the conning tower. Dorriss was the first one up the ladder; he snatched the *is-was* from its hook, draped it around his neck, and moved forward of the scope well. Stigwood, Vogel, and Hardy bolted up the ladder and slid behind the Torpedo Data Computer.

Frank waited for everyone to settle in.

"Sound, what's the bearing?"

"One propeller, bearing zero-nine-four relative, Captain."

Stigwood fed the information into the TDC. Frank

flicked thumbs-up to Lang, then stooped and pulled down the handles as the periscope slithered back up. He peered through the glass.

Rain obscured everything on the surface. It was so bad he couldn't see the horizon line. Great, he thought, all we need is a goddamned white wall.

"Bring me up," he said. "Three feet."

The sub rose, and his field of vision improved. A gray silhouette loomed out of the rain and mist.

"There she is," he muttered. "Bearing—mark!"

Dorriss checked the relative bearing line on the scope plates. "Zero-eight-zero relative."

"Range—mark!"

"Seven six hundred."

"Set!" The TDC ground away as Stigwood punched the information in. Dorriss computed more numbers on the *is-was*.

"Angle on the bow—port zero-four-four."

"Set!" Stigwood's voice crackled with tension.

"Down scope!" hollered Frank.

The whir of the periscope hydraulic blended with the clatter of the TDC. Frank stepped back to the computer.

Hardy's eyes scanned the tense faces of the other men. He was aware of the excitement rippling through the con, so thick he could almost taste it. Yet he felt a certain remoteness; he was still an outsider. But why? Was it because he had no assigned battle station? Ridiculous—that could be explained. Thirty years away from war, naturally they would relegate him to a backup role. Naturally.

He was the fifth leg on a four-legged horse. The intricate details of the attack were handled by more experienced hands, just as they had been during wartime. Except— No. No exceptions. This was as it should be.

The roles were reversed—that was all. Once again he was the passive scientist, the observer—while Frank and his crew were the active participants.

In what?

The clatter of the TDC startled him. Frank crouched over the scope and again rode it up from the deck.

The movement was so damned familiar—the way Frank stooped to pick up the scope. It jogged memories. He found himself admiring the way Frank had taken control—

"Control!" he blurted. "Jesus!" Hardy lunged for the ladder and slid down the metal rails, ignoring the sting in his palms.

He shot through the empty crew's quarters and burst into the forward engine room, startling Cassidy.

"Chief, get a tool kit and follow me."

Cassidy set his clipboard down and grabbed a heavy metal box. "What's the problem?" he called after Hardy, who was already retreating past the engines.

"NLO tanks! Come on!" Hardy pulled himself through to the after engine room. Cassidy scurried after him, wondering what in hell could go wrong with the Normal Lubricating Oil tanks.

He caught up with Hardy in the maneuvering room. He was down on one knee, lifting a deck hatch. He waved Cassidy over, and both of them horsed the hatch upright.

Hardy switched on a battle lantern and played the beam over the maze of lines and tanks that filled the motor room crawl space below.

"There!" His beam locked in on a cluster of pale green hoses leading from a T-shaped tank just behind the after bulkhead. "NLO tank number three. Those lines are the main oil feed to maneuvering. Get down there and watch them."

"For what?" asked Cassidy, suspiciously.

"For the leak. When it starts, you stop it."

"What leak?" Cassidy was astonished.

"Just get down there!"

Cassidy lowered himself into the open space and pulled the toolbox down after him. He took the battle lantern and fixed Hardy with a beady stare. "How do you know?"

Hardy stood up. "Just *watch* it. I *guarantee* you, it'll blow."

He swooped to the hatch and was gone, leaving Cassidy to squeeze himself and his toolbox into the cramped crawl space.

Hardy hurried back to the conning tower, wondering fleetingly why no one else had picked up on the NLO tank. After all, wasn't everybody studying his log?

Frank, still glued to the scope, was tracking the target on final approach. "All ahead dead slow," he said.

The helmsman rang it up on the MB.

"Range!"

"Two four hundred."

"We'll let her have it at two thousand."

Hardy read the anticipation on their faces. They were getting ready for the kill, feeling it build in their bones, their fingers.

"Captain, sonar reports a second target," announced Colby. "Bearing one-five-three relative."

Frank quickly walked the scope around, trying to penetrate the rain and mist astern. He saw a second gray shape emerging from a wall of spray far behind them.

"Christ! We can get two of 'em! Prepare stern tubes!"

"Stern tubes loading, sir." Frank ignored the talker as he swung back to line up on the first destroyer. "Open all outer doors."

"Ready all tubes, sir."

"All stop!"

They marked the bearing at 010, range 2100, speed 14 knots.

"Couldn't miss if we tried. Fire one! Fire two!"

Danby's hand stopped hovering over the firing keys. He slammed them down.

Isolated and uncomfortable in the cramped crawl space, Cassidy was debating with himself about sitting there any longer. He was shifting his body, trying to find a less tortuous position, when two torpedoes tore from the bow tubes.

The instant after they were fired, even before the boat finished its responsive shudder, he heard the *sprang!* A jet of warm oil spurted up, hitting him in the face.

"Shit!" he yelled, and groped for the cutoff valve. His oil-slick fingers slipped off twice before he could turn off the metal petcock. He found himself lying in a pool of oil. It soaked his pants, his shirt; he could taste it in his mouth.

He rummaged in the toolbox for a roll of friction tape. He found the break and was just starting to wrap it when the first torpedo struck its target, sending a metallic *ca-rrump* reverberating through the sub's hull.

The column of water marking their first hit soared still higher into the sky. The force of the blast had heeled the destroyer over, exposing her waterline. As she strove to right herself, the second torpedo slammed home.

Her midsection collapsed in a burst of flame and flying debris. In a convulsive eruption, the forward section leaped out of the water and flew apart. A gun turret detached from the deck and spun lazily into the air. Flaming chunks of wreckage showered the ocean, raising answering splashes where they fell.

The stern section, covered with sheets of flame, rolled over and slipped beneath the waves, leaving a cloud of oily black smoke and steam.

Frank yanked his head away from the scope and looked at Dorriss. "Son of a bitch," he said, in a voice filled with awe. "She's gone."

The Exec's face was wreathed in a toothy grin. "We got her! We got her!" he chanted.

"Direct hit. Both fish," Frank announced.

Stigwood let out a whoop, grabbed Vogel in a bear hug and pounded him on the back. Danby and Lang scrambled to shake Frank's hand. The other quartermaster was standing by Hardy, his sweat-streaked face glistening in the half light of the con. "How about that, Lieutenant?" he chanted at Hardy. "How about that?"

Hardy took no part in the celebration. He cocked his head and listened, hearing the faint *ping-ping* of search sonar. He left the hatchwell and moved to the periscope. He shouldered Dorriss away, grabbed the scope handles, and pressed his forehead against the soft rubber padding of the eyeshield.

Frank, his voice strident, shouted over the bedlam. "Okay, knock it off. Maneuvering says we've got a problem."

Hardy, pivoting, was trying to pierce the rain and scud that obscured his vision. "That's been taken care of," he said firmly, and hoped that Cassidy *had* taken care of it. "We've got another problem up here—that second destroyer."

Where the hell is it? he thought. There! Slashing through the water, her bow cleaving the storm-tossed seas and steaming straight toward them.

"Prepare for a stern shot!" he announced. "Bearing!"

What were they all waiting for? He pulled his head away and checked the bearing line. "I make it one-eight-four astern. Range, two three hun—"

"Stand away from that scope, mister."

Frank stood on top of Hardy, glaring at him, red-faced with anger. Surprised, Hardy let his fingers slip off the scope handles. He backed away, his mind a jumbled confusion of embarrassment. Frank took over the scope, fitting his body to it, as if he were made for it.

"Belay that last setup. Bearing—mark!"

"One-eight-zero relative."

"Range—mark!"

"One eight hundred."

Frank winced as the destroyer's forward turret opened up. There was a flat smack as the shell plowed into the ocean somewhere over their heads.

"It's going to be down-the-throat! All stern tubes—give me a two-degree spread."

Nadel must have turned his speakers up. The churning noise of the high-speed screws overrode the *pings* of the destroyer's sonar as it homed in on the return echo.

Through the scope Frank saw the forward turret flash again as the destroyer charged in and cut loose three salvoes in a row. He waited five more seconds, letting the range close even tighter while shell splashes dropped in on either side and rocked the hull. He waited for the motion to stop, then yelled: "Fire seven! Fire eight! Fire nine! Fire ten!"

Danby hit the firing keys, and the sub shuddered four times as four fish leaped from the stern tubes.

"Down scope! All ahead emergency! Left full rudder!" He whirled to the hatch and bellowed below, "Mr. Adler, take her deep!"

The *Candlefish* clawed for the safety of the depths,

trying to put as much ocean as possible between herself and the hard-closing destroyer before it could cut loose a string of depth charges.

On the surface the four fish raced toward their target, their ribbon wakes visible to the destroyer's lookouts, who spotted them and shouted—but it was already too late. The destroyer didn't have a chance.

The *Candlefish* was just passing the one-hundred-foot mark when two powerful explosions rumbled over the speakers.

Two hits.

Frank checked their dive, and the boat leveled off. The conning tower was hushed as everyone listened to the grinding metallic sounds of collapsing bulkheads giving way to the rush of tons of sea.

The noise trailed off, lost in the vastness of the ocean, but the cheering in the *Candlefish* surged and dipped in waves of emotion.

Frank took the role of hero as if he were born to it, lightly shrugging off the compliments from the surrounding circle of faces.

Hardy tried to wedge through the tightly bunched group, but Frank's face turned cold as their eyes locked. In the uncomfortable silence, his lips curled in a sneer.

"You never could do it right," he muttered.

Hardy felt a tightness grip his chest. His jaws worked back and forth, but he couldn't speak.

The last time he had seen hostility like that—naked and unchecked—it was on the face of Billy G. Basquine. The memory filled him with a mind-numbing horror.

The *Candlefish* surfaced in the squall; the rains pelted the sub, soaking the men who zipped up to the bridge. The stench of diesel oil filled the sodden air. A large patch was burning about a mile off the bow. Frank headed for it, intent on investigating the carnage he had created.

Forward and aft deck hatches were popped, and the men poured up, their elation still unchecked as they pointed out recognizable bits of wreckage floating by. But their laughter choked off at sight of the first bodies—oil-encrusted lumps of dead flesh, turning lifelessly in the water.

And then the living ones.

The throb of the *Candlefish*'s engines was muffled by the pounding rain. But neither of these sounds could drown out the screams of the dying. Bodies suspended in the sticky maw of diesel fuel bumped against the sides of the sub and spun like water bugs down the length of the hull, bouncing off the stern vanes and floating away.

Most of the submariners looked away. Billows of black smoke poured past and stung their eyes; the rain soaked them to the skin.

Frank was aware of their white faces. "What's the matter with them?" he demanded of no one in particular.

Dorriss tore his eyes away from a headless body draped over the charred remains of a life raft. "I—uh—I don't think they expected it to be like this, sir—"

Frank snorted. "Is that a fact?" He felt an anger—no, a hatred—for the seared and maimed shapes bobbing all around him.

Cassidy was feeling pretty good about the way he had seated the new hose in the NLO line. He came up the bridge hatch and found Hardy on the cigarette deck, standing in the rain. "Hey, Lieutenant, you were right! She really let go. How we doing up here?" He followed Hardy's gaze down to the water.

He saw the blackened bodies and recoiled in horror. He muttered a curse, his voice filled with revulsion.

Frank leaned over the bridge and roared: "Take a good look, gentlemen—and just remember, those sneaky bastards deserve everything they get." He waited for a positive response; none came.

"It didn't work then, Captain—and it won't work now."

Frank turned to the Professor. "Don't hand me that crap," he snarled. "If I had let a screwup like you make this shot, those sons of bitches might be looking at *us* in the water!"

He swung around to Dorriss. "Be sure every man below comes topside to see this—then hit the horn and take us down."

Dorriss nodded dumbly.

Frank dropped through the bridge hatch, leaving his stunned crew still lining the decks. Slowly they shuffled to the hatches and were swallowed back down into the hull. The on-duty watch straggled up, only because they had been ordered to.

Hardy and Cassidy stood apart, letting the rain wash down their bodies, in some sense hoping it might purify them of this disgrace. Finally, as an afterthought, Cassidy spoke. "The tank blew, Lieutenant, just the way you said it would." He blinked, shielding his eyes from the rain. "I gotta admit," he continued, "you have one hell of a memory."

Hardy smiled ruefully. "Sometimes it's too good, Chief."

In the quiet of the CPO cabin, Hardy shrugged into a dry shirt and tried to rationalize Frank's behavior.

Nothing normal could excuse the Captain's actions.

Granted, a man could become excited in the heat of combat. Most skippers were often guilty of things they later regretted, but Hardy sensed there would be no regret forthcoming.

The explanation? That could not have been Ed Frank.

But if it wasn't Ed Frank, then who?

He rolled into his bunk, facing the bulkhead; he shivered as the name formed on his lips.

"Basquine," he muttered, and wanted to retract it right away. It had to be Basquine. But how?

In all the excitement, Hardy had forgotten about his log and the fact that no one seemed to be following it any longer. He went looking for the copies, quietly checking the wardroom, the control room, forward torpedo . . . He couldn't find a single one.

He stopped Dorriss and made an offhand inquiry.

"Captain's got them. Picked them all up this morning."

"Before the attack? Why?"

"Says we're on our own now. We don't need any plans."

Plans? Hardy couldn't make sense out of that. They needed the log now more than ever. He paused, wondering if now was the proper time to confront Frank. He was reluctant to submit himself to more abuse. He felt shaky, and headed for the coffee galley.

Giroux fiddled with the tuning knob, winding it across the band. Static popped and crackled in his ears. Just as he was about to give up, the sweet strains of "Dancing in the Dark" filled his headset.

"We sure as hell are," he muttered. He flipped the

toggle switch that piped the music through the PA system.

Artie Shaw's clarinet soared and dipped, and the melody circumnavigated the boat. The song ended, and once again the silken voice of Tokyo Rose purred to them:

"That last song was for all you Marines whose dancing days are over—forever."

Hardy was leaning back against the coffee galley, and he looked up when Cookie growled, "Stuff it, lady," at the speaker. Her voice droned on:

"My next number is dedicated to the families of the crew of USS *Candlefish*—"

Men flaked out in their bunks suddenly sat up, confused.

"from the Japanese Imperial Navy—*condolences*. At fourteen hundred hours today, two of our destroyers sank your submarine. It's just an early Christmas present. And now, Glenn Miller's rendition of 'Adios.' "

"Son of a bitch!" Hardy heard someone yell. Cookie looked at Hardy, his face clouding with anger. Neither spoke; they were too stunned.

Frank's voice came from the speaker. "Congratulations, men, we've just been sunk. I think it's only proper that we permit ourselves . . . a moment of silence."

It lasted all of twenty seconds; then it was interrupted by the first snicker. There was a second, then a third; laughter rippled, then exploded.

Hardy turned and headed forward, shocked by the transformation.

The Captain, with the unwitting aid of a Japanese propagandist, had blown away the gloom that had settled over the crew that afternoon.

Out of eighty-four men, he was the only one aboard who realized that the original purpose of this voyage was now lost forever. This crew was not only reacting to World War Two, they were part of it.

Hardy found Frank on the bridge.

"I didn't get a chance to congratulate you," he began. "That was some shooting."

Frank regarded him out of the corner of his eye. "No thanks to you," he mumbled.

Hardy knew he had to reason with the man.

"Ed"—Hardy used his first name, leaning over the coaming to whisper conspiratorially—"don't you see what's happening? Today's action was a carbon copy of the original patrol." Frank's eyes shifted, centering on him, dark and unrevealing. "*You* didn't sink those destroyers; you went through the motions, but you weren't in control."

"And who is?"

"It's prearranged. You said it yourself—in the con—you couldn't have missed today even if you tried." He stopped, hoping against hope that he was getting through. "The only goal this boat has now is to return to Latitude Thirty. That much I'm sure of, but when it gets there—what's going to happen?"

"You tell me."

"If this pattern we're on holds true, the *Candlefish* is going to sink—again!"

Hardy searched Frank's eyes for a sign of understanding. But Frank turned away to stare over the side of the bridge at the night-dark ocean flowing past. "Lieutenant, I appreciate your concern, but let me worry about Latitude Thirty."

"There's another thing. My log. You had every copy confiscated."

"Captain's prerogative."

"But why?"

Frank's features smoothed out. "Don't you have a watch to stand at 0400?"

"Yes."

"You'd better pull some sack time." He gripped Hardy's shoulder and gave him a friendly smile. "We'll go over this later."

Hardy's shoulders sagged as he moved to the hatch and left the Captain on the bridge.

Frank reached for the intercom. "Exec to the bridge."

Dorriss climbed half out of the hatchwell and looked up.

Frank spoke slowly in a low voice that wouldn't carry to the lookouts or the Officer of the Deck. "I want you to keep a close eye on Lieutenant Hardy. He's got some cockeyed ideas, way off in left field, and I can't make any sense out of them. Just make sure he keeps them to himself. Understood?"

The faint glimmer of a wicked smile crossed the Exec's thin face. "I'll watch him, sir."

"Do that."

Dorriss dropped below. Frank remained on the bridge, his mind ticking off the possibilities that the future held for all of them.

CHAPTER 19

December 6

Dorriss hovered over the chart spread on the long wardroom table and worried his chin with one hand. He was staring at a copy of a Japanese map which outlined the layout of the harbor in Tokyo Bay. He ran a finger over the coordinates and then traced the coastline, shaking his head doubtfully. Adler stood at his side, the backs of his knees braced against the bench, rocking back and forth and frowning, trying to look more intelligent than he was.

Ed Frank sat at the head of the table. He already knew the chart by heart; he was just allowing the two younger officers time to convince themselves of something he had already decided. He shifted in his seat and spoke: "I'm waiting."

Dorriss unwound from his crouch and shook his head. "I wouldn't approach from the south," he said.

"But that's the only way in." Frank blinked.

"I know." Dorriss smiled.

Frank grew dark. "I didn't ask you in here for a humorous interlude. You've got a navigation background—give me a navigator's opinion."

"It's impossible," he said simply.

"No, it's not!" Frank slammed a fist down on the table. Then he relaxed and smiled thinly. *"We are going to do it.* So you better set your minds to it now. I want an approach worked out, in terms of weather conditions and physical environment—known quantities."

Frank came around the table and looked down at the chart himself. He glanced up at Adler. "Any opinions, Mr. Adler?"

"Sounds like a fine plan to me, sir."

Dorriss knew he was outnumbered. He shrugged and leaned over the chart with Frank. His skinny fingers tapped the knobby inlet, and he said, "I can get you weather and current details, and you can go in there. You'll be up to your ass in mines, but so what? If you do go in there, *sir* . . . you better go slow. You better *creep*."

Frank smiled. "Like a fucking pussycat."

Hardy was stripped down in the after head, about to step into the shower, when he caught a glimpse of the steward passing by with an armload of what looked to be trash. Hardy hesitated a second, not sure what he had seen, then turned and hurried to the hatch. The steward was already down the aisle, making his way aft. Hardy stepped through the hatch and followed. Cassidy looked up, and Brownhaver gave a wolf-whistle.

Hardy ignored them and swung into the aft engine room. The wolf-whistles picked up. Hardy ran the gauntlet down to the maneuvering cubicle, where the steward turned to see what he was missing. Hardy stopped and stared at the bundle in his arms.

It was the remains of the skewered globe and all of Ed Frank's carefully compiled notebooks and charts: his entire arsenal on the Devil's Triangle. And something else: all the copies of Hardy's log. Everything they had set out to follow—the very reason for their voyage.

Hardy stood rooted to the spot as the wolf-whistles

became raucous yowls and limp-wristed chortlings of "Whoops, my dear!" and "Oh my Gawd, it's a naked man!"

The steward grinned at Hardy and continued into the after torpedo room. Hardy watched from the hatch as the gear was stashed in one of the green bulkhead lockers. Ignoring the hecklers, he padded back to the head.

So Frank had decided to discard the scientific purpose behind this patrol, to store it away so it wouldn't be around to remind him, so he could concentrate on . . . *what?*

That elusive *what* again.

Hardy wondered if he should keep his mouth shut, let the *Candlefish* sail into Latitude 30°, and just see what would happen.

Wasn't that the scientific approach? And now, wasn't he the only true scientist left aboard? Frank was no longer interested—it was up to Hardy to pick up the pieces.

He stepped into the shower and let the water beat on his tense muscles. But as soon as he was dressed, he went back to the control room. He had to have another look at Frank's face.

He had to find out for certain just *who* the man *thought* he was.

He stopped to glance over Lang's shoulder. The quartermaster was checking the ship's log. He turned with it, and Hardy said, "I'm going up. You want me to have him sign it?"

"He already has."

Lang put the log down on the plotting desk and turned to consult with Scopes. Hardy's eyes rested on the OCS handbook protruding from Lang's back pocket, and he felt a shiver of discomfort. Then he turned to look down at the log.

The second shiver hit without any warning at all.

It was nothing in the report itself that shocked him. It was the signature at the bottom of the page: that hasty little scrawl, the name . . .

He couldn't look around, afraid of the faces he might see around him. A terror shrieked silently inside him, and he felt thirty years of life slipping out of his grasp, as if they had never occurred, as if he had never parted company with the *Candlefish* or her crew.

He shook himself. He had forgotten something again. He had come here with a purpose, and it had dribbled away from him. He felt like a man trying to scoop up a drink of water with open fingers. He was unable to hold on to anything. The *Candlefish* was all he had—the boat and her crew. It was wartime, and there was nothing he could do about it. There was no way to get off. He had to ride it out with the rest of them and endure the Captain's unstable ventures.

And he couldn't warn anyone—because he simply was not trusted.

December 7

There was only one bulb burning in the CPO quarters at 0200. Hardy was stretched out on his bunk, hands clasped over his stomach, somewhere between sleep and consciousness.

His eyelids fluttered as music wafted in over the speakers and came to him muffled by his drawn curtain. It was Glenn Miller's "Moonlight Serenade." Soft, sustained notes lulled him into dreams, recollections, summer nights in New Haven, the club near the pier, Elena dancing with him that last night before their departure for San Diego . . .

One eye came open, and he gazed up at her picture,

attached to the underside of Stanhill's bunk. Every time Stanhill came in, he would leap up to the bunk; it would sag, the picture would come loose, and he would have to replace it—

Stanhill? Not Stanhill. Stigwood.

Somebody turned up the volume, and Hardy felt himself being dragged away from sleep. The big-band sound had always been his favorite. But Stanhill was impossible. Every time he got his hands on the wardroom phonograph, it was Glenn Miller for three hours.

He became conscious of other sounds interfering with the music: feet tramping, shouts, laughter.

Hardy sat up slowly and listened. He parted the olive-green curtain shielding his bunk and peered out. The CPO quarters was deserted, but he saw something out in the corridor. Eerie shadows on the bulkheads, flickering lights . . .

He rose, pulled on his pants, and struggled into his shoes. There was something going on in the forward torpedo room. He stepped to the door and saw Lieutenant Dorriss appear in the entrance to officers' quarters, rubbing the sleep from his eyes.

Nadel came bounding aft, whizzed past Dorriss, and opened the door to the wardroom. Stigwood was inside, alone with the record player.

Nadel stood straight and barked, "Sir, Captain requests 'Anchors Aweigh' on the phonograph piped into all quarters immediately."

"Anchors a-what?" said Stigwood.

Nadel excused himself. "Permission to enter the wardroom, sir. Thank you, sir. Excuse me." He ripped Glenn Miller off the player, which brought a howl of indignation from Stigwood. Then he fumbled in the stack for an old seventy-eight. He found it and put it on the machine.

The march blasted out like a cannon. There was a matching roar from the forward torpedo room. Then a swarm of men tumbled into officers' country, carrying torches—rags stripped from old bedding, soaked in diesel fuel, and then wound onto sticks.

They poured into the corridor, led by Clampett and Cassidy, alternating in wild clamoring cheers:

"Ann Sheridan!"

"Betty Grable!"

Hardy and Dorriss had to avoid being crushed. Through the flames and smoke they could see that the crowd included nearly half the crew. A smile broadened Hardy's face. He remembered.

Cassidy shouted, "Grable's the one!"

Voices joined in support.

Clampett turned at the control room bulkhead and screeched, "Ann Sheridan!"

The steward, who was part Filipino, jumped up with a shout: "Carmen Miranda!"

"Git outta here!" growled Dankworth.

Dorriss dove into the crush of men and made his way across to Hardy. "What is *this?*"

"Submarine sweetheart contest." Hardy grinned. He swung out and joined the marching throng. Dorriss hustled after him.

As the crowd marched aft, past the radio room, the galley, the crew's quarters, they picked up more participants, who were promptly brow-beaten into support of one or the other candidate. Someone handed Clampett the Ann Sheridan poster, which he raised high in the air, turning his torch over to Witzgall. He marched backward and chanted, "Ann Sheridan! Ann Sheridan!"

The men in the rear started passing pencils and slips of paper forward through the crowd. Choices were marked and ballots were relayed to the front of the line. Some of the ballots disappeared into shirts—whole stacks of them never reached the polls. And Roybell kept pulling pre-marked ballots out of his shirt, shouting, "Here's one for Grable! Another one for Grable!"

In the forward engine room, Clampett turned the Ann Sheridan poster over to Lang. Brownhaver threw him the ballot box. It was a small carton with the word VOTE scrawled on one side. Clampett held it out in front of him and wedged his way back through the crowd, collecting the ballots.

"Put your votes in here! Right in the box! This ain't basketball, Googles, just drop it in!"

The steward held up his ballot, anxiously waved it in Clampett's direction, and yelled, "Carmen—" He was cut off by a rude shove from Dankworth.

Clampett was afraid the votes were going against him. When Giroux stepped up and proudly announced, "Grable," Clampett ducked him, then went on zig-zagging, picking up only Sheridan votes, bobbing under the torches until he was all the way back to the control room. He let the last of the men pass by and drop in their ballots—and then he faced Hardy and Dorriss.

"That's it?" he said. He glanced into the box; it was filled to the top with little slips of paper. He held it out to Hardy. "Sir—like to delegate you to tally the votes."

Hardy twinkled. "Oh, I'd be delighted, Corky—"

Clampett winked surreptitiously at Hardy. "Ann Sheridan's a shoo-in, don't you think, sir?"

"Fair chance," granted Hardy.

"Yup. Well, here they are." He handed over the box. "One man—one vote. Democracy."

Dorriss peered into the box, and his jaw fell. "Must be five hundred ballots in there."

* * *

Hardy looked up from the pile of counted ballots on the table in the crew's mess. "Betty Grable," he announced.

Cheers went up. They were as excited over this as they had been over blasting Japanese shipping out of the water. Clampett thrust through the crowd and confronted Hardy, wearing a look of chagrined disbelief.

Hardy pointed to the ballots. "Four hundred twenty-three to two hundred ninety-six."

There were more cheers from the Grable men. Cassidy whistled through his teeth. Cookie stepped forward and gaped bug-eyed at the ballots.

"*How* many votes?" he asked.

"Four hundred twenty-three to two hundred ninety-six," Hardy repeated.

"Shit! You mean I been feeding seven hundred men?"

He laughed right in Clampett's ear. Clampett turned red and grabbed the ballots, swirled to another table, and began a recount.

Hardy stared at him a long moment, a smile widening his scratchy old beard.

The Grable supporters let Clampett have it—a blast of jeers that only made him count faster.

Still grinning, Jack Hardy looked up and caught sight of Captain Frank, standing just inside the galley, coldly eyeing the proceedings. Dorriss appeared at his side; they had a short whispered conference. Once the Captain glanced at Hardy.

He felt another warning shiver.

The Captain chose his next big moment well. With the exception of Clampett, the crew's morale was the best it had been since the voyage began, so he decided to take advantage of it, to boost it and aim it in what he felt to be the right direction.

From the conning tower he switched on the intercom to all compartments. He lifted the battle phone and announced:

"This is the Captain. In case you have forgotten, today is December seventh." He was silent for a moment, then continued: "Three years ago our country suffered the most shameful episode of its entire military history. We do not recall this date with pride. There is no dignity in defeat."

His voice echoed around the boat. There was no compromise in his tone.

"We have had our fun tonight . . . While we all took part in it, we all recognize the insignificance of our brotherly feelings—because this is *not* a ship of men; it is a *weapon!* And by its proper application, we will attend to the destruction of our enemy with strength, dispatch, and skill! In memory of those who were killed at Pearl, we will from this date onward be the most formidable weapon in the Pacific!"

There was not a sound in the wardroom as Frank's voice crackled from the overhead speaker. But Hardy was not hearing the voice of Ed Frank; he was hearing Billy G. Basquine, the greatest rabblerouser in the Submarine Force.

"If those bastards still think that they have an island, a fortress, or a bay that they can call impregnable, then they haven't met *us!*" Frank's voice quavered.

"If they think they've sent us to the bottom of the sea, then let them think it! Let them make all the announcements and send all the condolences the airwaves will carry, but when we reappear—at a time and place they least suspect—we will exact a vengeance from them far beyond anything they have done to us!"

Hardy thought he was going to be sick. He left his breakfast and started toward the conning tower. What was the Captain talking about?

"We have a mandate from the Congress of the United States, from the Commander-in-Chief, and from the Almighty. With all those sanctions, whatever methods we use can be justified. The outcome is ordained, set, unalterable! We have only to fulfill it!"

Hardy stood with his head just above deck level in the hatch well, watching Frank bent over the intercom, the spread shoulders, the determined face and the mad, lunatic eyes.

December 7th. Four days to go. What *was* going to happen when they reached the area where they had gone down before? Did Frank know? But he wasn't Frank; he was Basquine. Did Basquine know?

"That is all, gentlemen." Frank finished his speech and closed down the intercom. His gaze fell on Hardy, and they stared at each other a long time, until the tiniest smile of triumph crept over Frank's face.

CHAPTER 20

December 10

The next three days proved depressingly uneventful to a crew charged up for the kill. The enemy was nowhere in sight. Frank became jumpy; his trigger finger itched. He took his frustrations out on Hardy, deliberately making it tough for him. In wardroom meetings he would drop hints to the other officers about Hardy's mental unreliability, and they took it as sanction for rumor-spreading.

Hardy realized what was happening, and took refuge in the forward engine room with Cassidy. He no longer had any confusion over the Chief's identity. Hardy saw him as he wanted to see him—as the friend Walinsky had been to him in 1944.

Hardy stood the night watch on December 10th, Officer of the Deck from 2000 to 2400, and stared out at the wallowing troughs, the frothy caps whipped up like cream, enduring the roll and pitch of the boat as she slugged through toughening seas, on course for the north of Japan, the Kurile Islands.

He huddled in his jacket and desperately tried to ignore everything except the job at hand. He had decided to divorce his mind from his duties, to perform as an automaton, to let the submarine take him where it wanted to, and to keep his opinions to himself. If he was being rebuffed because they all thought he was insane, then the safest course was to maintain a low profile. He would live this out to its conclusion, however awful that might be, and *whenever* it came . . .

But it turned December 11th, and Jack Hardy knew that the solution to his dilemma was less than a day away.

Since his log had been forgotten and disregarded for days, he appeared to be the only one aware of what was to come at 2130 the next night. If he wanted to, he could simply remain mute and smug and it would all come to its foregone conclusion. Or, if he truly was out of his mind, then nothing would happen when they reached that deadly spot in Latitude 30°. But if the submarine went to her demise a second time—well, Jack Hardy would be redeemed. He could die vindicated.

He smiled. It wasn't the best of all possible solutions.

He was relieved by Vogel, who took the OOD watch, and Dorriss, who tramped up to the bridge for a little midnight air. Neither said anything to Hardy. He went below in silence, marched straight to the CPO quarters, pulled off his clothes, and dove into the sack.

He was deep in slumber when something seemed to drift in and move against him, touching his shoulder. He thought he sensed light through the darkness, playing across his eyes, then a shadow covering it—fingers pressing him, more insistent. There was a reddish glow on his eyelids. He grumbled, and suddenly came awake to something shaking his shoulder.

The curtain was parted a few inches, and he could see the red glow of combat lights in the compartment beyond. Whatever had touched his shoulder was gone, but he heard another sound, a tapping . . . fingers drumming on the bulkhead outside, moving out of the

CPO quarters. He pulled the curtain. He was aware of a shadow fleeing down the corridor toward the control room. He rose, half asleep and puzzled. He slipped on his shoes and, dressed only in his underwear, stumbled out to the corridor.

The red lights were on throughout the boat. There wasn't a man to be seen in officers' country. He was alone, and it was deathly quiet. He moved aft, intending to follow that shadow to the control room.

He ducked through the hatch and stepped in, suddenly bathed in red light. He could make out the forms of the control-room crew . . . yet there was something odd. He froze in shock.

This wasn't the control-room crew at all . . .

He was exchanging stares with the officer contingent from the crew of 1944! They were gathered around the plotting table, white phantoms haloed in red, staring at him.

Bates stepped forward, and when he spoke his voice echoed as if it were coming from the bowels of the submarine itself.

"Cold feet again, Jack?"

Hardy's knees sagged; he couldn't stand up straight. He had to back against the hatch. Then Basquine stepped forward and, in the same terrifying voice, asked, *"Are you going all the way with us, Jack?"*

Hardy's mouth opened. He wanted to scream a defiant *No,* but he couldn't.

Basquine and Bates and the other apparitions began to fade from sight, blending in with the red illumination until they disappeared. Hardy was left cowering in a corner of the control room in his underwear, facing the regular watch detail under Stigwood and Roybell. They were staring at him in amazement.

My God! a voice shrieked inside him. It wasn't real!

You imagined it! Terrified, he could hardly choke the words out:

"The Cap—the Captain—where?"

"On the bridge," mumbled Stigwood.

Hardy climbed the ladder to the conning tower and stood shivering in the cold. He could see legs—the Captain's. Suddenly the cobwebs cleared from his mind and he could see—the truth. He *wasn't* crazy. He had experienced a *vision*. He had seen the *purpose,* and it was the purpose that was insane—not him. He whirled on the helmsman and bellowed fiercely: "Stop all engines!"

The helmsman turned and stared at him.

"Stop this boat!" Hardy shouted and, shoving the helmsman aside, reached for the MB and rang up ALL STOP. He punched the intercom to the engine rooms and hollered, "All stop! Secure all engines!"

As soon as his engines were shut down, Cassidy began to wonder why. He hurried forward to the control room.

Dorriss came down from the bridge and confronted the helmsman. "What the hell do you think—"

"Ask Mr. Hardy, sir."

"Hardy?" Dorriss turned on the Professor. "You better explain."

"Where's the Captain?"

"I'm the *Exec!* Explain to me!"

Ed Frank came down the ladder in silence. His eyes scanned Hardy. "What's so goddamned important you couldn't wait to put on your clothes?"

Hardy glanced self-consciously at his underwear. He rubbed his arms, aware of the bone-chilling cold.

Cassidy's head appeared in the hatchwell at their feet. "Okay," he said, "who did we kill?"

Hardy glanced from one to the other, afraid of how they would react.

"I know what's happening!"

"What is happening?" the Captain challenged him.

Hardy licked his lips. "The boat is after *me.*"

There was a stunned silence. "It's *what?*" croaked Dorriss.

"It's come back to get *me!*"

"Really?" said Frank smoothly. He never took his eyes off the Professor.

"It's true! That crew has returned to get the one man they left behind." He looked at Cassidy for support; Cassidy was aghast. "I was supposed to go down with this boat thirty years ago!"

Dead silence; then a snort of surprised laughter from the Captain. "Thirty years . . . ?" he said.

"Goddammit! I know I'm right!" Hardy grabbed Frank by the shoulders and spoke into his face. "If you and this crew stay aboard, they'll take you too! We've got to stop the boat and get everybody off!"

Frank pulled away. Hardy looked around wildly. "Listen to me! Today is December eleventh! There's less than *one* day to go!"

A smile that Hardy recognized as amused contempt appeared on Frank's face. Then Hardy noticed the Captain's hand: It was holding down the switches on the battle-phone circuit. Every word Hardy said was being transmitted to the crew. Hardy stared in anguish at the betraying fingers, then swept a gaze up to Frank's icy, determined face—and was confronted by the cold-blooded disdain of Billy G. Basquine.

"Well, Mr. Hardy, if you're through dispensing portents, perhaps you will return to your bunk and allow the rest of us to go about our business."

Hardy stared at the small group of strangers in the conning tower, realizing he must sound like a maniac to these men. Hardy moved to the well and started down, but Dorriss's mocking voice caught him short.

"Shouldn't stalk around in your shorts, Jack. Christ, if you'd only wear socks, you wouldn't get those damned cold feet all the time."

Hardy couldn't speak; even his breath stuck in his throat. He went below and heard Frank's voice over the intercom: "Resume speed. Ahead full on two engines."

Hardy glanced once at Cassidy, who could not meet his gaze and turned to go back to his station. Hardy looked at Lieutenant Stigwood. The surprise was gone from his face too, replaced by the sort of sniggering hostility that Hardy used to get from Stanhill and the rest of the 1944 crew. The other men in the control room, Roybell and the auxiliarymen, hardly even made an attempt to hide their derisory smiles. Everybody was in on the joke, and Hardy was the butt of it.

He hurried back to his quarters, more frightened than angry. He tried to pull on his pants, and discovered how badly he was shaking. His fingers refused to cooperate. He sat on the bunk, unable to stop the flow of tears.

Were they going to drag him back to Latitude 30°? Was that all there was to it? Seemed rather pointless— a purpose lacking in logic, even for ghosts. He felt the uncertainty again. If he wasn't crazy, surely this would drive him to it. Would the *Candlefish* really have come back just to get *him*? Or was there another purpose he had not yet seen?

PART V

CHAPTER 21

December 11

0212 hours.

Hardy stepped out of the CPO quarters and stood in the corridor trying to formulate a plan of attack. He had to stop this boat dead—had to cost them at least twenty-four hours of travel.

The conning tower was out. He had already made his move there. The helmsman would call for the Captain if he so much as set foot on the upper deck. The control room—Dorriss would have told Stigwood to keep an eye on him, so the central diving controls were out. He would not even be able to get near the planes, the manifolds, the valves . . .

The pump room, below decks directly under the control room? Impossible—he would have to go through the control-room hatch; he would be stopped, questioned. The batteries? He could increase the acid level—no! Increase the *load* level to a battery section, turn on the high-speed battery intake valves, take on sea water—yes! The salt water would get into the circuits, then into the cells—there would be massive electrolysis. He would have to see that at least five circuits were affected, and all of them yards apart. The result would be quantity emissions of noxious chlorine gas. Greenish-yellow vapors would seep up through the ventilating system into several compartments. They would have to seal off those compartments, turn off the vents, and eventually send a man down with a chlorine lung to determine which cell was the source. Then, one by one, they would have to track down the others.

Hardy smiled. It would take several hours for them to secure battery balance again. Several hours of costly, premium *time*. If he could just delay them enough so they wouldn't connect with Latitude 30° at the precise moment—

The only problem was—fore or aft? The forward battery was directly below officers' country. He could probably get down there and arrange some of the damage, but he ran a big risk by doing so. He would be alone. What if he made a slip and was overcome by the gas?

He would be better off going aft, to the battery compartment below the crew's quarters, where if something went wrong he could holler for help, make some excuse . . .

The beauty of it astounded him. Not only would Frank fly into a panic to make repairs, but he wouldn't be able to charge batteries sufficiently for a full daytime submergence in the morning, which meant they would have to lie low on the surface for several hours without making progress.

He stepped through the connecting hatch to the control room and nodded to Stigwood, whose eyes swung away. The silent treatment. Ostracism. So he was right back where he had been in 1944. Well, so what? It didn't matter now.

The entrance to the after battery compartment was a deck hatch in the forward section of the crew's quarters. It was normal procedure for an officer to check the acid level in the cells, so no one questioned Hardy when he lifted the hatch, stretched prone on the deck, then lowered the top part of his torso into the compartment, head first. He gazed down the long rows of enormous battery cells. Each lead-acid unit was almost as big as a small man, and there were dozens of them. He could just crawl around among them and pick and choose—

The alarm bell went off in his head: *time!* Too much time. It would take forever to organize all this and then have it come off at the right moment. It was no good; he needed speed and surprise.

Grimly he rose from the compartment.

"Anything wrong?"

It was Clampett, stretched out on a nearby bunk, watching him curiously.

"No. No . . . nothing." Hardy closed the hatch and smiled at the torpedoman, who responded with a sour look. Hardy made his way aft, heading for the engine room.

He pulled himself through the hatch and immediately began to examine dials and gauges on the bulkheads around him, his mind racing now to find another method of stopping the boat—before *he* could be stopped.

" Anything wrong?"

Good God, am I that obvious? Hardy asked himself. If they all ask the same question, pretty soon one of them is going to catch on. He swung around, face to face with Walinsky. The pipe was at an angle, hanging from the side of the Chief's mouth. He had asked the question with concern, rather than suspicion.

"Well?"

Hardy blinked at Walinsky. "You tell me—is everything up on the line?"

"Sure."

"No trouble spots?"

"You forget, I built this boat."

Hardy nodded, started around him, then stopped. He looked back at Walinsky. Walinsky? No—Cassidy! Hopalong Cassidy. He just said, "I built this boat." *Cassidy* had a hand in its construction—*not* Walinsky.

Hardy was convinced that each man aboard had become his counterpart from 1944: A massive personality exchange had taken place, with the substitute personalities quite drastic departures from the originals.

But Cassidy and Walinsky were practically the same man. Whatever differences there were between them were so minute as to be almost unnoticeable. They were both the old men of the boat, both had been mechanical wizards, both were Hardy's friend . . .

That was the key. Appeal to Cassidy's friendship—treat him as Cassidy—make him believe he is Cassidy—*drive Walinsky out of him.*

He stepped closer to Cassidy and looked into his eyes. "I need your help," he said.

He took Cassidy's elbow and led him back to his station. Huddled in a corner, out of earshot, Hardy poured out the details of the situation as he saw it, carefully feeding Cassidy morsels that couldn't be refuted: the series of coincidences, the sinking of the ships, the change that had come over the Captain.

"Naw. He's always been like that—"

"No, he hasn't," Hardy objected, "only since Byrnes was killed!"

"Byrnes?" Puzzlement filled Cassidy's eyes.

"Byrnes—the Captain!"

Cassidy looked blank. "Basquine's the Captain. Lieutenant—what the hell are you talking about?"

"Cassidy, I sailed on this boat in World War Two! Thirty years ago—when you were at Mare Island, building these boats. I served aboard the *Candlefish* two years after she was launched! *And you put her together!* You—*Cassidy!* Walinsky never worked in the yards."

"But that's not—but I—?"

Cassidy backed against the bulkhead, looking terribly confused. Hardy pressed on. "Did you read my log?"

"Your what?"

"Read it again! Locker number four in the aft torpedo room. Get one from there. Skim it. You'll see what I mean right away."

Cassidy nodded helplessly.

"Cassidy, I've been where we're going. Believe me, we can't go there again."

"Right."

"The boat will sink. Everyone will be killed. We have to stop it."

"You're right."

"Cassidy, look at me!" Cassidy looked. "We will hit Latitude Thirty and we'll just disappear." He snapped his fingers: "Just like that. You have to help me."

Cassidy stared at him. "How?"

"Get everyone off!"

"Only the Captain can do that."

"He won't."

"Well, then, the Exec—"

"*He* won't! You don't understand—they're not going to cooperate. It's down to you and me, and we've only got one day!"

"Well . . . what do you want to do?"

Hardy moved closer and whispered into Cassidy's ear, "Stop the boat. Right now—here. Sabotage . . ."

He missed the sudden flash of horror that shot across the Chief's face. Cassidy or Walinsky, the Chief was old-line Navy. You don't sink your ship unless it's already going down and you want to be sure it doesn't fall into enemy hands. There was no way he would be willing to endanger the sub. It was time to stop humoring Hardy. The old Chief gave him a shaky smile and gripped his arm in reassurance.

"Look—you just sit down, sir, and I'll go get us some coffee. Just sit right here and everything will be okay. I'll be right back."

Hardy sensed the tone. He was losing the one ally he had aboard the boat—losing him to the past. If Cassidy was about to betray him to the Captain, then Hardy wanted to plant at least the seed of doubt.

"Cassidy, listen to me. Your name is Cassidy. You sailed from Pearl on November twenty-first. Byrnes was the captain. Byrnes was killed on December second and Ed Frank took command. Is any of this coming back to you?"

Cassidy went blank for a moment, then seemed to react. "Ed Frank, yes."

"Okay, now go to the control room and *see how he signs the log!*"

Cassidy hesitated a moment, then hurried off to the galley. Hardy watched him go, the tightness going out of him, but he was still grim. He hoped it hadn't been a wasted effort. At least now he had a plan.

He turned and headed for the after torpedo room.

On his way to the galley, Cassidy struggled with what Hardy had told him. It was such a maze of contradictions, such a jumble of thoughts. The unfortunate part was that he liked Hardy. But if it came to a choice between Hardy and the sub, the boat got first consideration.

What was Hardy trying to tell him about the Captain? He stopped at the entrance to the crew's mess and scowled. How could one man think he was another man—how could an entire crew think they were some other crew? It was insane.

He went cold. Maybe all those stories that Stigwood and Dorriss had been spreading were true. Maybe Hardy *was* off his rocker. If so, he presented a potential threat to the sub.

Something Hardy had said was nagging at him, surging back and forth in his mind. One moment he was sure the Captain was right, that Hardy was going nuts; the next moment he wasn't even sure of his own identity. What the devil had Hardy said? Something about Cassidy having built the boat and Walinsky having served aboard her. How could the same man have done both?

Hardy had told him he was Cassidy—not Walinsky.

But the Captain had called him Walinsky.

All certainty seeped out of him; convictions departed like dust through a sieve.

He asked Cookie for two cups of coffee. Then, almost automatically, he started for the control room—and stopped himself. He was on his way to tell the Captain—yet here he was holding two cups of coffee, one for himself and the other intended for Hardy.

Why the goddamned hell couldn't he make up his mind? What was turning him around and around?

He never got the chance to make a decision. There was a loud thump from somewhere aft—a familiar sound—followed by an unfamiliar one: an explosion! Cassidy's feet almost went out from under him. The two cups of coffee went flying. He grabbed the radio room bulkhead for support. Someone yelled, "What in holy shit—?"

The collision alarm went off: great whooping snorts of the klaxon!

"Aft torpedo room!" Giroux yelled from the radio room.

Cassidy's eyes bulged. He jumped up.
Hardy!

Hardy stepped into the aft torpedo room. There was a small watch detail on duty: four men. And they were all the way aft, working around the tubes with rags. No officer.

Hardy frowned at the racks of torpedoes in the bays, then at the tubes. The giant brass doors were shut. He couldn't tell if they were loaded or not. He pushed away from the hatch and walked with as much confidence as he could muster down the line to the tubes.

"Fellas . . . gotta shoot some water slugs."

"Now, sir?" said one of the men, surprised.

"Right now. Let's hop to it. Any of these things loaded?"

"Number eight is surface-ready, sir."

"Eight, huh. Okay, we'll start with number seven. Let's go."

He moved to one side to man the firing keys. The torpedomen acted swiftly, preparing the tube for a routine slug test.

Hardy eyed them silently. They activated wheels and switches, closing the outer door on tube number seven and opening the inner door. Hardy gazed at the door indicators: Both inner and outer doors on tube number eight were shut. He smiled grimly. The torpedomen charged up the impulse tank for tube number seven, then lifted the safety interlock.

"Outer door closed, sir . . . inner door open . . . impulse tank charged . . . safety interlock set, sir. We're ready."

"Okay. Stand back there."

Three of them moved. The fourth man looked at Hardy, puzzled.

"I said, stand back!"

He moved. Hardy's hand swooped off the key for tube number seven and jabbed the one marked EIGHT. In the same movement, he leaped four feet down the deck, heading for the exit. He was followed by a thump and a sharp jolt.

The torpedo in tube number eight shot toward the closed outer door and crumpled it like cardboard. At the same time, the inner door was blown open.

The sub's collision alarm went off with loud shrieks of pain.

Water poured in through the damaged outer door and rushed past the stalled torpedo and out into the compartment, a cascading flood blowing the torpedomen back as they tried to reach the door to close it.

The torpedoman who had hesitated was the first to collect his wits. He whirled and raced down the deck after Hardy.

Cassidy dropped the second mug and scrambled through the galley. Cookie looked up in surprise, clutching a batch of stew that had threatened to christen his freshly swabbed deck. The men in the mess flew to their feet at the sound of the alarm. The Captain's voice came over the intercom: "This is the Captain. All compartments report damage!"

A chorus of answers came off the speakers as Cassidy made his way aft. "Forward torpedo room all secure, sir!" "Wardroom secure, sir." "Forward battery secure—"

Cassidy raced down the forward engine room and on through the aft engine room. He seemed to be flying— why? Of course! The deck was starting to tilt aft. "Down by the stern!" he heard Roybell's voice over the speaker, reacting to the inclinometers in the control room.

"Stern compartments—report damage!"

Cassidy knew it was the aft torpedo room. Why didn't somebody—Hardy at least—call the Captain?

There was a bottleneck in the maneuvering room. The controllermen were manning the watertight door, the entrance to the aft torpedo room, ready to close it if the order came.

"Lemme through!" Cassidy yelled.

He plunged past the controllermen and dove through the hatch, landing splash on the deck in four inches of water. He slid six feet and banged his head on one of the skids. They were down at the stern, all right. He got to his feet, and that was when he saw what the struggling was all about: Two crewmen were trying to hold Hardy down. The other two were fighting to close the tube door against a terrific flood of water.

Cassidy jumped for the battle phone and pressed the switch. "This is Cassidy. After torpedo room—taking on water."

The order came back right on top of his own words: "Seal off all stern compartments! Close all vents!"

The two controllermen pulled the watertight door shut and spun the wheel. Cassidy saw a face pressed to the sight glass, anxiously watching his next move. He called through the phone again. "Captain, it looks like an accident with tube number eight."

Captain Frank screamed down the hatchwell: "Blow main ballast tank number seven and the after trim tank! Blow it!"

Roybell complied.

Air blasted away around them, and Cassidy lost his balance again as the stern whipped up out of the sea. "Stop all engines!" Cassidy hollered back into the phone. Then he jumped to help the two torpedomen. The water stopped coming in for a moment, and they got the door shut. He thought he heard a funny metal click as they did.

"Son of a bitch! He did it on purpose!" One of the torpedomen had Hardy in an armlock. The Professor's head was whipping from side to side. Cassidy ran back to the battle phone. "Aft torpedo here. We're secure."

"On my way," the Captain hollered back.

It wasn't more than ten seconds before the dogs on the watertight door spun and it popped open. Captain Frank stepped through.

"What happened?" he asked.

The torpedoman nodded at Hardy. "Slug test—fired the wrong tube—tried to blow up the damned boat, sir!"

Suddenly Cassidy knew what that click was.

"Jesus!" he yelled, and reached for the inner door on tube eight. He pulled the locks. The door blasted open and more water rushed in, accompanied by a blast of steam. Cassidy swung to one side and pulled himself up on the tube until he could get his head down and see into it. Through the sheets of water and the blinding steam he could see the stern of the torpedo.

The prop blades were spinning madly, churning up the water—the steam was escaping gas.

"The blades are running!" he yelled. Frank looked stunned. "Tell Roybell to keep blowing ballast! Get me a crowbar!"

Those blades only had to spin the equivalent of four hundred yards and the torpedo would be fully armed. He could assume that the torpedo's nose was pressed up against the damaged outer door. That meant the warhead was already making contact. If this thing spins four hundred yards, he screamed to himself, the whole ass end of this boat will go sky-high!

So that was Hardy's great plan!

You son of a bitch! He cursed him out in his mind, then screamed for the crowbar again. A torpedoman ran forward and flung it to him.

Fighting the water, he pushed the crowbar into the tube and tried to shove it between the blades to disrupt the revolution mechanism. He knew he had only seconds. He missed. He jabbed again and again—he couldn't see through the churning water—then he heard another click. The water stopped churning.

But that crowbar would never stay. He needed something smaller. "Pair of clippers and a wrench!"

Cassidy strained all his muscles holding the crowbar in place until the torpedoman returned. "Hold the bar," he told the torpedoman, who grabbed it and stood right behind the open door. Cassidy clutched the wrench lengthwise in the jaws of the clippers. Then he squeezed part of his head and shoulders over the top of the tube and into it. He extended the wrench and the clippers inside, attempting to jam the wrench in where the crowbar was.

The water came back as the stern crashed down into the sea. With his free hand Cassidy clutched the tube. The torpedoman yelled; he was caught full in the face by a stream of water. Cassidy took a chance, jabbed in the wrench, and felt it drop into place.

"Pull the crowbar!"

Gladly the torpedoman yanked. The wrench snapped in—there was a metallic crunch—and the props were still.

The incredible, deafening sound of rushing water stopped. They stood in it to above their knees, but they stood there, alive, all breathing hard, and regarding each other with the look of survivors who know at last what a brush with death means. "Okay," said Cassidy. "We're secure now."

Frank had a tight look frozen on his face.

Hardy was still in the torpedoman's grip. His eyes met Cassidy's, and his lips parted to speak. He couldn't. He was still afraid. His hand went out and touched the Captain's arm. "It was an accident."

The silence became as deafening as the rushing tons of water had been. There was only the slop-slop against their knees.

Hardy quivered with frustration. Cassidy stared at him blankly. And Frank? The Captain shriveled him with a sneer, then whirled on Cassidy.

"Damage?"

"Uh . . . the fish is stuck in there, but she'll hold. We can pull her out later and dismantle. We'll need a repair crew topside to fix that door—probably two guys in rubber suits."

"You're in charge," Frank barked, then turned back to Hardy. "You're relieved. Confined to quarters," said Frank. He stepped to the battle phone and pressed the switch. "This is the Captain. The aft torpedo room is secure. Start the bilge pumps, switch on the vents, secure from emergency, open all compartments. Repair crews will be formed under Chief Walinsky." He paused, then glared right at Hardy as he spoke: "We have sustained a damaged torpedo tube. The fault lies with Mr. Hardy. He has been relieved of duties and confined to quarters."

The watertight door had swung open. Dorriss stepped through.

"Mister Bates, I want this man manacled to his bunk with a twenty-four-hour guard."

Dorriss nodded, and the torpedoman holding Hardy gave him a yank and dragged him through the water to the exit. Hardy stumbled to stay on his feet. He flung a look to Cassidy—a plea for help. Cassidy stood rooted to the spot. Hardy threw him a blast: "Someone's got to help me! You can't *all* be crazy!"

As he was pulled through the hatch, Dorriss gave him a grin of satisfaction. "You're all washed up, Jack."

Cassidy's hand shook as he pulled out his sopping kerchief and wiped his brow. He was sweating.

He had heard the Captain refer to him as Walinsky, and he had known the difference—because Hardy had told him. *I know who I am.* He stared at the men around him: *Do they know who they are?* He realized the truth:

He was an island of sanity in a madhouse. Even Hardy had finally gone around the bend. Cassidy could hear him screaming obscenities at the crew as he was hauled back to his quarters. He listened to the voice diminish.

I know who I am, he thought. *And I'm alone.*

0330 hours.

Nothing was going according to schedule. Cassidy coughed into his jacket and rubbed his hands. He ignored the sweeping sheets of rain and the unsteady plunging of the afterdeck. He gripped the antenna-cable stanchion and watched the repair crew at work around the stern vanes. The engines were off; the screws were not turning. The *Candlefish* rolled in a surging sea, taking a powerful buffeting every few seconds as the squall roared around them.

Two motor machinist's mates had donned rubber suits and jumped off the stern; they had been bobbing up and down around the vanes for the last forty-five minutes. Three more motor machinist's mates were lashed to the vanes, passing tools down. But Cassidy could tell it was fruitless. The outer door on number eight tube should be taken off, sent to a forge, and straightened. They would never be able to effect repairs from topside.

One of the divers popped up and grabbed the vanes. He ripped off his mask; his nose was bleeding.

"What's the matter?" Cassidy shouted.

"It's the altitude," the man gasped. "Can't take the heights."

Cassidy shook his head grimly. "It's too dangerous. Get your buddy and get below."

Cassidy went forward, letting go the antenna cables and striding uncertainly up the center of the top deck.

He would have to report to the Captain. And it was a good excuse to bring up the matter of Hardy; an appeal of some sort was worth a try. He climbed to the cigarette deck and glanced toward the first wisps of dawn. Soon the submarine would be visible, if anybody was looking. He would promise the Captain to have a crew at work tonight when they surfaced again, but they would work from within.

He went down the conning-tower hatch. Adler was on duty. "Captain's in his quarters."

"Thanks." Cassidy started down the control room ladder.

"Uh, Chief . . . can we get moving again? Captain wants to make up lost time."

"Sure. Just as soon as those men get below— Wait a minute! Don't we have to dive?"

"Captain wants speed."

He schucked his dripping jacket and went forward to the officer's head. He borrowed a towel and dried himself off. The sound of irritated voices drew him to the corridor. They were coming from the CPO quarters.

It was Dorriss reading Hardy the riot act.

Cassidy winced. It was a disgrace. Dorriss was pouring it on, and there was no response from Hardy. A royal shit-kicking, he thought, and wished that the tables could be reversed, that he could outrank that skinny lieutenant, if only for five minutes.

He flung the towel back to Stigwood or Stanhill or whatever he was calling himself now, and knocked on the Captain's door.

"Who is it?"

"Cas—" He hesitated. "Chief Walinsky to see you, sir."

"Come in."

Cassidy stepped in and waited for Frank to look up. The Captain was very busy composing a report. The fountain pen moved swiftly, spreading chicken scratches all over a sheet of paper.

"What is it?"

"The repairs, sir."

"Oh, yes." Frank looked up. "All fixed?"

"No, sir," said Cassidy. "It's not going to work that way. We should . . ."

"What?"

"Return to Pearl."

"Don't be an idiot, Walinsky. You know we can't do that."

"Then we'll have to run with a bad tube."

Frank leaned back and scratched his stomach. He seemed oddly composed for someone who had just suffered a setback.

"You'll fix it, Mr. Walinsky. You will take your repair crew aft and fix it from the *inside*. Understood?"

"Sir, the best we can do is pull that fish out of there and seal it up. You can't use it again—not on this—this patrol."

Frank thought a moment, then nodded. "All right. Do that."

"Look, Captain, in my opinion it's the worst of a bad set of options."

"Go on."

"To work on that tube at all, we're going to have to stay on the surface. Daylight's coming, and the storm won't last forever. We'll be sitting ducks. The repair crew will drown trying to fix that damned tube. And another thing: If we don't get it fixed right away, and you push this boat to the limit on the surface, there's going to be an awful lot of pressure coming down that tube through that bad outer door. There's no guarantee she'll hold—"

"Goddammit, Walinsky!" Frank flew to his feet, eyes blazing. "That's exactly what that bastard wanted! To force us into turning back. I will not! There is too much at stake, do you hear me? Too much!"

"Sir, it was an accident—"

"The hell it was!" Frank's eyes narrowed. He advanced on Cassidy, holding two fingers up in his face. "For two years Hardy's been a thorn in my side, and now I've had it! For the duration of this patrol we'll just forget about Mr. Hardy. He can stay right where he is. I don't want him interfering when things become crucial—"

"Crucial?" asked Cassidy. "How much more crucial can things get?"

Frank stepped to the door and held it open for him. "Get your ass aft and get busy on those repairs. We'll lie to until you've finished. As soon as you have that fish out of there, notify Bates."

There was nothing more to be said.

Cassidy moved away and went aft, ducking through the control room hatch and pausing there to think.

Why risk everything over one tube? It was the delay
that was costly to them, wasn't it? And the fact that
they might have to sit on the surface in broad daylight
while repairs were effected.

No. There was something bigger afoot, and Cassidy
knew he wasn't in on it.

0440.

The *Candlefish* sat hove to in the Pacific over the
area known on the charts as the Ramapo Depth. The
squall had moved on, leaving the submarine danger-
ously visible in the center of a spreading dawn. Adler
was on duty on the bridge, nervously shifting from port
to starboard to cover the horizon with binoculars.

Down in the after torpedo room, Cassidy and the repair crew were sweating like pigs. The compartment
was sealed off, the vents were closed, and water kept
pouring in through tube number eight. What had been
pumped out earlier had been rapidly replaced. They
were up to their knees again.

They had chains attached to the aft fins of the torpedo jammed into tube number eight. Cassidy had tied
off the prop blades so they couldn't move again. There
was seemingly no danger of the fish exploding, but no
one was breathing easy.

They were attempting to pry the torpedo free by
sheer manpower. Cassidy did not participate; he had
already contributed his share of muscle. Now he was
the brains of the operation.

"Oh, shit! My back!" The complaint came from
Clampett.

"Come on, Corky, you lazy bastard—lay into it!"

So Clampett was now called Corky. Oh, well,
thought Cassidy. Let 'em call each other what they
want. He glanced at his watch, hoping the operation

would take another hour. That would gain them the time Hardy had wanted.

But it was over in ten more minutes.

The torpedo gave an answering jerk and slid back in the tube. The men let out a yell of triumph. Using the chains as tackle, they hauled it back, foot by foot, and transferred it to the forward skid. When it was lashed in place, Cassidy told them to take a break. They drifted back out of the way.

Another surge of water came through the open tube, but nobody moved to close it. Cassidy was more interested in the damaged fish that lay on the skid at hip level. He leaned over to examine the crumpled warhead. The nose was dented, pushed back out of shape, as if somebody had clobbered it in a frantic basketball game. The paint had chipped off all around the head.

Then something very peculiar began to happen. Cassidy's stomach reacted first, then his eyes, bulging—

The torpedo's warhead returned to its original shape: The nose popped back, the dents disappeared, the paint smoothed back into place.

It was as if the damage had never occurred.

Cassidy turned to see if the other men had witnessed the transformation.

Most of them were gone. They had left the compartment. The hatch was open—though no one had given the order. The vents were on; the pumps were going; the water was disappearing into the bilges. The few men who were still around were calmly smoking cigarettes and chatting.

It was as if *nothing* had occurred.

Cassidy pointed a shaking finger at the torpedo and was about to say something—but no one seemed the least bit interested.

Then something else struck him.

The tube.

The door to tube number eight was still open. But there was no water coming out.

Cassidy stuck his head in the tube, but he couldn't see clearly. He turned and fumbled for a battle lantern.

The beam settled on the outer door. It was closed. *How had it closed?* There was a tiny, almost imperceptible movement: the rippling of metal, the spreading of paint. The dents were smoothing out by themselves— the paint reappearing over the damaged section—

Cassidy felt the breath constrict in his windpipe.

Was it happening to him now, too? Was he going crazy like Hardy? He managed to belch out a loud groan. His breath came back. He sucked in great lungsful.

The diving alarm came like a pair of shrieks in his ear. The klaxon roared twice. Then the Captain's voice over the speaker: "Clear the bridge. Dive! Dive!"

He heard the rush of footsteps, then the *pfush* of compressed air escaping, the whirr and clank of machinery starting up. But he hadn't even reported the repairs to the Captain!

Cassidy stumbled to the hatch and out of the after torpedo room. He was all the way up to his station before it got to him.

He gripped the overhead piping on main engine number one, stared at the bulkheads, at the shining, glossy gray paint, the curve of the overhead—and for the first time in his life aboard submarines, he felt claustrophobic. He lunged forward, and then so did his last meal—all over Brownhaver's freshly swabbed deck.

CHAPTER 22

December-11

Hardy lay quietly in the gloom of his bunk. The drawn curtain blocked out most of the light. He moved his foot and winced as sharp needles of pain shot up his leg; it was asleep. Gently he shifted his weight, rolling onto his side. The looped chain rattled as the links grated over the metal bunk frame, then grew taut, pulling on his handcuffs. Once again he felt the biting pressure from the steel clamped around both his wrists.

Voices filtering in through the closed cabin door distracted him. He couldn't pick out words, but he did recognize Dorriss's guttural chuckle. He strained to hear the conversation, but the door was too thick.

His eyes roamed upward, to the shadowy outline of Elena's photograph clipped to the bottom of the upper bunk. He groaned and tore his gaze away, eyes circling and homing in on the calendar taped to the bulkhead at his side.

The first ten days of December were crossed off, leaving the circled eleventh day standing out like a silent scream.

Not much longer, he thought, taking comfort—not much longer . . .

The Captain glared at the two officers across the plotting table. His fingers rapped on the table surface like hoofbeats on a wooden bridge.

"What the hell is the matter with you people? It's almost foolproof!"

"That's what gets me, Skipper. The *almost* part."

The Captain growled back at his Exec, tired of hearing the same objections repeated.

"Dammit, Bates," he hissed. "There's nothing left for us in this area—nothing up in the Kuriles either. I'm not going to waste any more time hoping for *them* to stumble over *us*. That's not the way to win a war!"

A red flame flushed over the Exec's face. "You're the Captain, sir," he said stiffly. "If those are your orders, we'll follow them." Then the Exec thrust a finger down on the chart: "But I might remind you that charging into an unknown area can end as a one-way trip!"

"Sure—if they're looking for us! But they think we're sunk! They've been broadcasting it for days!" He smiled, and his eyes twinkled. "We can get in our licks and beat it before they even know what hit 'em. Pearl Harbor in reverse."

At that he leaned back and judged the effect on the other officers. "Of course, we *could* get killed."

They all looked up at him, expecting him to assure them it wouldn't happen. The Captain smiled again and announced confidently, "But that's a risk you're all sworn to take."

Cassidy reached under the covers and dragged out the copy of Hardy's log he had "liberated" from the locker in the aft torpedo room. He cracked it open and began to read.

It wasn't until he was past the strafing that he began to feel the first faint stirrings of uneasy familiarity. Hardy's neat handwriting, his concise wording, the parallels—everything that had happened to them was written down, and it had all been written before they had left Pearl. How could that be?

Tonight—today—let's see . . . He flipped pages and froze on December 11th—the last entry. Latitude 30—there it was, a complete description, limited, of course, to the point of view of a man stranded on deck. But what he had heard! The sounds, vibrations, rolling and pitching. Cassidy's hackles stood up.

Earlier, twilight, sometime before surfacing—an attack. MADs. Christ, if this log was right— He checked his watch.

He sat up quickly.

Any moment now. His heart started thumping.

Maybe all that stuff Hardy had screamed after the slug-test mishap wasn't so damned insane.

The slug test!

Cassidy's eyes raced over the entry for December 10th. Yesterday.

On that date in 1944, there was no slug-test mishap—no slug test at all. No accident—no damage to the boat. Not a mention.

He closed the log and stared straight ahead, frantically trying to sort out the significance.

The log was complete, as Hardy had said it would be. Give the man one point. Therefore, he must have been there—thirty years ago? How could that be? But give him two points. December 11th and Latitude 30—yes, described in detail. But he didn't know yet if it was true. A half point.

What else had Hardy said?

Check the quartermaster's log. But why? He couldn't remember why. Never mind—better do it. He pitched himself out of the bunk and quickly padded toward the control room.

The skipper was hunched over some charts, his face puckered with anger, growling at his officers in a low voice. Cassidy avoided the Captain's gaze and slipped past, ducking into the quartermaster's tiny cubicle. It was empty. He lifted the official log off the rack, opened it, and hurriedly thumbed pages.

On the bottom of the entry dated December 3rd he found what he was looking for. Rapidly he leafed through the next seven pages, pausing at each one, his heart sinking.

Three and a half points.

Every single entry had been signed with a hastily scrawled "B. G. Basquine."

Cassidy was numb. He replaced the log and stared from the cubicle, examining the Captain, knowing that Hardy was right. He was not the man he should be. He had become someone else. Cassidy now knew for sure because he realized he too had been someone else. Or he wouldn't have forgotten the man whose signature was on every page prior to December 3rd: "L. F. Byrnes."

He stepped back into the control room. He was right behind Nadel when the sonar operator's head shot up and his voice rang out:

"Picking up sound, Skipper."

Cassidy's mouth opened.

All eyes swung around as Nadel fine-tuned his equipment.

"Screws?" asked the Captain.

"No, sir. Can't quite make it out—"

"Put it on the speaker."

He flicked a switch, and a distant buzzing clicked in, grew louder, filled the control room. The Captain acted instinctively:

"All ahead emergency! Take her deep! Right full rudder!"

The deck tilted beneath them. The *Candlefish* shoved downward. And Cassidy's arms sprang out. He clutched the instrument panels and shouted, "MADs!"

The Captain whirled and stared at him.

Four and a half points. Cassidy held on tight and waited for confirmation. Magnetic Airborne Detectors. The Japanese contribution to anti-submarine warfare—

"Two hundred feet, sir!"

Two distinct splashes pierced the buzzing that roared out of the speakers. Nadel whipped off his headphones, anticipating the shock. The Captain braced himself against the chart table.

Twin concussions slammed into the sub with stunning force. The air was filled with flying particles of insulation. Men who hadn't secured a firm handhold were knocked off their feet and sent sprawling.

The Captain hit the phone switches and barked, "All compartments report damage!"

Reports of "Secure" rattled back at him from stunned voices. The surprise had been complete, but the damage was minor.

It was all over in five minutes, and in less than an hour the submarine was secure. The two off-duty sections were released, and the *Candlefish* returned to normal operations.

Cassidy left the control room quietly, unnoticed. No one detected the new look of determination that had crept into his features. And no one suspected why he stopped in the forward engine room to pick up his toolbox.

Four and a half points, he was thinking. Shit, round it off to five and let's call it a day.

The jaws of the clippers closed around the line and bit down, slicing through the fabric at the joint leading from Normal Lubricating Oil Tank number three. Cassidy shifted his weight, trying for more leverage in the crawl space. He grunted and squeezed harder. The cutting head sheared through the last of the canvas and chewed into the hard rubber line.

With a final heave, he succeeded. The line parted. Oil spurted up, coating the bulkhead. He dropped the clippers and gazed happily at the flow.

Then the two halves of the severed line very slowly crept back together and sealed themselves up again.

His elation turned to horror as the oil sputtered, then stopped. Dazed, Cassidy observed helplessly. The canvas outer wrapping reknitted, and the oil-spattered bulkhead cleansed itself.

Shivers shot through his body. He gaped down at his clippers.

"What the hell are you doing down there, Walinsky?"

Cassidy swiveled and looked up. He bit his lip and swore under his breath. What the hell was the Captain calling the Exec . . . ? Bates!

"Nothing, Mr. Bates. Just thought I'd better check those NLO lines."

"How are they?"

Cassidy dropped the clippers into his toolbox and secured the snaps. "Holding fine, sir."

"You have the watch, don't you?"

"Yessir."

"You finished down there?"

Cassidy nodded. "Yessir."

"Then let's get with it."

The mess steward placed the tray on the deck beside Hardy's bunk and rapped twice on the bulkhead. Hardy waited till he left, then slid open the curtain with his manacled hands. He gave the food a disinterested glance, then began to pick at the spaghetti. The cuffs made it difficult, but since they hadn't given him a knife or a fork—potential weapons, he supposed—he had only the spoon to contend with. He took a few half-hearted bites and chewed thoughtfully. The coffee was good. Warmth flowed through, giving him a false sense of well-being. One look at his handcuffs, and that sensation evaporated.

He drained the mug, set it back on the tray, and began chopping the spaghetti into bites with the spoon.

Cassidy waited until the mess steward returned to the galley, then made his way forward, pausing to nod at the guard outside the CPO cabin. He slipped into the wardroom, helped himself to coffee, then plunked down at the farthest corner of the table. The seat gave him a view of the corridor while keeping him out of sight. He sipped his coffee and waited.

Hardy stared at the crumpled note resting in his spaghetti sauce. He fished it out with the spoon, wiped the grease off the edges, and carefully unfolded it. His eyes picked up the writing in the unstained center of the napkin.

NO SLUG TEST IN LOG DEC 10 1944—MUST SEE YOU—CREATE DIVERSION—CASSIDY.

Hardy studied the note, comprehension slowly dawning. The slug test—of course. The fact that he had been able to pull it off in the first place meant that *Candlefish was vulnerable.*

If he could catch the boat unawares once, why not a second time?

Suddenly he felt better, alive once again. He rolled the napkin into a ball and shoved it under his mattress, gauging the possibilities. It was overwhelming—maybe they had a chance after all.

* * *

Cassidy tensed and crouched down. He glanced over at the CPO cabin. The guard was turned away—

Come on, come on. What was Hardy waiting for?

The commotion started almost as if by signal. Hardy began bellowing to be released.

"Come on, will ya? I have to get to the can!"

The guard rushed in and saw his pained expression.

"You don't have to bust down the bulkheads, sir—"

"You want to see something bust, stick around another minute. Come on!" He held up his chains. "Let me out of these."

"Can't," said the guard.

Cassidy slipped in behind him.

"What do you mean you can't?" Hardy snapped.

"Have to get the key from Bates."

"Well, get a move on—my back teeth are starting to float!"

Cassidy spoke softly, right in the guard's ear. "I'll watch him, son."

The guard turned uncertainly, then nodded and took off.

Hardy dropped his chains and looked up at Cassidy, searching his eyes.

"That slug test broke the pattern, Hopalong."

"Uh-huh."

"Didn't happen on December tenth. I caught her off guard."

Cassidy shook his head. "Not for long. The damage repaired itself." Hardy blinked, not quite comprehending. "Repaired *itself*," Cassidy repeated. "And that's not all. I tried to cut the lines from the NLO tank. Sealed itself right back up in front of me. It was a nice try, but it's the wrong approach."

Hardy sagged.

"You were right about one thing. The Captain. Since

December third, he's been signing the log 'Billy G. Basquine.' "

Hardy struggled to a sitting position. "That's the day Byrnes was killed."

Cassidy nodded. "What about that? You didn't lose your Captain in '44. How come it happened now?"

Hardy hesitated to sort out his thoughts. Then it came to him, a disgusting realization of just how hopeless their situation was. "I know why—I don't exactly know how. Byrnes was the weak link. He was ready to turn us around and head back to Pearl. The sub didn't want that. Besides . . ." He paused, uncertain of what he was about to say. "We set out with an eighty-five-man crew, one more than we had in 1944. The boat killed two birds with one stone. Bumped off Byrnes and let Frank take over. It must have sensed that Frank would be easier to control."

"It might control Frank," Cassidy contended, "but Basquine?"

"What do you mean?"

"We're not dealing with Ed Frank anymore—it's Basquine. How could anything control *him?* I told you I knew him back at Mare Island. I thought he was crazy then, but *now?*"

Hardy struggled with it. Who or what was running things? The sub? Ed Frank? The ghosts of Basquine and Bates and the rest of the—

"My God!" Suddenly he knew it. "It's all of them! It's everything in tandem. The *Candlefish* is operating as it was meant to operate—*as a weapon!*"

Cassidy was blank.

"Christ, he said it himself. *Crew and machine—we* make up the weapon! This boat couldn't pull all that stuff on its own. It needs Basquine, and Basquine needs the boat! Deprive him of that—"

He stopped and scanned Cassidy's face for a response. "You've got to bust me out of here. We can still stop him, but I can't do a damned thing as long as I'm chained to this—"

The voice over the speaker interrupted him.

"This is the Captain speaking . . ."

They stiffened and waited. The hum of the air conditioners took on an ominous tone.

The Captain stood at the head of the torpedo skids, one hand on a green-and-yellow monster, the other clutching the battle phone. He was ringed by tired crewmen.

"Well, they've had a go at us again. Magnetic Airborne Detectors. Radio tells me they've reported us sunk once more . . ." He smiled, and the men around him smiled too. "So I think we should take advantage, don't you?"

There was no reply, but he could feel spirits rising.

"The pickings have been pretty slim for us these last few days. I intend to change that. We're not going to wait for them any longer, gentlemen. We're going to hit them right where they live—in their own ball park. We're coming off station this evening and setting course for Tokyo Bay."

He paused and nodded affirmation around the compartment. A cheer went up—then another.

"Where we'll shoot the shit out of anything flying the rising sun."

Hardy was stunned. "Oh, goddammit," he muttered.

Cassidy was smiling. He threw a palm up in Hardy's face. "Hey—we're off the hook! He's not going to Latitude Thirty. We're okay!"

"The hell we are. Can't you see what's going to happen?"

"Nothing—we're home free. He's going to bust right out of this pattern."

"You bet. Right out of 1944 and straight into 1974."

"I still don't—"

Hardy growled into his face. "This sub never *got* to Tokyo Bay. It was *thwarted*. At 2130 tonight, the recreation of that last patrol is over. There's nothing left to *re-create!* It's all new!" He paused, then added quietly, "Can you imagine the *Candlefish* on the prowl in Tokyo Bay—in 1974?"

Cassidy went white.

"A fully armed submarine on the loose in a crowded, unsuspecting harbor? It would be a disaster!"

"Okay . . ." Cassidy paced to the door, checking for the guard, then came back. "How come *he* can break the pattern and we can't?"

"We were interfering with *them*."

"So what do we do?" Cassidy asked helplessly.

"Now we've got to switch tactics. We have to force the boat *into* Latitude Thirty."

"*Into* it?" Cassidy returned his gaze painfully. "And sink?"

"That, or take the chance of killing an awful lot of innocent people."

"Awful lot of innocent people aboard this boat, too."

"I can't help that!" Hardy snarled between clenched teeth.

"How are we going to do it? Just tell him please forget about Tokyo Bay and stay on this course, please sir pretty please?"

"Just *get me out of here.*"

"Any trouble, Chief?"

Cassidy swung around. The guard came in, dangling a key ring.

"No. Just humoring him." He glanced sideways at Hardy, a look of bitterness. "Better keep those keys handy. The way he's been raving, he's gonna piss himself blue. In my opinion"—he gazed directly at Hardy, and Hardy thought he meant it—"he's a certified section eight. A maniac."

The guard unchained Hardy but kept the cuffs on.

Hardy glanced back at Cassidy as he was led from the cabin, his stomach contracting into a tight knot. Had he been suckered by the Chief? Strung along so that a report could be made to the Captain?

They broached at 2000 in a cold clear Pacific night. A bright moon bathed the superstructure and topside decks, giving the boat a shimmering, wraithlike appearance. The bridge watch came up subdued, lulled by the whine of pulsing diesels.

The Captain stood by the TBT, listening to the rhythm of the engines, drinking it all in, absorbing the strength of *his* submarine.

The roar of air that blew the main ballast tanks dry woke Hardy out of a frozen reverie. His mind was groggy, lethargic. With an effort he cleared the cobwebs and tried to concentrate. He was still trying to figure out how to stop the Captain. He hadn't thought of the time. Now it struck him like a blow below the belt.

2000.

Sixty minutes later, Hardy was losing hope. He had only thirty minutes left. And where was Cassidy? Soon it would be too late.

He couldn't even get to the door without Cassidy's help. Yet if he could somehow reach the control room, open the gun locker, grab a .45 and some grenades, then barrel up to the con . . .

The plan began to take shape. But it all depended on time. And he had less of that every second. Cassidy—

for God's sake! He didn't believe me. He's hiding in his fucking engine room, huddling there with Walinsky's pipes, trying to ignore everything. He's old! He wants to die.

Cassidy, please!

The thud shocked him upright. It was just outside. Then a sound like a sack of potatoes hitting the deck. Then the door closing . . . Footsteps . . .

A hand whipped the curtain aside. There stood Hopalong Cassidy, the clippers clutched in one hand and the key ring in the other. Behind him the guard lay sprawled on the deck. Hardy's eyes went gratefully to Cassidy's determined, grim face.

"Okay, Professor. Now what?"

CHAPTER 23

December 11

Hardy and Cassidy stood just inside the CPO quarters, Cassidy hefting the clippers, his only weapon. Hardy turned and spoke in a guarded murmur. "We're going to take the gun locker in control."

"Who is?"

"You are. Just take the key, open the locker, get a forty-five and two hand grenades, then call me."

"Call you? While they're climbing all over me?"

"Use the forty-five."

"I'm not going to shoot anybody!"

"Fine, just don't let *them* know that. Give me one of the grenades—I'll take the con. You set the demo charges on the electronic equipment."

"The what?"

"God, Cassidy—you said you built this thing!"

"I had nothing to do with electronics. That was Faber."

Hardy glared at him. "She carries self-destruct charges on all critical electronics, circuit-breakers marked with red and yellow stripes—you can't miss them. Just pull them down and the charges are armed."

"How many?"

"Two radar and one sonar."

"But that'll knock the sub right out of commission!"

"That's the idea."

Cassidy grabbed Hardy's shoulder; there was fear in his eyes.

"What about the crew?"

"We'll get them off, but it's going to take a very big scare to do it."

"Coming into fog, Captain."

The Captain acknowledged the report from the bridge, then turned back to Lieutenant Dorriss, who had the patrol chart spread out against the TDC casing.

"Fog," the Captain repeated, and displayed a faraway look of satisfaction, as though he was being reintroduced to an old friend.

"Course?" he asked the helmsman.

"Three-five-eight, Captain."

"All right, Mr. Bates, make your mark."

Dorriss looked down at the chart. Course 358, if they kept on it, would take them north to the Kuriles within three days. But that was not to be the way of it. Dorriss drew an extension of the red patrol line across the chart and stopped it just over the parallels and perpendiculars that marked latitude 30° north, longitude 146° east.

Then he inscribed it: 11 DEC 2100.

He put the red pen back in his pocket, folded the chart, and turned to deposit it in the mission locker. He closed the locker, then raised his hand, expecting to find his keys in the lock. He cursed.

Of course! He had loaned them to the guard, so he could unchain Hardy and walk him back to the can. The bastard had forgotten to return the keys. Dorriss turned to the Captain and said, "I'll be right back." He hurried below.

The Captain gripped the ladder and hauled himself up to the bridge, stepping out onto a cold, misty deck and squinting into the fog.

"I thought you said fog," he growled at the OOD.

"Sorry, sir. I meant soup."

It was thick. Terribly thick. As thick as the Captain had ever seen. But that was all right. He didn't have to see to know where he was going. And his course change was as much a matter of timing as location. He could risk anything right up until the last second—and he would. He felt giddy with the sort of exhilaration one should only feel in battle. But wasn't this a battle too? And he had it timed so well—down to the second. He glanced at his watch.

2108.

Dorriss ducked through the hatch to officers' country and stopped. He had sensed something: an imbalance, a tell-tale warmth from just behind him. He whirled and saw he was right: Two men stood there, wide-eyed, crouched in anticipation. Hardy and Cassidy, braced against the bulkhead, one on either side of the hatch. Hardy was free, without chains or cuffs, and Dorriss suddenly knew what had become of his keys.

His reaction was that of a man used to the crackle of immediate obedience. He stuck his hands on his hips and announced, "Mutiny, Mr. Hardy. Mutiny . . . *and* sabotage. That's going to look very nasty on a report."

"Is it now?" said Hardy.

"I could have you both thrown in the brig for the rest of your lives, so—"

Cassidy took a step forward. "Excuse me, sir, but we're late for an appointment."

Before his sentence was complete, the clippers were in motion. It was an overhand swing, and it came down hard on Dorriss's forehead. The Exec crumpled, blood welling up through the split skin.

"Watch that hatch," Cassidy hissed, then dropped the clippers, grabbed Dorriss under the arms, and dragged him into the CPO cabin. He was gone a long time.

Hardy waited for him, pressed against the bulkhead, his nerves shifting into high gear. What's keeping Cassidy, for Chrissakes—is he trying to revive that bastard?

Movement.

Men were leaving through the aft hatch, presumably for coffee.

Where was Cassidy?

He peered at the clock in control. 2111. My God, only four minutes, then the Captain will—

He jumped at the tugging on his sleeve and turned, fully expecting to see the ghost of Basquine or Bates. It was Cassidy.

"Let's go," he said.

At exactly 2112 Hopalong Cassidy stepped through the hatch into the control room, carrying his clippers. He eyed the five crewmen, sizing them up as adversaries. Roybell was nearest the gun locker. Stigwood was at the plotting table, penciling something into the log. The two auxiliarymen stood by the flood valves and the manifolds, lounging; there was nothing for them to do at the moment. Only Scopes was glued to his instruments.

What to do first?

The demo charges? The three circuit-breakers. He gazed about the instrument panels, seeking out the red-and-yellow-striped switches. He found the sonar switch and saw he had a clear path to it. He could just walk right by it, and give it a flick—

He smiled at Stigwood and slipped across the control room to the sonar equipment, and, raising the clippers to shoulder level in his left hand, he stretched with his right, yawned, and flipped the switch down, one quick movement.

He was past Scopes in a flash, reaching for the gun locker—

Goddamn!

The key. The key was in the wooden box attached to the periscope well over the plotting table. Back to Stigwood . . . Beginning to panic now. He flashed Stigwood another grin and was rewarded with a dull look, even as he opened the box. He knew exactly which key: the red-white coded one. He snatched it and swept back to the gun locker. He felt Stigwood's eyes on him—simple curiosity. Too late for you, bastard.

Cassidy jammed the key in the lock and had it open as Stigwood suddenly came alive and said, "Hey."

"Hey yourself," Cassidy muttered, flung the locker open, and grabbed the first .45-caliber pistol he saw. He slammed in a clip, pulled the slide, and swung it up at Stigwood.

"Hey!" Stigwood barked it this time.

"Hay is what horses and cows chew, bub. Were you born on a farm?" Cassidy moved the barrel of the gun around, letting it linger briefly on each man in the compartment. The two auxiliarymen stepped uncertainly away from their instruments; otherwise, no one moved.

"That's fine," said Cassidy. He pulled out two hand grenades, tucked the handle of one in his belt, gripped the pin of the other in his teeth, then—in his best John Wayne snarl—"Scopes, get your ass away from that station."

Scopes joined Stigwood at the plotting desk. Neither of them saw Jack Hardy step in behind them.

"All right," said Cassidy, pointing to the closed destruct switch above sonar. "Demolition charges are set. They'll go off in ten minutes."

Hardy stepped past Stigwood and Scopes. They stared at him, suddenly understanding. Roybell made a move to stop Hardy. Cassidy raised the .45 and said, "Don't." Roybell jumped back. Hardy moved to the radar station and flipped on the two destruct switches. He took the second grenade from Cassidy and climbed the ladder to the con.

Adler turned first and saw him—rather, saw the grenade coming up to his face. His mouth opened.

"You're confined to quarters," Adler said.

"Not any more I'm not. What's our position?"

Adler felt Hardy's foot connect with his backside. He moved to the position indicators.

He spoke shakily. "Latitude thirty degrees nineteen minutes north, longitude one hundred forty-six degrees thirty-eight minutes east."

"What's the heading?"

"Course three-five-eight," volunteered the helmsman, gaping at the grenade.

"All right, you hold this course—"

The Captain's binoculars were trained into the fog, scanning a completely invisible horizon. The Captain was feeling the first twinge of uncertainty. His eyes were useless in this muck. He listened for the regular slop-slop of waves against the bows as the sub made speed through the sea. He glanced at his watch once more.

2115.

The Captain turned and hollered down the open hatchwell, "Slow to one-third. Bring her around to course two-five-three!"

He felt a surge of excitement.

He was waiting for the answering call from below. But there was none. It was impossible that the helmsman hadn't heard him. Something was wrong . . .

He stared down the hatchwell and, from the foot of the ladder, Jack Hardy was looking back up at him.

2115.

The first effects of the geomagnetic anomaly they were passing through would occur at exactly 2132. Hardy had to keep the Captain at bay for seventeen minutes.

The Captain stepped into the hatch and went down the ladder. He turned and saw the grenade.

"Don't say anything," Hardy commanded. "I don't want to hear anything from you."

"Why? What are you going to do—pull that pin?"

Hardy hefted the grenade.

"Sure you are," the Captain sneered. "You're exactly the kind of man who would take a chance on destroying everyone aboard, right? That's the kind of maniac you are, Hardy. You don't give a damn about human life. Everything for your own crazy ends, isn't it? Who in hell did you convince to help you? What sucker's ear did you fill with your demented line of shit? *Who let you out?*" he roared.

"I did."

The Captain looked down the ladder to the control room. Hopalong Cassidy stood there, holding a .45 on the crewmen.

"You *listened* to him?" the Captain bellowed down the hatch. "Walinsky, you're a goddamned fool!"

"I'm not Walinsky! I'm Cassidy! Hopalong Cassidy!"

The Captain laughed and pointed at Hardy. "And who's this? The Lone Ranger? You're both out of your minds."

"Get your hand off that switch," Hardy said quietly. The Captain's hand shot back from the battle-phone switch. "Nobody has to hear this but us," said Hardy. He maneuvered the Captain away from the intercom circuit, backing him toward the helmsman. Adler retreated to a corner.

"Now, let me tell you what the crazies have in mind, Skipper. We have set the demolition charges on the radar and sonar stations. Without radar and sonar, you won't stand a chance chugging into Tokyo Bay—past the nets and the mine fields. Will you? *Will you?*"

He waited until the Captain nodded his head in agreement. "Now, I'll be willing to have Cassidy break those demo circuits—on one condition: We continue on this heading, course three-five-eight, without interruption for the next thirteen minutes. After that, I don't give a shit what you do, because it won't make one bit of difference. Either I'll be proved right, or you can pitch me overboard. But we're staying on this course!"

The Captain had turned purple. "Why?" he choked.

"Because if I let you take this boat west into Tokyo Bay, you're going to be in for the surprise of your life—"

"HARDY!!" the Captain screamed at him.

Hardy felt his whole body vibrate with the bone-chilling force of it. The Captain stepped forward and made as if to grab Hardy's neck with his bare hands. Hardy's arm came up sharply in reflex, and the grenade with it, connecting with the Captain's jaw. The Captain staggered back, then whirled on the helmsman.

"Left full rudder! Come about to course two-five-three! *Move!*"

The helmsman hesitated. The Captain screamed, "That's an order!"

The helmsman directed a shaking finger at Hardy. "That's a grenade!"

"Stay on course!" Now Hardy was yelling. It was the

only way he could keep control: match the Captain in rage and volume. "Captain," he said, "in five minutes your boat will start coming apart at the seams!"

The Captain looked back at him blankly.

"Did you think you could *beat it?* Just turn and run away from it? It has to happen! Can't you see? It's part of the pattern!"

"The pattern? You lunatic—there *is* no pattern! I'm in control of this boat!"

Hardy drew himself up with the assurance of one who has penetrated the last defense. "Then why are you so determined to change course?"

"I—I—" the Captain looked confused.

"We've got him!"

There were sounds of a struggle below. There was an explosion and a dull clang. Hardy jumped back, frightened. What was it? A bullet . . .

Cassidy's gun.

He whirled to the hatch, cutting around the ladder and looking down without turning his back on the Captain. It was all over below. Roybell and Scopes had Cassidy's arms pinned.

As Roybell swooped down to recover the pistol, he yelled at the others, "Cut those switches!"

He was too late. The explosion came on top of his voice. It was the sonar gear—the first switch Cassidy had pulled. The explosion was short and sharp, but it was followed by the sound of the gear splattering all over the compartment.

Roybell and the others were knocked over by the concussion, and the Chief jumped up again with the pistol.

Hardy yanked the pin from the grenade, then stepped back, clutching the spoon handle tightly so it wouldn't flip up.

"Forget it, Mr. Hardy. You've lost."

The Captain's voice had regained some composure.

"Control room secure, sir." It was Stigwood's voice, through the intercom.

"Damage?" the Captain shouted.

"Sonar is wiped out, sir. No one hurt. Should we alert the crew?"

"Yes!"

Stigwood's voice went out through the battle-phone circuit to every compartment in the boat. "Attention, attention. This is Control. We've had an accident with a demo charge. Equipment damage only. We still have hull integrity."

Stigwood switched off and called up the well, "Should I inform the crew of the mutiny, sir?" His voice was calm, not even an edge of distress.

"I don't think there's any need, Stanhill," the Captain said coolly. He was daring Hardy to let the grenade go. "It really is over, Mr. Hardy. I can have Stanhill make the course change himself, on the emergency helm. Why don't you be a smart fellow and throw that thing overboard? I wouldn't want to lose you."

Hardy checked the clock.

2130.

"Go ahead," he said.

"What?"

"Go ahead and have Stigwood or Stanhill or whoever change course. Do it from here if you like. You'll find out it's too late." He kept talking, stalling for time, rattling on like the madman they all thought he was, anything to hold them on this course another two minutes; that was all he wanted, he prayed for it through the babble coming out of his mouth.

The Captain turned to the helmsman.

"Course two-five-three. Now."

"Aye, aye, sir." He gripped the wheel and spun. Nothing happened.

The wheel didn't budge.

He strained. "Captain, she's not answering."

There was a moment of awkward, frightening silence. The Captain's eyes quivered. Hardy's muscles tightened.

The Captain grabbed the wheel himself. It held fast. He turned and snapped down the phone switch to control. "Emergency, Stanhill—left full rudder—come to course two-five-three."

"Aye, aye, sir."

Stigwood gripped the emergency helm and struggled with it. Nothing. It was frozen.

"Emergency controls jammed, Skipper. She won't respond!"

The Captain grabbed the phone and the motor telegraph at the same time. "All back full!" he yelled into the mouthpiece, and rang it up on the MB.

They waited seconds; then the controlled reply came from below: "Skipper, maneuvering reports engine switches won't answer."

Hardy let out an involuntary yelp of laughter. He had been right. "It's out of your hands, Mr. *Basquine!* It's not yours any more—the *Candlefish* is running herself! She's heading for latitude thirty degrees forty-nine minutes north, on course three-five-eight. When she gets there, she's going to disappear—and you and everybody else who's aboard will go with her!"

This time it was the Captain who yelled, "Get your hand off that thing!"

Hardy was holding down the intercom switch, spreading the word to the entire crew.

The Captain had just started to lunge for the hand grenade when the first tremor struck the boat.

The whole conning tower shook. All four men stumbled to one side.

A series of rattling shivers whipped the submarine from side to side.

The Captain's eyes met Hardy's. "All right, you son of a bitch," he screamed, "I'll take this thing through your fucking Latitude Thirty and still get to Tokyo Bay!"

CHAPTER 24

December 11

2132.

Hardy one-handed himself up to the bridge, still clutching the hand grenade. A thick gray mist covered the sea—a wall of cloud, obscuring everything as *Candlefish* cut deeper into Latitude 30.

The decks shook beneath his feet. The lookouts gripped their railings for support. Lieutenant Danby screamed an angry curse as the sub pitched violently.

Hardy took a long backswing and flung the grenade far out to sea. Seconds later he heard a dull thud. He turned and dropped back into the conning tower.

The Captain had shoved the helmsman aside and taken over the wheel himself, to no avail.

The inexplicable force whipped the submarine from side to side. The glass in the control-room clock shattered into a thousand fragments. Stigwood pulled himself up to the plotting table and grabbed the manifold controls.

And came away with a shout of pain.

They were red-hot.

Roybell managed to reach the indicator gauges, but his face twisted in surprise as he exclaimed, "Christ! She's doing twenty-one knots!"

Danby clung to the bridge coaming and gawked at the spray pitching off the bow. Top surface speed. But why? Nobody had given the order—and to charge ahead through this fog like an enraged bull—

The shakes became long, sustained vibrations gripping the submarine in a vise and heaving it to port, then starboard, then straight up into the air. She came down hard, bruising the sea, sending waves high into the fog.

The lights went out. Air conditioning shut down. The Captain called for emergency power, and the red combat lights came on. But then those lights started to flicker on and off.

The Captain grabbed the battle phone and called Maneuvering.

"What are you making back there?"

"All ahead full, sir!"

"Slow to one-third!"

The senior controllerman reached up for his motor telegraph and tried to pull it back. It wouldn't budge. He tried his panel levers. Nothing responded. He grabbed the speaker.

"Skipper, she won't respond!"

Again he grabbed the MB. The bell wouldn't move.

"Skipper, she's stuck on all ahead full."

In the forward engine room, Googles and Brownhaver checked dials and gauges. "She's heating up!" yelled Googles.

Brownhaver's feet slid out from under him. He shot across the deck and crashed ass first into main engine number one.

"Holy shit!" said a machinist at Googles's elbow. He was staring at the dials; they were spinning erratically.

Then there was a mind-rending shudder that began in the bow and worked its way aft, rattling through each compartment, flinging men to the deck, tossing them between torpedo bays, clobbering them with falling gear. Like billiard balls they caromed from one bulkhead to another.

The Captain was clinging to the periscope well. Hardy yelled to him, "Get everyone off! Abandon ship!"

The Captain turned possessed eyes on him and snapped angrily, "You're a coward, Hardy."

Hardy felt a cold chill blast down the open well. He jumped the Captain and clung to him. "Get everybody off!"

The Captain's hand shot out to the battle phone: *"Battle stations! All hands—battle stations!"*

The submarine began rolling and pitching as well as yawing left and right. Fixtures snapped off the bulkheads and crashed to the deck. Light bulbs popped and burst. Dial faces blew out of their settings.

High atop the conning tower masts, lookouts wrapped arms and legs about their railings and saw ocean rushing up to meet them, then falling away again as the submarine thrust itself faster through the waves.

In the control room, Stigwood shouted, "We're under attack! We're under attack!"

Scopes fumbled for his radar gear and switched it on. The entire radar installation shook in its mounting. The oscilloscopes came on; he saw green lights shooting in every direction at once.

Roybell pointed frantically at the Christmastree board, the life-pulse of the submarine. The warning lights were blinking, green to red, red to green.

Now they had no way of knowing the condition of hull integrity.

Cassidy stumbled back against the valve controls and stared at the instruments going wild around the control room.

He had seen enough. He made for the forward door,

yelling back over his shoulder, "Break out the life jackets!" He dove through the hatch and stumbled forward, repeating the message. He expected the order to abandon ship to follow him through the speakers.

The Captain felt the broken undulations rippling through the periscope shaft, rapping his body against the metal—yet he refused to relinquish his grip on the shaft.

Jack Hardy wobbled just beside him, clinging to the well ladder, regarding him with a resigned certainty. Hardy seemed to be waiting for him. The Captain felt boxed in, cornered by this bearded nemesis. He sprang from the scope and, shoving Hardy aside, clutched the ladder, staring up through the open hatch into the dark, swirling mist.

He thrust his head above deck level and stared, astonished, at the gyrating masts above the bridge. He was chilled by the rumble of creaking metal and the frightened yells of the lookouts. Frightened enough to back down, he turned and gazed below—and found Jack Hardy staring up at him, waiting, daring him to plunge on into absolute hopelessness.

"GOD DAMN YOU!" he screamed at the top of his lungs—and in one swift lurch he threw himself out of the hatch onto the unsteady bridge deck.

Even as he screamed into the battle phone, once again exhorting the crew to take up battle stations, he saw the terrible blinding flashes start up on the forward antenna cables, sparks lighting up the mist, turning it from ugly green to a golden brown, illuminating the sea as the bolts of electricity leaped from one cable to another, then ran up the length of each of them and shot toward the bridge. The sea was strangely calm and placid—except in the submarine's path. There it continued to churn feverishly, licking at the hull on all sides, as if stirred from beneath by some mad hand. And suddenly he knew the reason why.

The *Candlefish* was not moving.

She was doing twenty-one knots—standing still.

She was caught!

The submarine's communications system had broken down. No word could be passed from the bridge to below, or from compartment to compartment. The panic level rose.

In the forward engine room, Brownhaver and Googles fought to keep the engines under control. Googles got on the horn and hollered for Cassidy. It was then he realized the battle phones were dead. He threw the mouthpiece aside and lost his balance. The sub shook and quivered, and he could hear the rivets straining.

The lights were gone. Even the red combat lights could manage only an intermittent flicker. Brownhaver found a torch and switched it on.

"The hull!" Googles shouted at him, and struggled to his feet.

Brownhaver aimed the light at it, and they saw the inner hull bloat and stretch and push inward, pulsing. Tiny fingers of water shot in past stretched rivets. With a great lurch, main engine number one was ripped from its hold-down studs and belched out of the mounting, its metal casing screeching across the deck until it bashed into the forward bulkhead. Googles screamed a warning.

The other crewmen in the forward engine room tried frantically to get out before the entire compartment caved in. Diesel pumps and pistons twisted out of their casings, screeched and ground themselves to ruin below decks. The entire companionway was pushed up at an angle and vibrating with the unrelenting tremors that still coursed through the boat.

Brownhaver rushed to the intercom and yelled into it, "We've got a diesel loose down here!" But his voice never got beyond the engine room.

Then the pipelines started to go. Bitten, gnawed, chewed to shreds by main engine number one, they broke in a hundred places. Oil blasted into the compartment, filling it ankle-deep with an odorous slush.

As word was passed to the control room from the frantic crew about the extent of damage in all compartments, Hardy finally yelled up the hatch at the Captain, "She's breaking up! How much do you *want?*"

The Captain slid around the bridge to starboard.

It was time for Hardy to take over.

He ordered the helmsman to stand by to abandon ship: The helmsman was shaking with fright. "Aye, aye, sir!"

Hardy dropped below to control. It was a shambles.

Roybell was using a fire extinguisher on the diving-plane controls, trying to cool them down.

Hardy was struck by the absurdity of the situation. Thirty years ago he had missed all the action below. He had been topside, tumbling off the cigarette deck. This time he would get to see it all firsthand. He laughed. Nobody even noticed his laughter.

A savage voice boomed from above, roaring down the hatch funnel and resounding off the bulkheads:

"HOLD YOUR STATIONS! THERE WILL BE NO ABANDON SHIP!"

The officers froze for a moment, wavering between loyalty and common sense. Then Stigwood whirled to the after hatch and bellowed, "Hold your stations! Orders from the bridge!"

Hardy heard the order passed down the line. It rang

out over the hideous cacophony of sounds throughout the boat.

He turned and dove through the hatch on his way aft. Engine room. Cassidy. Had to find Cassidy.

Cassidy had made it to the forward torpedo room and was up on Clampett's shoulders, pulling the dogs on the forward escape hatch, when the submarine pitched and jerked back on itself.

Clampett flew out from under Cassidy's legs, and Cassidy crashed to the deck. Chains snapped, and men clawed to get out of the way; they knew the sound without even looking. The two torpedoes forward on the skids broke their restraints and shot down the rollers, crashed headlong into the closed tube doors, then fell to the deck. Clampett got up and ran to the intercom, but was stopped when a lubrication line burst. He backed away and turned, a mass of black slime.

"The hatch!" yelled Cassidy.

They got it open just in time. As they swung up out of the way, one of the rear torpedoes slipped its chains, flew off the bay, and ruptured the pressure hull.

Sea water burst through and cascaded down the deck.

"Switch on the bilge pump!" Cassidy yelled. "Get everyone out of here! Up the hatch!"

He turned; he slipped and slid across the sloshing deck toward the maneuvering room.

Hardy. He had to find Jack Hardy.

Hardy charged through the galley and the crew's mess, briefly joining a line from the control room passing life jackets aft.

Then he left the line and pushed his way into the crew's quarters. Vogel was there, pulling up the after battery hatch, thrusting his body below to check out damage to the cells. The vibrations were coming in rhythmic pulses, surging the boat back and forth on itself as if it were a bucking horse.

"Christ Almighty," said Vogel. "They're all rolling around down there. Must be a ton of sea water in the bilges. If those mothers crack——"

"Get everybody out of here," said Hardy. "Clear the compartment. Have men stand by the doors to seal it off. I'm going aft."

"Can't get through the forward engine room. Number one jumped its mounting——"

Hardy rushed the hatch anyway.

Cassidy had made it to the forward engine room. He was at the aft control stand, staring at his number one diesel sliding around on the crumpled deck plates. He couldn't believe the devastation. Oil lines, fuel lines—everything seemed to be going.

"Forget the engines! Get everybody aft! The batteries are gonna go!" Hardy shouted. He spotted Cassidy and grabbed him. "Go forward," he said. "See that they get the rest of the life jackets to the crew. Then send them up the forward hatch if you have to."

"Why not the bridge?"

"The Captain."

Hardy shoved past him and was gone before Cassidy could object. He went on through the aft engine room. Lights were out, and Hardy had to feel his way. He was going on blindly because he wanted to see . . .

"Captain—men coming up the after hatch!" one of the lookouts reported. The Captain stumbled to the cigarette deck and stared at the straggling bodies hoisting themselves topside. "Who told you to abandon ship? Get below!"

They hesitated. Then one of them cupped his hand

to his ear. The others followed his lead. Every time the Captain yelled for them to go below, they shook their heads and cupped their ears. And hoisted other men out.

Danby clung to the coaming, staring at the foaming sea around the hull, the electricity dancing on the antenna cables. He saw the deck plates straining, the strakes splintering, bits of wood flying off into the sea. And the constant, relentless shaking: cruel spasms shuddering through the boat. He was green and sick with fear, and he couldn't stand the wild look of determination on the Captain's face.

"Captain—what are we going to do?"

The answer seemed to come from the sub: an abrupt trouncing to starboard. Danby was whipped off his feet and thrown over the bridge. Only by clinging to the coaming did he prevent himself from being plunged into the churning sea below. He hung there, suspended. Then she heeled to port, and he managed to climb back aboard. The Captain was yelling at the men on the forward deck.

Danby pleaded with him, "Get us out of here!"

The Captain ignored him.

Hardy slipped past the maneuvering room, glancing through the dark at the controllermen still trying to hold the boat steady and keep the remaining engines running.

He ducked into the after torpedo room. Water was still pouring in through the ravaged hull. Torpedoes were racketing. Two men were risking their lives trying to lash the fish down. Hardy was suddenly whisked off his feet as pipes leading to the diving plane motors burst and spewed hydraulic oil over the deck.

"Clear out!" yelled Hardy.

The torpedomen scrambled for the after hatch. Hardy reached up to the nearest torpedo skid, pulled himself to his feet, and lurched toward the hatch.

The Captain screamed obscenities at the men from the bridge as the first life raft was inflated and flung out to sea. And then he heard voices below. More men were crowding into the conning tower, starting up the ladder. He appeared over them and stared them down. "Back to your stations!" he yelled.

"Captain—we can't! She's coming apart! Can't you hear it?"

"Abandon ship!"

It came from Danby. "All hands man your abandon-ship stations! Pass the word!" The Captain whirled, and Danby confronted him with all the courage he had ever mustered.

"Sir, I am taking responsibility for getting the men off. Abandon ship!" he screamed again, and there was an edge of terror in his voice.

He was drowned out by the sudden increase in vibrations. With a twitching, convulsive shudder, the *Candlefish* began to wobble on a gyrating axis.

The Captain was thrown back against the conning tower superstructure as he mouthed the words, "We'll get through—I swear it—"

The men started piling up to the bridge, charging up the ladders.

The Captain shuddered with rage, and the vibrations coursing through his body matched those rattling the submarine. He felt his mind become one with it—meeting it on equal terms—rushing forward to one last desperate act.

The diving alarm.

It went off with two resounding blasts: OOGA! OOGA! Danby whirled. "Who did that? We're not diving!"

The Captain was nowhere near the diving alarm, but he was smiling.

Danby leaned over the bridge hatch. "Who did that?" he yelled again.

Roybell stared at the vent indicators and the plane controls, and his eyes widened in horror. "She's diving herself! Get out of here!"

Danby jumped to his feet as men started to pour up from below. The forward torpedo loading hatch and the far forward escape hatch were popped, and men fought to get out.

Danby jumped to the deck, and ran forward to help pull men out of the hatches.

Hardy was standing by the controls at the maneuvering panel. At the order to abandon ship the controllermen had left their stations and rushed forward.

When the diving alarm sounded, Hardy grabbed the levers and tried to hold them. Propulsion. That's what he was hoping for. Strain the engines that are left—push this boat out of the grip. He knew it was hopeless—knew it for certain when Cassidy appeared around the edge of the panel and shone a battle lantern in his face.

"Hardy, forget it. Let's get out of here!"

"I'm trying to—"

His voice choked off as a thundering vibration struck the maneuvering panel. It creaked and groaned and then split in two.

"She's breaking up!" said Cassidy. "This way!"

Hardy followed him. "Can they keep her afloat?"

"Roybell's trying—up in control—but it won't work."

"They have to—until the men are off!"

Stigwood inflated two more life rafts and chucked

them clear of the churning water around the sub's hull. Men dove in after them; Stigwood guided them off the bridge to the side and then into the water, taking charge calmly, efficiently.

He looked down to see his ankles swirling in water. The sub was edging under, slowly but inevitably.

He wished the violent metallic creaking would stop, and those antenna cables. Every man who came to the side to jump hesitated a few costly seconds, afraid to cross that barrier of electricity, preferring the questionable safety of a flooding deck to death by electrocution.

Stigwood could not figure where in hell the electricity came from. The power in those cables was off. Communications below were out.

He looked up and saw the triple masts banging against each other; the lookouts climbed up their railings and jumped into the sea. Other men coming up the hatch from the con followed their lead.

The Captain stood on the bridge, gripped the coaming, and watched his men flee the *Candlefish*. He was motionless as he settled down to wait for Jack Hardy.

Googles and Brownhaver were the only ones left in the forward engine room when Cassidy and Hardy burst through.

"What the hell are you still doing here?" Cassidy yelled.

"Trying to keep up speed—bust out of this—"

"Bust out is right!" Cassidy flung them both toward the exit. "Get out of here!"

They picked their way past the sliding diesel, fighting the pitching deck, striving to reach the crew's quarters.

"Go straight to control—up through the con!" Cassidy hollered. He pulled Hardy along.

Brownhaver was the first to cough.

"Gas——" he said.

Cassidy stopped and looked down at the after battery hatch. Even in the half light he could see the wisps of greenish-yellow chlorine gas seeping up through the cracks. He shoved Hardy ahead of him, flinging him the lantern. "Get them through!"

They piled into the crew's mess, staggering out of the hatch, coughing and spluttering. Cassidy whirled and dogged the hatch, then went to the bulkhead flappers, closing off the vents from aft.

He turned and saw the others waiting for him. "Go!" he screamed, and pushed them on. They raced forward now, lunging into the control room. Roybell and the two auxiliarymen were still struggling with the flood valves.

"Blow all negative!" Cassidy barked.

"Blow it out your ass," growled Roybell. "We're losing depth control—forward must be flooding." He nodded toward the hatchwell. "Get moving—we can't hold it!"

Brownhaver and Googles joined the line of men streaming in from forward, men who couldn't make it up the forward hatch because of flooding. One of the machinist's mates was stuck in the well, sobbing. Cassidy shot up the con and ripped him bodily off the ladder.

"Never mind the wheel," he told the helmsman. "Pass these guys up the ladder." He yelled below. "You guys better move it—we've got chlorine gas in the after battery!"

He stayed in the con, pulling the men up in relays. "Dankworth, come on—that's fine—up you go. Get a jacket, Googles—in the stowage. One at a time, fellas! Any officers left aboard?"

Hardy stood at the bottom of the ladder, catching his

breath. Suddenly he remembered.

Bates.

No—Dorriss. Lieutenant Dorriss, socked by Cassidy, left—where? In the CPO cabin, on his bunk.

Can't let him stay there. He turned and rushed forward.

As he stepped into officers' country, a powerful tremor ripped through the compartments, jerking the deck plates apart. He heard a crashing sound and peered into the wardroom. The wall units lay in a heap on the deck, undulating with the waves of vibration. And now a new sound: rivets pulling apart with great ratchet shrieks.

The port side shuddered, and the bulkhead protecting the Captain's cabin ripped right in half, metal shredding like paper before Hardy's eyes. He stumbled toward the flapping door and peered inside as the boat gave another twitch to port—and the folding desk slammed down and all the Captain's papers poured out of it.

Hardy stiffened.

There was a groan from the CPO quarters.

He pulled himself along the trembling panels and stepped through. He stared at his bunk. The curtain was flapping as if whipped by a breeze—but there was no breeze. Dorriss wasn't there, nor was the guard. He stepped closer to the bunk. His wife's picture was on the deck, the glass shattered, ground into shards—by a boot heel. Who would do that?

"Knew you'd come back . . ."

Hardy whirled.

A wild man stood in front of him. A skinny wild man with blood on his shirt, hair matted with blood, more blood crusted on an open head wound, a twisted smile of triumph cut deep into his ghostly pale features—and a tightened fist that came up with a powerful sweep to the right, around and into Hardy's jaw, flinging him off his feet, back against the bunk, his head smacking the metal frame.

Lieutenant Dorriss watched him go down like a stone. His eyes blazed; then he turned and stumbled out of the cabin, slamming the door shut and feeling it jam. It was already twisted out of its frame.

He lurched toward the control room.

Danby had spotted the swirling green-yellow gas pouring up out of the open hatch. He spluttered water, then gasped as he got a lungful of the gas. He blew it out and reached for the hatch, slammed it down. He spun the dogs and looked up. The stern cables had broken and were dancing around the deck, threatening his feet with electricity. He dodged them and glanced out to sea. In the deepening golden fog he could see the life rafts tossing about, only yards from the hull.

Up on the bridge there were still a few men coming out. The Captain was watching from the starboard side. Danby saw a figure black with oil climb up to the bridge coaming, pause for a moment with the Ann Sheridan poster tucked under one arm. It was Clampett. He yelled, "Geronimo!" and flung himself clear of the sub.

The water was climbing up Danby's legs. Up to his knees now. He sloshed forward as fast as he could, grasped the deck gun for support and yelled up to the bridge, "She's going under! Clear the bridge! Abandon ship!"

The only one left on the bridge was the Captain. Stigwood was still forward, helping the last men out of the forward hatch. Danby tried to wade to the conning tower, intending to throw the Captain overboard if necessary.

He never made it. The sub took another jolt and

then an abrupt three-foot drop. A shower swept over the afterdeck and tore Danby off his footing. He was plunged into the sea. He came up spluttering, looking for a raft.

Witzgall's head popped through the hatch, and Cassidy pulled him up. "Where's Hardy?" Cassidy asked.

"Don't know. Think he went forward."

"Went where?"

Witzgall didn't wait to answer. He shot up to the bridge and went overboard.

"Can't hold her any more," said Roybell as he sent the two auxiliarymen up.

Then Cassidy saw who was next up the ladder. The skinny man with the blood encrusted on his head.

"Bates . . . ?"

It was involuntary. Cassidy had meant to say "Dorriss," but—

Dorriss quivered out of control; a vibration much like those convulsing the boat went through him. He tore past Cassidy and scrambled up the ladder to the bridge.

"Hardy!"

Cassidy yelled and squeezed down the ladder past Roybell, the last man up.

"Cassidy, come back!"

"HARDY!"

His voice echoed through the empty control room as he disappeared through the next hatch. Roybell continued up, pulling the helmsman after him. They got to the bridge. Dorriss was poised on the railing, afraid to jump. Roybell looked down and saw the forward deck awash—the strakes completely under—and pushed Dorriss. The lieutenant screamed as he plunged into the sea. The helmsman flung himself overboard, and Roybell climbed up after him. He was poised to jump when he heard Stigwood still yelling, "Jump! Jump!"

But it wasn't directed at him.

He turned and, in the split-second before the next shudder threw him overboard, saw the Captain step away from the starboard coaming and approach the bridge hatch, eyes coal-blazing, intent on that black circle at his feet, waiting—

Roybell pitched into the sea.

And at the bow Stigwood too let go and slipped over.

Cassidy plowed through officers' country, yelling "Hardy!" over and over. With another rending shudder the wardroom bulkhead split in two.

Cassidy sloshed into the forward torpedo room.

"Hardy?"

Sea water was plunging in through the open forward hatch. The compartment was dark with lights popping on intermittently—the red combat lights. Oil and steam blasted from broken pipes and filled the room with a black, sticky mist. Cassidy could hardly see.

"Hardy! For God's sake—no games!"

He hoped to God he would get a reply.

Jack Hardy's body rolled across the CPO cabin deck and came up against the forward bulkhead. He woke and moaned. There was a terrific throbbing at the back of his head. He dragged himself up. Shaky. He blinked around. Water sloshed at his feet. The boat was rolling and pitching violently—but the vibrations no longer came in waves. They were steady. Seventy-eight rpm's, he thought, and laughed to himself.

He shouldered aside the door and stepped into the corridor, stumbling past the crumpled wardroom bulkhead—and thought he heard someone calling his name. The ladder—in control—

He fell through the hatch into the control room. Instruments blinked back at him. Levers moved. The Christmas tree flashed strange green and red lights. Up the ladder—get to the con. No one there—deserted. Up the last ladder—get to the bridge.

He stood weakly on the bridge ladder and managed to move his head, to look up. The ladder shook in his hand. The open hatch—black sky. He wanted to see black sky.

Instead—fog. And a face.

Basquine.

Just a glimpse. That's all he got. Basquine's face—no, his look, his unmistakable expression on somebody else's face. He didn't know whose. It was unfamiliar. But the meaning was clear.

Even before the hatch slammed down on top of him, shutting out the sky and freedom.

He watched the dogs slowly spin around, then let go the ladder and collapsed to the deck.

The Captain rose from the deck of the bridge, his eyes gleaming with triumph. The sub rolled to port. The Captain flung his hands out but missed the coaming.

And the *Candlefish* expelled him into the sea.

CHAPTER 25

December 11

Cassidy found a battle lantern wedged between a torpedo and the forward skid. He switched it on and played it around the raging mess he was standing in. He felt the deck shift; he slipped and went down in the water, then was washed back toward the tubes. He thrust his arm up and held the lantern high. When he managed to regain his footing, he felt the deck tilting down by the bow. She was taking on water fast, going down. Sheets of it poured through the topside hatch.

"Hardy!"

Still no answer. He sloshed around the skids and searched up the other side. He was thigh-deep now, and frightened.

"HARDY!"

His voice broke. He felt a sob welling up in his throat.

"Hardy! For God's sake—"

Clang.

He heard it far back in the boat, resounding and final. A hatch slamming shut.

"Hardy?"

He whirled and floundered back around the skids, trying to beat the rising water to the after hatch. The water roared around him, drowning out his yells.

"HARDY!"

* * *

Hardy tumbled down the ladder and landed on his knee. He seemed to remember the pain from somewhere else. It was sharp and familiar, a shock of recognition that stopped him in his tracks for a moment. He stared at the aft controlroom hatch and suddenly knew he had to get through it, had to escape something that was following him, surrounding him . . .

Clang.

He saw it close even as he took his first faltering step to reach it. The dogs turned and locked it shut.

He couldn't steady himself. He collapsed to his knees and felt the pain throb in the bad one. His hands were under water. His clothes were drenched. His body surged with the insistent pounding rhythm around him. He glanced at the instruments and saw the valve controls moving. The inclinometer needle was creeping down. He felt another driving shudder rake through the boat, and then he saw the forward hatch waving at him.

He lunged across the deck and dove through it.

He was in officers' country again. The crumpled bulkheads of the wardroom threatened to collapse on him.

"Hardy!"

He heard the voice calling. From where?

"Hardy!"

He heard splashing forward. The torpedo room.

"HERE!" He heard himself yell the reply. He picked his way across the remains of officers' quarters, then thrust himself to his feet and thought he saw Hopalong Cassidy loping through the water in the forward torpedo room. He was within three feet of the hatch.

Clang.

He fell to his knee again and bellowed in pain and

frustration. The wheel spun slowly around to lock.

His hand shook at his side, creeping up to touch the wheel, to try to spin it back. He could do it; he knew he could; *he had to do it!* Why shouldn't he be *able* to do it?

He didn't want to.

He knew this was how it would end. He had always known it. Hemmed in, trapped, surrounded by his past, unforgiven . . .

He heard Cassidy calling, splashing up to the locked hatch, fingers clawing at it. Shoulders pushed into that wheel, desperately pushing it—pulling it—trying to get him out—

The red combat lights flickered around him.

Cassidy couldn't budge the wheel. He strained, nearly dislocating his shoulder. Through the sight glass he saw Hardy cowering just on the other side.

Cassidy screamed at the door in helpless rage.

"Christ—what's going on here!"

The lights went out. He backed away in fear and, turning, saw water and a bit of light pouring through the topside hatch. He was waist-deep now; in another moment he would have to swim for it. He whirled, flung himself at the door and screamed:

"HARDY! For God's sake!"

The red lights beyond the sight glass flickered on again, and he saw Jack Hardy staring at him from the other side, motionless, the fear replaced by a warm serenity on his boyish features—his beardless, slick, pudgy farmboy's face.

The shiver started in Cassidy's toes and gripped him all the way up to his scalp. The man looking back at him was a young, clean-shaven lieutenant in clean, pressed khakis.

Jack Hardy at age twenty-six. The Jack Hardy who had sailed aboard the *Candlefish* in 1944.

Once again Cassidy hurled himself at the door. But when he looked up he saw the young officer's back retreating to the control room, walking unsteadily, balancing himself against the settling tilt.

The sub went down by the bow again, and Cassidy fell back. He swam and spluttered toward the open topside hatch. He climbed on the skids to get above the swirling water. He stared at the shower of ocean coming down the hatch, then back at the forward door.

He reached for the ladder and hauled himself up.

Hardy staggered to the control room, stepping through the hatch. He heard it clang shut behind him, heard the final squeak of the dogging wheel. The instruments blinked silently back at him. The vibrations diminished, and with them the terrifying sounds.

Hardy looked at the ladder, then slowly mounted it and pulled himself up the well to the con.

Cassidy splashed out of the forward hatch and was plunged across the waves. In that brief harrowing moment, he remembered that he had saved no life jacket for himself. He was slammed into the hull of the conning tower, which was tilted forward at a forty-five-degree angle. He grasped a rail. The submarine screeched back at him, metal on metal. He pulled himself upright and looked down at his legs: water up to his thighs, his hips. He braced against the con and then flung himself clear of the boat.

Hardy stepped onto the conning-tower deck and waited in silence. He saw moisture condensing on the metal; the bulkheads were sweating.

The red lights popped on and stayed on. Then they came into view, all of them, eyeing him with their customary malevolence: the wartime crew of the *Candlefish* . . . the helmsman, the officers, Captain Basquine, Lieutenant Bates . . .

Their eyes bored into his. They said nothing, just stood looking at him, accusing. They had accused him once of responsibility in the death of the torpedoman Kenyon. Now they accused him of the death of their boat.

Basquine was the last to turn to him. When he did, his eyes blazed at Hardy for a moment. Then he drew himself up, stiff and craggy, every inch the hero of the seas—and then just seemed to deflate.

Hardy's face told Basquine, *There is nothing more you can do—you're stuck with me—you've lost.*

They both knew it.

Basquine pushed out a grudging hand in welcome. Hardy felt a surge of relief, as if the entire burden of thirty years had been lifted from his shoulders. Then Basquine's face came up, and his voice was filled with a strange sorrow:

"We had to have you back with us, Jack."

Cassidy groped and spluttered to stay afloat; he gulped sea water and spewed it out again, choking. He heard a terrifying growl over his head and looked up. Through the fog and churning water he saw the submarine upend herself, the stern rising out of the water, screws churning the air, metal creaking and whining in a last death roar. She was silhouetted against the sky. He braced himself for the blow that would crush him . . . but gracefully the submarine slid under the waves, as if pulled from below.

The churning stopped.

Cassidy was washed against something soft and pliant. Hands grabbed under his numb shoulders, hauled him up and over until he tumbled into the raft. He coughed and gagged. A gentle hand wiped his hair back; he blinked and looked up.

Ed Frank gazed down at him anxiously.

Beside him was Lieutenant Dorriss, his thin frame shivering, arms wrapped securely around his life jacket, fright embedded deep in his eyes.

Other rafts floated nearby in the fog, carrying more of the crew. Men were still being pulled out of the sea and helped to safety.

Cassidy looked again at Ed Frank. The man was staring at the spot where the *Candlefish* had gone down, turning pale with shock.

The sea becalmed. The men grew quiet, and one by one collapsed, exhausted.

Cassidy glanced suspiciously from Ed Frank to Dorriss. Frank spoke quietly in the dark.

"What about Hardy?"

"Gone," said Cassidy. "Went down with her."

"Oh, my God . . ."

It wasn't perfunctory; Frank's remorse was genuine. He sank back in the raft alongside Dorriss.

"It's all right," offered Cassidy. "He belonged there."

Frank didn't comment for a long time.

"Well . . . I know where *we* belong . . ." Frank sighed, gazing into the fog. "But I'm not so sure *we're* there."

"We're in the Pacific," said Dorriss. "Latitude Thirty."

"Uh-huh. But *when?*"

Cassidy chuckled, then laughed aloud. Same old Ed Frank. Practical, challenging . . . He dropped back in the raft, and his eyes closed. Of course, Frank was right.

When?

There was silence at last, and the life rafts were left to drift alone through the shrouding fog.

A chilly dawn broke and edged out the darkness. The fog had been too eerie for sleep, and the cold too bone-numbing. Cassidy and Frank stared out to sea and counted the life rafts adrift in the bedraggled group. They spent a full half-hour making silent head counts.

"I think we're all here," said Frank.

"Except Hardy," Cassidy mumbled.

An hour later Dorriss broke out the canned rations. Most of the men were awake but slugged with exhaustion. They fell to the food and ate voraciously. For dessert they stared out to sea.

"If we get picked up . . ." Frank began, then stopped, his short frame crouching into a corner, his eyes under a furrowed brow. He started over. "If we get picked up by the Japanese . . . we'll simply explain that we're Americans . . . the crew of the *Candlefish* . . . she sank last night in heavy seas . . . The worst that can happen is they chuck us into a prisoner-of-war camp . . ."

"That's the worst?" snorted Cassidy.

"Assuming . . ." Again Frank hesitated, for once in his life reluctant to assume anything. "Assuming that this is still . . . 1944."

Cassidy slowly looked up at him, grimly assessing the possibility.

Even if they were all stuck here in 1944 for the rest of their lives, unable to explain *why* to themselves or to anyone else—Hell, it wasn't a bad life, 1944. Not for a machinist. He bit his lip. Then the problems presented by the warp of time came showering down on his head.

"What happens when the war is over?" he asked. "And we go home?"

Frank's brow darkened in silent reproof. The other men shifted uncomfortably.

"Smoke on the horizon!"

The voice hailed them from another raft. One of the men stood up and pointed into the dawn.

They watched the sun spread across the sea, and the black dot sailing out of it.

They shielded their eyes and squinted. Silhouetted directly east of them, her black hull creeping closer, enlarging, the markings distressingly invisible. A single freighter . . .

She was huge, imposing, dwarfing them.

Cassidy felt a jiggle in his raft, glanced around to see Frank unsteadily getting to his feet, tears streaming down his cheeks. His hands dropped to his sides, and he confronted the ship, clenching his fists and growling under his breath, "Sitting duck."

The markings on her bow were Japanese. It wasn't until she loomed up in front of them and her officers came to the bow and she shifted broadside to take them aboard that the black silhouette disappeared and they saw her hull colors for the first time. Baby blue and cream, bright and sparkling, and there painted in giant block letters the entire length of the hull, the word that announced better than any other their fate, their ultimate destiny.

DATSUN.

Within seconds the Americans were aware of it. They gaped at the letters and spelled them out, read them to each other, breaking out in smiles, crying. Some threw up their hands and clasped them into fists, shaking them over their heads, cheering joyously.

Only a few stood up in the rafts and stared, comprehending the irony and sobered into frozen silence.

Cassidy and Frank in particular. Cassidy sneaked a look at the Captain and saw him suddenly small, insignificant, no longer the giant rock of authority—a walking aftermath.

It was 1974 again—and Ed Frank stood quietly considering his own diminished impact.

PART VI

CHAPTER 26

December 12, 1974

They were removed from the freighter by relays of Japanese helicopters and transferred to the aircraft carrier USS *Encounter*. All eighty-three men were taken to sick bay and examined head to toe. They were ordered not to talk of their ordeal among themselves. Admiral Begelman himself was flown out and made a special plea to "save it for the Board of Inquiry."

December 15, 1974

The crew was removed from the *Encounter* by two shifts of transport planes, then flown back to the Ford Island Naval Air Station at Pearl Harbor. Fit and rested and sobered, they were transferred to quarters at the Submarine Base. Ed Frank was put up at the BOQ in a small room much like the one Hardy had occupied. He got a telegram from Lieutenant Cook and realized that they hadn't sunk the *Frankland* on December 2nd after all. Hardy had been right: They must have dropped into 1944 early on the morning of December 2nd, dropped completely out of contact with the escort, then torpedoed the same Japanese submarine the *Candlefish* had sunk in World War Two. The *Frankland* had searched frantically for them until ordered to abandon the effort and return to Pearl.

He felt a twinge of guilt because the fate of the *Frankland* hadn't crossed his mind once in the four days since his rescue.

Lieutenant Cook had been transferred. The cable was couched in guarded language, advising Frank of the new assignment and thanking him for their past association, congratulations on a safe return. There was nothing even remotely resembling a "looking forward to a reunion and an update . . ."

Cook either was no longer interested or was not permitted to be.

December 18, 1974

The Board of Inquiry went into session and took depositions for four days, questioning each crew member about what he had seen and done. Most had only vague memories of their feelings, and all had shaky stories about their actions. To each man the entire patrol had proved a nightmare, and one they were not anxious to discuss.

Frank testified for a full day. He made his statements calmly and thoroughly and answered questions as best he could.

An admiral made the only comment: "You know, Commander, your story is corroborated in every respect save one. You were the only man on the bridge at the time Captain Byrnes was hit. Everyone else had gone below. Isn't it possible you only *thought* you saw him hit?"

"But the planes? The holes in the conning tower— the blood . . . ?"

The admiral was nudged by another admiral, and lapsed into silence.

Frank lapsed into indifference.

December 21, 1974

The Japanese Government quietly protested the maneuvers of an American submarine in their waters. Until the crew was picked up, the *Candlefish* had never been detected, by either radar or sonar. Somehow a submarine had penetrated their defenses, and the Japanese were rightfully upset about it.

By the time the official panic reached Smitty at NIS headquarters in Washington, he had already responded to the unofficial rumors. He prepared a statement for release to authorized agencies only:

The refit of number 284 had been improperly handled; she was a thirty-year-old boat that died suddenly of old age. As for the so-called maneuvers, the *Candlefish* was on an oceanographic research project led by Dr. Jack Hardy of Scripps Institution of Oceanography, who was unfortunately lost with the boat.

Eventually this version found its way into newspapers and became the accepted public explanation. But to the eighty-three survivors no explanation was acceptable. Twenty-one died within six months of the incident; thirteen immediately underwent extended psychiatric care. The remainder did their best to consign the voyage to the furthest recesses of their minds. Some suffered nightmares the rest of their lives. Some forgot, some coped—nine of them committed suicide.

Those who did manage to deal with it incorporated bits of unfamiliar personalities into their own lives. They became nostalgic for '40s music, fond of old war movies, prone to certain out-of-date epithets, and spiteful of all things Japanese . . .

Walter "Hopalong" Cassidy returned to Mare Island in his capacity as a civil-service mechanic and disappeared one month later. His body was found curled up in the crawl space beneath the maneuvering room of the USS *Pompanito*, the last surviving World War II submarine in the yard.

December 24, 1974

The day before Christmas, Ed Frank was flown back to Washington and driven to the Pentagon. He walked the halls to his office. Everything was just as he had left it—the photograph of Joanne in its sparkling silver frame still centered on his blotter. Cook's name was already gone from the other door; his cubicle was vacant.

Frank made several attempts to get through to Smitty. He was told that the Director of the NIS was away for the holidays.

Admiral Diminsky was in a doorway, chatting with an Air Force general.

Frank didn't stop to say hello; he went straight home.

He unlocked the door to his apartment, hoping to find a Christmas tree and other evidence of Joanne's holiday spirit.

He found only a note. Dated November 15th.

He spent Christmas Eve alone, nursing a bottle of Scotch, recalling that he hadn't written since he left for Pearl.

Maybe this was the way he had always wanted it.

January 15, 1975

Frank was advised in a curt note from Diminsky that the findings of the Board of Inquiry were not in his favor, that the NIS in particular was reprimanded for allowing a desk man to assume command of a Navy vessel, that in the future such matters would not come under the jurisdiction of that office.

The results of the Board of Inquiry were not surprising. But he finally understood why they had so easily accepted the stories: The case was too complex for them. They intended to hush it up and file it away. He knew it for sure when he was visited by the CIA and told point-blank that to speak of the *Candlefish* in public would be regarded as a treasonous act.

He received a letter from Jack Hardy's son in Seattle. It was a severe accusation, but he managed to deal with it.

February 20, 1975

But within two months he was having regular nightmares about the *Candlefish* and her crew, about what he had done, the parts he had played . . . and Jack Hardy.

For reasons he was never able to explain, he lost his ability to make firm, snap decisions. He became hesitant, cautious, worrisome.

He had inherited Jack Hardy's albatross.

On February 20th Diminsky sent him on an extended vacation.

On March 14th Ed Frank resigned from the Navy.

July 4, 1975

On Independence Day, one year before the two hundredth birthday of the United States, Scripps Director Dr. Edward Felanco set out from SUBDEVGRU ONE at San Diego in the AGSS-555 *Dolphin* with a team of oceanographic researchers. They were bound for

the area off the south coast of Japan known as the
Ramapo Depth on a classified project.

In thirty-one days of deep-sea exploration, they
found not a single trace of the phenomenon known as
Devil's Triangle. Nor did they find any trace of the USS
Candlefish.

But if they had been able to reach the sea bottom at
Latitude 30, their cameras and lights might have picked
out a shape mired in the deep silt of the Pacific floor.
An old, rotting, coral-encrusted hulk, the raised bolts
on her conning tower outlining a vaguely discernible
group of digits:

284.

BESTSELLERS
FROM DELL

fiction